A MAN WITH A MISSION

Nolan's air was running low when there was a sudden shout in his headset. He turned back quickly to see that a spacesuited figure was moving slowly away from the ship, pushed by an inverted yellow cone of high-pressure oil. Nolan bent his knees and launched himself after the man, but even with the suit's thrusters, he could see he would not reach the man in time.

The man's safety line was already taut against the ship's shield support. Nolan had never been good at mental arithmetic, but he knew that in a very short time that line would wrap itself around the support with steadily increasing speed until the radius became zero and the man crashed into the metal at a speed neither he nor his suit could survive . . .

By James White
Published by Ballantine Books:

AMBULANCE SHIP
ALL JUDGMENT FLED
CODE BLUE—EMERGENCY!
THE DREAM MILLENNIUM
FEDERATION WORLD
FUTURES PAST
HOSPITAL STATION
MAJOR OPERATION
SECTOR GENERAL
THE SILENT STARS GO BY
STAR HEALER
STAR SURGEON

THE SILENT STARS GO BY

James White

DEL REY

A Del Rey Book
BALLANTINE BOOKS • NEW YORK

A Del Rey Book
Published by Ballantine Books

Library of Congress Catalog Card Number: 91-91972

ISBN 0-345-37110-0

Manufactured in the United States of America

First Edition: September 1991

Cover Art by Vincent Di Fate

This book is dedicated to those fearless explorers of alternate Irish and Amerindian history, Andy, Billy, Heinrich, Ian, Jim, Joe, Michael, and Peggy, you know who you are and how very much you helped, and to the sainted Brendan the Navigator (A.D. 484–577), who is responsible for the original idea.

In Appreciation

Chapter 1

FROM the top of the wide marbled and mirrored entrance staircase, the mass audience chamber of the Imperial Court at Tara looked vast and incredibly crowded, except for the area covered by the processional carpet—onto which none dared tread until after the Seventh Maeve had done so—and which pointed like a broad, blood-red arrow to the distant golden blob that was the throne. Nolan paused for a moment while his name and district were announced, fighting an urge to turn and run as he performed a meticulous but inconspicuous check on his uniform in one of the nearby mirrors.

He was, after all, one of the two hundred officers for whom this Imperial reception was ostensibly being given.

The knee boots glittered like polished obsidian. No speck of lint marred the heavy black serge of the trousers, tunic, or the long silver-edged cloak, which was thrown back from both shoulders in the prescribed manner to reveal the epaulets—one retaining his carefully folded dress beret and the other carrying the crest of the Imperial district that was his country of origin, the badges of his ship and nonship specialties, and the proud emblem of his vessel. This blazon of arms was repeated on the hilt of his ceremonial sword, which, like the myriad other dress weapons on display all around him, was safely locked into its scabbard.

There was no easy way to become an Ard-Ri, or Ard-Rioghan, but there were always a few simpleminded, direct people around who thought that the old adage "To be a King one must kill a King" was a good way to start.

He moved slowly down the stairway and waded into the glittering, resplendent sea of Imperial and non-Citizen dignitaries, high-ranking officers of the Church and the military, and other personages whose exact ranks and powers were unknown to him, all of them wearing the full dress uniforms or elaborately decorated and bejeweled national costumes of their districts.

A few of the costumes were dazzling, he saw with appreciation, but very much abbreviated.

He had been instructed to wear at all times a pleasant, dignified, and approachable expression, but to answer all questions, particularly those relating to the financial, religious, or political aspects of the enterprise, politely and only in the most general terms. As a junior officer, he had been told, it was important that he guard his tongue.

Slowly, so as not to give anyone the impression that he had urgent business elsewhere and would therefore have no time to talk to anyone, Nolan moved into the crowd. He looked all around him with what must have appeared to be the stupid, benign expression of a half-wit on his gradually reddening face. Nobody seemed disposed to talk to him, or even to notice him, with one beautiful and all-too-brief exception.

From her distinctive and costly ornaments and the rich silks of her modest and all-concealing costume, he knew her to be a non-Citizen visitor from Cathay, and so exquisitely formed and flawless were her features that she looked for all the world like a life-size, living example of the justly acclaimed sculptural art of her nation. So smooth and unblemished was her skin that Nolan could not even guess at her age, and he had no way of knowing whether the personage, wearing the robes of a Mandarin of the Flamingo Rank, who was standing behind her was her husband, father, or owner.

In a voice that was soft and clear in spite of the high level of background noise, she looked up at him and asked shyly about the qualifications needed for non-crew members of the expedition. Stammering at first, he began to answer the question. Not knowing her degree of real interest or level of technical appreciation, and unwilling to risk offending her by oversimplifying and thus giving the impression that he was being patronizing, he answered in considerable and probably unnecessary detail. But within a few minutes it was plain that she was losing interest. Smiling apologetically, she dipped her head and backed away.

Over the heads of the crowd he could see a few patches of darkness floating in that dazzling, many-colored sea of costume—the uniformed backs or shoulders of his fellow officers. During one of the briefings he had been told that no tailor at or outside of Court could possibly design a uniform capable of competing with the finery that would be present at Tara, and that if one of them had been sufficiently inspired to build garments that were more tasteful, eye-catching, or flattering, he or she would have been banished to the Northern Wastes for not first offering them to the High-Queen. So it had been decided that a simple, tasteful, and cheap black uniform with minimal decoration would be both visually distinctive and politically inoffensive.

But even his fellow officers would not talk to him, because they had all been given strict orders to mix only with nonmembers of the crew. There would be ample time, far too much of it, perhaps, to talk to the other officers in the years to come. On this auspicious occasion their primary duty was to sell the project to the people who mattered and, as far as they were able, to speak only to the rich and influential.

Still trying to look pleasant and approachable, Nolan moved slowly toward the refreshment board.

The board, tastefully concealed by alternating sections of colorful imported vegetation and heavy drapes, occupied more than a quarter of the length of one wall, and the area was a little more secluded and a lot less crowded than the main hall. A large number of people had decided that it was a good place to have a quiet conversation, and they were doing just that and ignoring the lavish selection of food and drink laid out so enticingly before them. As he passed among them, none of the conversations were widened to include Nolan. After a lengthy period of being completely ignored, he swore under his breath and moved toward the stretch of board whose contents were contained in crystal flagons.

On his approach a large man, taller even than Nolan, detached himself from a small group of servants and came forward to attend him. He wore the servants' dark brown smock with one blue-and-white-striped sleeve, which probably meant that he was a supervisor of some kind, and suspended from his neck was the medallion that marked him as a member of the Imperial Household.

"It is an honor to serve you, sir," he said, glancing at the ship insignia on Nolan's shoulder. His bow was no deeper than a fraction of an inch, and there was respect in his tone but a distinct lack of subservience as he added, "My name is Ciaran, sir. What is your pleasure?"

Nolan indicated one of the distinctively labeled flagons and said, "A large one, please."

Ciaran stooped awkwardly, as if constrained by tight undergarments, then straightened with a similar degree of difficulty before placing a crystal goblet, already filled, before him. For a moment his eyes held Nolan's as he said, "I applaud your taste, sir. That is one of the better beverages distilled by our Caledonian cousins.

But this is a vastly inferior product, I'm afraid, and I would advise you not to drink it.''

Nolan stared at the man in surprise, then laughed. The stuff could not be too bad, he thought as he raised the goblet to his lips, or it would never have been served at an Imperial reception.

''How . . . how dare you!'' Nolan burst out, and only with the greatest difficulty did he refrain from spitting it onto the floor. ''It's . . . it tastes like cold tea!''

''It is cold tea, sir,'' Ciaran replied calmly. ''A blend from the Indies which, for the benefit of onlookers, most accurately reproduces the color of the original spirit. I am sorry, sir, but the ship's officers will not be served anything stronger until after the reception. Perhaps I can find you a slightly more palatable but regrettably nonalcoholic drink?''

Once again he bent stiffly to reach under the board, but Nolan put out a hand to restrain him. The man stiffened at his touch, then relaxed.

''You seem to be having some difficulty with your movements,'' he said, ''so please do not inconvenience yourself. However, if your duties allow it, I would be obliged for a few minutes' conversation before my tongue atrophies from sheer disuse. For some reason nobody here wants to talk to me.''

''You show consideration, sir,'' Ciaran replied, straightening up. ''Talking about your troubles to the bar-servant is a custom long hallowed by tradition, and in this instance I would be honored. What or who shall we talk about?''

Nolan set down the goblet and for a long moment looked straight into the other's eyes. ''If you've no objection,'' he said, ''I'd like to talk about you.''

Ciaran looked surprised, but he returned Nolan's stare without any sign of discomfort. ''You have the rank, sir.''

''I'm wondering about that . . .'' Nolan began dryly, then broke off as an Iberian nobleman and his lady moved up to the board beside him. One of the other servants came quickly forward to attend them, leaving Ciaran and Nolan free to go on talking.

''. . . because I wonder about you,'' he resumed quietly. ''At first I thought you were simply overweight and wearing an overtight corselet for reasons of vanity, but quickly discarded that idea.''

''Thank you, sir.''

''Then I thought that your general appearance suggested a military background,'' Nolan went on, ''and you had been wounded, invalided out, and rewarded with a good job in the palace for distinguished service. Not long service, because you are comparatively young. But menial jobs like that go to the lower ranks, and I don't see you as a foot soldier. And when I touched you just now I had the feeling that, for an instant, you were ready to react in a most unmenial fashion. I was fairly sure then that you were not wearing belly-strapping or artificial limbs, but weapons and probably armor. Because you were encumbered by all that equipment, I rejected the idea that you might be an assassin, and decided that if there was serious trouble, perhaps a threat to the life of the High Queen, you would discard that smock and, to minimize the ensuing confusion in the area, reveal yourself for what you really are. Am I right, so far?"

"No mere servant," said Ciaran in a neutral tone, "would dare to tell a palace guest that he was wrong."

"The reason you came forward to serve me," Nolan added, "was that no ordinary bar attendant would dare serve an officer of the ship with cold tea."

"That was one of the reasons," said Ciaran, without taking his eyes off him.

Nolan laughed uncomfortably, and went on, "It is possible that I'm completely wrong and that you will talk about me and laugh afterward. But I dislike untidiness, in things or events or people, and you are untidy as a person. No offense intended, Ciaran, but you are not what you seem. I think that you have two jobs, that you perform both of them very well, but you don't look like a servant."

"No offense, sir," said Ciaran, "but you don't look like a Healer."

Nolan felt his face growing hot as memories of all the stupid and narrow-minded female hostility he had suffered during and after his medical training came welling up, but the other laughed suddenly.

"It was not meant as a criticism of your professional competence, sir," he said, "just that you are not a woman."

"True," said Nolan, smiling in return.

"Not only do you not look like a Healer," Ciaran went on, "with your height and girth you could very easily be mistaken for one of my undercover Guardsmen. For security reasons a few of them have been given permission to wear a ship uniform, and the people here who think they know everything have taken one look at your size and unexpected insignia, and decided that you are just another Imperial Guardsman in disguise, and that asking you questions about the expedition would be a complete waste of time. So rest assured, the reason they didn't talk to you was not due to a forbidding visage, social discourtesy, or the omission of regular bathing.

"Sir," he added.

"I'm relieved," said Nolan dryly. "But earlier you implied that there were other reasons for you trying to poison me?"

Ciaran glanced over Nolan's shoulder as something in the main hall attracted his attention, then he said seriously, "I wanted to talk to you about the expedition. I've read all the published material, naturally, but was hoping for a less romanticized, inside view before I confirm my resignation from the Guards."

"You've already been accepted?"

"Yes, as a non-crew volunteer," said Ciaran, and laughed again in an attempt to conceal the pride and excitement in his voice. "Don't look so surprised. I have other accomplishments besides serving at a bar and keeping my armor polished. I have a certain amount of rank and influence here."

"How much rank and influence does a Guards officer carry?" asked Nolan curiously.

Ciaran looked faintly embarrassed as he replied, "This one is the Ionadacht."

Nolan shook his head in disbelief. This large, smiling, friendly man in a servant's smock was the second-in-command of the Imperial Guards. He stammered, "I—I'm surprised that you want to go, Ciaran. The life there will be very primitive, dangerous, and unpleasant in ways we cannot even guess at. If the navigation is faulty we might not even get to the New World, and with insufficient ship stores for the return voyage . . ." He lifted the goblet to his lips, then remembered in time and put it down again. "At Court you have position, authority, the trust of the High-Queen, wealth, comfort, security—"

"And boredom," the other broke in. "You're forgetting the awful, soul-destroying, never-ending boredom of watching petty squabbles and character assassinations, which is the closest these people ever come to an honest fight. I am an overdressed ornament most of the time, with nothing of any real importance to do. The comfort and security are driving me mad!"

"If you have volunteered," said Nolan, smiling, "it may already have done so."

Ciaran did not return his smile. Nolan sighed, and said, "Of course I'll talk to you about the expedition, as fully and honestly as I can. You appear to be in some mental distress and, as a

Healer, I'm obliged to do everything possible to relieve it. Beside, nobody else wants to talk to me, so I don't have much choice.

"And while we're talking," Nolan added, "you might consider ways of relieving my own distress with a therapeutic shot of something which only looks like cold tea."

Ciaran nodded and bent down behind the counter, then looked past Nolan and checked himself in midstoop. His expression was apologetic as he said quietly, "I'll have to leave you now; your chief has just arrived. He's about ten paces behind you and it is you, not me, he'll be wanting to talk to."

"The—the captain?" Nolan asked nervously. He had yet to meet that God-like being and he was not looking forward to it.

"I mean your real chief," Ciaran replied as he turned away, "O'Riordan."

Monsignor O'Riordan, the expedition's senior representative of the Sacred College for the Propagation of Faith, was not in uniform. He had chosen instead to wear the red-lined cape, cassock, and biretta favored by Romish prelates of his ecclesiastical rank. Apart from the small ship's crest appearing inconspicuously on his collar, he could have been any one of the dozens of middle-ranking clerics with reasons or good excuses for attending the reception. But if there was anyone present who did not know the rotund little priest with the deep, bass voice for who and what he was, then that person was remarkably ignorant.

"You look very well, my son," said the monsignor, his eyes moving slowly from Nolan's highly polished boots to his heat-flushed and equally shining face. He patted his waist gently, and added, "I lack the physique for that particular uniform, and must disguise the results of a lifetime of moderate gluttony by taking refuge inside this ecclesiastical bell-tent."

He smiled and looked over his shoulder into the reception area before turning back to Nolan. "For a man in your position this is a unique experience, but you don't look as if you are enjoying it very much. If something is worrying you, my son, please speak freely."

"I'm not worried, sir," Nolan began, then hesitated as the other's expression hardened momentarily at the omission of his ecclesiastical title. He went on quickly, "It's just that I feel, well, uncertain about this whole business. If the Imperial Treasury doesn't approve it after all the money that has already been spent . . ."

O'Riordan was holding up both hands. "Please forgive me, Healer Nolan. It was presumptuous of me to call you 'my son' when you are not of the Faith. I had forgotten that you are one of these heretics God has sent among us, I suspect, to test the quality of our own belief.

"And if I refer to you as 'my son' again," he went on, his eyes twinkling, "please forgive it as the irritating habit of a forgetful old man. Pardon the interruption, Healer. You were saying?"

O'Riordan was going out of his way to put him at his ease, but Nolan knew that one of the few things that the monsignor was not was forgetful.

"It isn't really my responsibility," Nolan resumed. "It is just that I wonder whether we are being entirely honest in our approach to the general public . . ."

O'Riordan was holding up his hands again. "If we are going to debate moral subtleties, please let us converse in your own native tongue. What you are doing to our beautiful Gaelic, had you been other than a Godless heathen, I would define as a mortal sin. Please go on."

All at once Nolan had the feeling that he should *not* go on; that, friendly and approachable as the monsignor might be, he was numbered among the ship's hierarchy and, although the graduations of priestly and professional rank on *Aisling Gheal* were often obscure, it was rumored that he was to be its second-in-command—and one who should not, therefore, be burdened with the minor anxieties of a very junior officer. He had not made any impression on the guests, probably for the reasons given by Ciaran, and he was in danger of making a very bad one on O'Riordan.

Nolan cursed himself for getting into this stupid and unnecessary predicament. He was not really worried by what was going on here, just proud and excited and concerned for its eventual success. But he had developed the habit of framing and answering questions, regardless of the subject, clearly and honestly and in complete detail so as to impress a succession of female Healers who otherwise would have had no time for a mere male trainee. It was a habit he was trying to curb. He should curb it now.

"I'm sorry," Nolan said. "You have more important matters to occupy your time than listening to me worrying aloud. Please forgive me, sir."

O'Riordan laughed quietly. "Forgive you, indeed? Dear me, that could be construed as the first step to hearing your confession. But if you were not a benighted unbeliever, you would know that it is my first and most important priestly duty, on or off the ship, to listen to my people worrying aloud. I'm sure that I would not risk excommunication by extending the same facility to you."

Nolan was beginning to like this friendly little monsignor, whose public reputation as a militant theologian and unrivaled debater was at such variance with his private manner. He said, "Possibly it is a legacy of my frugal past, sir, but the cost of all this is, is . . . I mean, we're pretending that the expedition is a certainty, that it simply needs a few details to be finalized for the ship to be ready to leave. The truth is that I feel we are taking part in a very expensive, and possibly necessary, confidence trick. It is said that the expedition lacks proper financial support, and I fear that it has very little real chance of success. I realize that the ship can be used for other purposes, but these people are going to be very angry with us if we disappoint—"

"You were made aware of all the risks, my son," O'Riordan broke in, and suddenly he was no longer genial. "Are you, perhaps, hoping that we will fail?"

"God, no!" Nolan burst out. "Honestly, I'm not afraid of what might happen when we arrive. It's not getting the chance to leave that frightens me."

O'Riordan was smiling again. He said, "The same thought frightens all of us. Perhaps your trouble stems from the, to me, unusual combination of a well-developed conscience and a serious lack of faith. But we will have to discuss this matter in detail at a more convenient time, Healer. Now I must leave you."

As the small red-cassocked figure slipped into and beneath the surface of the sea of people, Nolan became aware of a change in the atmosphere. An expectant near-hush had fallen, and a tidal surge of brightly garbed bodies moved toward the edges of the processional carpet.

Ciaran jumped to the top surface of the board and stood among the crystal goblets, wearing the expression of some stupid amadan of a servant with no other thought in his head than to see his Queen Empress. He appeared to be a most slovenly and untidy servant, because his smock fastenings were loose and it would have needed a keen eye and foreknowledge to see the dull gleam of metal between the partially open folds. The drapes enclosing the refreshment area had moved silently apart so that the disguised *Ionadacht na Garda* had an unobstructed view all the way from the entrance stairs to the throne.

Nolan, as politely as possible, used his considerable advantages of weight, size, and uniform to push forward to the carpet's edge.

A double line of trumpeters in Imperial livery had taken up positions along both sides of the staircase; so still and precisely spaced were they that they might have been part of the ornamental statuary. Suddenly their instruments swept upward as one and the Imperial Fanfare pealed out.

Maeve VII was about to walk among them.

In spite of himself Nolan felt his scalp prickle and a shiver go crawling along his spine as that splendid music reached its stirring climax. Then, as the trumpets were silenced, the musicians positioned under the entrance balcony went smoothly into the equally stirring, but more stately, "Brendan's Victory," muted so as to enable the strong, beautifully modulated voice of the Master of Protocol to carry clearly to the farthest corners of the great hall.

"Her Most Puissant and Imperial Majesty, Maeve the Seventh, High-Queen of the Provinces of Ulster, Munster, Leinster, and Connaught, of the island Kingdom of Man, and of Cymri and Caledonia . . ."

With the first few words she moved forward onto the stairs and began her stately, measured descent in time with the music, the long, formal cloak flowing over the marble steps like a dark green and gold river behind her. She had chosen to wear a simple emerald tiara with the golden, jewel-incrusted armor and accoutrements of a warrior queen, which, because of the constant battle being waged so successfully between her advancing years and the Court cosmeticians, showed to the best advantage her striking, waist-length red hair, renowned comeliness of face, and splendid physique.

". . . Ruler of the Great and Glorious Empire of the West, of the Protectorates, Dependencies, and Mandated Territories of Skandia, Arctica, Amundsenland and of Mex. Empress Mother of the Common Weals of . . ."

The visiting dignitaries were bowing or curtseying low, while the Imperial Citizens exercised their prerogative of remaining standing and holding their heads high in the presence of their High-Queen. As a result, Nolan had an even better view as Maeve drew abreast of him.

". . . Knight Commander of the Noble Orders of the Red and of the Green Branch, Defender of the Faith and Guardian of the Pax Hibernia . . ."

It was not Maeve, however, who claimed Nolan's attention, but the man in crew uniform who walked two paces to her left and one pace behind her. He had not been announced, because no lesser person accompanying her, whether they were a lowly guard or a high-ranking minister of state, could have their name coupled with that of the most powerful ruler in the world, the Ard-Rioghan of Tara and Empress of the Westland.

A tall, graying, stern-featured man who moved with a barely perceptible limp, he carried himself with an air of authority rivaling that of the Empress. He wore only his badges of rank, displaying none of the many decorations and awards bestowed on him by seats of learning all over the civilized world. Had it not been for that limp—the legacy of a prenatal accident to his mother—and the strict rules governing the physical, as well as the mental and moral, requirements for election, he would not have been walking one pace behind his temporal ruler, because the crown of the High-King Emperor would have been resting on his own head.

There had been no surprise when, following his narrow defeat at the election, he had entered the Church as a member of one of the confraternities devoted to the scientific and technical disciplines so that his many and varied talents could be put to use in the Imperial Civil Service, where his rise in both the ecclesiastical and scientific rankings was deservedly rapid. And even though there was no constitutional way of exchanging rulers, there were many who still made unfavorable comparisons between his abilities, accomplishments, and blameless private life and those of the reigning Empress, who tried very hard to surpass, on the scented battleground of the silken bed, the conquests of the first Ard-Rioghan to bear her name.

That, it was rumored, more than any other consideration being weighed here today, was the reason why Maeve was lending her active support and that of her treasury to the project. It was the only safe and legal means by which she could rid herself of this man and the constant embarrassment his presence caused her.

In spite of her faults, Maeve was not a bad Empress. Even though she was a staunch traditionalist who bitterly fought against the changes forced on her by a constantly changing world—as witness the archaic trappings ordered for today's reception—she was far from being the worst to occupy the Seat of the Ard-Ri at Tara, and she had accomplished much good during her reign.

Maeve's place in the history books was assured.

But so also would be that of His Eminence Padair, Cardinal Keon, priest-scientist and statesman, commanding officer and driving force behind Project Aisling Gheal, Earth's first starship.

Chapter 2

FROM the project's inception it had been realized that *Aisling Gheal*, the Bright Vision, would have to be Earth's first starship rather than be exclusive property of the Hibernian Empire, for not even the richest and most advanced civilization that the world had ever known possessed the financial and technical resources needed to launch a project of such size and complexity. And because the proud and powerful Empire had been forced to seek the help of its weaker contemporaries, the major problems encountered were political rather than scientific.

Hibernia, however, the Great Empire of the West, had existed in a stable if not always peaceful condition for more than five centuries, and knew more than a little about the art of politics.

"But this is just a friendly get-together," Nolan went on pleasantly, in answer to the question of a guest seated opposite. "Thankfully, the more complex diplomatic and financial negotiations are not in either of my areas of responsibility. All I am supposed to do right now is be nice to everyone and answer all their nonpolitical questions."

Beside him Ciaran cleared his throat and said, "What exactly are your areas of responsibility, sir? I mean, are you a spasaire with medical qualifications or a Healer with astronaut training?"

A number of specially chosen guests had been moved discreetly from the mass audience chamber to the palace's state banqueting hall, and the ship's officers had been scattered not quite at random among these important personages. During the very few minutes between their arrival and taking their places, Ciaran had been able to exchange his original seat for the position on Nolan's right so as to continue, he had explained blandly, the conversation interrupted by the arrival of the monsignor.

Somehow he looked even larger now that the loose, barservant's smock was no longer hiding his uniform, and it was obvious that not one ounce of that weight was adipose. Ciaran, it seemed, was a very potent individual indeed, and it made Nolan feel uncomfortable that the Ionadacht insisted on calling him "sir."

"If the question is not proper . . ." began Ciaran apologetically. He must have mistaken the other's hesitation for reluctance to answer.

"No, no, quite proper," Nolan replied. He made a show of glancing at the strikingly beautiful occupant of the seat on his left. "I'm sorry, my mind was elsewhere."

Ciaran smiled his understanding and Nolan went on, "I was given basic spasaire training, but the Healer qualification, in certain areas, has given rise to adverse comment."

If Ciaran had detected a defensive tone in Nolan's voice, he ignored it—or perhaps the Guard captain knew that there were times when the best way to be tactful was to appear to be brash.

"I can understand that," he said, laughing. "However, I've had personal experience of one of your kind treating me during the immigrant riots on Brendan's Island in '73. It wasn't a full-scale rebellion, of course, but the hand-to-hand work was rough, and at the time I didn't have either the rank or the good sense to stay out of it. I was badly cut up and . . ."

Plainly the incident was unpleasant to recall. Ciaran shook his head and laughed again as he continued, "He was the only Healer available at the time, his stitching was neat even though it was in places where it wouldn't often show, and I was bleeding so much that it wouldn't have mattered to me if it was a medically qualified baboon doing the job.

"They had my face covered so that I wouldn't be distressed by seeing him at work," he went on very seriously, "so that I never saw his face. He might have been a medically qualified baboon for all I could tell. But definitely a male one, because I heard them call him sir."

Before Nolan could respond, the girl on his left began laughing, but quietly so that the sound was overlaid by the subdued rattling of the gold and jeweled ornaments that covered, very inadequately, her neck and chest. "Please excuse the interruption," she said, "and my obvious eavesdropping on a personal conversation."

The gold-on-black place card before her said that she was the Princess Ulechitzl, of the Royal Court of Tenochtitlan, and she wore the winged serpent medallion of an Adept of the First Level of the Order of Quetzalcoatl—a degree respected by universities all over the world. She was, therefore, something more than an exquisite and high-born decoration.

"My apologies are due to you, Your Highness," Nolan said, turning to her, "for excluding you from our not-very-interesting conversation, and for ignoring your presence. My problem was that had I looked at you, even briefly, I would have continued to look at you to the exclusion of all else, and risked giving even greater offense of another kind. Please forgive me."

The tall, slender headdress that sprang from the crest of her helmet like a feathery many-colored fountain shivered as she laughed again.

"Never have I encountered a more pleasing reason for being ignored, Healer," she said. "Delicacy of manner is unexpected in a—in such a large . . ."

"Baboon?" Ciaran finished for her.

Ulechitzl smiled faintly, then went on, "The original purpose of this archaic costume was to make men look, and continue to look, at me. I do not feel offended when it does what it was designed to do. In any event I am simply obeying the wishes of your High-Queen. In Tenochtitlan I normally wear coveralls."

"In coveralls, Your Highness," said Ciaran, leaning forward so that he could see her past Nolan, "men would continue to look at you."

She acknowledged the compliment with the smallest possible nod, and said, "We do not qualify baboons in our kingdom, but our Healers have been predominantly male since the earliest times. Their professional philosophy has always been that a doctor should remove the cause of the trouble, not risk poisoning and weakening the patient with obscure herbal treatments until the person is too weak, more often than not, to benefit from the surgical treatment which should have been given in the first place."

She smiled again and went on, "Our Healers have been surgeons rather than physicians since the bad old days when we practiced nonelective cardiac surgery to ensure that Huitzilopochtli would allow the sun to come up every morning.

"I would be quite content, Healer Nolan," she added seriously, "to entrust my physical well-being to you."

Nolan could feel his face growing hot. "You are too kind, Your Highness," he said. "I am very sure that you would receive much better attention from your Court healers in Tenochtitlan."

"To you," she said firmly, "rather than any other Healer on the ship."

There was the small sound of crystal striking gold plate as Ciaran knocked over his goblet, painting a dark-red fan on the expanse of snow-white linen before him. He ignored it, even though it was one of the better vintages from Gaul and not the nonalcoholic near-poison being served to Nolan, and said incredulously, "*You* are going?"

With the quiet self-assurance that only an Aztec Princess Royal could command, she said, "There are very few of my race who will be fortunate enough to share in your Bright Vision, and they have been chosen from the best that is available. Naturally, I shall be going."

For the next few minutes Nolan could only sit back in his chair and listen to them talking past him. He had been concerned over Ciaran's reasons for going. They had been based principally on the natural boredom of an active young man forced into physical inactivity, and Nolan had not thought them strong enough—unless, of course, there were other reasons which he had not revealed. Ciaran had active service experience, at least, which would prepare him for some of the aspects of the new life. But a Royal Princess of the blood, a delicate beauty who was protected at every turn from the harsher realities of the Old World, would not, he thought, be well fitted for life on the New.

Still, she might not be completely without protection. Whether or not Ciaran himself realized it, the interest he was showing in Ulechitzl seemed more personal than the discovery of a shared interest would warrant. It might well be that she had found in Ciaran a most resourceful and able protector.

Nolan sighed and asked himself, not for the first time, whether he was more interested in reaching the New World than in escaping from the old one. He was still wondering when the Imperial Fanfare crashed out again, putting an end to the conversations of Ulechitzl and Ciaran and everyone else. It was followed by a sound like a great wave breaking over rocks as all present pushed back their seats and stood to face the Royal Table.

Maeve inclined her head graciously and rose to her feet. Everyone else sat down.

She was flanked by the cardinal-captain and her former Court Healer, Dervla, and a handful of the top-ranking specialist officers. With the exceptions of Monsignor O'Riordan and herself, all were in the black and silver uniform of the ship. Plainly she wanted no doubt in the minds of any of her audience regarding the subject of this evening's Imperial Address or where her support lay.

Nolan was not looking forward to meeting Cardinal Keon or

Dervla. And while it was possible that the captain might never have occasion to speak to one of Nolan's lowly rank, the cool, lovely, utterly dedicated, and reputedly sexless Dervla would be his chief of department on the ship.

To join the expedition she was relinquishing her position as Physician Director of the Tara House of Sorrows, which was probably the largest and most advanced hospital in the world. She was indisputably the Empire's foremost Healer, for had this not been so, a woman other than herself would have been ministering to the medical needs of Maeve VII. And those steady blue eyes would be watching Nolan's every move and, staunch traditionalist that she was, finding fault at every opportunity with this male person who had joined the most honored of professions through a foreign back door.

He hoped that her red hair, a darker and less artificial color than that of the High-Queen, was not indicative of the same hypershort temper.

The shuffling of feet and the nervous, anticipatory coughing faded into stillness, and Maeve said, "*A Daoine Uasial, Gael agus Goll.*

"Noble People, Gaels, and Visitors," she went on in ritual fashion. "With this warm and personal and most grateful greeting to every one of you here present, may I call down the blessing of the One True and Many-natured God on our deliberations and on the glorious enterprise in which you will all, I firmly believe, want to take part. So strongly do I believe this that I shall dispense with the diplomatic niceties, the individual expressions of pleasure at the presence of my brothers within and without our great Empire, and discuss without further preamble my reasons for bringing together this distinguished gathering."

She had the voice and bearing that in the old days would have inspired warriors to deeds of valor against impossible odds, Nolan thought, and the costume of a warrior queen had probably been chosen with just that effect in mind.

Suddenly she flung up a slender, well-muscled arm and pointed toward the great, arching, beautifully executed ceiling panels depicting the major episodes in Imperial history, and beyond. The ring of the legendary O'Donnell the Brave on her stiffly extended index finger caught the light and shone symbolically against the decp blue of the background drapes like the flashing of a many-hued variable star.

"Out there," she went on, "orbits the spasarthach *Aisling*

Gheal, the greatest and most complex space vehicle to be envisaged by the mind of man. It began as a vision of my predecessor, Dairmuid VI, that was given substance during my own reign. But it is a vision still clouded and incomplete, a dream that remains unfulfilled, a great, near-empty shell, a spore pod which is as yet unable to carry its seed. This glorious dream will surely die unless we have your help."

She paused and looked down for a moment, with an expression that might have been embarrassment on her regal features, then shook her head and looked up at them again.

"Never before in the long and proud history of the Hibernian Empire," she continued, "has an immeasurably wealthy and powerful High-Queen and Empress had to ask for alms like a lowly beggar. But now, and I will not try to obscure the fact with high-sounding, diplomatic phrases, that I and the army of priest-scientists and specialist technicians charged with the completion of the project are pleading for your help.

"The help we need is not purely financial, although funding is a vitally important aspect of the endeavor. Unlike the beggar, we will return much more than simple insubstantial gratitude for your assistance, because we will be sharing with you the finest fruits of the Empire's technology as well as our most closely guarded industrial secrets . . ."

"The few," murmured Ciaran, "that they haven't already stolen from us."

". . . Not only will we be planting the green, white, and bronze standard of the Empire on another world," she went on, giving a little smile, "we will be raising the living standards of everyone who remains on this one."

At the other side of the table a Redman chief was looking slightly more impassive than usual. Beside him a Maori lord and his lady were staring at each other, their expressions hidden by thick daubs of ceremonial mud, and Ulechitzl was making no attempt to hide her displeasure. The reference to planting the Imperial standard had been a mistake, but while the High-Queen's advisers who had prepared the speech could make suggestions, nobody could tell Maeve exactly what to say and hope to draw his pension.

Ignoring the suddenly congealing atmosphere in the room, she went on smoothly, "But with our Imperial emblem other flags will proudly fly, for Hibernia is subordinating any Imperial or expansionist aspirations we may earlier have harbored, and are now satisfied and, indeed, proud to provide little more than the vehicle itself, the great metal womb that will carry and protect the embryo of all that is best of the richly varied cultures and philosophies that go to make up the human race."

The Redman's features had relaxed and Ulechitzl was looking excited rather than displeased. Verbally, Nolan thought admiringly, Maeve was fast on her golden-shod feet. She lowered her hand, and her voice became serious and almost sad when she went on.

"No empire of this world will last forever," she said, "not even this one. Already the signs are obvious to my learned monks who study these things that we have reached our peak of progress and culture and are about to go into a slow decline. Our colonies have come of age, are leaving the parental control and influence, and are demanding self-rule. The process has been a stable and amicable one on the whole, but the signs of dissolution are clear for all to see, and competition for the world's diminishing natural resources is becoming more intense. This, you must agree, is the Golden Age, and it will not be long with us."

Her voice deepened and shook with feeling, and her hand was raised again in the manner of a teacher stressing an important point in a lesson as she went on, "It is this Golden Age which must be preserved, and planted anew on a mineral-rich and verdant young world. The seed we will plant must represent the best this old world can provide of its arts, culture, history, and traditions.

"Not only will our Imperial Citizens, our long-beloved brothers of the Nations of the Redmen, the proud members of the Aztec and Mayan kingdoms, the Icelanders, the Skandians, the loyal Saxons, and all the others which time alone forbids my mentioning, be represented. The ancient and gifted peoples of the twin Empires of Cathay and Nippon, long recognized as the undisputed masters of both nuclear and micro-technology, will play a most important part. Naturally, since our Empire remains the farthest advanced in space sciences, the ship, with a few important exceptions, will be crewed by Hibernians. The number and composition of the colonists has not yet been decided . . ."

And the more a nation contributes, Nolan thought wryly, the larger will be the number of passenger tickets it buys.

". . . But everyone who volunteers," she continued, "and especially the ship's officers, whose space training will be redundant once the landing is accomplished, must have mastered at least one additional and most important discipline, that of the teacher.

"For on the New World," Maeve went on, a warning note

creeping into her tone, "the methods of mass dissemination of information which we take so much for granted here and now will not always be available. The communication and other electronic equipment taken from the ship will wear out or be drained of power in time, and the suppliers of spare parts will be far away and their delivery dates proportionately untrustworthy . . ."

She paused for a moment to smile, but there was no response to her little pleasantry. They were hanging on her every word, Nolan saw, so intently that they did not want to waste even a few seconds on polite laughter. He could well understand their feelings, because it was their people's future and hope of racial immortality that she was talking about, and the hair at the back of his neck was beginning to prickle again.

"It is expected that some period of time, perhaps three or more generations, will elapse before the worn-out mechanisms from the ship will be replaced, gradually, by the colony-developed technology," she resumed, "and if the teachers are faithful and dedicated in their duties, the period may be even shorter. For they will not simply be teachers in the presently understood meaning of the word. Instead, they will inherit the mantles of the bards, of the legendary Homer, of Seamus the Wise, and of the great poet Far Falling Water, and they will be able to recall and recite, accurately and in meticulous detail, not only the exploits of the great men and women of our past and present, but the elements of the science, technology, and culture which has made our Earth what it is today."

She looked around, slowly enough to make everyone feel sure that, if only for an instant, her eyes were on them alone. The silence spoke much more eloquently than could the wildest of applause.

"Nothing of us will be lost or forgotten," she went on. "This tremendous star pod will carry not only the most physically and mentally perfect of our sons and daughters and the technology which has made mankind great, it will also contain the replicating seed of the incredibly rich and varied philosophies, cultures, and art which is the true reason for that greatness. This tired old Earth will produce a seed which will be wondrous beyond imagining.

"As in every birth, there is labor, sacrifice, and pain for all of us. But, my friends and fellow laborers, what a glorious seed we and the *Aisling Gheal* will plant in that new and virgin world.

"That," she ended simply, "is our Bright Vision."

As she sat down, the opening notes of the fanfare blared out, bringing everyone else to their feet. But it was clear from the start that the trumpeters were fighting a losing battle against the rising storm of shouting, cheering, and pounding of fists and feet against floor and furniture—a din to which Nolan was contributing no small part.

Chapter 3

PALE and feeling like the wrath of all the Gods worshipped throughout the Empire, Nolan took his seat at the breakfast board next morning. After the Imperial Address had come the presentation of ship's officers and, following the withdrawal of the ecclesiastical crew-members, the strictures regarding the consumption of alcohol had been removed and it had become a gaudy night—what he could recollect of it. Ciaran, who had obviously been waiting for his arrival, took the seat next to his.

"If you're feeling bad, sir," he said sympathetically, "there is a concoction, rumor has it, used by Maeve herself and prescribed by Dervla and called the fur of stag. But even better is strong coffee, some light food, merely for the purpose of alcohol absorption, and fresh air."

"Thank you, Healer," said Nolan dryly.

Embarrassed, Ciaran said, "I'm sorry. It's just that on the subject of cures for the aftereffects of dissipation and depravity, I am a specialist. What are your duties for today?"

"None," said Nolan. "I plan to get some fresh air as you suggest and do a little quiet sightseeing, visit the university and . . . well, this is my first chance to see the Imperial City. Perhaps you could advise me on how best to spend my limited time here?"

"You won't find much fresh air in Atha Cliath," said Ciaran. "But I, too, am free today and would be delighted to be your guide. And don't worry, Healer, I shall not escort you dressed in all this finery. But you can wear uniform if you like. Everyone we meet will want to shake your hand and take you into the nearest tavern to drink your health in ten languages—"

Nolan shuddered and raised a hand gently to his throbbing head. "I'll wear civilian dress," he said.

"But wear your Healer's insignia and ship medallion with it," Ciaran said, laughing. "They will help if you should become unruly and annoy the Peace Guards."

The high-speed train that took them from Tara to the center of Atha Cliath was stoned only once as it skirted the Imperial College complex, a strange conglomeration of buildings in which soaring towers of steel and glass grew like enormous glittering trees from the cracks between the gray, tradition-steeped buildings of the original establishment. Even though the sun was shining, the outlines of the buildings were obscured by a golden haze which gave them a dreamlike quality that was quite beautiful.

"Just wait until you smell it," said Ciaran, making Nolan realize that he had been thinking aloud. "It is industrial and domestic smoke. Why do you want to go to the university?"

"I'm interested in the library," Nolan replied, "because it should give me some idea of the size of my problem and, with luck, point toward a solution."

"A serious problem?" asked Ciaran.

Nolan smiled. "I may have to teach subjects about which I know very little, and so I must begin by teaching myself."

"You are off duty," Ciaran protested. "This is Atha Cliath. There are much more interesting things to do here than looking at a lot of musty old books."

"And I look forward to doing them, and soon," Nolan agreed. "But you are forgetting that to many people, myself included, the Imperial College Library is the most wonderful place in the world. I shall be trying to find out how the teachers of old were able to pass on their knowledge, without benefit of books and modern visual aids, so effectively that even today we remember their lessons. The trouble is, history has always been an interest of mine, so I know just how large the problem is."

The train was slowing and rattling over the switches on the approach to Hero station, and in the corridor the black-cloaked senior civil servants with business in the city were jostling each other, politely as behooved ecclesiastics, for positions by the doors. Even though the train was crowded, the Guards' captain had arranged that they had the compartment to themselves.

"Will I be expected to teach?" Ciaran asked suddenly.

Nolan shook his head. "The crew, most of whom are of the priesthood and celibate, are charged with the propagation of knowledge while you are expected to propagate the race, an easy job by comparison. All you have to do, Ionadacht, is carve an outpost of Empire out of a new, raw world, with a plowshare in one hand and comely partner, possibly an incredibly beautiful Aztec Princess, clinging lovingly to the other."

Strangely the remark seemed to embarrass the other, and Nolan felt sure that his words were not those he wanted to speak as he said, "Healer, my name is Ciaran."

And there were other names as well, Nolan had learned from one of the palace servants—names that explained the reason for his influence over virtually everyone below the level of Imperial Adviser. He was Ciaran Conhair O'Rahilly, Ionadacht of the clan that had jealously served the High-Kings and High-Queens of Tara as personal guards for more than five centuries, although only the finest of its young men were chosen for service at the palace

In the old days his father would have been called a King in his own right, and Ciaran his royal lieutenant. The fact that he had never mentioned his family name might have been due to his father, for personal or family reasons, not approving of his high-born son and heir leaving Earth, and he was in disgrace. In any event, Nolan had been fortunate that such an influential young man had decided to pick on him, a mere male Healer and a heretic, to befriend.

Nolan wondered whether their meeting had been through good fortune or design, and then he wondered if he should visit a Healer of the Mind to have his paranoia exorcised before it reached the acute stage.

The station concourse had seemed to be crowded until Nolan came to the staircase leading down to street level and he was confronted by the sight of pavements so thickly covered by a moving, many-colored carpet of people that the ground itself was invisible. The noisy, slow-flowing vehicular traffic, horse-drawn as well as powered, seemed only a little less congested.

"It's worse than usual because of the games," said Ciaran. "Faster if we walk, I think."

As they pushed their way through the crowd Nolan rubbed shoulders with, or frequently walked on the feet of, every racial type known to him. With very few exceptions they were all wearing the distinctive souvenir caps, badges, or rosettes of the Eighty-seventh Tailteann Games, which in the past century had been widened to include not only native Gaels and Imperial Citizens, but athletes from all over the world. There was a rumor circulating, which the palace press monsignor had on several occasions refused to deny, that Imperial gold medalists would automatically be offered places on *Aisling Gheal.*

"Be advised," said Ciaran, when they found themselves in a particularly thick press of bodies which ranged from infants-in-arms to octogenarians, "that the pickpockets of Atha Cliath are reputed to be the most proficient and daring in the world. Their apprenticeship begins before they can walk, and they improve with age."

"Do they have long arms, too?" asked Nolan, laughing. "My few valuables are back at the palace."

Ciaran smiled approvingly and said, "Stay close behind me; it should be less crowded by the river."

As the crowd divided before his enormous shoulders like a living and loudly protesting bow-wave, Ciaran seemed to feel it necessary to apologize to Nolan for virtually everything. The streets were too narrow and winding for the volume of traffic they had to carry, and were always being dug up because the sewers were as old as the buildings they had been designed to serve many centuries earlier, and a less popular High-Queen would have leveled the lot and started over. But whenever the senior planning engineers advanced any such suggestion, the historians, archeologists, and Maeve herself threatened to hang them by their clerical collars from the most convenient streetlamp. A completely new and properly laid out Imperial City should have been built a century ago, he said with great feeling. For a lot less gold than it took to maintain Atha Cliath as an imperfectly functioning Imperial capital, the old city could have been classified as a living museum and roofed over in plastic.

"It is a great pity that they didn't," said Nolan, holding out a hand palm upward. "It's starting to rain."

The traffic congestion and the smell increased as they neared the river which, in its lower reaches, was crossed by more than a hundred bridges, so that the larger ships tied up alongside the ancient quays had nowhere to go except down when, as occasionally happened, one of them caught fire and sank at its moorings. Jostled at every turn, they pushed their way past lines of houseboats, floating souvenir shops, and the odd vessel that looked so inconspicuous and purposeless it had to be engaged in something illegal.

"Unsavory or undesirable rather than illegal," said Ciaran when he pointed to one of them. "If some of our nonbelieving Citizens state that destroying their minds and bodies with happy powder is something that they firmly believe in, there isn't much that the Peace Guard can do about it. We live in a liberal and enlightened age, Healer, but this is one part of our culture which must not be transplanted to the New World. Ah, I see that you have already noticed the Swans of the Sweet Dreamers."

There were five of the long, low barges tied up in line along the quayside, each one decorated extravagantly in gilt and the bright lacquers of Cathay. Neither the gray overcast nor the thick vapors drifting above the river could dull those bright, rich colors or the delicate artistry of the detail work. It was like walking beside a floating art gallery whose large, square ports framed three-dimensional portraits of unsurpassable charm and beauty. The gallery attendants stationed at the bottom of each vessel's gangway were quietly and conservatively dressed, respectful in manner and very, very muscular.

"Those barges never go anywhere," said Ciaran delicately, "but if they did, their navigation lights would burn red whether you approached them from port or starboard."

Nolan stumbled because he was looking at one of the living portraits which was inclining its beautifully adorned head and smiling as it looked back at him. He sighed and said, "A visit to one of them would be a very pleasant way of sheltering from the rain. Have you ever . . . ?"

"Not recently, Healer," said Ciaran. "This is another aspect of Imperial culture which will not be transplanted to the New World."

Nolan stopped suddenly and pointed at the vessel tied up on the opposite bank of the river. It was an incredibly ancient and fragile ship gleaming in its all-over coat of the clear, protective varnish that would inhibit further deterioration. The outlines and rigging of the ship were unmistakable, as were the sections of burned upper hull and superstructure that had been replaced with the Westland timber, and explained the endless line of sightseers who moved slowly along the dockside and past it. They were kept from touching any part of that fabulous vessel by a low rope barrier and some very tall guards, neither of which interfered with the view.

His words were not so much a question as an awed statement. "That is the *Sea Dragon*?"

"Small, isn't it?" said Ciaran. "Would you like to go on board?"

"Now you're tempting me," said Nolan, without taking his eyes off that ridiculously tiny ship which, close on six centuries earlier, had carried Brendan the Navigator, the legendary priest-captain who had been responsible for the founding and formation of the Empire of the West. He cleared his throat noisily and asked, "To be allowed on board, to actually walk the deck . . . Dammit, does your influence extend as far as *that*?"

"Unfortunately, no," said Ciaran, "but yours might."

Nolan looked at the Guards captain in astonishment, and the other went on, "Come now, remember what rather than who you are. A crew-member of the *Aisling Gheal*, a ship whose purpose is also the discovery and exploration of a new world. The analogies must be plain even to you, and if Brendan himself were on board he could not, nor would he want to, forbid it."

Nolan hesitated, thinking of the thousands of words and the multitude of still and moving pictures he, and more than half the schoolchildren of the world, had absorbed covering every fact, detail, aspect, and legend concerning this historic ship. But to walk its deck and touch its rigging and move, bent almost double, through its tiny, low-beamed cabins was something he had only dreamed about. The thought that he might actually live that dream left his feelings in utter confusion, but the strongest and most easily identified feeling was that of caution.

If Ciaran and himself were to push their way through that crowd of sightseers to identify himself to a guard, and the guard had the kind of routine-indoctrinated mind which was incapable of responding to the situation other than by taking refuge behind his simple orders, then Nolan would have to withdraw. But Ciaran was too proud to allow that and would almost certainly respond, physically or with heavily weighted words. A very embarrassing situation might develop which, considering the number of onlookers and the two individuals at its center, would certainly be reported back to the palace and might even make the newscasts.

Nolan was an officer on a ship whose crew was composed entirely of officers, but he could not think of a single one of them who was subordinate to him. Perhaps Ciaran had a more inflated idea of the Healer's importance than had Nolan himself.

"Later, perhaps," he said, "after I've been to the library."

Ciaran, who had been watching his expression closely, nodded his head but did not speak.

There was no argument or embarrassment involved in gaining access to the history shelves of the Imperial Library because it was the chief librarian himself who met and led them quickly through the stacks to his private study, where he immediately offered hospitality of the spiritous kind. Nolan was not surprised that he knew Ciaran—practically everyone in the Imperial City seemed to know the Ionadacht—but it did surprise him that the chief librarian knew who Nolan was and virtually everything about him.

"So your job will be to bring healing, enlightenment, and knowledge to the colonists and their offspring," said the little man, in a voice that was as old and dry and fragile as the parchments in the display cases all around them. "What better man could the cardinal-captain entrust with the duty than an unbeliever."

"That," said Nolan, "sounds vaguely heretical."

The little man's eyes twinkled and his surprisingly white, uneven, and probably real teeth showed in a smile that seemed impossibly bright in that incredibly ancient and wrinkled face. He said, "Heresy in high places is what keeps the Faith pure, or so our more ungodly students tell me. But we do not have the time to debate the benefits of therapeutic heresy, and while I would like to help you as much as I can, regrettably your time with me is limited to a few moments."

Nolan said quickly, "The time for study and mental self-training will be very long indeed. But right now I need guidance on how best to use that time . . ."

The chief librarian listened sympathetically as Nolan detailed his needs and, by inference, his many problems. Ciaran was beginning to look worried and seemed ready to interrupt, especially when the long-term nonavailability of teaching aids and the power to run them was assumed. But it was the old man who raised one faintly trembling hand and brought Nolan gently to a halt.

"The teaching discipline you intend to practice is possible," he said gently, "because it has been used with success in the past, as we well know, to promulgate our nonwritten histories. But few indeed were the sages and poets who were capable, as were the predecessors of Homer, of retaining in their minds those tribal and family histories, or the great stories and epic poems which often required many hours or days to recite to completion. The people to whom this ability was passed were required to study under their masters throughout childhood and into middle age before they could hope to match the proficiency of their mentors. Great though it was even then, the capacity of the minds concerned was limited, and there must be very few minds of the present day that are capable of emulating them.

"Which means," the chief librarian went on, "that you and the other teachers may be forced to edit, alter, or perhaps attempt to improve or simply not pass on certain areas of knowledge. This leads to the interesting question of who will decide, for practical as well as philosophical reasons, on the precise contents of the teaching syllabus. There would be the danger that—"

"Your pardon," Nolan broke in, trying to head off what could have been an interesting but lengthy debate, "I realize that I cannot equal the accomplishments of the bards of old . . ."

"Such engaging modesty in one so young," murmured the old man.

". . . But I thought," Nolan concluded, "that a study of the Druidic disciplines might be helpful."

"Are you thinking of the pre-Christian Druidic practices," the librarian said, "several of which have been modified, although they would be the last to admit it, for use by those members of our own clergy seeking major promotion in the civil service. One such exercise, I seem to remember, involved the singing or recitation of epic poems or detailed astronomical information concerning the times for planting crops, while the reciter was immersed, but for the nose and lips, in a bath of near-freezing water. The purpose of the cold soak was to help focust he mind and ensure its optimum functioning in spite of bodily discomforts. Had you something like this in mind, Healer?"

"Could the water be warm and soapy?" asked Nolan, laughing. "In that situation I have been known to sing."

The old man shook his head. Without smiling he went on, "I am unable to help you, not at present, and must apologize for detaining you here. Had I acted correctly I should have turned you back at the main gate. But I was most anxious to meet and talk with an officer of the ship, however briefly, before sending you away."

Nolan stared at the old man, who until then had seemed to be so friendly and cooperative. His surprise must have been plain for the other to read.

"It was a great honor and pleasure to meet you, Healer," the chief librarian went on. "I have a clear idea of your requirements and will personally assemble material which I am sure will be helpful, and forward it to you as soon as possible. But without any further delay on my own selfish part, I must pass on an urgent message to you from Monsignor O'Riordan. It is to the effect that the time of the technical presentation and reception for newsgatherers on Brendan's Island has been advanced, that your flight leaves Tara International one hour before dawn tomorrow morning, and that you should return forthwith to the palace for briefings. I am truly sorry that you could not stay long enough to let me show you the library, but the message seemed urgent and important."

"I understand, and thank you," said Nolan. To Ciaran he added, "The monsignor did not know I was coming here."

"As a trained psychologist and Healer of the Mind, among other things," said Ciaran dryly, "the monsignor is aware of how his charges think. He must have decided that the Imperial College Library was the first place to find Healer Nolan."

"The second place," said the old man with equal dryness. "At the risk of making your reverend psychologist seem something less than omniscient, a few minutes before the message from the palace arrived here, an identical one was relayed to me by a friend on the Swans of the Sweet Dreamers."

Later, as the great airliner climbed steeply and turned westward into a sky still dark and glittering with stars, Nolan watched the tall, floodlit gantries of the Tara space complex and the jeweled carpet that was Atha Cliath unrolling below them. The pilot, concerned with the strict ordinances against sound pollution, maintained subsonic mode while the dark central plain with its irregular scattering of town lights slid past, the sleep of those below uninterrupted by any sonic shock wave rolling over them.

Less than a century ago, when few indeed were the nations who came close to matching the world-girdling technology of the Empire, it had been decided that the Hibernian Thunder in the skies would be dampened only over the motherland herself. Now, however, the laggards had caught up. They were snapping like science-starved wolves at the Hibernian heels and they, too, were flaunting their own supersonic thunder all over the world.

As they overflew the Connemara coast, whose scenic grandeur was hidden by the dark cloak of night, he leaned back into his seat, closed his eyes, and tried to test the functioning of his memory.

The remembered scene was bright and beautiful and barely eight hours old. Between the afternoon and evening briefings Ciaran had taken him up to the observation blister atop the cloud-piercing central tower of Tara, although on that occasion the sky was clear.

He had gazed downward into the rolling acres of the palace parklands, tracing the outlines of the ramparts and ditches that had fortified the Royal Hill in bygone times. He had looked east and south across Atha Cliath, whose streets and buildings were given a more-than-three-dimensional clarity by the bright, orange light of the westering sun, to the dark blue sea; south and southwest over the provinces of Leinster and Munster; westward across the great central plain and Connaught; and north to the rounded, dark-blue mountains of the old Kingdom of Mourne in Ulster. He had been looking for a very long time when Ciaran broke the silence.

"There is much history to be remembered here," he said.

"You may not see me again, Ciaran," Nolan said quietly, "until we meet on the New World."

The other hesitated, then said, "But you will see me before then?"

"Oh, yes," said Nolan.

"And Ulechitzl?" Ciaran asked quietly. "I am concerned for her. She is not fitted for an enterprise such as this, Healer, and has need of a guardian."

"Yes," Nolan repeated, and smiled, although there was no hint of laughter in his voice as he went on, "both of you can rest easy. Whether you are cold or warm, asleep or newly awakened and confused, I will watch over you."

"Then, I shall rest easy, Healer," said Ciaran.

The Ionadacht's hands had come up and he had clasped Nolan's wrist and shoulder firmly, as he would at the parting of a close member of the family. And even now a shiver had run along his spine with the realization that he had not been speaking a few words of professional reassurance to a worried colonist, but had instead bound himself, at least in the Ionadacht's mind, to a most solemn and immutable promise.

Chapter 4

As their aircraft outstripped the rising sun and bored deeper into the western night, Nolan's memory of that final few minutes with Ciaran would not leave him. It remained clear in every word and tone, sharp in every movement and subtle play of expression, and more inexplicable with every moment that passed. For the Ionadacht was not the type of person to be frightened by the unknown, by the threat of some imaginary space monster or any other phantasm that was conjured up by his own mind. If there was some aspect of the flight of the *Aisling Gheal* that seriously worried him—frightened was not a word one associated with the onetime Captain of the Imperial Guards—it was most assuredly not composed of insubstantial imaginings.

Nolan muttered to himself in self-annoyance, and wondered, not for the first time, if the insubstantial imaginings were exclusively his own.

"Talking to yourself," said a well-remembered voice, "is a habit which you must assiduously cultivate, since there will be many times when you will be the only person able to hear you. But then, as now, you should make it a practice to speak in a clear voice so that others besides myself, who happens to be blessed with unusually acute hearing, are able to benefit from what you say."

The monsignor, who had been moving along the narrow aisle toward the flight deck, smiled gently at the officer sitting beside Nolan, and the man rose silently and gave O'Riordan his seat.

"If something is troubling you," said the monsignor quietly, when he was settled into place and the safety belt extended to accommodate his portly form, "I am always ready to help you."

"Thank you, no, sir," Nolan said. "It is a minor matter, neither urgent nor significant, and I apologize for any irritation suffered by those around me. I will be silent for the remainder of the trip."

"You will not be silent," said O'Riordan, smiling again, "because I came forward expressly to see you and request otherwise. It seems that I am one of the few ship's officers who has not heard you, ah, perform, and I am anxious to remedy this omission as well as to assess your qualities as a teacher. My next two hours are at your disposal, my son. To begin with, perhaps you have a favorite lecture or story, or an historical incident which you find of particular interest?"

"I wasn't expecting . . ." Nolan began, and fell silent. His face felt so hot that it must be elevating the temperature of the entire cabin.

"Hesitancy and shyness," O'Riordan said quietly, "are not desirable qualities in a teacher. The choice of subject will not always be yours."

Nolan took a deep breath, then said, "There is the War of the Red Brothers, or the coming of the first Hero to Tara or . . . or could I relate the Story of Brendan?"

"Since this is your first visit to the Westland, the choice does not surprise me," said O'Riordan, smiling. "May the Holy Spirit guide your tongue in the path of truth."

Nolan closed his eyes, the better to concentrate as well as to avoid the distraction of having to look at the priest's face, and began to speak.

"Under the command and spiritual guidance of Brendan the Navigator," he began, "the *Sea Dragon*, his flagship, accompanied by the sailing vessels *White Heron* and *Sinead*, the expedition left Atha Cliath on a course northward past the Kingdom of Man toward—"

"The date," O'Riordan said gently.

Nolan kept his eyes closed and a tight rein on his temper. Throughout the Empire and beyond, there was not an educated child above the age of three or an adult who did not know that particular date, which rivaled—in popularity, general celebration, and excessive gluttony, if not in true importance—the day of Christ's Mass. The omission had not been due to a lapse in memory but an unwillingness to include unnecessary information, and the monsignor must know that as well as did Nolan himself.

He gave the date, time, and relevant tidal information, and went on, "Two days out they encountered very bad weather, a sudden and unseasonable northwesterly gale which forced him to take refuge in the Lough of Belfast . . ."

Awkwardly at first but with growing confidence and feeling, Nolan went on to describe the pictures that research and imagination were combining to project onto the blank screen that was his closed eyelids—the words that accompanied them had, of necessity, to be his own. But to Nolan's mind, Brendan, the gifted visionary but essentially simple monk known variously as the Navigator, the Traitor, the Heretic, and ultimately the Exile, was arguably the most important, and certainly Nolan's own favorite, historical figure.

While he spoke Nolan tried hard to modulate his voice, to let it rise and fall as the incidents warranted it, and to make of the story what a thespian friend had once called a song without music. He did not try to conceal his enthusiasm. And it seemed to be going well, because the monsignor did not interrupt again, and from the officers in the seats behind and in front of him, and from across the central aisle, there was a silence which he hoped was attentive.

The interruption, when it came, took the form of an apologetic cough.

Nolan opened his eyes to see the officer who was seated across the aisle from him raise a hand and point forward to where, now that he had stopped talking, he could hear the sounds of the approaching meal trolley. The man said quietly, "Healer, I think this is the proper moment to break off, so that we can digest food as well as your history lesson."

The reason for his softness of voice, Nolan saw, was the slumped figure of the monsignor beside him. O'Riordan's hands lay palms upward on his crimson-garbed ample lap, his chin rested on his chest just above the pectoral cross, and his eyes were closed.

"Yes," Nolan agreed softly, and forced his lips to smile. "How many others have I sent to sleep?"

The monsignor opened one eye and smiled without raising his head. "I was resting, not sleeping," he said, "and I am sorry if my seeming unconsciousness was mistaken for an implied criticism."

Before Nolan could reply, O'Riordan went on. "My critical response so far is that you go more deeply than is necessary into the feelings of your characters—feelings which no historian however learned may know with accuracy—and are therefore guilty of fictionalizing the incidents to this extent. Our libraries are full of weighty tomes which purport to examine the character and motivations of Brendan. He is long dead, God rest his soul, and the nuances of his character are of no importance compared with his far-reaching effect on subsequent history. Your lessons should be aimed at children, and at non-Hibernian adults with little or no appreciation of the subtleties of—"

"But I thought that a fuller understanding of the characters concerned would increase the interest of—" began Nolan, and broke off as O'Riordan raised his head to look at him.

"Brendan was a truly great and humble man who might have been a saint," the monsignor went on in a voice that made Nolan feel uncomfortable without knowing why. "But a man can be too thoughtful, too humble, and too liberal. He can respect the rights and beliefs of others so much that he forgets that he has any of his own. That kind of thinking is dangerous and must be avoided, because it can make heretics of us all."

Nolan would have liked to argue that point, but the arrival of the food trays left only enough time for O'Riordan to have the last word.

"Try for a little more action and less introspection," the monsignor said, and smiled suddenly. "Having said that, I am reminded of the old-time bards, who were frequently required to sing or otherwise perform for their suppers. After due consideration, my son, I would say that you may enjoy yours with a clear conscience."

Pleased at the compliment, Nolan hurried through his meal and waited impatiently for the trays to be cleared so that he could resume.

This time he did not close his eyes, and neither did the monsignor, as he related the well-documented actions of the principal characters rather than the probable thinking behind those actions. It was a story of high adventure and dauntless, but never blind, courage which covered the initial abduction of Brendan, the so-called conversion of the Redmen chiefs, the last of the intertribal wars, the commercial interdiction of all non-Hibernian trading vessels, and Brendan's climactic act of disobedience to both his High-King and the Holy See.

By the time Nolan reached the great and stirring and, many still thought, tragic conclusion with the simple and stubborn and by then incredibly aged monk and Paramount Chief no longer able to enjoy the rewards that were so justly his, the aircraft was nose-up and subsonic on its final approach to Shining Sea airport.

They were met outside the aircraft with the news that their baggage would be taken directly to the world-renowned guest longhouse, the Algonquin Hibernia, where they would be accommodated during their stay on the Island, and escorted to a large, deeply carpeted lounge where their guides awaited them.

Unless she happened to be a close blood relation, it was still considered an insult by the conservative-minded Westlanders for a visitor to be met by a female. The guides were men, therefore, and dressed in the dark, close-fitting leggings, fringed matching tunics, and soft, beaded boots that aspiring Brendan's Island executives were wearing this season. There was a guide assigned to every five or six visitors, and the one who approached Nolan to stumble through the ritual greeting was young, very tall, and very, very nervous. The nervousness was possibly due to the fact that his Gaelic was even worse than Nolan's own.

"And I am happy to greet Wanachtee, my Redman brother," Nolan responded. He smiled reassuringly and added, "It is especially pleasant to be welcomed by another person of average height. I have a theory, supported by much observational evidence, that the majority of the human race are dwarves."

The Redman looked confused for a moment, then he relaxed and laughed. "You speak truth, Healer. There is also evidence that the smallest of stature often hold the greatest authority, and one of these . . ." His eyes looked briefly to one side. ". . . is probably wondering why the most recent member of the company tribe is laughing and at ease before an officer of the starship, instead of doing what he is supposed to be doing."

"Which is what?" asked Nolan.

From the inner pocket of his beautifully crafted jacket Wanachtee produced a handful of decorated fabric headbands. When he replied, the Redman raised his voice so as to include the officers standing close to Nolan.

"We would be honored if you would wear these during your stay with us," he said, in a respectful tone that still managed to convey the message that his people would be most gravely insulted if they were *not* worn. "The fitting is adjustable, and there is a small opening which allows the ship insignia to be seen when you wear them with your uniform berets. They should be worn at all times in public, whether you are in or out of uniform, and great care must be taken not to lose them."

One of the officers beside Nolan, a non-ecclesiastic Middle European called Brenner, was examining the delicate embroidery on the band. He said, "And what would happen to me if I did lose it?"

Politely the Redman disregarded the question, but answered it with a further explanation. "The fact that you are officers of the starship gives you the status of warrior and technical or administrative sub-chief, which is the highest level attainable by any person who is not a full-blooded Redman. A wearer of the band is accorded much respect and has access to many places and people of importance, and if his band should find its way into the wrong hands . . ."

He broke off to look around at the many uniformed attendants who were constantly coming and going all around them, then went on apologetically. "We have a large immigrant population here, lower-class paleskins for the most part. The majority of them are hard-working, honest people who respect the law and the teachings of their various gods. But there is a small criminal element among them who would willingly kill you to gain possession of the symbol of a chief."

Brenner was looking suitably chastened as they were ushered out of the lounge and into their vehicle. But Nolan was also looking at their guide's band, which was a narrower headpiece, in quieter but more intricately worked colors and with a single, short feather stitched into the pattern. None of the other guides' headbands that he could see included this inconspicuous decoration, so it was possible that in spite of his earlier shyness and pretension to subordinate rank, this young man belonged to one of the noble families.

Their vehicle was one of a convoy that raced along the wide, brightly lit streets, their path cleared of pedestrian and wheeled traffic by an escort of motorized peacekeepers in vehicles that wailed like demented banshees. The pavements were thronged by people whose skin coloration and costumes rivaled those seen in the Imperial City, but not once did he see a headband being worn by anyone on foot.

Since Brendan's time the longhouses of the Algonquin had grown much longer and very much higher. So tall were the buildings in the commercial district that the Islanders boasted that direct sunlight never reached the streets between, but was reflected back and forth from their steel and glass flanks until it reached the pavement.

The guides saw to it that they were settled into their longhouse accommodation, whose furnishings were only slightly less opulent than those of the ambassadorial suites at Tara, and withdrew with the polite reminder that they would return early on the morrow. A number of short tours would precede an important business meeting, it was explained, to enable the menial Islanders as well as the news-gatherers to see that the officers of the ship were physically present in the city. To ensure maximum effect, the touring officers would be divided into small groups.

"The duty is not onerous and you may even find it interesting," Wanachtee said as he was turning to leave, "and you need not speak unless you choose to do so. Now I would advise my pale brother to sleep, or at least rest."

"But I'm not tired," Nolan protested, staring through a window as clear as air at the most famous and beautiful night skyline in the world, "and too excited, I expect, by my first visit to sleep. My body thinks that it is only a few hours after midday!"

Wanachtee gave a small smile of sympathy. "Those who race the sun must pay a penalty for winning," he said, and left.

The bed furs were so deep and soft that when Nolan closed his eyes he could almost believe that he was in free-fall, but so far as inducing sleep was concerned he might as well have been lying on a penitential bed of nails. He felt in turn excited by the night sounds and sights of the city beyond and beneath his window, confused by images of the gentle but very tough little monk who had given it his name, and worried, needlessly perhaps, by the monsignor's lack of response to his story. After a couple of hours that had stretched subjectively into an eternity, he dressed.

At the other end of his corridor he made two discoveries: a guest lounge, which served refreshments throughout the night, and that he was not the only crew-member who could not sleep.

It was a large room with low, comfortable chairs and conveniently positioned tables scattered around it. The outer wall was a single, panoramic window and opposite it was a refreshment board that displayed a rich variety of solid and liquid nourishment. The lighting was tasteful and subdued, neither dim enough to make pedestrian navigation difficult nor so bright that it would spoil the occupants' view of the city.

There were about twenty officer-ecclesiastics scattered about the room, singly and in small groups, and none of them looked up when he entered. The single officers were reading their Breviaries, and Nolan had an aversion amounting to superstitious fear of interrupting a priest at prayer; the others were talking shop so intently that, deliberately or otherwise, they excluded him. Close by the window he could see Brenner and two other noncleric lander pilots having an animated conversation with a broad-shouldered man in a white tunic who was probably the bar-servant. There was food on their table as well as three large, near-empty flagons of what was almost certainly Brenner's native Teutonic beer. Like the others they were much too busy to notice him.

Nolan sighed and chose a seat within ten paces of them to wait for the bar-servant to attend him. He shared Brenner's liking for beer, but as the minutes passed and the servant made no attempt to leave the other table, his anticipation changed to irritation and then to a deepening concern.

The voices at the other table had risen so that he could hear every word, and it was clear that the discussion had developed into an argument which had become so angry that if it was not ended quickly it must ultimately lead to violence.

Nolan hesitated, waiting for one of the more senior officers in the room to intervene, but none of them seemed disposed to do so. The harshest words were being exchanged by Brenner and the bar-servant, who, it had transpired, was a non-Citizen countryman of his. A friendly and inebriated inquiry about the servant's background had apparently been taken as a gross condescension and implied criticism of the person occupying the menial position. One of the other pilots, who was wearing the district crest of Mex, was moving his head from side to side and clearly enjoying the argument even though the language must have been unfamiliar to him while the other, a fellow Teuton, was looking worried as he gripped Brenner's arm and spoke quietly to him. Both the restraining hand and the words were being ignored.

Struggling out of his low and sinfully comfortable chair, Nolan walked slowly toward the other table. As yet he had no idea what he was going to do or say.

Brenner's face was a study in primary colors—tightly curled yellow hair, pale blue eyes, and red, near-apoplectic features—as he said angrily, "I do *not* consider you a menial! But if you had stayed in the old country and worked and studied hard, as I had to do, instead of taking the easy option of leaving for the Golden West, golden insofar as the rewards for simple work which does not involve the use of great intelligence is concerned . . ."

Brenner had been one of the few crew-members to befriend Nolan during training, even though the pilot's first words had been to ask if it was true that all male Healers, because of the high degree of sympathy and gentleness necessary for the practice of their art, were closer to being women than men, and if many of them were voluntary *castrati*? Brenner was a simple, direct, and far from stupid man who was acknowledged to be the best of *Aisling Gheal*'s lander pilots, but diplomatic he was not.

". . . You bear a proud and honorable name," the lander pilot went on, somehow managing to make the compliment sound like an insult. "Had you remained at home to work for our people instead of for yourself, you might have been in my position now with no reason to envy me—"

"I would *not* be in your position!" the servant broke in. His hair was dark and, though closely shaven, the bluish shadowing around his mouth and chin gave him an unkempt look, and his face matched the angry red of Brenner's own. "I would not be wearing a pretty uniform, the medallion of a Citizen, and the band of a Redman chief which requires that I abase myself before you as I would to a Landgraaf or Knight. I would not be taking part in your stupid and wasteful enterprise. The gold needed to train you, nay even to lift you as far as the orbit of your vessel, would feed and warm the poor of our home city throughout an entire winter. And the horrendous cost of that ship could better have been directed toward improving the conditions of countless millions here on Earth instead of squandering it on a stupid piece of national self-aggrandizement by—"

Nolan moved up to the edge of the table, which was the closest he could come to getting between them. He was looking hard at Brenner as he said, "Gentlemen, please moderate your voices. No doubt your discussion is interesting, but you may be inconveniencing others who do not share that interest, and who may complain to higher authority if it continues."

That might already be happening, Nolan thought worriedly, because one of the other officers had moved to the refreshment board and was using its farspeaker. He glared at Brenner, trying by the sheer intensity of his thoughts to remind the other that they were honored guests in this city, that they were expected to behave accordingly, and that the ecclesiastics would almost certainly report any serious transgression to the monsignor with probably dire consequences for the lander pilot regardless of who was at fault.

The briefings had stressed the importance and diplomatic delicacy of their visit to Brendan's Island and the necessity of making a favorable impression on the Redmen. If he did not quickly return to his senses, Brenner might be fortunate not to be expelled from the project and left to spend the rest of his days as a bar-servant like his argumentative countryman.

But the men were responding neither to his physical presence nor to the intensity of his unspoken warnings.

". . . If the ship had never been built," Brenner was saying in a scornful voice, "and the horrendous cost, as you describe it, had been distributed among the world's needy, we would have succeeded in keeping them warm and well-fed for no more than a few days, and then the problem would be as bad as ever. If you argue in that way then we should never have put up the orbiters, flown the first heavier-than-air machines, or wasted time and money on heroes. The ship, all these things, ultimately benefit everyone."

"They benefit a few," the servant broke in angrily. "They benefit only the men of science, the spasaires and the specialist artisans who support them, and the rich merchants and chiefs who supply the material to . . ."

At least, Nolan thought with relief, they were moving from the area of personal criticism to political argument, which was well-trodden and much safer ground. Shouting them down would attract even more of the attention he wanted to avoid, so he waited for a break in the conversation that would enable him to try again.

". . . That may be true if you consider only the short-term benefits," Brenner was saying with the passionate intensity of the believer who is preaching one of the prime tenets of his faith. "But surely you are able to see beyond your selfish concerns of today to a future so glorious that it is beyond imagining? Did not the teachers of natural philosophy impart the knowledge that this is only one world among the myriads that populate the galaxy?"

"One of the short-term benefits I missed," said the bar-servant, in a voice that was lower but even angrier, "was your education at one of those accursed and seditious colleges supported by our country's Empire-lovers. Neither my father nor mother, I am pleased to say, were Citizens."

"I won my place at the college," Brenner replied proudly, "and was granted Citizenship only after qualifying as a spasaire. Neither of my parents were Citizens."

Brenner was matching the quieter tone of his countryman, and Nolan had begun to wonder whether his intervention was necessary. It seemed to him that their argument was becoming only that, and no longer the prelude to a fight.

He was wrong.

"You won your place," the bar-servant said coldly, "only because you were allowed to win. Everyone knows that the colleges are for the children of Citizens, whether or not their fathers publicly acknowledge them as such, and a few places are given to non-Citizens so that the dishonored mothers will not make trouble . . ."

Oh, no, thought Nolan. Telling a man that he was a bastard was the mildest of insults, unless he happened to be one, but insulting his mother was asking for serious and immediate trouble. It was too late now to stop them with words. He leaned quickly across the table, placed a large, open palm on each man's chest, and pushed them apart as hard as he could.

Brenner was already throwing a punch at the other's face and his fist scraped painfully across Nolan's nose, which immediately began to bleed. Through tear-misted eyes, he saw the bar-servant stagger backward, his own wild swing wasted on the empty air, but remaining upright while the pilot, unbalanced by the force of his attempted blow, spun round, tripped over his own feet, and fell. He demolished a chair and struck the top of his head on the edge of a nearby table on his way to the floor.

For a moment the pilot lay face downward and motionless amid the wreckage of the chair. Then a spasm shook his body and his head was encircled suddenly by a spreading yellow halo of vomit.

All of the ship's officers were on their feet, prayers and private conversations forgotten as they began to crowd forward. The bar-servant was staring down at Brenner, and at the beret and head-band lying on the floor; his facial pallor matched exactly that of his white tunic with the realization of what he had done. He had offered insult and injury not only to a crew-member of *Aisling Gheal* but to a person with the honorary rank, powers, and privileges of a Redman chief. Nolan could not imagine what the man's punishment would be for such an offense, but it was obvious that the bar-servant could.

Nolan grasped the man's arm gently and shook it until he had the other's attention, then he said quietly, "You are fortunate in that you did not strike the spasaire, and he did not strike you. Doubly fortunate in that we do not want to report this incident to your superiors or ours, unless a very serious injury is involved, because as guests of this city we are expected to behave like responsible, civilized people.

"Nobody here is interested in ordering further refreshment," he ended. "So go now, and remain out of sight until this matter is cleared up. Go at once."

Without waiting for a reply he turned quickly to kneel beside Brenner.

He rolled the pilot onto his side and checked that the breathing passages were unobstructed before examining the head injury. He could feel a small bump and an abrasion which was bleeding enough to barely stain the hair. There were no indications of a depressed fracture, but he looked for uneven dilation of the pupils as verification. While he was doing that, Brenner wakened and began struggling weakly and cursing very strongly. Relieved, Nolan grasped one arm and leg and began pulling him clear of the mess on the floor.

From behind Nolan a female voice said sharply, "Don't move him, you stupid man, you risk compounding his injuries. Stand clear."

Without rising, Nolan looked over his shoulder to see Dervla glaring down at him. He said quickly, "There's no danger of that. The only injury is a superficial scalp wound with a small localized swelling, from which he may suffer at most a mild concussion. The regurgitation was due to overindulgence and is not symptomatic of cranial damage. As you can hear, the patient is conscious and able to, ah, speak."

"Considering your advantages of size and reach," Dervla said angrily, "I expect to find much graver injuries to your opponent, and I'm only surprised that he was able to bloody your nose before you knocked him down. Now stand clear."

Nolan stood up angrily and began, "I wasn't fighting and I had no wish to hurt him—"

"And I have no wish to listen to excuses for a drunken brawl," she broke in, kneeling beside Brenner, "especially from a . . . Healer."

Her momentary hesitation and the inflexion she placed on the word made Nolan want to use language not normally directed toward a female.

"I am not making excuses," he said, controlling his temper with a mighty effort. "The reason he struck his head was—"

"Nor have I time to listen to reasons," she said without looking up. "Please be quiet."

Nolan stared hard at the back of her head and at the long, red-bronze hair spilling over the collar of her cloak, which had been thrown back to leave her hands unencumbered. The hair was her only attractive feature, he thought, because her expression had been so stiff and cold when she looked at him that the face might have been prematurely frozen by cold sleep. The black uniform made the thin body look even thinner and the only curvature visible was the swelling of her gluteus maximus. He had a sudden, fearful urge to kick that area as hard as he could.

But a calmer part of his mind, one less affected by his anger and hurt pride, reminded him that such a kick would probably send her sprawling halfway across the room, that it might seriously injure her lower spine, and that, at the very least, it would ensure his losing his place on *Aisling Gheal*. The imaginary administration of that one swift kick was a beautiful and immensely satisfying mental picture to contemplate, however, and while he was taking pleasure in it his anger began to fade.

He watched her repeat the examination that he had just carried out, but with the difference that when her fingers touched Brenner's scalp he became quiet, opened his eyes, and looked up at her as a young child would look at its mother. Suddenly she slipped her hands behind the pilot's knees and shoulders and stood up, apparently without effort, with him cradled in her arms. She had muscles, Nolan thought, and wondered where she was hiding them.

He moved forward to help her, but she shook her head and fixed one of the two pilots with her cold blue eyes.

"If you know his room number, lead the way," she said briskly. "The rest of you, return to your rooms and sleep. That is the considered professional advice of your Healer. It is also an order.

"As for you," she went on, turning to Nolan. "Clean up your bloody face and uniform. If there is a mark on either of them in the morning, you will not be allowed to parade your battle scars during tomorrow's tour, which means that the monsignor will have to be told all about this stupid business. Are you capable of self-administering the appropriate medication or are you only good with the knife and your fists?"

"It's only a minor nosebleed . . ." Nolan began, but she was already striding toward the door, with Brenner in her arms and the Mex pilot leading the way.

Nolan felt a hand on his arm and turned to see the other pilot, the one who had been trying to calm Brenner when the argument had begun to get out of control, smiling sympathetically at him.

"Thank you, Healer," he said. "That was a piece of very quick thinking on your part, and it saved us from an awful lot of grief. But don't concern yourself about Healer Dervla jumping to wrong conclusions. The monsignor will soon learn the truth"—he nodded toward the officers who were already leaving—"which means that she will learn it as well. You have nothing to worry about."

"That . . . that *woman*!" said Nolan, scarcely hearing him. "Is she a human being at all, or some kind of organic robot with—"

"I have been told that she has a very human side," the pilot said dryly, "but the only people allowed to see it are her patients."

Chapter 5

HE saw Brenner and Dervla at a distance in the breakfasting room next morning. The lander pilot appeared to be physically fit but psychologically subdued, and apart from giving Nolan an apologetic smile, he did not raise his eyes from the platter. When he looked toward Dervla's table, he found her looking in his direction. She gave him a barely perceptible nod and then turned her head away. Nolan did not know whether it was a nod of apology for having misjudged him or a sign that his unblemished face and spotless uniform had passed inspection as being suitable for exhibition to the public.

When the meal was finished he saw her rise and move toward him, but the guides arrived at that moment to shepherd their charges to the waiting vehicles and he lost sight of her.

Once again his guide was Wanachtee, but when the convoy of vehicles reached its destination, Nolan did not have to be told where they were.

The Trading Place of Coshawnee was the tallest building in the world, occupying two city blocks and housing, in its first thirty-two floors, a store in which everything imaginable could be bought, from the smallest trinkets to the largest airliners, although the latter were not, of course, kept on the shelves. A deep basement, sectioned off by triple tiers of service and observation galleries, was devoted to toys and indoor hobbycrafts. It was a fabulous treasure house that Nolan had longed vainly to visit since he had first learned of its existence as a child, and now, incredibly, it had become his duty to fulfill that dream.

The guides were ushering the officers between the endless rows of display and demonstration tables at a brisk although dignified pace, but much too quickly for Nolan's liking. He kept hanging back for a longer look, with the result that his group was falling behind the others.

At the model display devoted to transportation through the ages, Nolan stopped. He felt like a child again with his first, crudely carved model of *Sea Dragon* that, in his youthful imagination, had seemed every bit as exciting as the replica before him which must have required hundreds of hours of painstaking work to build. Like that child, he was oblivious to the nonvocal signals of impatience being generated by the adults around him.

Wanachtee's face was showing the impassive anxiety of the Redman as he looked with increasing frequency at the newsgatherers on the galleries, whose sound and vision senders seemed to be focused exclusively on their party now that it had stopped moving, and at the crowd of noisy customers and store staff who had begun to press closer.

With the exception of the ship's officers and guides there was no person that he could see who was wearing a headband. Nolan reminded himself of the fact that as wearers of the bands they were assumed to be warriors capable of defending themselves against close, physical attack. Unless a warrior was a very senior Chief, and ailing or infirm, a Redman considered it demeaning to employ personal bodyguards.

With a brief look over the display of intricately detailed ships, iron horses, aircraft, and space vehicles, and a last and more lingering one at the *Sea Dragon* model, he turned away and said, "My apologies for delaying you, Brother, but that is a truly beautiful model."

Wanachtee smiled and nodded to the store assistant on duty at the display, a shy young man who looked as though he was as enthusiastic about the models in his charge as was Nolan, then said, "It is yours, Healer."

"I cannot accept such a gift!" Nolan burst out in instinctive protest. He turned back once again to regard the near-priceless model, whose length was more than twice his own height. Even the differences in the grains of the native Hibernian woods and the Westland varieties that had been used to replace the material burned in *Sea Dragon*'s furnace during the latter part of its epic voyage had been meticulously reproduced in color and texture. But as he reached forward to touch it he became aware that the young attendant's face had grown pale, that the people within hearing had become strangely quiet, and that the expression of their guide had cooled to the point where it could have congealed hot lava.

Under his breath, Nolan cursed himself for an unthinking, loose-tongued amadan, and wondered angrily how such an abysmal fool could ever have become a Healer much less an officer on *Aisling Gheal*. In the full view and hearing of hundreds of people, including the dozens of news-gatherers who were broadcasting the sight and sounds to a countless multitude of others, he had refused the gift which had been offered to him as a first-time visitor to the country.

Whether the present was the smallest of tokens or a priceless work of art, one did not refuse a Redman's Gift of First Meeting. To do so was considered, in less civilized times, a studied insult that usually preceded an intertribal war. Even if he was to apologize immediately for his hasty and unthinking words and accept the gift, irreparable harm had already been done, because many would view the apology and belated acceptance as an act of cowardice.

This was supposed to be a goodwill visit aimed at gaining wider public support for the starship project in the Westland Federation of Redman Nations, as well as hammering out a number of less glamorous financial agreements behind the scenes, and Nolan was responsible for getting it off to the worst possible start. He could not even imagine the reaction of Monsignor O'Riordan or of their awesome and omnipotent cardinal-captain. Almost certainly Nolan would be kicked off *Aisling Gheal*, perhaps without benefit of a spacesuit.

He had to *think*.

"Such . . . such a fine present is wasted on me," he began hesitantly, trying desperately to make the earlier refusal and insult into an explanation. "It is an object which I would delight in, and keep in a place of honor in my home. But I no longer have a home on Earth, and on the ship there are restrictions regarding the size and weight of the personal possessions allowed on the voyage . . ."

An idea came to him as he was speaking, and he reached into the display quickly to lift out another model. Costing only a tiny fraction of the *Sea Dragon*, it was a lightweight plastic self-assembly model already completed and painted by a craftsman for display purposes. Some of the finer details had been omitted, but the configuration and structural complexity of *Aisling Gheal* were unmistakable. Because the vision senders had him in close-up, he held the model motionless in one hand while he used the index finger of the other to point out the modules comprising the main hull.

"This is the control, astrogation, and long-range sensor module," he went on, "which includes the on-watch and cold sleep accommodation for the entire crew. Just astern of Control is the vessel's spine, which supports the great hibernation modules which will contain the colonists, livestock, seed stores, and other perishable materials. These, and the life-support, cryogenic, and communication systems they contain, are the brain and the main body of the ship. They are the most advanced, stringently tested and reliable structure ever produced by Westland Federation technology. The number of our brothers, Redman and paleskins alike, who have given willingly of their time and their knowledge and the sweat of their bodies to build these structures, in greater or lesser part, is larger than we can imagine, and much too large for all of you to be thanked in person as you deserve."

With his index finger he tapped on the complex, bulbous shapes of the model's forward and midships hull, and ended quietly, "We have already received your Gift of First Meeting. It is the greatest and most valuable present that you could possibly have given us. It—it is accepted."

He concentrated his attention on replacing the model, afraid to look at the still-silent crowd. Then suddenly the attendant was beside him, his face red instead of pale, and stuttering and waving his arms in great agitation. One hand held a pen and the other the illustrated booklet of assembly instructions.

"No, I must refuse this model, too," said Nolan kindly, and smiled. "I'll be busy working on the original."

The young man's mouth was open, but there were no coherent sounds coming from it. Wanachtee's expression had warmed a little, so presumably Nolan had been able to retrieve something from what could well have been an utterly disastrous situation, but it was plain that the Redman was anxious to move on. The store attendant was still stammering helplessly and waving the instruction book.

"*Now* I understand," said Nolan suddenly. "You want me to write something in it?"

The dammed-up words poured out in a flood which was a continuous "Yes, please." But before Nolan could complete his signature under a few brief words of greeting, what seemed like every customer in sight, many of whom were quite elderly, came surging forward, waving books, old envelopes, and odd bits of paper and asking for one of the spasaires to sign them.

For a moment Nolan felt sorry for the other officers even though he, too, had no previous experience of this kind of thing. They were priest-academics and specialist members of the Church's various scientific and technical confraternities, and their laboratories had been as cloistered as any monastery. Probably their only experience of a public occasion was when, newly ordained and still unspecialized, they had officiated at a friend's wedding. But the people crowding in on them knew only that they wore the uniform of the starship, with all that that implied, and cared nothing for their ecclesiastic rank. They were coping with the situation very well, however, and might even have been enjoying it—until the sound of excited voices began to die away.

Wanachtee was holding up his arms, slightly outstretched, and waiting for silence. Nolan did not know the exact level of rank indicated by the other's headband, but the people there knew and were quiet.

"The visiting brothers have urgent matters to discuss with Silver Elk," the Redman said in a quiet but far-carrying voice. "They are too polite to mention this to you, so I am forced to do so. Please clear a path to the elevators."

That elevator ride, which reminded Nolan of a shuttle takeoff, took them past the store levels and through the higher sections devoted to accounting and administration to the top of the building and the sumptuous family and business accommodation of Silver Elk, the present Paramount Chief of the Coshawnee Corporation. The monsignor was waiting for them at the entrance of the main conference room.

O'Riordan waved the other crew-members past and stopped Nolan with an angry gesture. Smiling, he said, "I had need of you, Healer, to treat an impending cardiac arrest which your own stupid behavior caused. We watched it on the screens and I still don't know the extent of the harm you have done us, or the repercussions of—"

"I am very sorry, sir," said Nolan.

"Take your place," said O'Riordan. He was still smiling, possibly because Wanachtee was waiting nearby, but there was more anger contained in that quiet voice than Nolan would have believed possible. "And for God's sake, so far as it is possible for an overgrown amadan like you, try to remain physically and verbally inconspicuous. And if you are too stupid to understand what I have said, I'll make it simpler for you. Sit down and don't talk."

Wanachtee took a chair beside Nolan. The closest of Nolan's fellow officers were seated three places away on either side, giving the impression that he was the carrier of some dreadful contagion. He found it difficult to return the Redman's polite conversation during the brief pauses between the presentation of proposed advertising campaigns, market-research projections, and demonstrations of the best—and sometimes the cheapest and worst—examples of the toymaker's art. He saw *Aisling Gheal* in several sizes and qualities of self-assembly kits; as a soft, plastic model that could be towed on a string or floated in the bath by the very young; as a helium-filled balloon; and as a small, beautifully detailed, and fantastically expensive replica in crystal and onyx designed as an ornament for a high executive's desk. There were innumerable models of landers, space tugs and two-man scooters, accommodation modules, some of which lit up and made noises—in space? Then there were the widely differing qualities and prices of the uniform reproductions for sale to all age groups. There were badges, transfers, watches bearing a stylized representation of the ship which made it look, he thought, like a particularly nasty, fat-bellied insect.

Comments were invited after every presentation, but Nolan was under strict orders to decline such invitations, even though he felt that he could have contributed a few useful ideas. Instead he listened to the Redmen marketing people waging a polite but utterly merciless war with *Aisling Gheal*'s financial advisers while they tried to agree on profit percentages for the manufacturers, home and overseas retailers, and, more importantly, the project itself.

In spite of heavy tax levies throughout the Empire and major contributions by the other rich nations, the starship project was seriously underfunded. It badly needed the financial support of the world population, no matter how small the individual contributions or how they were obtained, if *Aisling Gheal* was to be launched as mankind's first attempt at interstellar colonization and was not to be downgraded to a mere Earth-orbiting research-and-manufacturing complex. Worse, after close on two decades since work on the main structure had begun, public interest was on the wane, and with it the political influence that ensured that the project's incredible and endless appetite for scientific resources, specialist manpower, material, and, most of all, money would be fed. Even the pennies of children would make a difference, if there were enough of them, which was the reason why they were meeting atop the Toyshop of the World.

Nolan's attention drifted from the warriors locked in verbal conflict to the great wall of glass that formed one side of the conference room. The slim, glittering, cloud-piercing commercial lodges of Brendan's Island, many of them rivaling in height the Great Tower of Tara, rose skyward, their acres of windows reflecting the lightlike details in some vast jeweled tapestry.

"You seem restless, Healer," said Wanachtee quietly. "It will soon be over. Silver Elk speaks."

The Paramount Chief and the others present drew lengths of flexible tubing from recesses in the conference table and took the first ritual puffs. When Silver Elk stopped smoking and laid down his section of the meeting's Pipe of Peace, the others did likewise.

"We are in broad agreement," said Silver Elk, speaking for the first time. His voice was thin and weak and very, very angry. "And the finer details will be the concern of others. But before our brothers leave us we must apologize for the disgraceful behavior of a member of our junior staff and customers toward a group of the officers.

"We were hoping," he went on, with a slow look along each side of the long table, "that our brothers would meet and speak to many of our non-Redmen, because we are aware of an increasing stratification in our society which is causing the paleskins to lose interest in anything that does not directly affect their own personal concerns. But this premature and undignified interference with your persons was inexcusable, ill-mannered, and embarrassing. Rest assured that the young man who initiated this incident will be severely disciplined."

"Not . . . not *too* severely, I hope," Nolan said hesitantly, when it was obvious that nobody else was going to respond. He felt O'Riordan's eyes boring into him, but he ignored them and went on. "The young man was not disinterested, far from it, and the enthusiasm for the project shown by him and the others who mobbed us was a most pleasant surprise. I am sure that I speak for the other officers concerned when I say that the minor embarrassment caused by the incident was far outweighed by the high compliment it represented."

There were murmurs of agreement from several parts of the table. Even the monsignor was nodding in benign assent.

"Very well," Silver Elk replied, his sharp, old eyes fixed on Nolan. "No action will be taken. But I wonder if that young man will ever know that his case was pleaded by such a gifted advocate, one who is so expert at turning major insults into compliments. However, your seeming refusal of a Gift of First Meeting was, in the words of my public-relations people, such an effective attention-grabber that it ensured maximum impact for the subsequent and highly complimentary things you said about the Westland Federation's contribution to *Aisling Gheal*.

"As a direct result of this incident," he went on, indicating the farseer screen before him, "the itinerary for your visit will have to be replanned. As well as the round of high-level formal receptions for the crew, our marketing people suggest that in addition a large number of single-person, informal interviews be given to groups of non-Redmen would be effective. Such interviews, the guidelines for which have already been established by you, will go a long way toward bridging the gap, so far as the project is concerned at least, between the Redmen so-called technocrats and the paleskin population. It will also sell more toys."

Silver Elk allowed himself a small smile, then resumed, "But we would feel much happier if the interviews did not begin so dangerously. On this occasion, Healer, the timing was perfect and your words gave every indication of spontaneity and sincerity, but I am afraid that there may be brother officers who are not the consummate actor that you are, and so in the future we would prefer you to omit the attention-grabbing preliminaries."

"But . . ." began Nolan, then broke off as Silver Elk raised a hand so thin and brown and fragile that it might have belonged to one of the mummmified Kings of Egypt.

"I would not like to hear that your performance was spontaneous," said the Chief, "or that your insult was spoken without thought, and that you had to think very quickly indeed to retrieve a most delicate and dangerous situation. We expect resourcefulness, and the ability to react positively in the face of danger, from our brothers of the starship. But such hazards are normally faced in the airless immensity of space, not in a toy store. Were you about to speak, Healer?"

"No, Great Chief," Nolan lied.

He got to his feet with the others as Silver Elk's powered chair backed away from the table and rolled smoothly toward an inner door. Because of his late arrival at the meeting he had not known that the Paramount Chief could not use his legs. But of two things he was very sure: There was nothing wrong with those tired, old eyes, because they had seen right through him; and, among the Redmen executives who still remained in the room, Nolan had the reddest face.

None of his fellow officers seemed anxious to join him, and even Wanachtee had left his side. Unsure of what to do next, he wondered whether he should join the group around the monsignor to await instructions and the expected tongue-lashing which the meeting had merely postponed. Then he saw Wanachtee reenter by the door Silver Elk had used to leave and walk quickly toward O'Riordan. They spoke together for a few minutes, but Nolan was not able to see the monsignor's expression. Then the guide turned and came toward him.

"Please sit down, Healer," said Wanachtee, "and wait until the others leave. There is something I must ask you."

Probably, thought Nolan, you want to know what I would like for my last meal. He had the feeling that Wanachtee would be speaking the words of both Silver Elk and O'Riordan, and no matter how politely the Redman delivered them, they would not be kind words.

"Ask," he said.

Hesitantly, Wanachtee said, "I wish to be assigned exclusively to you, Healer, for the period of your stay in Westland. Without first consulting you, I suggested it to Silver Elk, and both he and Monsignor O'Riordan approved the idea subject, naturally, to your agreement. It means that you would be separated from your fellow officers, and that you would be forgoing the luxury of the Algonquin Hibernia for the city lodge of Wanachtee, which is moderately luxurious and much more comfortable, and the view over the city is unsurpassed. Owing to the absence of my squaw, Golden Rain, the place is dreadfully untidy—"

"Enough!" said Nolan, laughing. "I agree with pleasure." The last few officers who were leaving the room turned to stare at him, plainly wondering what someone who had incurred the extreme displeasure of O'Riordan could find to laugh at. He went on, "But I suspect that you have been ordered by Silver Elk to undertake this duty to make sure that I don't get into any more trouble."

"You are right, Healer," said Wanachtee. "Silver Elk is old and wise, and he understands much because he was not always old, nor wise."

Nolan's confusion must have been clear in his face.

"You are a brother and first-time visitor to this great city," Wanachtee explained, "and if your off-duty time here is to be spent as enjoyably as possible, you will need a guide. I am told that your philosophy and living habits are not shared by the majority of your fellow officers, whose behavior is restricted because they are priests, strivers after sinlessness, and No-Squaws to a man. This and my purely selfish desire to talk to you about the project are the reasons why I asked Silver Elk and the monsignor to be your personal guide."

"Glad I am that you did," said Nolan, laughing again. "I have the feeling that O'Riordan would make me spend the rest of my time here in sackcloth and ashes."

As they rose to leave, Wanachtee regarded him with an expression of great solemnity and said, "As for keeping you out of trouble, were I to do that I would be failing in my obligation to my brother and to this very exciting and wicked city which he is visiting for the first time. So first you will eat and rest in my lodge, Healer, and then you will tell me what kinds of trouble you prefer."

Chapter 6

NOLAN stayed at Wanachtee's lodge for the first eight days of the visit to Brendan's Island. He was much in demand for public appearances at stores, schools, and sports complexes, and at the evening feastings of medium-level businessmen's organizations. His approach to all of them was informal; and rather than giving a prepared lecture followed by a few minutes' mingling, he soon found that inviting and answering questions from the start worked best for him. At none of these functions did he share the limelight with another ship's officer, although he knew that they, too, were appearing at similar gatherings. The few instructions he received from O'Riordan were relayed through Silver Elk's people, and he often wondered if the monsignor was trying to isolate him and make him feel unwanted as a prelude to removing him from the project.

After one long and especially gaudy night when his reticence was anesthetized by Wanachtee's alcohol, he began worrying about it aloud.

"You are missing the company and the technical shoptalk of your fellow officers," said the Redman, in exactly the tone of voice Nolan used when he was making a considered diagnosis, "you may also be missing, although you yourself may not realize it, the support and guidance of the ship's Healer of the Mind."

"Never!" said Nolan, with alcoholic firmness. "My shoptalk would be that of a Healer, not a technologist, and you yourself already understand the essentials of the healing art, which is listening to other people's troubles." He laughed suddenly. "As for missing O'Riordan, let me say only that, had I not been a Godless heretic, my behavior earlier this evening would be most decidedly a matter for confession."

"I understand," said Wanachtee sagely. "Some of our Christian Redmen feel the need to confess their misdemeanors to a holy man. And you, being an unbeliever and feeling guilty over this evening's sinning which, I must say at the risk of offending you, was not on a grand scale, have nobody to confess to or—"

He hiccupped suddenly, looked apologetic for the interruption, and went on, "You may confess any misdemeanors which we did not share to me. Or you may speak freely to me about anything that concerns you. This visit, your hopes for the colony on the New World, your feelings about the project as a whole. All of this will interest me now, for tomorrow my head will contain nothing but pain."

Nolan doubted that Wanachtee would have any difficulty in recalling any detail of what he might be told, regardless of the size of the hangover that might intervene and itself be an additional cause for worry. He was reminded suddenly that Ciaran, whose rank would have given him ready access to the project's most senior officers, had also wanted Nolan to talk freely. And there had been other people of varying importance who had wanted to talk to *Aisling Gheal*'s junior Healer rather than to more senior officers.

"I talk too much," said Nolan miserably.

"Then, Healer," said Wanachtee, topping up both their glasses, "let us maintain the silence of friends."

Nolan sipped his drink, coughed, and thought that the savagely potent beverage should be given a blanket contraindication for all persons and conditions. But it was enabling him to enjoy his misery, and it no longer seemed to matter that he talked too much.

"Much too much," he repeated. "I think they look on me as a great, shambling, amiable buffoon, an oversized performing bear who is excluded from the serious business of the project, and can be turned loose with safety because he does not know the answers if awkward questions are asked. But now I think I have become an embarrassment to them, and they would prefer me to resign rather than wait until—"

"Your analysis of the situation is substantially correct," Wanachtee broke in. All at once the look in his eyes was keen and sharp, and for some reason it was clearing the alcoholic fog between them.

"I did not," said Nolan, "expect you to agree so quickly that I was a fool."

The Redman watched him silently for a moment, his head slightly inclined and his expression both sympathetic and clinical, then he put down his glass and spoke.

"I agree with your assessment of the situation," he said quietly, "not that you are a fool. You are dedicated, enthusiastic, socially immature in some areas, transparently honest, and outspoken. You have had to be silent before inferiors during much of your training, but now your position as an officer of the ship is so elevated that, understandably, you have gone far in the other direction and are outspoken at the wrong times. You must be an embarrassment to the monsignor at these times, but . . . Did anyone with great power, temporal or ecclesiastic, use their influence to see that your name appeared on the final crew roster?"

Nolan's expression answered that question without him having to speak.

"Competition for crew positions was even fiercer than for the colonists' cold-beds," Wanachtee continued, "and rumor has it that the assassination weapon was used more than once. So your position was gained solely because of professional competence . . ."

"But there are much better qualified people in the specialty than I am," Nolan protested.

". . . And other personal qualities which the monsignor found desirable at the time," Wanachtee continued, ignoring the interruption. "I'd say that O'Riordan studied your psychic profile very carefully, and decided to take a calculated risk. For public-relations reasons he must have decided that the crew needed someone who was honest and incapable of guarding his tongue. By now you must have realized that you are being used, and not simply as a Healer?"

"Yes," said Nolan. He felt physically relaxed and mentally alert, so much so that he wondered if he was about to say the wrong thing again, but he said it anyway.

"I am sure that I have been used by several people for their own purposes," he said. "I think I am about to be used by you."

Wanachtee's face became very still for a moment, then he sighed and said, "You *do* take risks, Healer. But when a question is asked of an honest man, all of the answer must be accepted, so I will not take offense."

"Thank you," said Nolan, making no attempt to hide his relief.

"Because of their religious and political training for high administrative positions in the Empire's service," the Redman went on, apparently changing the subject, "your ecclesiastical colleagues arouse a certain amount of distrust among us. But Maeve insisted that this be so even though she was forced to agree to reduce her quota of Hibernian colonists by that same number.

"Our Aztec brothers," he continued, "feel that their share of the colonist payload is not in proportion to their financial support. And the Emperors of Nippon and Cathay also want a larger allocation because the project would not be possible without the deep-space engines they have developed. But there are feelings other than greed among us. There are misgivings regarding the basic philosophy of the project, worries that the interests of the different colonist groups will not be properly represented, fears that the ship would go off course and its people become eternally rather than temporarily frozen. To those of us, Redmen and paleskins alike, whose religious beliefs include some form of afterlife, what would happen to the spirits of these eternally nondead is of grave concern.

"And on the purely material side," he concluded, "there is the feeling that we are making fools of ourselves by pouring resources into a project which will show no return, resources which would go a long way to improving life on Earth for a great many people."

Nolan shook his head vigorously, and said, "Of course there will be no return, not for many centuries if ever. But one does not count the cost, or expect a return, on the time and effort and self-induced poverty spent in educating one's children so that they can make a successful life for themselves and their children's children in a far country. We are considering the future success of the far-traveling children of mankind, and no personal sacrifice is too great for them.

"This question was expected and we were given many answers to it in our briefings," Nolan went on quickly, "but that answer is the simplest and, I believe, true. As for your worries about the afterlife, there are many reassuring things that I have been instructed to say, but as an unbeliever I would have difficulty making them sound sincere. My own position is much too subordinate for me to have any influence on the composition of the colonist payload, but their interests are being represented by myself and other officers with teaching qualifications, so that their history and culture will not be lost to them. On the New

World they will marry and raise children and, in time, find their own people to represent their interests in the traditional ways.

"But there are risks at every stage," Nolan rushed on, "many of which will be unforeseen, and there is no certainty that our children's children and those of you who remain on Earth will ever meet. And there can be no material return other than the deep, philosophical satisfaction of knowing that we have made of ourselves a star-traveling race who may one day—"

He broke off as Wanachtee abruptly held up his hand.

"Peace, Brother," he said dryly, then went on, "These are the answers, unpleasant as some of them are, that I want to hear. But between our superiors the questions and answers are more wordy, more statesmanlike, more uncertain, and, perhaps, more subject to change and negotiation. That is why many of us prefer to hear them from a junior officer with no political or theological constraints, one who believes them to be true, and who has complete faith in the rightness of the project. I do not suggest that any of your superiors are dishonest, simply that you give the same answers with more feeling and conviction, so that even your doubts carry reassurance by their very honesty. Whether you realize it or not, you are a major asset to the project at the present time, and the monsignor—"

"Please," Nolan broke in with an embarrassed laugh. "If all this flattery is the prelude to asking a favor, well, anything I have is yours up to and including both legs. The arms I need for surgery. But you yourself have just admitted that I am useful to O'Riordan at the present time. But my usefulness is coming to an end. The qualities which you find so laudable will become unnecessary once the voyage begins. Hell and damnation, Wanachtee, no amount of well-meant flattery will affect that situation. Or make me forget it for more than a few minutes."

He had expected the other to show anger, but instead the Redman smiled and said, "Please allow me to flatter you further, by reminding you of a very basic psychological truth. People facing the unknown, or any other danger or difficulty that they think might be beyond their capacity to handle, seek the help of a friend, someone they can trust to protect them. You may have more friends and influence than you realize. You told me about your promise to Ciaran, which must include the Aztec Princess, and there is—"

"As an ex-Captain of the Imperial Guard," Nolan broke in, "he would have great influence with the Empress, as would the

Princess of a nation which is a major contributor to the project. But they will be in cold sleep, and any prior instructions they might have given about me could be safely ignored. When they awaken on the New World, I will have been dead for centuries, on Earth, and they could do nothing about it."

"I had been about to say," Wanachtee resumed patiently, "that there is Silver Elk."

Nolan stared at the Redman in astonished disbelief. "Your . . . your Great Chief would speak for *me*?"

Wanachtee sat forward in his chair, his features relaxed but his body displaying the stillness of concealed tension as he said, "Silver Elk is old and frail. The worn moccasin which serves him as a heart is feeble and erratic in its beating. The Healers have forbidden him all the pleasures that make life endurable, he says, and your performance with the *Sea Dragon* model made his old heart skip several beats. For the few moments of excitement you gave him, and for the first time in many years seriously endangering his life, he is most grateful. Had you been less committed to the project, he would have offered you a high position in the Corporation.

"Silver Elk is a Great Chief," the Redman went on, a note of almost savage pride creeping into his voice, "and his influence throughout the Federated Nations is great. The contribution of Westland to the project is second only to that of Hibernia herself. Neither O'Riordan, the cardinal-captain, nor the Empress will refuse him. If you want to fly on *Aisling Gheal* then fly you shall."

"Oh, come now . . ." began Nolan.

"If you do not go," Wanachtee ended simply, "nobody will go. Silver Elk has that power."

Nolan stared at the Redman, feeling both reassured and frightened and no longer disbelieving. If Wanachtee said that his Great Chief had the power to abort the *Aisling Gheal* program, then it was so. That such power could be wielded on his behalf was an idea he had difficulty in accepting, and there was still a certain tension, perhaps an embarrassment or some other mental discomfort, emanating from the other's body that told Nolan that once again he was being used.

For a long moment Nolan looked into Wanachtee's eyes, then he said quietly, "I am most grateful for the support of Silver Elk. If there is any small favor I can do for him in return, he has only to ask."

Wanachtee leaned back into his chair. "You are not a fool, Healer," he said. "But please believe this. You have Silver Elk's favor, whether or not you do as he asks, and your place on the ship is assured whether or not you do what he asks."

"Then I shall certainly do as he asks," said Nolan. "Will you be involved?"

"Yes, my brother," said Wanachtee. "Nothing in the world will stop me from being involved."

He smiled and stood up. Plainly excited now, he went on, "There are urgent arrangements I must make. A message must be left for the monsignor telling him that you are doing a favor for the Great Chief. We will say that one of the influential Plains Chieftains, a grandson of Silver Elk, has asked for a private visit by you to the younger members of his family. That story will explain your absence until your people leave for Cathay. An aircraft must be made immediately available and trusted friends at the complex warned to expect us . . ."

Nolan held up a hand. With an edge to his voice he said, "I have two questions. What exactly am I going to do? And is there time to finish my drink?"

Wanachtee chose to ignore the sarcasm. "I'm sorry, Healer, your briefing would best be given nearer the time and place. I do hope Mojave Center has a spacesuit large enough to fit you. And no, but we can take the bottle with us."

They did not take the bottle with them nor, after boarding a company aircraft less than an hour later, had Wanachtee or himself shown any interest in the contents of its well-stocked bar. It was a subsonic aircraft bearing the emblem of a black buffalo and three black arrows on a red field, the mark of the family that virtually owned the land and facilities of the Mojave Space Center. He did not meet or even see the pilot.

Nolan slept during most of the trip, and was wakened by the Redman shaking his shoulder. Wanachtee pushed a suit of coveralls and a cap at him and told him to put them on quickly. But when Nolan started to remove his headband to transfer it to the cap, the other shook his head. Wanachtee's cap was already in place, concealing the band, and its long peak and the shoulder-length suncloth covered his ears, neck, and most of his face.

By the time Nolan was similarly dressed they were descending steeply toward the floodlit gantries, safety bunkers, and square, unlovely administration blocks of the launch facility that was second only to that of the Imperial Spaceport at Tara. Sunrise was still two hours away.

"Now," said Nolan, rubbing the last traces of sleep from his eyes, "are we near enough to the time and place for me to be told what is going on?"

Wanachtee was silent for so long that Nolan assumed the answer was no, but when the Redman did finally speak, there was more doubt and pain in it than any human voice had a right to contain.

"Are we doing the right thing?" he said, not looking at Nolan. "Silver Elk believes in the project. You believe in it. The Empress, the cardinal-captain, the monsignor . . ."

"Not necessarily in that order of importance," Nolan broke in, trying to inject a lighter note, and failing. Awkwardly, he went on, "I did not train as a Healer of the Mind, Red Brother, but I will listen while you talk out your hurt."

"As does everyone else whose wisdom and experience I respect," Wanachtee went on, as if he had not spoken. "We are trying to plant anew the seed of mankind, with all the rich variety of its people and cultures squeezed into a tiny cluster of metal pods. But sometimes I wonder if the seedpods are too small, too tightly packed with mutually reactive constituents, too much like one of the nuclear bombs used in the old Cathay-Nippon wars."

There was a sudden bump and a rumble as the aircraft touched down. Automatically, Nolan released his seat belt, but the other man did not move.

He went on soberly, "We are expecting the proud Redmen to live in complete accord with our even prouder and more autocratic Aztec brothers, with the tradition-dominated colonists of Nippon and Cathay, with the colonist minorities of Europe and Greater Nubia whose differing cultures and traditions have led to conflict in the past. Our colonists are not all low-level menials who will accept and adapt to any changes which may be forced on them by others. For the most part they are people who gained their places through influence, sheer ability, or both. It is not a mixture that will combine easily."

Nolan looked at Wanachtee's impassive face and into the tortured, pleading eyes and gave the answer that for the first time since he had joined the project seemed dreadfully inadequate. Reassuringly, he said, "The plan is to give all of the colonists instruction in the history and culture of all the groups, so that the violent lessons of the past will not have to be relearned, and we will go forward together in peace to even greater things."

But Wanachtee was not reassured. He said, "That is a noble intention. But it could be that we are transplanting the seeds of a small and bloody civil war, which will be followed by a descent into savagery, the loss of all wisdom and traditions, and, if enough of the colonists survive it, a long and even more bloody climb back to civilization. Is that to be the fate of the finest and most able of our people, of our friends and loved ones?''

Nolan had not expected Wanachtee, outwardly the epitome of the worldly wise and ambitious young executive of a major Redman corporation, to be capable of such deep, patriotic feeling. His concern for the future of his people on the New World seemed almost personal.

They avoided the brightly lit passenger reception gate and entered through the aircraft maintenance area. Nobody gave them a second glance as Wanachtee led him along endless corridors whose directional signs and office-door titles changed gradually from the language of air to that of space transport. A headbanded technician avoided looking at their faces as he took them along another short corridor, up boarding steps, and through the narrow hatch of a shuttle's control deck.

Wanachtee did not introduce the two men waiting there. Pointing at the larger of the two spacesuits clipped to the aft bulkhead, he said, ''Take off the coveralls and put that on, everything but the helmet. It will save time later. Our brothers will assist you to dress. Payload ready?''

The question was not for Nolan. The two men nodded and, still without speaking or reacting in any way to his pale face and black starship uniform under his coveralls, began dressing both of them. Through the cargo-bay port he could see two spacesuited figures strapped into temporary seating and several large, space-sealed containers. When the two men were finished, they put on the coveralls Nolan and Wanachtee had been wearing and left.

''Time to go,'' said Wanachtee, taking the control position. He looked completely at home there.

Chapter 7

FROM a distance of five miles it looked exactly like the beautifully detailed, self-assembly model in the toy basement of Coshawnee's. Like the model, it had been put together from a large number of prefabricated parts. Unlike the model, it was not mounted against a background of black velvet sprinkled with crystal chips to represent the stars, for behind this vast and complex structure the stars were real, incredibly numerous, and unreachable with, hopefully, the one exception which was its destination.

Aisling Gheal hung in orbit like some grotesque and monstrous stick insect with far too many wings, legs, and feelers. Bulbous and lumpy and fringed with the projecting sensor and communications antennas, and with a glittering many-faceted eye which was the brightly lit direct vision panel of Control and the on-duty crew quarters. The great head was joined by a ridiculously narrow neck to the first of the ten cold sleep modules, each one of which was capable of transporting in its spherical belly one thousand refrigerated colonists with their seed stores and livestock, and each with its own lander docking bay. Aft of the colonist modules the spine was more strongly braced to support the lander hangar and fuel reservoirs. Clustered around the lower spine like a bunch of bright red grapes were the heavy water tanks, and beyond them the power module, main thruster, and its blast shield.

As they continued their approach a number of fuzzy patches appeared to spoil the clean, hard outlines of the ship—temporary frameworks erected for the purposes of final assembly and inspection, some of which were already being dismantled. Then the distance shrank rapidly and the structure of the great starship became distorted by perspective until all that could be seen was the smooth, white wall of a colonist module and its docking bay moving slowly closer.

"You'll need your helmet now," said Wanachtee. "When we're in the air, keep it on unless I tell you to take it off. Use the number-three sun filter on your visor; that should let you see clearly enough as well as hiding your pale face."

"Since you told me what Silver Elk wants done," Nolan said grimly, "I expect it is paler than usual."

The Redman did not reply. Wanachtee's visor was already down, hiding an expression that would probably have been unreadable anyway.

They remained on the control deck while a spacesuited team arrived to help the two men who had traveled up with them to move their payload—eleven cold sleep caskets and sundry other equipment—into the module. All of them were either hypersensitive to light or intent on concealing their features. When the containers had been immobilized by deck clamps, he followed Wanachtee outside.

One by one he flipped back the covers of the casket telltales to check that the systems were functioning properly and the temperature of the contents had not risen during the transfer from the cryogenics facility to orbit. As soon as he finished with each container, it was wrapped in a thick, insulated, and heavily padded cover to protect it against accidental damage or temperature increase during the next stage of the transfer. Throughout the proceedings, Wanachtee remained beside one of the caskets, and when the others were being moved from the dock, he ordered that it be taken last.

Moving it easily and expertly in the weightless condition, the two men who had traveled with them guided it toward the colonist stacks in the wake of the other caskets. But they had been moving only a few minutes when Wanachtee diverted them into the hyperthermia-systems test and inspection room. There they attached the casket to the inspection frame alongside another casket which was already in position, then they left without speaking.

Nolan looked at the familiar equipment ranged around and above him. It was possible that he had never before visited this compartment, but it was identical in all respects to the examination room where he had completed his training.

The air in the room was bitingly cold. Wanachtee opened his visor and Nolan removed his helmet and gauntlets. Pressing his upper lip forward and down over the lower in an attempt to keep the thick clouds of condensing breath from obscuring his vision, he moved to the first casket, pushed his boots into a set of floor stirrups, and flipped open the telltales panel.

It was not a pleasant tale that they told.

He lifted back the casket cover and began moving his bare

hands over the surface of the ice-cold, naked body, working from the feet up. The left thigh, hip, and abdomen felt noticeably warmer than the rest of the body, and it was in these areas that the smooth, bronzed skin showed evidence of subdermal bleeding. He reached above him and swung down the X-ray and thermal scanners, but they merely confirmed what he already knew had happened. He sighed, then began a careful check of the casket's systems and wiring. He straightened up and sighed again.

Wanachtee's look was a silent question.

Using his most clinical voice, Nolan said, "You can see for yourself that there is widespread tissue damage and necrosis in the blood-supply network, musculature, and underlying organs in the areas of the left leg, hip, and abdomen. The sleeper was cold at the time of the malfunction, so he could not tell us why it happened even if he had the specialized knowledge to do so. He can be wakened, but, considering his condition, he would survive for no more than ten minutes in extreme physical discomfort, so I would strongly advise against it. But I would like to make a thorough investigation of the casket in case—"

"There isn't time, Healer," Wanachtee said firmly. "It was only by chance that one of our technicians, who had no business looking into a casket sealed for the voyage, noticed the skin discoloration. But now we have the chance to send a live rather than a dying colonist to the New World."

"A living colonist greatly beloved by Silver Elk," said Nolan, and added dryly, "if the accident had not occurred, would she have remained on Earth?"

"Perhaps another, more complicated and dangerous way would have been found," said Wanachtee in a neutral voice, "to place her on the ship."

"Who are they," Nolan asked as he began a meticulous systems check on the other casket. "Or would you rather not tell me?"

"The man was gifted in many ways," said the Redman sadly, "and his talents would have been invaluable to our people on the New World. His qualifications ensured his immediate acceptance as a colonist." A defensive note crept into his tone as he went on, "The girl, too, is most highly qualified, but could not gain a place because of a small technicality."

He had not named names nor had he specified the technicality. But if she had the friendship and influence of Silver Elk behind her, it would not be a minor one.

"I shall open the casket for a few minutes to check the placing of the freeze-thaw pads. This can be done without risk to the sleeper since the temperature here is low. Would you mind turning your back?''

Wanachtee made a derogatory sound and said, ''Healer, we do not subscribe to the nudity taboos of the paleskins. I shall stand beside you. If the girl finds my presence an embarrassment, I hope that she will awaken and say so.''

Nolan shrugged, a useless gesture inside a spacesuit, and lifted the cover.

He did not blame Wanachtee for wanting to look at her. He enjoyed looking at her himself, even though he was forbidden by his calling to take pleasure in the sight or touch of any patient. She was tall for a woman, but delightfully proportioned in body and lovely of face—a beautiful, dark-haired, red-bronze Venus who could have been the work of the greatest of the old Grecian sculptors. But this was no flawless Aphrodite imprisoned forever in marble, because it would require but the pressure of a finger on the manual revivification switch to bring this frozen dream to warm and pulsing life. Wanachtee was staring with such intensity at the girl that Nolan began to feel uneasy. Perhaps the Redman was having similar thoughts.

''If this girl should waken or be wakened,'' said Nolan, apparently continuing the conversation, but allowing a note of warning to enter his voice, ''she would have to remain awake until another casket was prepared for her at your cryogenics facility. These are colonist caskets, remember, and designed for one freeze-and-thaw cycle only, and it would be very difficult for you to maintain secrecy while moving a living, unclad female back to the—''

''Healer,'' said Wanachtee in a voice that shook with suppressed emotion, ''I know all this.''

At last Nolan was beginning to understand. Deliberately he allowed the casket cover to remain open for another few minutes before resealing it, then left the examination room pushing the girl's casket ahead of them. The two men who were waiting in the corridor helped them move it quickly into the passenger stacks and to the empty recess where the casket of the spoiled colonist had been located, then they left to collect the other casket from the examination room and move it to the shuttle, for the body's cremation above the Old World rather than the hoped-for burial on the New World.

''It is the strictest of the project's rules,'' said Nolan very seriously, ''that in order to obtain maximum benefit from the available genetic pool, all colonists be healthy, unmarried, and with no family or prior emotional attachments. The effects of long-term hibernation anesthesia on a recently conceived human fetus, about which we have no data, had also to be considered. Pairing off is expressly forbidden until after the colony has been established. Yet here we have a girl who is sleeping, unclothed, in a stack with hundreds of similarly undraped men.

"Granted," he went on, and tried to lighten his tone with a gentle laugh, "it is unlikely that anything unseemly would occur at a few degrees above absolute zero. But our ecclesiastic friends are not noted for their flexibility of mind on moral issues and might—"

"We have made very good time, Healer," Wanachtee broke in sharply. His tone suggested that he saw nothing humorous in the situation. "You will be back on Earth long before anyone realizes you've been gone."

Two hours later they were shuddering through the upper layers of the atmosphere, the jettisoned casket and its spoiled contents falling far ahead of them and already burning up. Nolan watched as it blazed incandescently for a few moments before dissolving into nothingness.

The cremation of one nameless cold sleeping would-be colonist was complete.

"Now *that* bothers me," he said, breaking his long silence. "A person should know, should have some warning, that he is going to die. There must be feelings, memories, thoughts which he must think, and know that he is thinking, for the last time. Even the victim of a street accident, or an assassination, has a little time to know that life is ending. But, dammit, that man was—is—expecting to wake up."

Inside the heavy suit he gave a single, uncontrollable shiver.

"You are a Healer," said Wanachtee gravely. "But are you sure that you are an unbeliever?"

"I'm sure that I'm a Healer," Nolan replied, ignoring the question and trying to keep the irritation he had felt since leaving the ship from showing in his voice. "As a Healer I expect people to make use of me. They know that I have certain abilities, knowledge, and constraints. They know that anything I may discover from a patient, or deduce as a result of treating that patient, may not be spoken to any other person."

The Redman was watching him closely, even though there were only a few minutes before he would have to concentrate all of his attention on the final approach. When the attention is divided, Nolan reminded himself, answers tend to be less guarded.

He went on, "Let us consider the strange case of the Corporation executive who is also a shuttle pilot. A Redman who has great power and influence in his nation and, no doubt, many other abilities still hidden from me. Such a person would be sure to volunteer for *Aisling Gheal*, either as a ship's officer or as a colonist. The names of the unsuccessful crew applicants are known to me, and I am sure that if a colonist was also a trained spasaire, that would also be known. But for some reason this colonist has concealed from me the fact that he will be among the last applicants to be cooled, and he has concealed from the project's selectors, probably by changing his name, the fact that he is an astronaut."

"Healer," said Wanachtee, "there are fewer places for ship's officers than for colonists, and more competition."

"That is not the only reason," said Nolan. "Let me remind you that I am medically responsible for this female colonist, as well as for all the other cold sleepers in the ship, and the more I know or am able to deduce about my patients the better I shall be able to care for them. It doesn't matter to me if they have a guilty secret, like contravening a not-so-minor technicality by marrying before departure. Such secrets are safe with me.

"So rest your mind," he added in a gentler voice, "I shall take good care of both of you."

The desert was spread out before them, brown and heat-hazed and almost featureless under the early afternoon sun, and they were falling along their unnervingly steep glidepath like an aerodynamically clean brick. It was more comforting to keep his eyes on Wanachtee.

"I am truly sorry that I wasn't able to meet Golden Rain," said Nolan, "at your lodge."

Chapter 8

THE streets of the Imperial and Open City of Peiping had been planned at a time when the Emperor's civil engineers had only pedestrian traffic plus the usual proportion of two- or four-legged draft animals to worry about. It had not, because of its centuries-old status as an open city, had the benefit of periodic large-scale demolition and reconstruction which would normally have followed in the wake of Cathay's many wars.

The young officer walking beside him sounded nervous and apologetic, as if the bloody and untidy histories of both nations were somehow his fault. He said, "Kyoto is even more congested, and less solidly built because of the earthquakes. Kyoto is the Imperial capital of Nippon, and since the time of the Shogun, Hamaseya, when it was mutually agreed that—"

"They taught me a little geography in school," Nolan broke in, "and history."

The freshly scrubbed and shaved face above the uniform collar went an even deeper shade of pink, and the priest said, "I'm sorry, Healer. It's just that the Twin Empires are of special interest to me, and sometimes I forget that other people do know quite a lot about them."

He was small and slightly built, and either talked incessantly or fell into long, embarrassed silences as he was about to do now. Nolan had seen him a few times during training, but had not known his name until the monsignor had introduced him as Father Quinn of the long-range sensor department. O'Riordan had given Nolan the smile of a worried parent and said that the young priest had some business to conduct in the city, but that his secondary concern would be to show Nolan the sights and keep him out of trouble.

Unlike Wanachtee, this earnest and intense young priest would do just that.

Nolan had not wanted to hurt the other's feelings, so he smiled and said, "My school taught only the basics, and a boring job they made of it. I'm delighted at the chance to reduce my level of ignorance of the subject, Father. Cathay is one of the few histories that for some reason I am not required to teach."

"The reason," said the priest, beginning to relax, "is that I will be teaching the subject. I've been attached to the College of Computing here in Peiping, with the Confraternity for the Regulation of the Hibernian Treasury Abroad, since my ordination ten years ago. The banking duties took me all over Cathay and, whenever there was a chance, I tried to help some of the poor and bring them the Word of God. Perhaps I learned too much about the people I was trying to teach."

Nolan quickly revised upward his estimate of Father Quinn's age and of his degree of intelligence. He said, "Maybe you can begin by telling me why, in spite of these rather splendid full-dress uniforms we're wearing, nobody is looking at us?"

"Without wanting to hurt your feelings, Healer," the priest replied, with the hint of an apology creeping back into his voice, "the majority of them don't consider us worth their attention, and the rest will not look at us because it is considered ill-mannered to do so. Quickly, please, step down into the street."

Nolan gave him a questioning look, but did as he was told.

"Move naturally," the priest continued quietly, "as if we have decided to take another look at the pagoda we just passed. Those carvings are well worth a second look, anyhow. Do not look at the group moving along the pavement toward us."

There were seven of them, all dressed in dull brown street cloaks stretching to the ankles and wearing flat, round hats which were also free of all decoration. Six of the men were spaced loosely around a seventh, who had a wispy gray beard and mustache. As Nolan turned his face toward the brightly lacquered carvings fringing the upper roofing of the pagoda, he had a second, indirect look and saw that the fingers and thumbs of the older man were black.

"Even I know the significance of covered fingers," said Nolan dryly. "A person of some importance passes us."

"A Mandarin of the Osprey Rank, no less, with guardians," the other replied in an awed voice. He took Nolan's arm, and pointing at nothing in particular on the other side of the street, he turned so that the group passed unseen behind them, then went on, "Please don't look at him again. The guards react very quickly to any threat, real or imagined, because if the slightest harm occurred to their master, they would expect to have their hands, feet, and heads cut off. In that order."

Nolan did not ask what would happen to them if some serious harm befell their master—it might be better not to know. He said softly, "And this is supposedly a civilized country."

"It *is* a civilized country, Healer," Father Quinn said bitterly. "It was civilized for two thousand years before the Greeks or the Romans or the Hibernians knew the meaning of the word. Long before the Coming of Christ, it was the equal of Rome in power and influence. There was trade along the Golden Road through Samarkand and India. Persian carpets decorated the palaces of the Han Emperors, and the wives of the Roman senators wore the silks of Far Cathay. The trade was profitable in spite of the brigands who plagued the caravan routes, until our own High-Kings became increasingly angered at having to buy their costly silks and spices and jade ornaments through the money-hungry merchants of the Levant, and decided that they would open up their own direct trade route around southernmost Africa to Cathay. Despite the many vessels that foundered in the early days, the enterprise was successful. We profited and learned much from them, and they from us, including the art of naval combat waged by vessels which were independent of the wind or tide or ocean currents, ships which were subsequently armed with the machines of war that spoke only in the one, dreadful language, the Thunder of Cathay.

"And if that was not enough," the priest went on angrily, "we initiated the war between Nippon and Cathay which has raged until this day."

"Oh, come now," said Nolan uncomfortably. It was unusual for a cleric of today to display such personal shame and anger over the mistakes of long-dead brethren. "They were traditional enemies to begin with, and war was inevitable even if that dreadfully mismanaged meeting we arranged between the Emperors had never taken place. And anyway, there has been peace between them for six decades."

"You think so, Healer?"

The scorn in the other's tone made Nolan's face grow hot with embarrassment. He said, "No, I *don't* think so. When two decades of continuous aerial bombing and long-range artillery bombardment became a limited nuclear exchange, they stopped when eighteen cities of each nation were obliterated and the countryside surrounding them poisoned. Since then they have been improving—if that is the right word—their weapons to the point where they cannot use them without bringing about immediate mutual obliteration, as well as sickening to ultimate death all living things on Earth. No, it isn't peace, but neither is it war."

The other man did not speak. Unlike the crowd of passersby moving so closely around them who did not appear to see the strangers because obvious curiosity would have been impolite, he was seeing only the conflict of ideals and ethics that was his own inner war, and the single casualty that was himself.

"There was much good that came out of their endless war," Nolan went on, wondering if the priest's ears were as deaf to the Healer's words as the eyes of the passersby were blind. "It was Cathay explosives which opened the ship channel in the Egyptian desert, so that trade between East and West flourished. Their dirigible kites gave us air transport, their long-range bombardment missiles showed us the way into space, and their great knowledge, much of which we stole from them, gave us nuclear power plants, nuclear medicine, suspended animation, and, ultimately, the *Aisling Gheal*. It isn't your fault, Father, that some civilized nations do not always behave in a civilized fashion."

"We had the chance," said Quinn, still engaged in his own private battle. "But we didn't have a Brendan to live with them, to tell them tales of brotherhood and past glories shared, to confront two honorable but warlike peoples with the ultimate challenge of living together in peace. Instead we had captains and adventurers and merchants who were little more than pirates.

"We used the people of the Twin Empires," he went on, "and were used by them. But we were never allowed close to them in the areas which really mattered. The religious among them listen to the teachings of Buddha instead of Christ, even though both deities are equally foreign. Few, indeed, will be the martyrs' crowns earned among the missionaries to Cathay, or even Nippon, because we are ignored.

"Politely, of course," he added bitterly.

Nolan gave a sympathetic and probably unnoticed smile and said gently, "I would not have thought, bearing in mind your specialized scientific training, that a martyr's crown ranked high in your list of priorities."

"A martyr's crown is the surest way into Heaven," said the priest, forcing himself to smile, "but I would prefer to wait for it until I was, say, seventy or eighty years old."

Nolan laughed a little louder than was necessary. But the other's tone became serious again as he said, "You must understand that whatever else I am or have been trained to do, the priestly duty comes first, and last. The same applies to the other priest-officers on the ship. Please do not forget that, Healer.

"And I apologize for the recent morbid tone of my conversation," he went on quickly. "No doubt I am lacking in true humility, but sometimes the way these people treat us annoys me. Them and their covered fingers . . . !"

He broke off, smiled again, then went on to explain that in the reign of the early Emperors it was the custom for high-ranking Mandarins to allow their fingernails to grow unchecked as an outward indication of their status. It was said that the nails were grown to the length of their forearms, like thin, curving talons which were protected by sheaths of jewel-encrusted gold. They sat or lay with hands resting palm upward in their laps, unable to move unaided for fear of damaging their nails, or to bathe or dress or eat or, the priest added delicately, do anything without the assistance of servants. It was their total dependence on others to perform the most personal and intimate tasks for them that was seen as the true measure of their nobility.

Nowadays they wore only a token covering on the fingers, but they still retained a great many personal servants who would kill and do who knew what else for them, instantly and without question.

"There is a cautionary tale regarding a young Hibernian noncleric," Father Quinn went on, with his smile still held firmly in place, "who was transferred to our bank here as a junior teller. To help him more easily count the paper money he decided to wear a couple of rubber finger-grips he had brought with him from home. He holds the record for the shortest term of employment in Cathay banking circles. But don't worry, Healer. At the proper time and place, a foreigner wearing surgical gloves is quite acceptable."

They continued walking through a well-tended park which was thronged with quiet adults and very noisy children who, in the course of their games, did not despoil in any way the floral beauty all around them. At the center of the park, partially concealed by a screen of ornamental shrubs and trees, there was a low, wide, and completely featureless dome of dazzling white. The entrance to the structure, which was well below ground level, was reached by a descending ramp lined with statues carved in jade and wood.

"The outer flash-shield of a nuclear bomb shelter," said Quinn, answering the question before Nolan could ask it. "They have them in Kyoto as well as Peiping. Even though the two Imperial Cities, which both house the illustrious and deified persons of the Emperors and are the true treasure houses of the art, culture, and written histories of both great civilizations, are open and never to be subjected to nuclear bombardment or any other form of physical attack. But they never will trust each other."

Nolan took a few more paces in silence, then said, "Where we are going there will be no worries about the final nuclear war breaking out. And you will certainly have to give up your hopes of a glorious martyrdom."

The priest gave him an odd, intent look and seemed about to say something. Then he shook his head, smiled, and visibly changed his mind to say something entirely different.

"I have to give a lecture over there," he said, indicating a large many-roofed building decorated in rich, dark colors, whose outlines were further softened by a delicate, almost transparent screen of trees. "You should sit beside me . . ."

And stay out of trouble, Nolan added silently.

". . . so as to enjoy the best view," Father Quinn went on. "The monsignor tells me that you are one of the few ship's officers who has not seen the New World at close range."

Inlaid in gold on black marble, the name of the quietly resplendent establishment appeared three times above the entrance—in Mandarin, Latin, and Gaelic. This was the Imperial School of Lensmakers of Cathay, whose graduates had for more than three centuries produced the finest telescopes in the world, and one that orbited far beyond it.

The priest was very respectful toward the girl who conducted them to the main lecture theater, but Nolan did not know whether it was simple politeness to a female student or the honor due a member of the faculty—it was difficult to guess the degree of seniority from the ageless beauty of that face. When they took their seats beside the lectern, the projection equipment and the audience were ready and waiting even though the priest was not scheduled to begin his lecture for another ten minutes.

Before the lights dimmed, Nolan was able to see only two people in the audience wearing finger covers. In both cases it was the tips of the index finger and thumb only that were hidden, and the two men were encircled by empty chairs rather than bodyguards. Plainly they were of a fairly low order of Mandarin. Relieved, Nolan settled back in his chair.

As a specialist in the computer processing and image enhancement of data from long-range sensors, Father Quinn left no doubt that he knew his subject and was quietly and intensely enthusiastic about it. Whether he was communicating his enthusiasm to the overly polite and quiet audience was another matter, but Nolan was enjoying the lecture and visuals too much to care.

The priest spent little time on the Earth-based telescopes of the past, which had shown only blurred images of a few super-giant planets of the nearer stars and, understandably, even less on the few early Christian astronomers who had suffered excommunication and worse for describing what they had seen in them. Only one subject was of interest to this audience, and they were as anxious to hear about the findings of this ultimate in optical instruments as Father Quinn was to describe them.

The incredibly sharp and minutely detailed pictures he showed them made even this politely undemonstrative audience gasp, and had Nolan instinctively gripping his chair to keep from falling endlessly into the interplanetary space that opened out suddenly before him. He told himself that the projection equipment used in the Imperial School of Lensmakers would be well-nigh perfect, but he had not expected such breathtaking, three-dimensional clarity over interstellar distances.

Space Observatory One had been positioned thirty degrees above the plane of the ecliptic some ten million miles beyond the orbit of Mars—a compromise position that balanced the disadvantages of distance against the advantages of reduced structural damage and lens deformation from meteorite collisions and solar heating. Seen from a distance of five miles, it hung like an enormous silver parasol whose gossamer structure seemed much too fragile to support the weight of a reflecting lens that was just under half a mile in diameter. The observation pod at the instrument's point of focus seemed totally unsupported, but that was because the members holding it in position had been painted matte black to minimize structural reflection into the mirror. At closer range the instrument looked even weaker and more insubstantial.

But on *Space Observatory One* they did not have to worry about weight. The reflector itself was gigantic but not massive, simply an incredibly thin membrane of mirror plastic whose curvature and optical properties were maintained by tiny movements of the framework on which it was stretched. As a feat of space engineering it was rivaled only by the building of *Aisling Gheal* herself, and it was a structure of almost infinite complexity, delicacy, and great artistry which was totally in character for the nation that had built it.

They were shown film taken during its construction, including the dramatic sequence when a malfunction in the positioning controls caused the great mirror to face the sun for several seconds during which the hastily evacuated observation pod at the point of focus had flared into incandescent gas. There were pictures, incredibly sharp and detailed, of surface features on the moons of Jupiter and Saturn and on the outer planets; there were exposures that showed the strangely ordered distribution and structure of the galaxies at the outer limit of the Universe, and the hint of something even greater beyond. And there were the results of the increasingly successful search for extra-solar planets, culminating in the discovery of a small bluish-white world, the second of a seven-planet system, orbiting an inconspicuous star in the southern constellation of the Sword of Tao.

The New World.

Distant it was in space and time, but to the tremendous fabrication that was *Aisling Gheal* and to the engines that would drive it, the time separating it from Earth would be less than six centuries. And even over that vast distance, the computer-enhanced resolution of *Space Observatory One*'s mirror was such that the pictures were as clear as, and often clearer than, those taken of the Earth's surface by the first manned orbiting vehicles.

It was the most recently acquired photographs of the New World that the priest was showing now, and it was the first time that anyone, himself included, had seen them displayed to such good effect.

There were as many different names for it as there were languages on Earth, but all of the translations had the same basic meaning—the New World, the New Home, or the New Future. Even when the hemisphere it presented to the space telescope was covered by the clear, still air of high-pressure systems, it still looked remarkably like the Old World. But the enlarged photographs showed the outlines of oceans, clusters of islands, and continents that did not fit into any Earth atlas.

Largest of these was the long, irregularly shaped landmass that intersected the planet's equator at an angle of about thirty degrees and extended well into the north and south polar regions. By general agreement, and there had been very little of that regarding the other place–names on the New World, it was called Dragonia because its outline resembled a rampant dragon and nothing else. The head and fiery tongue, icy cold in this case, occupied the north polar wastes, while the long neck and landmasses making up the forelegs and upper body extended through the temperate latitudes to the equator. The afterbody and rear legs reached through the south temperate zone, and the tip of the heavy curving tail was, like the head, also cooled by polar ice.

Running like a long uneven spine down the center of both the neck and tail were two high mountain ranges. But in the equatorial region they divided, the peaks become lower, more rounded and numerous, and separated by large tracts of jungle or lakes varying from a few miles across to the dimensions of inland seas, which gave the visual effect of a dragon with a fat, mottled green belly.

Compared with that single major continent, the remaining landmasses were small and insignificant.

"The proportion of sea to land surface is greater than on Earth," the priest said, "and we could expect it to be cooler were it not for the fact that the planet orbits much closer to its sun. There is no axial tilt and, therefore, no seasonal changes for the farmers to worry about. The world rotates approximately once every twenty-nine and one-half hours, its year is two hundred and ninety-six planetary days, and the lengths of day and night are equal. Spectroanalysis shows the atmospheric composition and pressure to be so close to our own that you would not be able to detect the difference without instruments.

"The longer we observe it," the priest said with quiet enthusiasm, "the more perfect it becomes."

A member of the audience stood up suddenly, indicating that he wished to speak. He was one of the two whose index fingers and thumbs were covered.

"Respected officer," he said in a tone that was anything but respectful, "are you absolutely sure that it is uninhabited, and inhabitable by us?"

From the confident way the priest replied, it was clear that the question was neither new nor unexpected. He began by admitting that he could not be absolutely sure of anything, but that the probability that the New World was uninhabited was so high that there was no significant difference between it and a certainty.

The areas where intelligent life would be most likely to show itself had been scrutinized repeatedly and most carefully. On Earth the primitives had sheltered in caves, usually situated on high ground, which gave protection from the weather and wild beasts as well as allowing pestilence-carrying wastes to drain away safely.

Less primitive people settled on riverbanks, so that their crops would have water and there would be fish as well as flesh to eat, or, if fishing was more profitable or less dangerous than hunting, they built their early villages on sheltered inlets and river estuaries, settlements which would later become the sites of modern cities.

"But even the most primitive of cave dwellers leave traces of their presence," the priest went on, "and none of this evidence could be hidden from us. The traces of more advanced settlements, the unnaturally cleared ground for planting, and the well-used trails would be even easier to detect. Except for a few smoke traces which were directly and indisputably associated with lightning strikes in the areas, there is no evidence of unnatural combustion occurring anywhere on the planet.

"Many small herds have been observed, well scattered across the subtemperate grasslands," he continued, "and maximum image enhancement used when the sun was low and the shadows long has shown us that individually they are no larger than Earthly sheep. Schools of sea creatures with the approximate mass of large whales have been observed, but so far as we know there is no birdlife. Naturally, we cannot resolve the images of the individual birds, but a flock of them would show as a small area of moving haze that changed direction too erratically for it to be wind-blown mist. The larger and more obvious cliff markings left by flocks of nesting seabirds are likewise absent.

"It is a clean, untainted, and very beautiful world," he ended, in a voice that made the words sound like a prayer. "Without a doubt it is habitable, and uninhabited."

Nolan moved restively in his chair—people who spoke with such absolute certainty worried him. The questioner with the covered finger and thumb also seemed dissatisfied, because he had not resumed his seat.

"Perhaps, respected officer," he said in his condescending voice, "there could be a danger from inhabitants too small for you to see?"

Before the priest could reply, the Mandarin turned his head to look haughtily toward another member of the audience, then sat down.

The man he had indicated stood up quickly. He was swathed in a pale blue cloak whose edges were decorated with ideographs in black and red. The face was old but the eyes were clear and dark, and, Nolan saw with relief, his fingers were uncovered.

"Respected officer," he said, in a voice that was respectful, "I am but the humble mouth and mind which asks the questions of the others here. I am Hseng Hwa."

"Your name is known to me, Doctor Hseng, and greatly respected," said the priest. His tone was equally polite, but Nolan could detect the anxiety in his voice as he went on, "I shall answer your questions to the best of my poor ability."

"With respect," said Hseng, "our questions have little relevance to your most interesting and informative lecture on the long-range examination of the target world. Our primary concerns relate to the continued health of our people and the actions they should or should not take when we get there. For this reason we would prefer that they be answered by Healer Nolan, who is not yet known to us, but whose position in the ship and on the New World are worthy of respect.''

The priest was silent for a moment, and when he spoke, his face had grown pink with embarrassment

''I was not expecting this sudden change of subject midway through the lecture,'' he said ''I am sorry, but you will understand that adequate preparation is needed if such an important subject is to be treated properly, and the time remaining to me is short. At a later date, perhaps, I can arrange for Healer Dervla herself to answer your questions. If you will pardon me, I shall confer with my fellow officer.''

Nolan had been tugging gently at the priest's cloak. He kept his voice low as he said, ''There's no need for a conference. If I'm not adequately prepared now I never will be, so let him ask his questions. Besides, have you forgotten that in Cathay they still prefer their Healers to be male?''

''I have not forgotten,'' the priest said in a voice that was equally soft, but very angry. ''Nor have I forgotten the monsignor's instructions to me, which were that you would be allowed to attend this lecture as an observer only, and that you must not be allowed to speak other than the few words required by good manners.

''The most delicate negotiations are taking place in the Imperial Palace as we speak,'' he went on quickly. ''They are aimed at balancing the overall value of their nuclear thrusters to the project against the number of Cathay colonists who are to travel. The number they demand is unreasonably high and ours, because we are bargaining from a position of strength, somewhat low. For this reason they will try to weaken our position in every way possible, by discrediting the project, its management, and officers, which will include you if you give them the chance.

''Refusing what seems like a polite and spontaneous request will also reflect discredit on us,'' he added in a worried voice, ''but it will be a minor embarrassment compared with—''

''My apologies for the intrusion,'' Hseng Hwa broke in. ''I can assure you that my questions will be few, and very simple.''

''And I, Father,'' Nolan said softly as he rose to his feet, ''shall be speaking on matters well within my area of competence. Is everyone in the audience a colonist?''

"I sincerely hope," said Father Quinn, with a glance toward the men wearing finger covers, "that two of them aren't. Hseng Hwa is, among other things, the chief scientific adviser to the Emperor and a longtime friend of our cardinal-captain. You will remember that I advised against this, Healer, so please be careful."

Nolan forced himself to smile, and said, "What is your first question, respected Doctor?"

"As has been already indicated by my illustrious predecessor," Hseng Hwa said, bowing politely toward one of the Mandarins, "my question concerns the probable dangers to our people from native creatures too small to be resolved either by our great telescope or the enhancements of your colleague's long-range sensors.

"I refer," he went on gently, "to the small creatures that burrow and bite, to the winged insects that swarm and sting, and to the disabling or lethal poisons that are even smaller, those which must be viewed with a microscope rather than a telescope and which, on Earth, have all too often been the carriers of plague and pestilence that have decimated the proudest and most populous nations. How may we overcome this small but multitudinous population of your beautiful and uninhabited New World?"

Hseng Hwa sat down and there was stillness throughout the auditorium. Even the priest behind him seemed to be holding his breath. Nolan sighed, and thought sadly about his area of competence, which was being attacked at its weakest point.

Chapter 9

"YOU will understand," said Nolan, in a voice that projected a confidence he did not feel, "that the microbiology, parasitology, and immunology of the New World, and the associated bacterial and viral organisms, assuming them to be present and effective against human life and/or the animals we shall take with us, can only be deduced by behavioral observations, and in particular deviations from the behavioral norm, of life-forms affected—''

Nolan broke off because the blue-cloaked doctor was rising to his feet again.

''I apologize for this interruption,'' Hseng Hwa said politely, ''and for the additional burden I must place upon you. I realize that in order to answer our questions properly you must speak with precision of meaning. Regrettably, the majority of our people here are simple colonists, trained in husbandry and the coarser manual crafts, who are not familiar with the nomenclature of the medical art. You should speak to us as you would while teaching older children.''

Which meant, Nolan thought, that he would not be allowed to conceal his professional uncertainties behind a cloak of polysyllables. He doubted very much that his listeners were as ignorant as the respected doctor pretended, but the wording Hseng Hwa had used suggested that it might be his ability as a teacher rather than his professional competence that was being tested.

''I am grateful for the timely reminder,'' he said, with a small bow in the direction of Hseng Hwa, ''that it is the instructor's responsibility to make his meaning clear to those he wishes to instruct. I shall begin, therefore, with a simple and perhaps frightening statement. It is that we do not know with certainty how the tiny insects and even smaller disease carriers of the New World will affect us, but there are reasons why these fears may be without substance.''

He paused for a moment to allow the coughing, throat-clearing, and small body movements that invariably preceded a lecture to subside, then went on. ''Many wise men and women have deliberated long and earnestly on the question you have raised, and many of them have reached a conclusion that is comforting to all of us.

''They believe that there is a very strong probability,'' Nolan continued, '' that the microscopic forms of life which inhabit all living creatures, and dwell in the soil, seas, and air of the New World, will have no effect on us whatsoever. They believe that the germs which may have caused pestilence among the creatures of the New World since the dawn of its history would find our bodies, and those of our breeding animals, so strange and unworldly that they would simply ignore us. Similarly, any germs which we chanced to bring with us, in spite of the many precautions we are taking to ensure that the colonists and crew are disease-free, would have no effect on the creatures that live there. In short, they believe that we can ignore this problem because it may not exist.''

As he paused for a moment to arrange his thoughts, Nolan heard Father Quinn give a long, quiet sigh. It was a pity, he thought, that the priest's relief was a little premature.

''Personally,'' he resumed, ''I consider this view to be too optimistic and therefore untrustworthy. But there is evidence of a much more substantial kind which points toward the same comforting conclusion . . .''

As it was on Earth, he went on to explain, there was constant competition between creatures great and small for personal survival and for the survival of their various offspring. The land creatures and burrowers, those they had been unable to see because of forest cover, and the dwellers in the oceans, were expected to behave in a similar manner. Insects defended themselves with bites and stings, and the vegetation had its thorns to discourage grazers and blooms to encourage the pollen-carrying insects.

''. . . The creatures of Dragonia have been under continual observation for many years,'' Nolan continued. ''They have been seen to die, after lengthy periods of reduced activity, a condition almost certainly caused by old age, or as a result of accidental injury or attacks by others of their own or perhaps a different kind. At no time during these observations have any large numbers of them behaved as if they were being affected by a fatal or even disabling disease.

''I consider this negative evidence,'' he ended quietly, ''to be much more trustworthy, and reassuring.''

Hseng Hwa was on his feet again. ''Is it possible, respected officer, that these Dragonian creatures have become so accustomed to their native pestilences that they are no longer affected by them? And could these New World germs wage successful war on us?''

''That is a possibility,'' Nolan replied. ''But from our experience with Earthly diseases we know that such wars can be won, frequently by the intended victims. There are many uncertainties in the old world, and I expect that the same will hold true on the new one. But in my own opinion it would be impossible to find a world more suitable for colonization, for it is clean, fresh, and in the very morning of its life.''

Without rising to his feet, one of the Mandarins held up a hand and said quietly, ''Is there an implication in your words that the New World resembles very closely your fabled Garden of Eden? And if this should be so, are you worried by the possibility that you may not be allowed to land colonists there, or that you might be prevented from reaching it, or even from making the attempt to leave?''

Nolan inclined his head toward the speaker and said, ''My apologies. Since I am an unbeliever, my thoughts on this matter would be without value. Perhaps Father Quinn, who has much more competence in this subject, will answer you?''

He turned to look at the priest, who made a small movement of the head that could have been one of affirmation or irritation. But before he could rise to his feet, the Mandarin spoke again.

''It is of no consequence to me,'' he said in a bored voice, ''and it was impolite of me to force you to display incompetence in any area. Since you are a Healer from the ship, and an unexpected but welcome visitor because of that, there must be other questions that we can ask that you are competent to answer.''

The Mandarin looked at Hseng Hwa, who was already on his feet. Nolan felt as though he was once again undergoing his final examinations for the qualification of Surgeon-Healer. These questions were much more politely worded, but they were equally searching.

''We would all like to believe, respected officer,'' said Hseng Hwa, ''that there are no harmful diseases on the New World and, if there are, that they will be impotent against beings from this one. But there are other hidden dangers which concern us, other dangers which cannot be detected at a distance. I am thinking not only of the insects, and the effects of their bites and stings on us, but of the venom of the serpents which hang from the trees and the burrowers which strike from the ground. These creatures inject poison as their natural weapons, not disease. Or are you saying that the toxic chemicals of the New World will likewise be ineffective against the natives of another?''

Both of the Mandarins were watching him, faint smiles on their hitherto impassive faces. It was quite obvious that they were trying to discredit him. He should have heeded the priest's advice and accepted the earlier, minor embarrassment to avoid what might well be a later and greater one.

Before Nolan could reply, Hseng Hwa went on. ''Calculations have been made which suggest that the quantity of seed-grain carried on *Aisling Gheal* is more than sufficient for the planting of a large variety of edible crops on the New World, but they also suggest that the surplus will fall short of the quantity needed to feed the colonists until the first harvest is in. Would they then be forced for many months to survive wholly or partly on native vegetation, a large proportion of which we must expect to be inedible or even poisonous? Is this a true description of the post-landing situation? And if this be so, what actions must be taken to guard against the triple threat of lethal poisoning by insect, serpent, and plant?''

Like one of Cathay's own heat-seeking missiles, Hseng Hwa had gone unerringly to his one area of weakness. Nolan used words under his breath that would have shocked the patrons of even the most depraved of the Reykjavík harbor taverns.

He could feel his face growing warm with embarrassment as he said, ''Regrettably, I do not possess the knowledge to answer these questions. The exact disposition and quantities of stores have never been my concern, and the answers to your medical questions should properly come from Healer Dervla, who is accompanying us on our visit to Peiping and who, I am sure, would be pleased to answer these questions . . .''

Nolan stopped talking as he became aware of the utter stillness and silence in the room. It seemed that Father Quinn had forgotten how to breathe, and he was giving Nolan no indication of what he expected the Healer to do or say, and both of the Mandarins were smiling their inscrutable smiles. He looked again at them and, briefly harboring the un-Healerlike wish that their fingers had been amputated at birth, smiled in return.

''If such an arrangement is not convenient for you,'' he went on, ''I am willing to give you the answers that I think Dervla would give, although not, you will understand, with the same degree of authority and prior experience. But I am making two assumptions. They are that you have no other and more important demands on your time, and that Father Quinn has not already scheduled another meeting which will not allow me sufficient time to deal adequately with the subject.''

He turned to look appealingly at the priest, wondering if the officer would or could rescue him.

''The time for learning should end only with death,'' said one of the Mandarins before Father Quinn could reply, ''as should the time for teaching . . .''

Nolan had a wild, ridiculous thought that he was going to stand there answering questions until everyone died of old age, and with difficulty he kept himself from laughing aloud. But he found nothing to laugh at in the words that followed.

''. . . There are many things we would learn from you,'' the Mandarin went on. ''We would all like to learn why you, a Healer chosen above all others except Dervla, admit to incompetence in a specific area which, you imply, is the prerogative of and has been mastered only by female Healers. This is an important question about which our people would like information and reassurance. Later, if we have the time to spare for it, we will listen to the answers Dervla might or might not give to this question."

The yellow face was bland but the insult was not even a polite one. Nolan looked slowly around the audience, trying to impose a feeling of calm on himself that would keep the anger in him from reaching his voice. Hseng Hwa, who, it had been obvious, had up until then been merely directing the missiles that his superiors had fabricated, had resumed his seat and was regarding Nolan with a mixture of apology and sympathy. With the exception of Father Quinn, who seemed to be staring into a near future where all was desolation, Hseng Hwa's was the only friendly face in the room.

Nolan looked back to the Mandarin who had spoken, made a bow that was no deeper than a fraction of an inch, and said, "It is a very simple question, but the answer is complicated and lengthy, and would involve matters which are historical rather than medical."

"Then, you must make your answer understandable to everyone," said the Mandarin. "But you should also bear constantly in mind the fact that the level of ignorance among the members of your audience is unequal, and that although your words should be simple enough to enable the untutored among them to understand you, they must also be accurate, because there are also those among us who will be able to detect any falsehood or lesser form of verbal distortion. You should fully understand this before you begin to instruct us. You may begin."

For a moment Nolan looked at the rows of bland faces in a silence that was a feeble attempt at registering his independence of mind and resistance to psychological pressure rather than any pause for dramatic effect. He tried to pretend that these were the faces of pupils who had confronted him in disinterested or unashamedly bored rows during his nonspace teaching training in the low schools. Then he had tried to kindle the interest or at least relieve the boredom of those young men. But here the faces were so completely expressionless that he would never know whether or not he was succeeding.

He drew a long, silent breath, joined his hands loosely on top of the lectern, and began. "One of the most polite and potent curses that a person of Cathay can use against another is that he should live in interesting times, and in Hibernia the times had been interesting indeed for close on three centuries.

"It was a period of civil conflict that was as continuous and bitter as it was confused, and of social and industrial unrest that split not only the farming and manufacturing tuaths but the members of families that comprised them. Sea raids by the Roman self-styled conquerors of Saxon Britain, whose purpose was to capture Hibernian machines for the military, civil, and political benefit of distant Caesars whose Empire was already beginning to crumble, were answered by counterraids which returned with few of the lost machines but a great many captured slaves. With the slaves there also came a strange new malady, a disease which did not waste the body so much as undermine the spirit by calling into question the right of the strong to impose their will on the weak. It was an infection against which the members of no Mediterranean race, nation, or Empire had been able to develop an immunity since the crucifixion of the Christ.

"It was the time when the proud Druidic and bardic traditions had still to merge with these Christian teachings of the Sainted and long-dead Padraig to produce the coda which would impose order and responsibility, as well as honor and ultimate authority, on the High-Kingship of Tara.

"It was the time of the heroes . . ."

Chapter 10

ORLA had never been a beautiful child, and as a young woman she was remarkably lacking in comeliness—so much so that when the hero raiders overran the tuath's House of Sorrows, she narrowly escaped being slain along with all the male attendants and wounded because she had been mistaken at first sight for a thin and sickly young man. Only when her breast was bared to receive the sword's thrust was the truth discovered, and she was left unharmed and unmolested among her silent dead and unquietly dying menfolk.

The raiders would kill with dedication, enthusiasm, and the most bitter hatred any man, be he a young boy-child or a toothless ancient no longer capable of fathering children, whom they found in the tuaths and families of Followers of the Old Way. With a special zeal they dismembered the grievously wounded, the warriors whose time among the living could be numbered in the minutes or hours, in case a miracle of healing occurred and they lived to fight and kill another day. But the raiders were not without honor. They would not harm a female, regardless of age, unless she openly professed to be, and was armed and accoutered, as a warrior.

For a long time Orla knelt beside the butchered remains of Liam, her youngest and, until this morning's hero raid, only surviving brother. Her eyes were closed and she did not weep, because she was seeing Liam as the baby she had helped her long-dead mother to nurse, as the child who had swum and climbed trees and fought with wooden swords against his brothers and fosterlings, as the not-yet man who had proudly exercised with a sword and shield that had remained too heavy for him, and lastly as the writhing, agonized boy-warrior ambushed and pierced in the thigh by an arrow whose head, according to their recently slain medical Druid, had been smeared with the excrement of pigs.

It had been cowardly and disgusting and a terrible way to take a life, even though Orla, much to the shame and displeasure of her surviving male relatives, had stated loudly and often that there were no admirable ways to inflict violent death. But Liam's end on one of the crude, mass-produced swords of the heroes had eased his suffering much more effectively than her own comforting words or the soothing herbs and poultices which, in her brother's condition, had been as so much wet and rotting straw.

She knew with a dreadful certainty that all of the men were dead now, that the once proud and peaceful tuath was populated only by women, whose wailing and keening she could hear through the thick wicker and mud walls, because the House of Sorrows would not have been visited until all of the healthy males had been slain. Even the well-loved male fosterlings, hostages of neighboring Kingdoms whose presence in her father's tuath was supposed to join their families in friendship and ensure the borders against sudden and treacherous attack, had perished. For the attacks had not been mounted by neighboring tuaths greedy for land and cattle but by warriors from the mighty Northern Kingdom of Dalriada, armed with weapons and engines of war produced by the steaming, smoke-blackened cities of Emain Macha and Baelfairste that the thick-tongued Saxon mercenaries called Armagh and Belfast.

In vain she tried to bring back pictures of the old days, and the stories that had been told of the Old Way: of wars that had been fought by prior arrangement on a sunny afternoon, to settle a land dispute or because of an unpaid dowry or some similar matter of great moment, or of battles in which great deeds of valor were performed that rarely, if ever, resulted in fatal injury, and which gave to the bards and storytellers the bare fabric on which their imaginations wove the rich tapestries of song and epic poem that were carried to the farthest shores of the land, and beyond. In those far-off days, she was told, the heroes had been little more than a nuisance that could have been abated at any time, provided the great and powerful kings of the five provinces could agree together on it.

But they had not agreed because the heroes were already in their great houses, welcomed there because of the novelty and entertainment and prestige they gave. They had entered like the purveyors of those insidious, Eastern drugs, approaching shyly as a slave promising only pleasure and an easement of the more monotonous forms of toil, but in the end becoming the most terrible and cruel of masters who exacted a price paid in the blood of those whose livelihood lay in the performance of such monotonous tasks.

In spite of Orla's eyes being tightly closed, the slow, warm tears pushed between her lashes and onto her cheeks. The old days and the Old Ways were gone and would never return, because over the years she had come to realize that the only way to vanquish a hero was to use a stronger and more able hero. Some of the menfolk had come to the same conclusion, but not enough to change the ways of her father and the other traditionalists, and those who had not changed had perished to a man.

When her eyes were dry enough for her to see again, Orla searched the House of Sorrows for a warrior's shoulder harness and belt that would fit her and hung it front and back, not with weapons but with small sacks into which she had packed a warm cloak and sandals, food that would not soon perish, curative herbs from the cabinet of the Druid, and a few body ornaments given to her by her father. Then she left the place with its sweet, sickly smell of the blood of the newly dead and the loud, excited buzzing of the insects.

She walked slowly and without hindrance between the fallen warriors who lay like tumbled, man-sized dolls, past the keening or silently grieving women, and through the groups of raiders who were alike unmindful of her passing. Even the ground was bloodied and littered with the beautifully crafted and decorated weapons of her people, swords no more nor less effective than the crude, inartistic and soulless blades of Emain Macha.

The majority of the raiders had moved away from the decimated village and were already lighting fires and setting up camps inside the encircling protection of their heroes. Orla knew that in a few days' time, when hunger began to overlay and dull ache of grief, some of the raiders' women would come among the female survivors to offer sympathy and food and the protection of a hero tuath, always provided they were properly subservient and did not try by word, deed, or omission to avenge themselves on the warriors or machines who had slain their men. But that protection would be little more than a life of backbreaking labor in the fields and mines of the Black North, or of the slow rotting of the lungs that came from working in the smoke-belching factories of the larger hero tuaths.

The offer of food and shelter was a kindness of sorts, and the best Orla could hope for in the circumstances, but it was not for her. There was a great and terrible anger in her, so deep and all-consuming that no pretense of soft words and submissive manners would be able to conceal it, because she thought that her very eyes must be blazing with the fires of it. A female with eyes like that would not be offered the protection of a hero tuath.

But it was a helpless anger, a fury without clear direction or focus, a hatred that singled out for vengeance no man or men.

It was not even the raiders all around her that she hated, because they had done what they believed to be necessary and would claim, with some truth, that the Followers of the Old Way had been the first to begin the slaying without mercy of all male supporters and users of the accursed heroes, regardless of age or physical condition. It was the terrible times they were living through, the stupid way that things were, the cruel, senseless civil war that was tearing the heart out of her lovely and once-populous country—that was what she hated, bitterly and helplessly, but not blindly.

Orla kept her eyes only upon the ground as she picked her way among the deep, muddy hero tracks. Smoke billowed suddenly around her. She coughed, blinked the stinging from her eyes, and looked in time to keep from walking into a large overturned hero.

During the initial, predawn attack on the village, it must have run into the trap, rolled onto its side, and set itself on fire, because there were no fallen warriors around it or other evidence of an external attack. The wooden structure had burned away, leaving the blackened metal skeleton projecting from the pit like disordered bones from an unfilled grave. The smell of burned wood, grease, and coal was mixed with an odor of roasting meat that belonged to the kitchen rather than to a field of battle, which meant that at least one of the occupants had died with his mount.

Feeling even angrier, Orla moved to windward of that terrible, appetizing smell and continued until her shadow began to walk far ahead of her. She could not wander forever without direction like some strayed calf, but where could she go that was not as bad or worse than the desolation behind her?

To the north lay Emain Macha, which was so busy fabricating the weapons of war that the city itself was at peace. But it was said that the people there outnumbered the heroes by less than three hundred to one, and that they suffered like the sinners in the Hell of the Christians. To the northwest she could see, blue with distance, the dark and brooding mountains of the Kingdom of Mourne. That powerful tuath had supported the heroes for two generations, and for that time its thickly forested mountains sheltered bands of marauding rebels who still held true to the Old Ways. A stranger in Mourne, whether male or female, would almost certainly be considered a spy by either side and treated with great dishonor.

Westward lay Connaught, a province divided within itself and where the heroes were gaining support and where the fighting was bitter indeed and without any pretense of honor. And to the east lay the coastal villages that supported neither faction, but accepted help from both sides because of continual harassment by raiders from across the Celtic Sea.

The rampaging Vikings came regularly from their northern homeland to loot and pillage and gather slaves, and, with greater frequency, from the island fortress and Kingdom they had established on Man, which could be seen on a clear day from many of Hibernia's east-facing mountain slopes. The Romans, who did not sail as often as the Norsemen and did not handle their ships well, also took slaves or warriors experienced in using the Hibernian heroes so as to improve their outdated and clumsy engines of war.

If a slave she was destined to be, then Orla would prefer not to be enslaved to strangers. But it was highly probable that, considering her unpleasing physical appearance and a demeanor that had never been servile, she would not long survive as a slave to anyone.

There was always the south, and Tara.

In the south there were many who still supported the Old Ways, even though it was said that the heroes, albeit only a few innocuous and unwarlike toys used for pumping water and other innocent domestic purposes, had invaded even legendary Tara. There the High-King had been trying to keep his fiercely independent and often quarrelsome lesser kings at the Tables of Council rather than on the field of battle, but to little avail.

She did not know if Connair still sat on the Chair of the Ard-Ri at Tara. He had been a roaring, red-faced giant of a man whose game with his Little Orla had been to toss her so high into the air that it seemed for a brief, joyful moment that she was a bird, before catching and hugging her, laughing, in his enormous arms. A mist that was not of the damp earth underfoot rose before her eyes. To the small girl-child who had been visiting Court with her father all fully grown men were giants, strong and good and perfect in every way. Now she knew better, and in retrospect she also knew that Connair had been brave and honorable but not the subtlest of men. It was likely that another sat on the Throne of the High-King and that she might not find a welcome at Tara.

Even so, something would be done for her, if for no other reason than out of respect for her father. The tuath he had ruled was small, with little power and few fighting men, but until his death in battle he had been greatly loved by his own people, and his counsel had been sought by many throughout the land. The High-King, whoever he might be, would feel it his duty to help her. But the war had left many fatherless children of royal blood, and she would be only one of many hundreds—by now they must outnumber the palace warriors and menials—of such refugees.

As the youngest daughter of a King, Orla would be treated with all due respect, but her loss of respect for herself would be great indeed. She did not want to be a slave, but better that than to become a highborn beggar, an unwanted embarrassment and a nuisance.

She began to walk again, taking no particular direction because there was nowhere that she wanted to go.

By the time the gray, frowning sky had darkened into twilight, a fine mist of rain had begun to fall. Orla headed for a wooded hill that she had already chosen as her resting place for the night, taking shelter under a mighty tree that stood on a carpet of leaves so thick and dry that she doubted whether even the heaviest rain could find a way through its branches. There were sounds of many warriors moving in the area, so she did not light a fire, but ate her food cold. She wrapped her head and body tightly in her cloak so as to discourage the entrance of the ground insects, and lay down on the crackling softness. But the pictures of the morning's raid returned again, bright and clear and terrible despite the layered darkness of her thick cloak and the night enclosing her, and drove away all thought of sleep. But she was weary and her bed of leaves was soft, and the raucous sound of birds in the branches above wakened her to a new day that she would have preferred not to see.

For many days she wandered through a countryside scarred with the tracks of heroes and covered with the stinking, buzzing sores that were the bodies of the fallen. The only shelter to be found in that desolate land was under trees or in the lee of high rocks, because the farm buildings of stone and mud and wicker had been tumbled and burned lest they be used to conceal ambushers. When the food she carried with her was gone, Orla ate as did the creatures of the land and the air all around her.

She had been taught many things by her father's aged Druid Healer, even before it became certain that he would not live long enough to select and train a suitable male apprentice to whom he could pass on his store of sacred and secret knowledge. She knew, therefore, the different roots and leaves and berries that were harmful, and which possessed healing or palliative properties, or were simply good to eat. She grew very thin, but stronger rather than weaker, stronger than she had ever been before, and more lonely and homesick than she had believed it possible for anyone to feel.

Then one hot, bright morning as she was rounding the shoulder of a low hill that rose out of the surrounding bogland and forest, Orla found the shelter that was destined to be her home for the next two years. It lay like a wrinkled, harvest-yellow flag on the spring-green lower slope of the hillside, a large and long-abandoned hero trap whose concealing roof of foliage had been allowed to wither and die.

The position of the trap had been carefully considered, placed as it had been to lie beneath the only convenient hero path between the steep upper slopes of the hill and the rock-strewn bed of the river below. But now that it was revealed for what it was, the heroes and, Orla hoped, everyone else would avoid it.

By peering through holes in the covering thatch, she was able to find the steeply sloping earthen wall that had enabled the constructors to climb in and out while the pit was being dug, and she soon discovered that this had been a most unusual hero trap. Enough sunlight was coming through the holes in the cover to show that the center of the pit was piled high with straw and thin untrimmed branches of trees rather than sharpened stakes, and that short tunnels had been cut in three of the walls leading to artificial caves fully half as large as the pit itself. The tunnel and cave roofs were supported by wood, as in a mine, and the caves contained remnants of dismantled heroes as well as the litter of many living occupants.

She decided that it had been a trap designed to capture and study rather than to simply destroy heroes, although their warrior occupants would not have fared so well, and the signs were that it had been put to this use many times before being abandoned. This must surely mean that there had been a group of warriors, Followers of the Old Way, who had decided that they would learn how to fight with heroes of their own and no longer pit their unprotected flesh and blood and sinew against steam-driven metal.

Many small animals were using the place as their home, Orla saw as she explored the side caves. Some of them could be used as food, and others would be allowed to remain because they hunted and lived off the more troublesome insects who were also trying to make a home there. But her first task was to clear the center of the pit of its branches, which she did by breaking the sapless wood and twigs into small pieces and stacking them in one of the caves where they would serve as a supply of dry firewood for a long time to come. One of the bushier twigs she used to sweep the hard-packed earthen floor. Then she made a bed from pit props and covered it thickly with straw from which she had shaken out most of the insects, kindled a small fire, and climbed out onto the hillside.

Night had fallen and the color of the thatch cover was bleached almost white by the light of a full moon. Orla circled the trap many times, viewing it from different angles and distances. The smoke that filtered through the holes in the cover was just barely visible, so it would be safer if she did not light fires during daylight or on moonlit nights. But when thick clouds passed across the moon, rolling a thick, dark blanket over the hill and surrounding countryside, not the smallest gleam or firelight was to be seen.

Satisfied, she returned to the pit to eat and to smother the fire, lest a spark ignite her great store of dry firewood and straw, and to sleep. She was sure that her presence here would go unnoticed and that because it was so plainly exposed to view for what it was, her trap shelter would be violated only by the elements.

She was awakened next morning by the bright, early sunlight slanting through the holes in the thatch and by the unmistakable sounds, some of them strange and very frightening, of battle.

Chapter 11

THE battle was strange in that heroes were opposing heroes, frightening in that hero weapons were being used of a kind that Orla had never before seen or heard or even imagined in her most terrifying dreams.

She was able to view every movement and encounter in that confused and terrible battle as it slowly approached her position on the hillside and moved past. There was a large group of heroes, of a kind she knew and recognized, attacking and trying to encircle a much smaller group. In spite of their broad spiked wheels, the first group's machines, loaded as they were with warriors and bowmen, were making difficult progress over the soft, peaty ground. The second group was much smaller; its heroes were fewer, stranger, and more terrifying. This group moved more easily because its warriors and bowmen were on foot, using the vehicles only as moving shields against the opponents' spears and arrows, while its strange heroes reached out to wreak dreadful havoc against the enemy men and machines alike.

The smaller group's heroes were composed of two distinct kinds of machines. The first was mounted on eight wheels, each pair of which was joined together by long wooden and cleated planks to make a roller that gripped the soft ground while not sinking into it, and the second type was being towed by the first. This one had similar roller wheels and a flat platform on top which carried its hero. Shoulder-high wooden shields concealed the details of the machine and protected the few heavily cowled men who served it, and through the cloud of steam hanging over each vehicle, Orla could see something resembling a squat metal barrel with one end open that could be turned to any angle or direction.

Every few minutes there would come the sharp, whistling hiss of a steam explosion, and rocks would be hurled upward from the open barrel to fall on the men and machines of the enemy. Some of the new heroes hurled not rocks, but jars of burning pitch that broke up and scattered in the air before falling and clinging to the bodies of the opposing warriors and to the wooden parts of their vehicles.

Orla turned her face away from the sight, but she could not stop her ears from hearing the sounds made by the terribly burned men. Many attempts were made to ram and disable the fiendish new heroes, or warriors would try to charge and capture them on foot. But time after time the opposing vehicles would be evaded or they themselves rammed and tipped over, while the numbers of charging warriors were thinned by falling rocks and fire and arrows, and the remainder slain with spear and sword.

She lay amid the bushes on her hillside while the sun rose higher and the only clouds to be seen were those of the smoke and steam hanging over the battle, which had moved far away. She had made the decision to be alone, to hide in this secret place, and to ignore this senseless war and everyone engaged in it. But now she felt that the decision had dishonored her, and without hesitation she returned to the pit for her bag of medicinal herbs and two water gourds that she would fill at the river before searching the ground of battle for survivors.

The sky darkened, as if the sun was ashamed to look upon the scene below, and the rain steamed where it fell on the patches of hot pitch. In the beginning she found only the tumbled, burned, and bloody dead and those so close to death that they neither heard her consoling words nor felt the comfort of the water on their lips. Then she came upon one who was bleeding from many wounds, but breathing deeply and unevenly as did a warrior who had nothing to fight but his own death.

He was lying on his back with one arm wrapped in his cloak because his shield had been lost or broken in battle. His sword, a finely crafted weapon with its hilt inlaid with gold and precious stones, lay close to the other hand. A long, straight wound diagonally bisected his face, opening the left side of his forehead, nose, and right cheek down to the jaw, and blood had made bright red pools of his eyes. The body leather had protected his chest and stomach, but when she unwrapped the heavy and richly decorated cloak from his arm, she found that it was the only limb not covered with wounds. Carefully she washed the blood from his face, finding that the eyes themselves were undamaged, then she raised his head gently and tried to make him drink.

He began to shiver violently, causing the congealing blood in some of the wounds to flow again, but there was no other response. She decided that the wound across his face, if it had been inflicted by the swinging of a heavy sword, could have broken his head and would certainly have rendered him insensible. It was plain that he needed shelter and a warm fire before anything else could be done for him, but he was a tall and heavily muscled young man, and much too heavy for Orla to lift or even drag without increasing the severity of his wounds.

Nearby there was an overturned hero. She pulled off one of its shields to use as a litter, discovering that someone still lived inside the machine. She spoke comforting words to him, promising that she would return to help him as speedily as possible. Then, carefully, she rolled the first warrior into the makeshift litter and wrapped him tightly in his once-beautiful bloodstained cloak. But the sword she left where it lay.

As she began to move the first warrior toward the hillside it began to rain heavily, soaking her to the skin but making it easier to drag the litter over the ground. On the way to the shelter she came on two more warriors. Both were grievously wounded and burned, one so badly that she hoped he would not be alive when she came back for them.

Her wish, and no doubt that of the burned man, was not granted.

By the time she had the four of them moved into the hero trap it was dusk and rain was dripping steadily through the holes in the thatch. So wearied was she by her exertions that she wanted only to sleep, but she knew that her work was only beginning.

Gently she cut away and removed the charred or bloody clothing, then carefully cleaned the wounds and applied the prescribed healing herbs before binding them, because the work had to be performed according to the strict practices of the Druidic Healers if the flesh around them was not to rot and die. The burns she did not cover, because the mind-dulling herbs she had given to those warriors were keeping them in the veriest shallows of sleep, and to let anything but a breath of air touch that bright red or charred flesh would have been an unnecessary torture.

The warrior from the hero had arrow wounds in the shoulder and upper arm and had suffered a broken leg when his machine overturned. He remained conscious and silent, his face a pale, sickly orange in the firelight, while she treated the wounds and straightened and bound the leg to a pit prop. Finally she caught one of the small animals that had ventured too close, paying for its curiosity with its life. When she had cleaned and cooked it over the fire, she fed him and told him that she wanted to sleep and that he should do the same.

The warrior ate as if he had not done so for many days, then he looked around the firelit earthen walls and at the thatch overhead, and began to speak the words that Orla knew would come and for which she was prepared.

"I have been welcomed and treated as a friend here, nay, as a blood relation," he said softly, so as not to disturb the sleepers. "Know that Seamus, of the tuath and family of the Tain of—"

"No!" said Orla with quiet intensity. "I have no wish to know the name of your family, your tuath, or its King, or the names of anyone here. To know these things is to know what as well as who you are, whether you are Followers of the Old Way or supporters of the heroes. Here there will be no names, no boasting about past battles, no arguments and recriminations, and no continuance in words of this stupid and increasingly dishonorable war!"

Seamus stared silently into the fire for a long time before he looked up at her and said, "Know, nevertheless, that I am grateful and that whether these wounds heal cleanly or they putrify and take me off in fever and pain, my debt to you for all that has been done for me will not be easily repaid. But there may come a time when you, also, will need succor. That is why I would like to tell you of my family so that should I die, you can tell them the manner of it and claim that which is rightly your due."

There was a weariness on her and a sadness and a despair so deep that she was unable to guard her tongue. She whispered fiercely, "You will heal, never fear, and doubtless live to kill or die in another stupid battle. I have had much experience at caring for the bloody wreckage of battle, and I have seen warriors more grievously wounded than you who survived, or who would have survived had not raiders slain them where they lay on their beds of pain. And what if your family had a part in that slaughter, which took from me the last of my family? How would they discharge that greater debt?"

Seamus did not speak, and the small unsteady flames of the dying fire made it difficult to read his face. In a whisper that was less charged with anger she went on, "I, also, have decided to fight a war, and I care not whether I live or die. It is a very strange war because my enemy is both sides, and my only small victories will be when by my skills and knowledge I cause someone like you not to die. But I must not concern myself as to the sides for which the wounded have fought, because I am human and, if such knowledge was mine, I might be tempted to anger and revenge. And I would be very angry indeed if you, or any of the other wounded, were to name names to each other and argue and try to continue your stupid war in this place.

"And now I am weary," she said. "Let us both try to heal our wounds with sleep."

But Seamus was restless, or perhaps his wounds were troubling. For several minutes his eyes remained open, regarding her closely, before he whispered, "Curiosity eats at my stomach like a great, hungry worm. I know not who you are but I think I know what you are, a follower of the Christus, and your family was converted by the onetime slave and missionary zealot, Padraig. Is this not so?"

"My name is Orla," she replied wearily. The name was in common use among many families, and no purpose would be served by concealing it. "That is a morsel for your hungry worm, but it is all that you will learn about me. And now you must rest your mind as well as your body and be silent."

"The Christians," his whisper persisted, "are a strange, unworldly sect which, many years after the death of Padraig, is still growing in numbers throughout the land. It is said that one of the prime tenets of their faith is that they must love and not hate their enemies, no matter how great or how many the wrongs inflicted upon them. In spite of this incredible belief, which gives the advantage in time of war entirely to their enemies, it is said that they are neither cowardly nor a weak-willed people and hold to their beliefs as strongly as do the Druidic Followers of the Old Way. If you are indeed a Christian, it would explain why you are not concerned with the sides on which your wounded have fought. Is this not so?"

Wearily, Orla said, "Must I bind your mouth as well as your wounds to ensure your silence?"

"No, Orla the Unknown," Seamus replied quietly. "But I tell you again that I am grateful, that my debt to you is great, and that there is only one way that I can discharge a small part of it. Know, therefore, that if and when I am healed and the time comes for me to leave you, I swear by whatever God you hold sacred that I shall not speak of this place to any other, whether they be family, friend, or stranger."

The words brought her a feeling of such relief that it gave her voice an unaccustomed warmth as she said, "Thank you, Seamus. You may depart whenever we can both agree that you are well enough to undertake the journey home, wherever that may be. And now, for the sake of whatever God *you* hold sacred, let me rest."

Orla fell into a sleep that was to be the longest and most satisfying that she was to know for many days, because the condition of one of the burned warriors grew steadily worse as the fires of fever and infection raged within a body already charred and blistered over half its surface. Neither Seamus, who tried constantly to console him with words, nor she blamed the man for his inability to suffer as a warrior should in silence. Neither did she blame herself for the pain-dulling potions that she coaxed him to drink even though she knew that the mixture of poisonous roots and berries would, in the strength and quantity administered, end his life as surely, albeit more comfortably, than would the drying out of his body and the infections in those terrible burns.

When the merciful cloak of Death fell over him, bringing at last the stillness and peace he craved, Orla's first thought was to remove all evidence of her attempts to heal him and then simply leave his body with the other unburied dead that were lying in the bog and forest, lest kinfolk came looking for him. But in the days since she had found him she had begun to feel a responsibility toward this nameless warrior that was almost that of a blood relation. When she made plain her intention to bury the man, Seamus, who had been trying constantly by means direct or devious to make her reveal more about herself, bound two pieces of firewood together with reeds to form a cross, which he gave to her. He said that the dead warrior she had tried so hard to cure was unlikely to be a follower of the Christus, but he thought that she might gain some consolation if his grave was marked with the symbol held by many to give promise of another and happier life.

Orla thanked him, but left his curiosity unsatisfied by politely refusing the gift.

The other burned warrior mended slowly, but he did not speak, and tried not to move his head, because the burned flesh had tightened so that half his face looked like the bright red bark of a tree, and it was painful for him to move his lips. The warrior with the sword slash across his face had awakened, and remained so for longer each day, but spoke not at all. He lay looking around the walls and thatch of the pit and at Seamus and Orla with the soft, curious eyes of a small child. And like a child, he whimpered with fear when he saw the face of the burned warrior. She thought that the blow with the heavy sword might have addled his wits, and wondered if he would be stricken dumb for the remainder of his life.

There were times when Orla thought that the rest of his life would be numbered in the days rather than the years. One of his leg wounds was very slow to heal, and remained inflamed and open and oozing constantly with pus instead of filling and drying out as had the others. But she persevered, with poultices which she had learned would withdraw even the most stubborn of poisons, with herbs and mosses of the earth to aid the healing, and, more than any other regimen, by exposing it to the fresh, clean air and sunlight of the hilltop.

Every morning, unless rain or the presence of warriors in the area threatened, she dragged the three litters up the beaten-earth ramp and to the top of the hill. There her charges kept watch for intruders while she hunted in the lowland for food animals and gathered edible roots and berries and the medicinal herbs which were at their most potent when they were pulled fresh. But it was their youth and thirst for life and the steadily increasing amounts of food that they were eating, food that they had begun to hunt and gather for themselves, more than her Druidic potions, that were healing them. And so it was that before another moon had waned, both Seamus and the burned warrior left her, renewing their promises of silence and speaking the shy, awkward words of thanks that grown men use when ashamed of their own sincerity.

The third warrior also healed, albeit more slowly. Sword slashes that had opened wounds all over his straight, young body closed into pale, healthy scars. The bones of his shattered leg grew together and the limb, withered from long disuse, grew flesh and muscle to match its twin. Even the terrible scar traversing the face healed, but in so doing it pulled his features into a thing out of nightmare. And behind that fearful, living mask the mind also healed, but not completely.

Nevertheless, the eyes in that ruined face shone brightly, and the young man talked with wit and intelligence, occasionally slipping without effort into Latin, which meant that he was well traveled or at least well educated. He gave no name, neither personal nor family, but not because it was forbidden by Orla. His life had begun when he had awakened inside the hero trap and he knew nothing beyond that time, except for the things he saw in his dreams which often caused him to struggle and cry out in his sleep so that he had to be held and comforted as a child. Of all the warriors who came under Orla's care to limp home with their wounds healing, he alone did not want to leave the only world he knew.

Orla was both saddened and pleased by this. She knew that the earthen walls and thatched roof of the pit were not the surroundings that befitted him, even though he could remember nothing else. But he had proven himself an adept with bow and spear, weapons that lay discarded on the boggy ground of battle below her hill. He had become the far-ranging hunter and provider of food for the wounded, leaving Orla to spend more of her time gathering the healing herbs and medicaments that coaxed her wounded warriors back to health and strength.

There was no dearth of the burned and bleeding bodies for her to treat and heal and, all too often, to bury. After one particular bitter and bloody battle had rolled around and past her hill she cared for more than a score of warriors, only three of whom perished from their wounds. While her nameless hunter and one-time warrior was helping her tend them one night, he said that their hill overlooked an area of valueless ground on the borders of two warring tuaths. Although the surface was too soft and uneven for hero battles, he said, this could reduce the advantage of the larger force if, as had happened on previous occasions recently, the smaller force was more intelligently led. He had spoken in the voice of one who is sure of his knowledge.

Then one day he found his sword, and he began to change.

The blade was rusted to the color of congealed blood by more than a year's exposure to rain and snow, but the inlay of precious metal and gems on the hilt was unmistakable—it was the weapon Orla had hurled from her when she had first seen his broken and bleeding body. When the work of the day was over he spent more and more time rubbing it and cleaning it with flat stones and coarse earth until it shone once again as the beautiful and cruel bringer of death that it once had been. He washed as best as he was able the stains of mud and blood from his cloak, and he mended the many cuts it had taken when it had been wrapped tightly around his arm as a shield. As well as throwing it carelessly over his body before sleeping, he had taken to wearing it during the day with its precious-metal clasps fastened tightly at the neck. And when he looked at her, his eyes were no longer those of an innocent, empty-headed child but of a deeply troubled young man.

Then one evening when the wounded had been brought in from the hillside, fed, and made comfortable for the night, he sat down cross-legged beside her. He still wore the cloak in spite of the warmth of the fire, and the sword gleamed red and amber where it lay across his knees.

"My name is Dairmuid," he said very softly, "and I must leave this place. I have duties, obligations, to my family and my people. But even greater is the obligation that I owe to you. It is the strongest and most binding ageas of all, because you have given back to me my life."

He did not try to name his family, as some of the others had done, because if he had tried she would have forbidden it or stopped her ears. All at once there was too much in her heart and mind for the right words to be chosen, and she was silent.

"We will wait until the wounded are able to return to their families, then I shall do the same," he said, putting an arm slowly around her shoulders. She felt the great muscle harden with his effort to be gentle as he went on. "You, too, should leave this place and come with me and, if you would, stay with me and bear my children, Orla. I give you my body and would take yours in honor and with love as my wife."

It was not the slow tightening of his arm around her shoulders that was making it difficult to breathe. For she more than anyone else alive had come to know that tall, splendid body, knew the breadth and power of those shoulders, knew every muscle and sinew that drove those long, beautifully proportioned limbs, and she could not help knowing, because it was she who had aided its return to full strength. Nor could she help her deeply buried, womanly feelings when the treatment of the wounded had kept Dairmuid and herself working closely together for many hours at a time, or the hot intensity of her dreams when she laid herself on her lonely litter at night. It was the terrible effort of refusal rather than anger that put the harshness into her voice.

"Don't be an amadan, Dairmuid," she said. "I am honored, but you owe me no great obligation, certainly not one of marriage, for healing a body that was wanting so badly to heal itself. What I did for you I have done for many other men, who were grateful and discharged their obligation by swearing silence about this place. They did not feel it necessary to marry me.

"You would not speak of or to me in these words," she went on in a gentler voice, "but I may speak them of myself. As you can see I have the withered and warty countenance of a young but nonetheless ugly witch, and my body, which you will never be allowed to see, has all the beauty of a starved and scrawny plucked fowl. There are many women, far too many with little hope of finding men since the slaying of boy children became a custom of war, and all of them are more comely of face and form than I. You will find one who is able to see deeper than the disfigurements of your face, and who will comfort and cherish you, and bear you strong, tall sons and comely daughters instead of the runtish litter you would beget from me."

"Tall and fair and loving she might be," said Dairmuid, in a voice that was both fierce and quiet so that he would not disturb the sleepers, "but she would not be as loving and gentle as you. Or as hard and unyielding as the Rock of Cashel in word and deed when it is the strengthening and encouragement of a failing spirit that is needed. You have been thus with every warrior you have brought into this blessed haven. You have battled with the soft words and the gentle touches of a mother and with your wondrous arts of healing against Death itself, and many times you have won. Orla, it is you I want by me, to love, to instruct, to strengthen and inspire me as you have already done, and to continue the battle beside me and my family until—"

She silenced him with one upraised hand, too angry at that moment to realize that the fiercely imperious gesture and the habit of obedience it represented would tell Dairmuid more about her than she had ever revealed in words, and said firmly, "I will battle for no man again, be he King or kinsfolk, for all of those I have lost in this senseless and shameful and unending war."

Before he could answer she went on in a gentler voice. "You have likened my caring for you, and the others that have passed through my hands, to the love of a mother. This pleases, nay, greatly honors me. But the love of a son for his mother is very strong and completely blind. He sees not the wrinkled and blemished skin, the coarse hair, the ugliness of face, or the bent and toil-worn body, for he sees only with his feelings. I fear, Dairmuid, that you have mistaken the strength of your gratitude for love, that and the natural alchemy which makes a man and a woman who have been together for a time want to stay together.

"You will find that with separation," she ended softly, "the spell will quickly fade. Now lie back, compose yourself for slumber, and clear your mind of this foolishness."

He remained lying on his side and propped up on one massive arm. The cloak had slipped down to his waist and his sleeveless tunic was unfastened because of the warmth of the evening. She wished that his eyes were not so blue and did not look at her so long and steadily.

Finally, he said, "I know that you would not offer harm to

anyone, or allow anyone to be harmed if you could do ought to prevent it. But the battle we would fight together is the same one that you wage here alone. You will have charge of my father's House of Sorrows, where many who are wounded in battle or afflicted with agues and fevers will be brought to you for healing instead of these few. You will have many helpers to aid your work, and if you so will it, to instruct them in your art. My father will honor you as will I, and give you a high position in our tuath and family to console you, in part, for the family and position you have lost."

"And if the tuath you would have me join," she said sadly, "is the one responsible, even in part, for slaying to the last man-child my own family, what consolation would I find there? Here no allegiance is owed to family or tuath, because there are no names. Surely you know my mind well enough to also know that I would not practice my art on the warriors of one tuath and not another."

Dairmuid's gaze remained fixed on her, and his face deepened in color so that the scar traversing his forehead, eyebrow, nose, and opposite cheek looked like a pale ravine of uneven depth in his flesh.

He said, "Orla, I would prefer that we speak of more personal matters, but you raise a wall between us which must first be broken down. My family, whose name I will not speak lest you wriggle and spit at me like a weasel, have long been Followers of the Old Way as, I feel sure, were yours. Unlike yours, we learned the new ways as well and, for a time, lost respect and were called traitors and my father a half man and half hero, although not to his face, while we were finding the new strength which returned our respect. My father, as do you and, now that I have sought far for meat and curing herbs and have helped you feed and tend with my own killing hands these nameless warriors around us, I myself find no honor or glory in fighting this war. Quickly would I bring it to an end. But tuath has been set against tuath, even families have been divided, and there is much hatred and bitterness and thoughts of righting terrible wrongs. These wounds of the mind will be long in the healing, but it may be that you have shown how even they can be eased of their pain, cured, and closed over with the healthy flesh of forgiveness.

"You will not find it easy to make our people care for and cherish our enemies as we do our friends," he went on gravely. "That is, not in the beginning. But a few of our people follow the teachings of the Christus. They will support you, as will my father and myself. Together we can break down even that great wall.

That is why I need you for my wife, and for much more than wife.

"Think on my words, Orla, and give answer."

Slowly she lay back on her litter and put a hand over the side of her face, sure that it was glowing more hotly than the bright embers of the fire. It was as if her head was a soft anvil on which a smithy was playing his hammer with steadily increasing strength, and she realized, when several moments had passed, that her mind was fighting with itself so mightily that she had forgotten to breathe. In the end she forced herself to say the right words, not those that she wanted to say.

"Dairmuid," she said, "you honor me beyond any words that I can speak. You are a great and brave warrior, and a wise and gentle man, and I will do all that is in my power to help you break down your great wall. But . . ." With her other hand she struck herself angrily on the belly. "But I fear that my fate is to be a mother to many men, and no man's wife. When must you leave?"

"Soon," he replied. Even in the brightest light it was not possible to read that mutilated face, but the hurt was plain in his voice. "But not until we have spoken of this again, and you have given another answer."

Dairmuid lay back and closed his eyes, but she knew by the fast, uneven breathing that his appearance of sleep was a pretense, as was hers. Onto the blackness of her closed eyelids her mind was painting pictures that were like the hot, bright, repetitious dreams seen in a fever where all is endless confusion. In her young life she had given herself to no man, because of her certainty that no man would accept the gift. But Dairmuid had asked her, Orla the Ugly, for her mind and skills and the feelings they shared as well as her runtish and unbeautiful body. In spite of her every argument and appeal to his good sense, he had asked again. Those arguments were still valid but, should he cease his pretense of sleep and ask her again, she was no longer sure that her answer would be the same.

It seemed that many hours passed before his breathing slowed and she knew that he slept. By then she wanted him to speak to her again, wanted to give him another answer, wanted to lie with her body under his and do that which would make a later change of mind impossible. But she would not awaken him deliberately to prompt him to the question because that would be as if she were asking him. And on this of all nights, the wounded were sleeping, so that she could not waken him by making a noise while going to attend them. Thus it was that she lay wakeful and tortured in her mind and miserably lonely in a pit filled with sleeping men, watching as the night-black holes in the thatch changed slowly to gray and pale blue and become golden-edged with early morning sunshine.

Orla rose quietly and stood by Dairmuid's litter, gazing long and lovingly and sadly at the peaceful, disfigured face, and knowing that if he was to awaken now and ask his question her answer would not have changed. She was still watching him when there came rustling and crackling sounds from above. She turned to see the thatch and supporting twigs being torn down and cast aside, and many men with swords drawn moving silently down the earthen ramp.

"*No!*" she cried, and ran between the litters to the bottom of the ramp, arms outspread. "Don't harm them, they are wounded!"

Ignoring her words they pushed her back from the bottom of the ramp. Some of them were staring at the men on the litters, who were beginning to waken, while the others looked back toward the top of the ramp to where a small flat cart with large wheels was moving through the hole in the thatch.

Fastened to the middle of the cart was a chair without legs, on which there sat a man who would have been tall if his wasted lower limbs had enabled him to stand. She watched as his hands grasped the wheel-rims, in turn checking, pushing, and guiding the cart with the certainty of an adept, until it came to rest before her.

Orla had heard of people like this, victims of the early days of the war when the raiders still felt uncomfortable with the thought of slaying boy-children, and had ensured that they would not grow into warriors by cutting their hamstrings. Looking down at the graying hair and the marks of long suffering on those strong, proud features, she wondered if the warrior who had done this to him had lived or died regretting that act of mercy. But she could tell at once that this was a man who did not need to stand to cast a long shadow, and that it was to him alone that she should speak.

"I entreat you," she said quietly, "let no harm come to these men. They have fallen in battle and are grievously wounded. They are warriors no longer and powerless to defend themselves or to harm you. I know not their names, but some may be your friends or kinsmen."

"One of them is still a warrior," he said harshly, looking past her. "This giant with the face of a devil who carries a sword."

She turned quickly, already knowing and dreading what she would see. Instead of lying on his litter and pretending to be one of the wounded as she had hoped he would do, Dairmuid was walking slowly and with great deliberation toward the man in the cart, the blade of his brightly burnished sword held across his chest. He came up behind her and she felt his hand grip on her shoulder.

"Move aside, Orla."

The warriors around the cart moved forward, weapons raised for use, but he did not attack. Instead he grasped the top of the blade in his free hand—carefully, because he had made the edge very sharp—and extended the sword hilt foremost toward the man in the cart.

The man stretched out an arm and looked down at the richly decorated and jeweled hilt that was resting on his open hand, then he pushed it aside. His head bent forward until the chin rested against his chest and for a long moment he remained thus, and when he looked up again his eyes were shining and it was as if his careworn face had been washed in the legendary Waters of Youth.

"For these past two years," he said softly, "we had thought you slain."

Quickly, Orla said, "He was sorely wounded, much more than any of these others, and his head was cracked. Only in the past few days has he begun to remember who he is. But this is a place of healing, not war, and there must be no killing here . . ." She stopped as the man on the cart held up his hand.

"Enough, young Orla," he said. "Know that I, Cahill, King of the tuath of O'Rhaillaghy, owe a debt to you that is beyond the ability of mortal man to discharge. Know also that your fallen warriors will suffer no harm at my hands, either now or while they travel my lands on their journeys home.

"I broke my own journey at this place out of curiosity," he went on, "because of the strange stories being told about the battles fought around this hill of mine. Stories of a witch or fairy who heals wounds and so enchants the warrior that he cannot say how and where he was healed. Stories of grieving womenfolk returning to bring back the bodies of their loved ones for burial, to find only unmarked graves. We had assumed that it was the enemy who had thus honored our dead, and they assumed the same of us. And so we were able to throw words, sometimes very angry and bitter words, at each other instead of spears and fireballs. As a result of this hill will see no more battles, and all the mechanisms and appurtances of war will be removed from our adjoining lands, including this pit that I built so many years ago that has become a secret House of Sorrows. That is another and greater debt we all owe you, for by burying our warriors you unknowingly sowed the seeds of peace.

"We had no wish to disorder the bones of the dead in the hope of discovering their names," he went on, his gaze shifting for a moment to Dairmuid, "and if this peace is maintained there will be no addition to their number. But the healer and peace-bringer, Orla, will not be allowed to live in a hole in the ground, and eat roots and berries and small creatures like an animal, nor to waste her arts on a few when many are in need of them . . ."

"We do not eat like animals . . . !" Orla began, to be silenced again, this time by Cahill's smile.

"This I know," he said. "When we were raising our tents last night our cooking women could smell last evening's meal from a great distance downwind, and were greatly envious. But we will speak of your future at another time, Orla. Now I must resume my journey to Tara, to help elect the new Ard-Ri."

For a moment there was silence as he looked up at Dairmuid, who looked down at him through wet eyes, and smiled but did not speak. Cahill frowned, and Orla wondered if he was worried lest Dairmuid's head wound had permanently affected his wits. She was about to tell him that his concern was needless when he began speaking again, in a voice that a tutor uses toward a simpleminded or forgetful child.

"Much has happened since last we spoke," he said. "The war of the heroes has become a war between heroes, because now the tuaths of both sides use them, and a war that neither side can win. If it cannot be won then it must be stopped, ended before we are so weakened by self-inflicted wounds that we can offer no defenses against slave raids or invaders from Rome or Cymri or the Vikings of the North. We need a High-King who is strong, both of will and in the support he commands, brave in battle, honorable, and just, if he is to impose peace on those tuaths who have forgotten all else but the waging of war. I myself have the strength of purpose and enough support to accomplish this . . ."

"You have all the qualities save one," said Dairmuid in a gentle voice. "I have no wish to hurt you, but surely to be considered for the Chair of the Ard-Ri, the candidate must be—"

"I know, I know," Cahill said impatiently. "He must be strong, brave, unblemished, and untainted in body, mind, and character. Few of us are without physical blemish in these terrible times, so the honorable scars suffered in battle are no longer considered a bar.'' He slapped angrily at his useless legs and went on. ''When I suffered these wounds I was still in the cradle, and certainly not defending myself in battle, so the Chair is not for half a man who has wheels for legs. But when we travel to Tara I shall support the election of an Ard-Ri whose mind is and has always been alike to my own. Do you understand me, Dairmuid?''

''Father,'' said Dairmuid, standing straight and still and seeming to grow even taller, ''I understand you well.''

And so it was that they journeyed to Tara where Cahill, called Half-hero, saw his youngest and only surviving son, the First Dairmuid, ascend the throne of the High-King, where he was to reign for close on half a century. In that time he ended the war and the even more bitter though less bloody conflict of ideas that followed between the Druids and the growing numbers of the followers of the Christus, the merging of which led to the formation of what was to become the Imperial Civil Service. The heroes that had once devastated the land were harnessed to the machines and ships like that of the legendary *Sea Dragon* of Brendan the Navigator, which brought increasing prosperity so that the power and influence of Hibernia as a trading nation became known all over the world. He was the first High-King to set foot on the Westland for the historic meetings with Running Bear which brought into being the Great Empire of the West, although to his dying day he refused to call himself Emperor.

After much debate and argument, Orla followed him to Tara, where she was given charge of both its House of Sorrows and its kitchens as well as acting as his adviser in many important matters. In Cathay a Healer's worth is measured by the number maintained in good health rather than by those cured. Orla knew well the importance of food in this respect, and she taught the people how to live off a land seemingly scoured bare by the war until the crops and food animals could be made to grow and thrive again. It was also her firm belief that women alone, with their gentleness of touch and unsparing sympathy with the ills of others, were best suited to healing, and in her time she taught and trained and tested to her own high standards many thousands of women of all ages before allowing them to travel the length and breadth of Hibernia and beyond in the practice of their art, so much so that for many centuries the citizens of the Empire regarded the male Healers of other Kingdoms as inferior. With but a very few exceptions her Healers were, as was said of Orla herself, mother to all but wife to no man.

As a matter of statecraft, Dairmuid took as his Ard-Rioghan the Princess Siobhan of Connaught, who loved and served him faithfully and gave him many fine children. When he died, there was great mourning by the people of his own and many distant lands, even those of the Redmen of the West. Orla outlived him by less than a day.

As he paused for a moment, and the bright pictures of Orla and Dairmuid and Cahill lost color and substance in his mind, Nolan was surprised to find that the auditorium had grown dark with the approach of night. The faces were like rows of gray smudges in the darkness, and no one had moved to turn on the lighting. They were at all times a most polite race, and perhaps such a movement while he had been speaking would have been considered both a distraction and a breach of good manners.

When their polite silence continued for a moment, Nolan cleared his throat and said, "There is little more that I can tell you about the female Healers, other than that to this day the final test before qualification, even for the lowliest and least ambitious of their number, is to be abandoned with nothing but a cloak and sandals in a land that is strange to them. It could be the slopes of a bare mountain, a lifeless desert, or a jungle teeming with too much dangerous life. But for a period lengthy enough to prove that they could live off that land, if necessary for the remainder of their lives, they must use only their training and their highly developed instincts to find and identify as beneficial or dangerous the fruits and plants, if such are present, or the grubs and slugs and burrowing insects, if that is all there is, that would enable them to survive indefinitely and in good health.

"Fortunately for me," he went on, smiling into the gloom, "my tutors were not so tightly bound by tradition and did not require me to take this test, and, in any case, the medical resources presently available on Earth and in *Aisling Gheal* make it unnecessary. But in Hibernia even the lowest grades of Healer have undergone it, and Dervla is Healer to the Empress. On the New World we will be in very good hands.

"Are there any other questions?"

The silence lengthened and slowly the lights came up. Rising from their chairs the two Mandarins each gave him a small bow, then left without speaking. Hseng Hwa stood up but did not leave.

"Our apologies, respected Healer, for detaining you so long," he said blandly, as if the fault had been his rather than Nolan's. "You have not told us that our safety on the New World is assured, and had you done so, there are many here who would have been so impolite as to doubt your words. Instead you have spoken words which we cannot doubt because you have made no extravagant promises, and our people are more reassured by them. You have reminded us also that uncertainty is the salt that gives life its savor, and we thank you and are content."

Without further speech, Hseng Hwa led the audience quietly from the lecture hall.

Chapter 12

A FEW days later they flew on to Kyoto for more high-level technical and financial discussions from which, for obvious reasons, Healer Nolan was excluded. But this did not mean that he could do as he wished with his time. There were invitations to visit and speak at the foremost universities and ship-related industrial complexes or to go sightseeing, many more than there had been in Cathay, and everywhere he was received with friendship and polite enthusiasm. But at all times he was accompanied by Father Quinn or one of the other officers, which placed unwarranted constraints on his free time. Only when he lay down on his low, wood-block Nipponese bed was he alone, and there were times when that had not been his intention.

As he and the priest were returning to their hotel along the narrow streets past the rows of graceful and incredibly fragile houses and, in contrast to the overly polite pedestrians of Cathay, being stared and smiled at wherever they went, Nolan decided to broach the subject without any of the customary Oriental circumlocution.

"If I asked at the hotel," he said, "do you think that they could have a sign painted for me? It would be fairly small, tastefully executed, and suitable for attaching to my cloak, informing anyone who might be interested of the fact that, while I am an officer of the ship, I am neither a holy man nor celibate."

"O'Riordan wouldn't want you to do that," said Father Quinn, his pink complexion deepening in color until it must have matched that of the monsignor's cassock. Delicately, he went on, "If you were to do such a thing, when we are all trying so hard to make a good impression on these people, he would probably have you rendered involuntarily celibate."

Nolan laughed quietly, but it was plain that it was at the joke rather than the situation. They walked for about twenty paces before the priest spoke again.

"The monsignor is uncertain of your future behavior, Healer," he said. "On Brendan's Island your unthinking words nearly caused a diplomatic incident, although you were able to retrieve the situation. At the College of Lensmakers, and during the interviews here, you have done very well for us. But I have the feeling that Monsignor O'Riordan is afraid that your open and, at times, disquietingly honest response to questions, especially those you aren't really qualified to answer, will cause serious embarrassment if you don't have a guardian angel continually at your elbow."

Nolan tried not to allow the irritation he was feeling to show in his voice as he said, "If you were thinking of that question about who would be responsible for teaching the Nipponese Empire's history to the local and other non-Hibernian colonists, it seemed like a fair question, especially as I'd just finished giving them a potted history of our Empire of the West. I knew from talking to you over the past few weeks that you are capable of teaching the subject, and I said so. Was I wrong?"

"They would have preferred an Oriental tutor for such an important subject," said the priest, without giving a direct answer to the question. "I am an Occidental, and you should not have reminded them of that. You gave my name without asking permission or knowing what my noncrew responsibilities are to be."

They continued walking for several minutes, then Nolan said, "There has been no direct mention of it, but I assume that, as well as ex–ship's officers, there will be colonist teachers charged with the instruction of members of the children of their own races?"

"It may well be," the priest replied, "that the parents will be kept too busy with the day-to-day work of the colony to teach anything but the basics to their children, so we might have to provide the formal and advanced education."

He laughed softly and went on, "To return to your original problem, Healer, as a priest I can neither condone nor encourage the kind of carnal activity you have in mind. But if you wanted to get away from your guardian angel for a while, why didn't you simply leave during this afternoon's lecture? I couldn't very well have left the hall to chase after you."

"I wouldn't have missed that lecture for anything," said Nolan.

"Considering your current state of sexual frustration," the priest said gravely, "that is indeed a compliment."

It was Nolan's turn to laugh. He said, "I didn't realize that your specialty in computer banking could be widened to include the freezing and unfreezing of people rather than their monetary assets. But you explain complex operations so that they sound simple, or at least understandable to a nonspecialist. Would you mind continuing the lecture, to a limited audience of one, this evening? It might be one way of getting my mind on higher things."

"And you," said the priest, "might be sorry you asked. I really love my subject."

"In that case," said Nolan, knowing that Father Quinn had only the one vice which he indulged in moderation, "I'll buy the saki."

"You are too generous, Healer," said the priest, smiling again. "We both know that the only payment these people will accept from ship's officers is our permission to let them photograph us patronizing their shops."

They were moving away from the residential district around the university so that the private dwellings were outnumbered by the even more colorful shops and pavement stalls. Had he been an ordinary visitor to Kyoto, Nolan knew that he would have rapidly impoverished himself buying the delicately executed paintings on parchment and the wood carvings that seemed almost alive to the eye and the touch. But in Kyoto even the spending of money was a forbidden pleasure.

"You sigh as if all of your relatives had just died," said Father Quinn. "What parts of the lecture did you want clarified, Healer, so that I'll know which files to bring to your room?"

"I don't want to become an expert in your specialty, Father," Nolan replied. "It's just that, in case of accidents, I would like to know if individuals can be thawed and removed from their caskets before your multiple resuscitation system takes over prior to their boarding the landers. That first resuscitation, when they are all feeling post-hypothermia debilitation and nausea, would not be a good time for them to discover a spoiled friend among them. You seemed to skate around that one, Father, and you did not even mention the predicted figures for colonist casket malfunction. Instead you told them that you had implicit faith in the excellence and dependability of Nipponese equipment. Sooner or later someone is going to ask me that question, and I'd like to have a nice, simple, reassuring answer to it."

"So would I," the priest said with great feeling, then went on. "But that is one of the questions you must not even try to answer. Nor should you avoid it by referring the questioner to another member of the crew. Just say nothing, reassuringly, in the manner of your profession."

Nolan tried to hide his irritation as he said, "Are there any other questions that I should not answer?"

"Yes," Father Quinn said dryly, "almost certainly the one you are about to ask now."

"I doubt that," said Nolan. "It is about the sequence of warming each lander load of colonists, and how long you expect to keep them in orbit before the survey crew declares the site ready for occupation . . ."

They walked and talked until suddenly the beautifully barbered and scented grounds of the hotel were all around them. In the lobby there were several groups of officers talking quietly and intently together, and a uniformed page was waiting just inside the entrance with an envelope for Father Quinn. While he was opening it, O'Riordan stepped out of the elevator and came straight toward Nolan.

"Good evening, Healer," said the monsignor briskly. "It seems that once again we must forgo the pleasure of your company for a time. Cathay has advanced the launch of its next colonist shuttle by three days, and has asked us as a special favor that a Healer from the ship go up with it and supervise the transfer of the caskets. It is a public-relations exercise, I'm sure, aimed at reassuring the colonists' relatives. We are still engaged in some delicate negotiations with their people, which makes it desirable to grant this favor, even though Hseng Hwa's hypothermia technicians are the equal of our own and there is no real need. Healer Dervla has been recalled to Tara, so it is fortunate that Doctor Hseng has asked for you. A transonic aircraft will take you to the Xian complex two hours before lift-off. When the favor has been done, do not return on the Cathay shuttle. We will be traveling shortly to Mojave complex, and if we were to put them to the inconvenience of flying you to Westland, they might decide that the small favor we had done for them had been discharged.

"We will let you know when we need you again," he went on, giving Nolan's shoulder a friendly squeeze, "when you can ride down in a Westland vehicle. Until then you may as well stay on board and make yourself professionally available if required. The structural and inspection people are forever dropping heavy, weightless objects on each other."

Nolan gave a small, dutiful laugh and said, "I understand, sir."

"Good," said the monsignor. "You will be driven to your aircraft at six tomorrow morning, so get a good night's sleep. A safe flight to you, my son."

The monsignor moved away and Nolan said, "Why would Hseng Hwa ask for me? He was polite to me at the College of Lensmakers, but telling the story of Orla kept them waiting for an awful long time, and I thought Doctor Hseng would have seen and heard enough of me."

"It was probably because of your lecture," said Father Quinn. "You spoke as if you had authority in both your subject and your person, and sounded as they expected a Black Mandarin to sound. That is how many of the Cathay colonists think of and behave toward *Aisling Gheal*'s officers, as the Mandarins of the starship. That being the case, if you are ever unsure what to do or say at any time, it would be best if you maintained an aloof and inactive silence. Otherwise some technician is likely to do exactly as you say without argument even though he knows it to be wrong. Please remember that, Healer."

"Thank you, Father, I will," said Nolan. "But you must be hungry. Are you ready to dine?"

"Not yet and not here," the priest replied, and smiled. "A meeting has been called at short notice at the university. All astrogation and communications officers must attend. I know you will forgive me if I don't talk to you as I promised. Tonight I am afraid your guardian angel will be otherwise engaged."

"Are you telling me . . . ?" began Nolan.

"I'm telling you that tonight I don't care where you go or what you do," said Father Quinn, "so long as you don't answer questions while you're doing it."

That night in Kyoto, which he had been able to enlarge until an hour before breakfast next day, Nolan had been free to do exactly as he pleased. His uniform opened all doors in that colorful and exotic city. But it was a uniform that he did not wish to dishonor and so his behavior, although a trifle exuberant at times, would not have caused his absent guardian angel to raise a priestly eyebrow.

In retrospect he knew that he had enjoyed himself very much, but that he would have tried much harder had he known at the time that it was to be his last evening on Earth.

Chapter 13

ON the flight to Xian launch complex Nolan had plenty of time to think and no need to guard his tongue, because he was the aircraft's only passenger. And in the vehicle that was waiting to take him to the loading gantry he was also separated from the driver so that he did not get a chance to speak until he was met by Hseng Hwa.

Many polite words were spoken while they walked to the dressing room, but nothing was said. It was an unexpected pleasure to see Hseng Hwa again, Nolan said, and he was accustoming himself with difficulty to the thought that he was seeing many people for the last time; and Hseng hoped that the measure of the Healer's inconvenience would not outweigh the inestimable favor he was performing for all of Cathay by coming here at such short notice. Nolan waited patiently to discover the precise nature of the favor, but no mention was made of it, and whenever he tried to ask questions about it, he was politely steered onto another subject by both Hseng and the technician who was helping him dress.

He was surprised to discover that they had a spacesuit that was large enough to fit him and very comfortable, so much so that he wondered if it had been specially made for him. The project's spacesuits were of uniform specification and design so that all components and attachments would be interchangeable, but it seemed to him that the workmanship of this garment was particularly fine, as were the delicately executed and nonstandard embellishments, which he was unable to read, decorating the front of his helmet and the back of one gauntlet. Just before they left the dressing room, Hseng Hwa hung a bejeweled yellow-metal brassard around his neck so that it rested on the center of his chest, securing it with silken cords tied at his back. Then he closed his sun visor in such a politely firm manner that Nolan knew that it would be considered a grave impoliteness if he were to open it again without permission.

In the elevator that took them up to the loading bay, Nolan

looked down at Hseng's gray unmarked robe and sandals and said, "I had assumed, wrongly as I can see now, that you would be traveling with me."

"Regrettably, no," Hseng Hwa replied. "I can neither accompany you on this vehicle nor in the ship. Too many duties and too many years preclude my leaving Earth."

Within a few minutes of them entering the loading bay, the first of the hypothermia caskets arrived. The technicians in attendance treated Nolan as if he weren't there and he, because there was nothing they were doing that would arouse the slightest professional criticism, had no way of registering his presence with them. During the time taken to move them up and transfer them to ship power, the caskets used their own batteries. So far as Nolan could see, the power and refrigeration levels were at optimum, and the colonist property compartments at the base of each casket contained only the specified quantities of personal effects and clothing which would remain frozen like their undressed owners until required to await their landfall five hundred years hence.

He well remembered the debate that had raged between the higher ecclesiastics and their brethren of the scientific confraternities about the advantages and disadvantages of the colonists wearing their own clothing while in cold sleep. There was no reason why they should not wear clothing, and be ready to move to their assigned landing vehicles within moments of thawing out, instead of struggling in the restricted space available to dress themselves and fill their backpacks. But it was a statistical certainty that a small number of caskets would suffer malfunctions, and the earliest indication of such failures would be changes in the cold sleeper's skin coloration, which would not be seen if the body was covered by anything but the padded restraining straps. For once scientific prudence had won against ecclesiastical prudery, although not completely. A thin, opaque shell covered the caskets occupied by females so that only the head and upper chest were revealed.

Even so, it was rumored that several of the ship's officers intended to wear uniform in cold sleep and put their trust in God and the more sophisticated design of the crew caskets.

With Hseng at his side Nolan paced up and down the line of caskets that were waiting their turn to be hoisted so slowly and carefully into their positions on the shuttle. Occasionally he would stop, meaning to look more closely into one of them, but somehow his companion was always able to interpose either his small body or a large question to direct Nolan's attention elsewhere.

Impatience finally overcame his desire to be polite and he said quietly, "Hseng Hwa, your people are performing all the handling drills and safety checks with meticulous precision, and the well-being of your cold sleepers could not be in safer hands even if those hands were my own. What am I supposed to be doing here?"

"That is a high compliment indeed," said Hseng Hwa, "coming from an officer of the—"

"Please," said Nolan firmly, "will you, or can you, answer the question?"

Hseng Hwa was silent for a moment during which the last casket of the present consignment was brought in and readied for loading, and Nolan wondered if the question was about to answer itself. For if the technicians had been precise and gentle in their handling of the other caskets, they had been as maddened Westland buffalo when compared with their behavior toward this one.

The top of the casket bore the opaque, hinged cover and head-level cutout that indicated that it contained a female sleeper, and the proportions were slightly different from those that had gone before. Only when it came closer did he realize that apart from the timers, which gave a multiple freeze-thaw capability to the officers charged with the operation of the ship, this was in all other respects a triple-fail-safe casket. This time, when he moved forward, Hseng Hwa remained beside him, and the technicians withdrew quickly as though anxious not to obstruct his movements. He bent over the casket and was about to raise his sun filter when he felt Hseng's gently restraining hand on his arm.

He was being allowed to look into this particular casket, but for some reason, the technicians present were not supposed to look at him.

The hair of the sleeper was cut short in the colonist fashion, and the smooth pale-yellow skin, facial features, and the flat chest were those of a prepubescent ten-year-old. When he proceeded to check the casket instrumentation, the indicators confirmed the presence of a body of just over half the average adult mass. When he examined the underside storage compartment, which was twice as capacious as those in the colonist caskets, he found the regulation allowance of clothing and stores, and a lot of empty space. He looked up at Hseng Hwa, whose face looked even more impassive than usual, then he stood up and, feeling like the worst and most despicable kind of moral coward, silently waved the technicians back to their work.

Hseng Hwa actually smiled in his relief.

First it had been the Ionadacht Ciaran and the Princess Ulechitzl who had been forming an emotional bond, which was expressly forbidden prior to the landing on the New World. Then there had been the young Redman chieftain Wanachtee who, with Nolan's assistance, had smuggled his wife onto the ship. It was a strict rule that all colonists be single, virtual strangers to each other, and mature in body and mind. But here was another and much greater infringement of the rules. This sleeper was probably a favorite daughter of Hseng Hwa, just as Golden Rain had been beloved of the similarly powerful Silver Elk, but this one was not even an adult. Reminding himself that he must not say or do anything that would place the project at risk did not make him feel any better about his moral cowardice, or the fact that once again he was being used.

The hypothermia technicians had moved into the shuttle with the young girl's casket when Hseng Hwa said quietly, "Respected Healer, the partial answer to your earlier question is that a treasure of immeasurable value is being sent on a great journey. The times of greatest risk on this particular journey are at the beginning and the end, during the first few steps into space and the last few down to the New World. It was considered necessary and proper that no person of lesser standing than an honored officer of the ship, one who is known to us to be deeply concerned for the survival of the sleepers, yourself, be entrusted with the safety of this great treasure now and, it is hoped and believed, prior to the landing.

"You are a Healer," he went on very seriously, "whose duty it is to protect the life of this child and, for political reasons, you will do that best if no other person, on Earth or in the ship, knows of it."

"I understand," said Nolan, but his irritation at what the doctor was doing to him was becoming overshadowed by sympathy for the very obvious concern on the other's normally expressionless features. "And I promise to do everything in my power to keep your child safe and well through the journey. But you must also understand that my duty extends equally to the others."

Doctor Hseng inclined his head in what might have been polite agreement, and said, "We are all deeply indebted to you, Healer. But as yet you do *not* understand."

When it was clear that Hseng Hwa was not going to explain further, Nolan moved toward the shuttle and at the same time altered the direction of his questioning. He said, "When your sleepers have been transferred, my orders are to remain on the ship. I don't understand why you have given me this very fine spacesuit to wear, since both the shuttle and the ship casket modules are pressurized and none of your technicians are wearing them, or why I have been decorated with this chest emblem. But I shall send them back to you with the returning technicians."

"No!" said Hseng Hwa sharply. Then in a milder voice he went on, "Please accept them as our gifts, Healer, which you may find helpful in the future. And do not remove either of them while the technicians are present."

Who, Nolan wondered, was supposed to be inside this unnecessary spacesuit with its permanently lowered sun visor?

Hseng Hwa did not answer the unspoken question.

Nolan was still wondering when he entered the shuttle and strapped himself into his seat, a position close to the child's casket and separated from the technicians by the width of the hold. They did not look across at him, and his visor ensured that they could not see him looking at them. It was a great pity, he thought as the lift-off warning sounded, that Father Quinn was not present to tell him the meaning of the markings on his helmet and the emblem on his chest.

The child's casket had been the last to be loaded and the first to be unloaded. He accompanied it while the technicians transferred it to its assigned position on the ship. After carefully and very obtrusively checking its instrumentation, Nolan remained close to it until the other sleepers were moved in. He had not spoken to the technicians since his arrival, and the rule of silence was coming more easily to him.

When their work was finished they returned to the shuttle dock, holding back respectfully so as to allow Nolan to precede them into the vessel. With a disdainful gesture that would have been the envy of the most highborn of Mandarins, he waved them away and sealed the lock behind them and returned quickly to the child's casket.

Something had been nagging at the back of his mind since he had first seen the child, something about the bone structure and features of the cranium and face, and he wondered if he had been jumping to conclusions where the young sleeper was concerned. He was also remembering that it had been a crew casket with a triple personal-storage space, only a fraction of which had been used. The gift of the spacesuit would pose another problem, because there was supposed to be only one issued to each ship's officer, and unless he was to give a detailed explanation of the whole incident to the monsignor, it would be better to hide the suit in this casket's storage space and say nothing. But first he wanted to take a closer look at the child.

As soon as he removed the light plastic screen, Nolan saw at once that the small head-and-shoulders cutout had been present not to protect the maidenly modesty of a girl-child but to conceal the lower half of a young male, and specifically the right hand.

At last Nolan's understanding was complete. Now he knew the reason for his presence as a guardian and ship-equivalent of a Mandarin of the highest rank during the loading, for he had indeed been guarding a treasure of great price. In common with everyone in the world who could read or had access to the farspeaker or farseer broadcasts, he knew that Cathay's dying Emperor had long since named his eldest son as his successor, so that this child who was destined for the New World must be the eldest son of the future Celestial Majesty.

Nolan did not need Father Quinn and his wide knowledge of Cathay affairs to tell him the significance of the covering on that hand, because few and ignorant indeed were the people on Earth who did not know what it signified.

It was the black silken glove of an Heir Apparent.

Chapter 14

DURING the three weeks that followed, Nolan was not recalled to the surface, but the number of ship's officers using the warm dormitory increased while the construction men and their space-tethered accommodations grew proportionately less. His own sleeping quarters, a wide padded and curtained shelf in the ship's surgical-treatments room, were too close to his patients to allow him much sleep. There was nothing like the close proximity of a Healer to remind a suffering or sleepless patient awaiting transfer to an Earthside House of Sorrows of his troubles, and make him want to share them.

Even though the majority of the construction people had been working on the project from the beginning and had had years of assembly experience, there had still been a constant flow of minor fractures or torn muscles to keep Nolan busy. He did not mind the work, because it was only while treating a patient that he had a legitimate excuse for shortening his time in the anti-atrophication harness. He more than any of the others knew the importance of wearing that cramping and uncomfortable arrangement of straps and pneumatic cylinders that was designed to counter the physiological effects of prolonged weightlessness. But, then, knowledge of the long-term deleterious effects of alcohol on the liver did not mean that a Healer did not imbibe occasionally.

The indulgence of slow and enjoyable self-destruction, Nolan had always thought, was an inalienable human right.

When he tried taking off the exercise unit for reasons other than to sleep, treat patients, or transfer into a spacesuit, O'Riordan usually found out about it within minutes. When it had happened three times in a week, he had asked the monsignor if it was obligatory for the ecclesiastics to be in such a hurry to confess to a fellow officer's venial sin.

The monsignor had smiled gently and reminded him that unbelievers like Healer Nolan did not commit venial sins, they developed minor bad habits that, if they were not checked at the onset, could quickly become major and health-threatening, and that unbelievers were also bound by the ship's regulations. The fact that the priest-psychiatrist was quite right did not make Nolan feel any better.

The officers who were coming on board in steadily increasing numbers were not unfriendly, but they seemed to be continually and frenetically engaged on their specialist duties, testing and calibrating their systems and instruments while speaking a language that automatically excluded Nolan. When they were off duty they talked among themselves in the same language, or withdrew behind an invisible wall of silence to perform their religious exercises, or slept the sleep of the exhausted.

When there were no patients to treat or talk to, Nolan kept out of the crew's way by spending a few hours each day in the colonist modules checking the caskets of the most recently arrived cold sleepers. If the exercise harness become too irksome, he changed, as now, into his spacesuit and explored the outer hull.

There it did not matter if there was nobody to talk to him, because the grandeur spread out all around him was enough to render any man speechless.

So far as a nontechnical spasaire like himself could judge, the ship was very close to flight-readiness. The frenetic activity and quiet excitement of the other officers, the fact that less than three hundred of the casket spaces were unfilled, and that the only external work currently in progress was on the drive's blast shield and its fuel delivery system, all supported that judgment.

That was one reason why he liked to spend his time outside at the stern, so that he could watch the work nearing completion. Another and equally childish reason was that—unlike the topologically uniform and virtually featureless structures of the ten colonist modules and the eleventh that housed the dismantled agricultural machinery, cold sleeping livestock, and the seed stores—the lander docks, their gigantic spherical tanks of chemical fuel, the vast, grapelike clusters of the main drive's disposable heavy-water tanks, and the great, tubular support members for the blast shield made of the whole stern section an adventure playground for adults.

For one adult at least.

There was one of the unpressurized engineering-support vehicles clinging like a multilegged insect to the rim of the blast shield which occluded the stars astern like a enormous metal planet. A spacesuited figure working on the oil reservoir for one of the fuel-delivery systems, mechanisms built with the precision of watches guaranteed to run for a thousand years, and the legs of three other men were projecting from an open access hatch on the power module. All of the suits were lightweight and unpowered, of the type designed to give maximum freedom of movement to the wearer and all, he noted with approval, were tethered by long safety lines to their five-hundred-feet-distant support vehicle. He switched on his headset for a moment, but heard only voices speaking in the clipped, esoteric language of yet another engineering specialty.

Nolan's air was running low and he was turning to retrace his steps when there was a sudden burst of language in his headset that was nonspecialized and indicated that at least one of the working party was not a cleric. He turned back quickly to see that the first spacesuited figure was moving slowly away from his work station, pushed by a pale-yellow inverted cone of escaping high-pressure oil. He heard laughter, a voice complaining angrily of being covered in oil, and another, more authoritative voice ordering the one with the profane vocabulary to be quiet and pull himself back to the support vessel, and for one of the others to deal with the fault.

Within a few moments the thick spray of oil wavered and disappeared, and the man it had knocked loose tumbled slowly amid an expanding haze of droplets. The slack in his safety rope was like a crooked white line drawn on a star-spotted blackboard linking him to the support vehicle. He was not falling directly toward the vehicle but at a wide angle to it, and between him and his tether point stretched the long tubular shape of one of the shield supports.

Nolan used a few profanities of his own, knowing that his set was switched off and the words would not find their way back to the monsignor, then he bent his knees as deeply as the heavy suit would allow and launched himself after the man, feeling only a slight tug as the boot magnets pulled free.

He thought of using the farspeaker, then decided against it until he had a clearer idea of what he could do. The falling man was unaware of his own danger because his visor was obscured, and the others could do nothing to help because they were in lightweight suits. Only someone wearing a powered suit had any hope of stopping what was to come.

But even with the suit thrusters augmenting the force of his initial jump, Nolan could see that he would not be able to reach the man in time. The other's safety line was already lying loosely against the inner face of the shield support, with the slack being taken up as he continued to fall outward. As yet he had given no sign of realizing his danger. Then suddenly, the loose twists and turns in the safety line between the service vehicle and the shield support, and from the support to the falling man became tight, straight lines and he was jerked to one side as his outward, linear motion was abruptly converted to radial with its center of rotation the shield support.

Nolan had never been good at mental arithmetic and could not calculate the radial velocities involved, but he knew that in a very short time that line would wrap itself around the support with steadily increasing speed until the radius became zero and the man crashed into the metal at a speed that neither he nor his suit could survive.

Then he saw that a slower and perhaps no less fatal collision would occur even sooner than that, because the safety line was so long that the first, wide swing around the shield support would send the man crashing into the main hull. Nolan changed direction awkwardly, overcompensating and cursing his lack of experience with self-powered suits, and headed for the point on the shield support where the line was beginning to wind. By the time he reached it the members of the working party were moving toward the expected point of impact, probably with the intention of fending the man off or trying to catch him, but they would not be able to reach it in time.

By now they had told the faller what was happening, because Nolan could see the man turning and twisting helplessly as he rubbed furiously at the oil-covered visor and wrestled with the equally oily fastenings of his safety line, and someone was telling him what Nolan was trying to do to avert the first collision, at least.

He switched off his suit farspeaker the better to concentrate on what he had to do, then began pulling in the safety line one-handed and coiling it tightly between the back of his elbow and the other opened hand, at the same time moving slowly around the shield support so as to keep the spacesuited figure above him and continually in sight. Fortunately the man was not yet moving fast enough for centrifugal force to be a problem, because the pull on the safety line was less than a quarter of the other's body weight, and Nolan judged that he had been able to shorten the line by about twenty feet when the man swept in a slow, flat arc toward the hull structure. Even through a badly smeared visor the other must have been able to see something the size of the hull coming at him, because at the last moment he brought his arms and legs forward in a frantic attempt to reduce the force of the impact. Then Nolan saw the figure strike the metal plating a glancing blow, bounce away, and continue on its circular path like a limp, slowly spinning doll.

Nolan watched for the fogging or sudden explosion of vapor that would have indicated a ruptured suit, but without seeing anything. He knew that such a collision would certainly have opened the joints in his own suit, but the flexibility of the lighter garment had enabled it to survive without serious damage, although the same might not be true of its wearer. He released the line coiled around his arm knowing that because of the thickness of the shield support under him, next time around the line would be much more than twenty feet shorter and there would be no risk of a second collision—at least, not against the hull. When the weight at the other end had pulled the line out straight, he grasped it in both hands, detached his boot magnets, and swung his legs out and upward until they, too, were wrapped loosely around the line.

Hand over hand and feetfirst, Nolan pulled himself toward the man. With every movement the line twisted and vibrated slowly, threatening to escape from between his hands and tightly crossed legs. But the farther outward he traveled the more he was affected by the centrifugal force, which began to pull so strongly that the line was slipping uncontrollably between his hands, and he came to a sudden halt with his feet against the injured man's backpack tanks.

For a moment Nolan clung to the line while they both swayed and spun around the new center of gravity, then he lowered himself carefully until he had his legs locked around the other's waist. Gripping the line with one hand to steady himself, he used the other to cover his visor briefly as their circular path intersected the cloud of oily fog. It had dispersed into a fine mist by then, but Nolan was taking no risks, because he needed very badly to see what he was doing.

They were no longer moving slowly. The stern section of the ship was whirling past them with steadily increasing frequency as the line wrapped more and more of itself around the shield support, and with the decrease in the radius of the swing, the centrifugal force and Nolan's apparent weight also increased. If his legs and hand once lost their grip on the man's oil-covered spacesuit and rope, the Healer would be flung away like a stone from a slingshot. If he was released at the wrong moment he would hit the metal of the ship at high speed instead of shooting safely into space.

Nolan looked and felt around for the safety rope's quick-release stud and tried not to think about anything else.

The trouble was that by its very nature a safety rope should not be too easy to release lest it happen by accident. This particular fitting was a noncrew type and strange to him, and by the time he discovered that two overlapping safety latches had to be moved aside before the quick-release stud was revealed, more than half of the line had wound itself around the shield support and their speed did not bear thinking about. His apparent weight was increasing by the moment, and the stern section of the ship was whirling around them so fast that it was next to impossible to calculate a precise moment when it would be safe to let go, and the longer he delayed the more impossible the calculation became.

He waited only for the few seconds it took for the gap between the hull and the adjoining shield support to come around again, then pressed his thumb down hard on the release stud, simultaneously changing his grip from the safety line to the other man's equipment belt. Wherever they were going, he thought, they were going together.

The safety line whipped away behind them and suddenly they were free, weightless, spinning slowly about their common center of gravity and shooting toward the metal horizon that was the edge of the hull. Nolan was able to see individual rivets as it whipped past them and they shot toward the shield support on the opposite side, which they missed by about fifty feet. Then the ship was contracting slowly behind them and Nolan remembered to breathe again.

Still holding on to the other man's equipment belt, Nolan used his thrusters to kill their spin, then he carried out a quick visual examination without otherwise touching him. Normally the pressure within the suit would cause the limbs to drift apart starfish fashion, he knew, but in this case there was restricted movement in three of the limbs. He moved his head closer to the oily visor, and saw that the man's eyes were closed and his mouth slightly open, and there was no sign of the bleeding that would have signaled a decompression. The farspeaker indicator was still showing, which meant that the headset was still functioning. Nolan turned up the volume control to maximum and then switched on his own set.

He counted at least five voices talking at once and the consequent distortion rendered them all incomprehensible. Slowly and clearly he said, "Priority Yellow Five. Quiet, please. Priority Yellow Five . . ."

It was the code for a single-person medical emergency not involving a radiation hazard, and Nolan repeated the message until only he was talking. Then he went on, "I'm trying to find out if this man is still alive. When I count to three, will all of you please take a deep breath and hold it so that I can hear if the casualty is breathing. One, two, three . . ."

In the hissing silence of his earpiece it was like a faint, uncertain breeze blowing through long grass. Nolan contributed a loud sigh of relief.

"Thank you," said Nolan, and went on briskly, "You may resume breathing now. He is alive, unconscious, and, judging by the uneven respiration, going into shock. He has sustained fractures, probably multiple, to the lower legs and right forearm, and the subsequent motion will have caused severe crepitation, so he is fortunate to be unconscious. For that reason I don't want to risk complicating the injuries by subjecting him to the deceleration of my suit thrusters, gentle as it is . . ."

"At your present velocity you wouldn't have enough power to get back," said the authoritative voice Nolan had heard earlier. "We'll come after you in our scow as soon as we can board it."

"How soon . . . ?" began Nolan.

"About twenty minutes to match velocities with you," came the reply, "and close on an hour to decelerate and return to the ship. You built up a lot of speed on that merry-go-round. And . . . and that rescue was very well done, friend. In a hot spot you keep a very cool head."

If my head was cool, Nolan thought, why is the rest of me half-drowning in sweat? A sudden reaction to what had happened was making him shake inside his spacesuit, so that he felt embarrassed by what he considered an undeserved compliment and did not reply.

"We reported the accident to Control," the voice went on, "and since then they've been trying to contact Healer Nolan on the ship frequency but he isn't answering. They seem to have lost him . . ."

"And now you've found him," said Nolan, more sharply than he had intended. The thought of yet another smiling, friendly rebuke from the monsignor, this time for not observing proper farspeaker procedure, had angered him for a moment. In a softer voice he went on, "We have enough air to last until you arrive. But I must immobilize the limbs before the transfer into surgery, to reduce the risk of further complicating the fractures. Holding the arm across the chest with the safety harness is no problem, but I'll need a rigid splint to bind between the legs. Do you understand what I want? A piece of rigid bar or tubing, metal or stiff plastic, about four feet long. And some tape or cable to hold it in position. Can do?"

There was an uncertain sound to the formerly authoritative voice as it replied, "The cable is no problem, but the only item we have that is long and strong enough to serve as a splint is . . . well, it's an extremely important and valuable component we were delivering to the power module."

"Is it radioactive?" asked Nolan.

"No, but—"

"I'll be careful not to damage it," said Nolan impatiently. He was more concerned about the broken bones of the man floating beside him at that moment than with any possible damage to equipment. He went on, "I think I can see your vehicle moving away from the blast shield now. Can you still see us or shall I light a flare?"

"We see you, Healer."

With increasing distance the ship had lost the major distortions of perspective and had again become like the plastic model that had enabled him to get out of trouble on Brendan's Island. It was at times like this that Nolan wondered if everything he said, thought, did, or did not do would ultimately land him in trouble with the monsignor. Which reminded him of yet another sin of omission, that of failing to maintain contact with the ship.

"Healer Nolan," he said, changing to the ship frequency. "Please prepare the surgical treatment room to receive one casualty, unconscious, probably with multiple fractures to both legs and one arm, and with the possibility of thoracic damage presently concealed by the suit, arriving one hour from now. I will need help with this one, so please have two healing assistants standing by."

"Communications. Please wait," said a voice in his earpiece.

It was a cool, impersonal voice of the kind favored by all officers from the communications department; a voice, he had heard it said, that was supposed to remain calm and unemotional whether it was discussing the cataclysmic detonation of the Earth below them or the Second Coming of the Christus. Naturally it gave no indication of either approving or disapproving of Nolan's recent activities.

"Communications," it said again. "Fathers Conlon and Sanchez are being excused from their other duties. They will make the necessary preparations and will meet you at lock three. Have you any other instructions?"

"Nolan," he replied. "Thank you, no."

Both Fathers Conlon and Sanchez had chosen medicine as their noncrew specialty, and Nolan had found them to be particularly adept as surgical assistants. But being ecclesiastics and traditionalists in such matters, neither had aspired to full Healer status. And it was only during medical emergencies that Nolan could tell them what to do—at all other times the Healer was gently and continually reminded that he was the subordinate.

"Communications," said the voice again, and this time there was just a hint of unsteadiness. "Healer Nolan. As soon as you are finished treating your casualty, His Eminence would like to see you."

Chapter 15

BY the time the leg fractures had been reduced and immobilized, the weightless traction necessitated by the absence of gravity had been applied, and the casualty was no longer giving any cause for concern, Nolan was much too weary to care whether the cardinal-captain wanted to officially compliment him on the rescue or to kick him ceremoniously off the ship. He did, however, want to know which it was to be as quickly as possible.

"Thank you, Fathers," he said gratefully, taking his attention from the patient for the first time in three hours. "That was a long and difficult procedure and both of you performed very well indeed."

"It was at your direction, Healer," Father Conlon said quietly.

"Nevertheless," said Nolan, "you have every right to feel as pleased with yourselves as I am with you. There was a time, just after we cut his suit away, that I thought he might lose the right leg at least, but we were able to save it. Now, however, I would like one of you to stay with him until I return. Do either of you know where the captain is just now? I've an overdue appointment with him and must leave at once."

"We were told that he would be spending most of today in the power module," said Father Sanchez. "You could begin by looking there."

"There is no need," said Father Conlon in a very quiet voice. He was looking past the Healer's shoulder and seemed to be trying to stand at attention, a difficult feat in the weightless condition while one's boots were detached from the floor stirrups. Nolan turned quickly to see Cardinal-Captain Keon floating a short distance behind him.

"Sir," Nolan began, "I was about to—"

'I overheard you, so there is no necessity to repeat yourself," said the cardinal in a voice that sounded quietly stern and very impatient. "Since you have been too busy to visit me, Healer, I must emulate Muhammad and come to the mountain. Where is it?"

"I—I'm sorry, sir . . ." began Nolan.

"I am speaking, Healer," said the captain, as if he were talking to a not-very-intelligent child, "of the ceramic tube that you used in such cavalier fashion as a splint, not Muhammad's hypothetical mountain. Are you about to tell me you smashed it?"

"Oh no, sir," said Nolan. He slid open the door of the wall storage compartment beside him and reached inside. "Once it had served its purpose I took good care of it. And I've already looked at it in case it had been cracked or warped during—"

For an instant there was a sudden bone-crushing grip around his wrist, and it was the cardinal who used his other hand to reach within for the tube that was floating weightless among the remains of the casualty's spacesuit. Then Nolan's wrist was released and His Eminence began to slide the tube gently through his hands, and look along and through the hollow center at the smooth, annular projections on the tube walls, and at the finely worked inserts of copper and gold that decorated both the outer and inner surfaces. To Nolan's overtired mind it resembled nothing so much as a wand, a magic wand capable of wonders undreamed of except in the imaginations of children and, perhaps, in those of full-grown men who would use it in some arcane fashion to help guide their starship.

"A magic wand is as good a description as any, Healer," said His Eminence, making Nolan realize that he had been thinking aloud, "at least from one who is not engaged on this somewhat theoretical work, and there are few enough who are. My friends at the University of Peiping required more than three years to produce this particular wand, to devise and accurately position the circuitry in a rigid ceramic structure of precise dimensions and—But I'm sure the details are of small interest to you, Healer, other than that it would shatter and not bend. Now you have some understanding of my concern."

Nolan's mouth had gone dry and he could scarcely recognize his own voice as he said, "Yes, sir. But—but I didn't know. I mean, that I could have delayed the departure of the ship by three years . . . !"

The captain shook his head quickly and said, "You would not have affected the time of departure in any way. But you would have wrecked a project of my own which has engaged me for more than a decade, and you would have displeased me greatly which, so far as you yourself are concerned, might have proved to be an even greater calamity. But it seems you have a talent for extricating yourself from dangerous situations. You are a most fortunate man, Healer, and from what I have heard, so is your patient. How fares he?"

"Very well, sir," said Nolan. He gave a brief report on the man's treatment and present condition, then went on enthusiastically, "at first we thought he would have to lose one leg, and he would have, if we had not been able to immobilize the limb before bringing him in. But as it is, he'll be ready for transfer to his local House of Sorrows in three or four days, and to resume work in two months with only a slight limp to show for—"

Nolan shut his mouth so quickly that the other must have heard his teeth come together. Cardinal-Captain Keon also had a limp, a very minor deformity that had kept him from ascending the throne of the High-King at Tara, and it was a matter about which he must feel very sensitive. Nolan wished that he had done the job properly and bitten off his tongue.

The captain looked at the fiery discomfort of Nolan's face without any change of expression, then he said mildly, "In the weightless condition a limp will not be noticed. He is very lucky to be alive, and it might aid his nonphysical recovery if you were to tell him that for a short time his legs were attached to a splint worth more than three times his body's weight in gold. His friends may disbelieve him, but his children and grandchildren will have no trouble believing in magic wands, or in the heroic figure of the Healer who braved the wrath of a starship captain to . . . But why go on? Before we leave orbit you will have created a legend."

Nolan could feel the heat leaving his face, and he knew that the relief was apparent in his voice as he said, "I shall certainly tell him as soon as he wakes. But, sir, I was told that you wanted to see me as soon as possible. When and where shall I report?"

The thin, stern line of the cardinal-captain's mouth twisted into the faintest of smiles. He said, "I have already seen you and I now have no reason to see you again. But I would appreciate it, Healer, if henceforth you tried to perform your duties without creating any more legends."

The captain departed with his much-prized ceramic device held protectedly against his chest, followed shortly thereafter by Fathers Conlon and Sanchez, leaving Nolan alone with the patient to consider his good fortune. His Eminence might not entirely approve of his junior Healer, but neither was he actively displeased with him. It was likely that Monsignor O'Riordan would have something to say about the matter, but compared to what the captain could have said and done, that was a minor concern for the future. The strength and frequency of his yawning were threatening to dislocate his lower mandible, and he realized that he was becoming too tired even to think. He checked the patient's vital signs once again, placed padded calipers around his head to detect the movements that would signal his awakening, connected them to an audible warning, and then strapped himself loosely into his bunk.

But sleep did not come easily nor, at first, did it stay for long. Twice he dreamed that he was out on the shield support, dizzy and confused and fearful as he whirled around on the end of a safety line that was twist-shortening and threatening to smash his puny body against unyielding metal, to awaken sweating and struggling against his straps. On the third occasion he wakened because there was a hand shaking his shoulder.

He opened his eyes to see two faces looking down on him. The clock above his bunk told him that five hours had passed and the other face, which belonged to Healer Dervla, said, "It seems that both patient and Healer are resting comfortably. Nevertheless, if it isn't too inconvenient for you, I would like your report."

"Of course, Healer," he said, wriggling out of his straps. But before he could go on, she held up her hand.

"The clinical picture only," she said, "not the prior circumstances. I was made aware of those in great detail within a few minutes of my coming on board. Also, you have been in charge here long enough to tell me about the general run of minor injuries and ailments you have encountered up to now, so that I'll know what to expect as the on-board crew comes up to full strength and you take your last Earthside leave."

She moved, turned away from the bunk, and the long, earth brown cloak that had been drifting in untidy folds behind her immediately began wrapping itself around her head and one shoulder. She pushed it clear and said irritably, "This uniform needs gravity to look well. Like you, I'll wear my ship coveralls from now on and keep this for formal occasions, if there are any where we're going. Well, Healer?"

But unlike me, Nolan thought as he began his report, her coveralls would be the dull brown color signifying that she was qualified in the strict and exclusive healing disciples of the Hibernian Order of Orla, while he wore the whites of a mere surgeon. At least it set them apart from the other ship's officers, who wore black at all times, relieved only by their departmental insignia.

While he was speaking she paid close attention to him, asking pertinent questions from time to time but moving around the treatment room with her eyes missing nothing. Finally she asked to see the patient's pre- and post-operative X rays which she studied briefly before handing them back to him. Then she turned to leave, took an angry swipe at her misbehaving cloak, and said, "That was well done, Healer."

"Thank you," said Nolan, "but Fathers Sanchez and Conlon helped . . ."

She paused for a moment in the entrance to say, "This time I wasn't referring to the clinical picture."

Three days passed and still the monsignor had not sent for him. It was possible that O'Riordan was too busy to waste time on a calamity that had not happened. More than two-thirds of the ship's complement were on board now, so that the two warm dormitories were beginning to resemble birdhouses that were rapidly filling with their white-faced, off-duty ravens. The crew's warm accommodation was both cramped and Spartan, for the good reason that they would be spending only a tiny fraction of the voyage there, because the remainder of the time they would be in their cold sleep caskets and totally uncaring of creature comforts. But if O'Riordan did not want to see Nolan, the Healer needed to see the monsignor.

O'Riordan's compartment was larger by half than Nolan's surgical treatment room, decorated in pleasant, restful colors and furnished with a desk and two deep, old, and comfortable chairs fitted inconspicuously with retaining straps. To enhance the feeling of being in the office of a Healer of the Mind, the monsignor insisted that his visitors use the straps to remain seated and, hopefully, at ease while he was talking to them. Nolan took the indicated chair and strapped in, but he did not feel at ease.

"Yes, my son," said the monsignor with a gentle, fatherly smile. "How may I help you?"

"Sir, thank you for seeing me at once," said Nolan quickly, "especially as there are officers who were already waiting before I arrived. For that reason I would like to waste as little of your time as possible and come directly to the point. Healer Dervla has already given her permission for a seven-day leave of absence from my ship duties, and it requires only your own approval to . . ."

The Monsignor was holding up his hand. He smiled benignly and said, "No, my son."

"But—but *why*?" said Nolan, too surprised to feel anger. "I assumed your permission would be granted as a matter of course. What possible reason . . . ?"

"One possible reason," the monsignor said quietly, "might be that you have no living relatives on Earth and have, therefore, no pressing need to go there."

Nolan said, "But there are other people and places I would like to see for the last time, and hopefully others for the first and only time. I missed the chance to visit the Imperial Library because of the Westland visit."

"Another reason," said the monsignor, "might be that you are a person who seems to attract trouble and, with all but a few of the ship's officers already on board, there would be no steadying influence that I could bring to bear on you. Let us face it, my son, in your situation the whole planet is likely to be an occasion of sin."

"That's nonsense!" Nolan protested. "I've no intention of going on the rampage like a bull in heat. Please believe me, I would not say or do anything that would reflect badly on the project . . ."

"No doubt your present intentions are exemplary," said the priest, his smile still firmly in place, "but the flesh of an unbeliever is weaker than most. And the remark about occasions of sin was a small, ecclesiastical joke which would not be appreciated by such as yourself, and for which I apologize. But you might consider another possible reason for refusing you, and everyone else presently on board, leave to visit Earth.

"You, and they, must accustom yourselves to the thought that you are no longer of Earth," he went on, "and for very good psychological reasons it should be sooner rather than later. To this end there will be a general tightening of discipline, an increasing emphasis on and orientation toward individual crew responsibilities and the purpose for which we are all here. To aid the process, farspeaker traffic between the ship and the surface will be reduced to a minimum, and then it will deal with the technical aspects of the project rather than personal matters. Farseer broadcasts, even news coverage, will not be relayed to the crew except in very special circumstances. Direct vision ports will be covered to all but the astrogation officers, to reinforce the fact that *Aisling Gheal* is the only world we have until we reach the new one. Naturally there will be a few of you who feel homesick, or suffer related emotional problems, but I expect these difficulties will be minor and easily controlled, because the crew's dedication to the success of Project Aisling Gheal is as strong as their vocation to the priesthood. As an unbeliever you lack this spiritual strength, but

I believe that your commitment to the project comes close to equaling theirs.''

There was no trace of a smile on the priest-psychologist's round, pink face as he went on, ''You already know that, with a very few exceptions, every officer will be required to assume watch-keeping responsibilities at least three times during the course of the voyage. It is for that reason I am advising all of you to begin developing the mental habits of solitude and silence during off-duty periods, or while performing duties which do not in themselves require verbal communication. The psychological advantages of this prior preparation are obvious. However, I am making it a strong recommendation rather than an order, because acquiring the habit of silence will be harder for some than others. But if there is anyone who cannot overcome his feelings of homesickness, or who has other psychological difficulties in this respect, it would be better to know about it while we are still in Earth orbit.''

Nolan was silent. The other's words contained a warning that was not even thinly veiled. If the Healer insisted on leaving the ship for any reason at all, he might not be allowed to return to it.

Then suddenly the monsignor was smiling again.

''But there is another reason for keeping you from the libraries and the fleshpots of the Imperial City,'' he said in a voice of gentle dismissal, ''but I have neither the time nor the intention to go into it now. I will say only that your application for leave is refused, and that one day you will thank me for it.''

''When Hell freezes over,'' Nolan muttered softly, but not quite softly enough.

''Oh, much sooner than that,'' said O'Riordan.

Chapter 16

THE week that followed Nolan's interview with the monsignor was such a busy one for both Healer Dervla and himself that they scarcely met and rarely had the chance to speak to each other; one had to remain on call while the other slept, and when they happened to be awake at the same time, she was usually treating the steady flow of minor injuries associated with weightlessness while he concentrated on the casket inspections.

It would have been a very good week to be on leave.

All of the spaces in the colonist modules were full. The warm dormitories of the crew had also filled up as the few remaining officers with business on the surface returned to *Aisling Gheal*, and the noncrew technical and inspection people had moved their support vessels, their equipment, and themselves clear of the ship or back to Earth. There was the feeling of increasingly purposeful activity in progress from everyone Nolan met, together with an air of excitement that was both intense and very, very quiet.

The monsignor had insisted that he had been making a helpful suggestion rather than giving an order, but by the middle of that week the voluntary vow of silence was already showing its effects. As fewer and fewer officers seemed willing to talk to him, Nolan took to spending more time in his surgical treatments room even though the contagion of silence had spread to the patients. When there were no patients needing attention he studied. He would position the terminal so that he could study in his bunk, and sometimes he closed his eyes to rest them from the intricate diagrams on-screen and to help him think.

It was at one of those moments that he heard a nonsymptomatic and not very polite cough.

"Healer Nolan," said Dervla when he opened his eyes, "I don't really blame you for taking to your bunk and sleeping, especially when there is nothing else to do, but for the reputation of my department I do not want anyone else to catch you at it. No, don't get up. I came for conversation, not treatment."

Nolan waited for her to go on, but when she remained silent he said, "I was studying, not sleeping. And I'm in my bunk because it is more convenient than floating about and making the place look untidy. You can use the examination table if you like."

He watched as she tethered herself loosely to the table, thinking that Dervla was surely the most manlike woman he had ever seen. She was very tall, flat-chested, and any of the female physical attributes she might have possessed were hidden by her coveralls. The face was well-formed, smooth of skin and liberally dusted with the freckles that plagued the majority of people with red hair and blue eyes, and her expression was that of a person who is permanently close to anger. Since coming on board the luxuriant waist-length and, in the weightless condition, unmanageable hair had been cropped to within an inch of the scalp, further adding to her mannish appearance. Only the dull, earthen brown of her coveralls, a color that could be worn by no man, and the hands revealed her femininity. They were slim and strong and beautifully formed, and assured and economical in their movements as they fastened the table straps around her. As a surgeon Nolan liked to watch hands that knew what they were doing.

"Thank you," said Dervla, when the table had been adjusted so that they faced each other. She hesitated for a moment as if uncertain of what she wanted to say, then went on, "What are you studying, Healer?"

"I'm trying to learn another language," said Nolan.

"A waste of time, surely," she said, frowning, "when everyone on the ship, crew and colonists alike, has one language in common. Perhaps a few speak it with a worse accent than yours, but you know as well as I that they are all required to be fluent in Gaelic."

Dervla had told him that she had come here for conversation, but had not said whether or not it would be polite. Nolan sighed, and swung out the display screen to a position where she could read it easily.

"My problem is that if a fellow officer admits to my presence and allows himself to speak to me," he said, "the language is familiar but the words are foreign. If I'm to have any chance of talking to some of them, and I do like talking to people, I decided that it would be a good idea to learn at least one of their languages. This one, considering the length and dangers of the voyage ahead and the possibility of supposedly foolproof systems breaking down, seemed as if it would prove particularly useful. But it is becoming plain that I could have chosen an easier one."

Dervla smiled suddenly, and said, "I understand you well, Healer, for I have the same problem. Because of my vocation and shipboard rank, they cannot treat me with the same polite silence as they do you. But neither, because of that position, can I force conversation upon them. It would not be seemly. But you at least speak the same language as I, the language of medicine."

"Again," said Nolan, smiling, "I speak it with a heavy accent, on surgery."

Dervla laughed quietly. It was the first time that Nolan had seen her teeth, which were small and even and well-nigh perfect. She said, "One does not expect a quick wit in such a large and seemingly slow man. But I may be able to help you study your new language which, fortunately, is not dependent on a proper accent for a full understanding. I had much to do with the computer system of Tara's House of Sorrows, which in many respects equaled the ship's in complexity. One early lesson you must learn is that computers do exactly as they are told which, unless you word your instructions properly, may not be what you want. But I have no intention of beginning your lessons here and now. I have been given information, which I feel should be passed to you, that is interesting, inexact, and with highly restricted circulation."

"That sounds like the definition of a juicy piece of gossip," said Nolan. "Please go on, Healer."

"His Eminence does not gossip and neither do I," said Dervla sharply, then went on, "Every few days the cardinal invites me to dine with him, even though custom dictates that the officer in command of a vessel and its Healer dine alone, and separately. On these occasions Monsignor O'Riordan is also present, but has little to say because the captain likes to talk about the activities of the people we both knew at Court . . ."

So His Eminence never gossips, Nolan said, but silently to himself.

". . . and I suspect that the monsignor is there to observe the proprieties," she continued, "although it is not clear whether the concern is for my honor or the captain's. This time His Eminence did not want to speak of Tara but only of the ship, and the preparations for the first testing of the main drive and blast shield, which is imminent. The exact timing is uncertain, since delays must be expected in such a complex operation, but the captain's expectation is that it will occur not later than ten hours from now and no sooner than four. When the time is known with certainty, the officers who are not already involved with the test will be told officially about it one hour before the event. The reason for this is that the monsignor thinks that delays and periods of uncertainty, however short, would unsettle and give rise to unnecessary speculation among the non-engineering crew members. Until the official announcement has been made, you will therefore keep this information to yourself."

"Of course," said Nolan, his excitement at the news forcing him into physical activity. He was drawing up his legs prior to leaving the bunk when Dervla leaned forward and pressed down hard on his kneecaps, forcing him flat again.

"I told you to stay where you are," she said, as if he were a disobedient child, then went on, "I have already seen that your department is prepared for any emergency; had it not been, I would have had unkind things to say to you, so the most sensible thing you can do is rest. Do not study or even think, just sleep. I shall try to do the same."

She unstrapped and was about to push herself toward the entrance when Nolan said quickly, "Healer, wait please. I have the kind of peculiar mind that needs something tangible to worry about or it will not go to sleep at all. What types of casualties can we expect, and in what numbers?"

Dervla steadied herself with a hand on the table edge. She gave a small albeit impatient smile and said, "I understand. The Healers of the Mind tell us that it is much better if a patient has something to worry about than if he worries about nothing. I had intended briefing you when you wakened, but there's no reason not to do it now."

"Theoretically," she went on quickly, "if everything functions as it should and everyone obeys the safety regulations, there will be no casualties. My present understanding of the situation is that there is no radiation hazard, but in the event of a catastrophic malfunction in the power module, we will all be casualties. Decompressions are also unlikely since the operation is controlled remotely by personnel inside the ship. Which leaves us with traumatic injuries associated with local structural failures. It is possible that the initial detonation will cause the structure aft to crumple and telescope forward, slowly of course, and the rearmost colonist modules will be involved, which is not a pleasant thought.

"I realize," she went on, "that this will be in your specialty rather than mine, so I will assist if and when required. You will use my treatment room as a base, since it has more patient accommodation and a better communications link with Central Control One than this place. You will go to the accident site if a casualty needs attention before he can be moved, while I remain with the other patients. Both of us are going to be on duty, possibly for several days with little possibility of sleep if there is a major accident, which is the reason we must rest while we have the chance. Now have I given your peculiar mind enough to worry about for you to rest easy?''

''Thank you, Healer,'' said Nolan. ''I think you've given it enough to have nightmares.''

''Sleep well, Healer.''

Strangely, he found no difficulty in sleeping, until Dervla wakened him with an unladylike punch in the stomach and told him that the test would begin in fifty minutes and to come to the medical treatment room at once.

In spite of her comparative youth—she had not yet seen twenty-five summers—Dervla had been Palace Healer to the Seventh Maeve, High-Queen of Hibernia and Empress of the West. She was a friend of Padair, Cardinal Keon, whose power, so far as *Aisling Gheal* was concerned, was even greater. She was also a very strong-willed woman who would not take kindly to suggestions, however gently worded they might have been, of a mere monsignor regarding the running of her department.

Any or all of those factors could have been the reason why the direct vision panel of the medical treatments room had been left uncovered, but Nolan felt sure that the last one was the most likely. It was unfortunate that, in their present orbital position, the panel was on the side of the ship looking away from the planetary surface.

The room was lit only by the dim, red night-lighting so that the black field speckled with the brighter stars showed to good advantage, as did the wall screen which reproduced Control's ship status display. Centered above that screen, there was yet another refinement not available in his surgical treatments room, a small vision screen which also showed a full-length image of *Aisling Gheal* that was wavering and indistinct because it was being relayed from a surface observation station.

During the final moments of the countdown, the calm, muted voices that had been pouring from the wall speaker like a quietly flowing river had been reduced to a trickle. Suddenly there came a voice so cool and impersonal that Nolan did not immediately recognize it as belonging to the captain.

''Central Control One, seventy-five seconds to initial detonation. Silence from all departments except those specified, or if reporting an emergency condition. Gunroom Control, come in.''

''Gunroom Control Three,'' came the prompt reply. ''Remote

firing controls and cameras functioning. Lasers powered up and focused. No technical holds expected. Standing by."

"Very well. Gunroom Three, you have the count at sixty-three seconds, and permission to proceed to first detonation."

A voice that sounded less calm than that of the captain took up the count, and Nolan felt his hands beginning to sweat. Apart from Central Control One, Communications Two, Gunroom Control Three, and the four unmanned laser gunrooms in the power module aft, all of which showed the blue operational indications, the diagrammatic representation of the ship was a solid mass of yellow standby lights. Astrogation Two, Maneuvering Thrust Six, and Lander Docks Seven and Eight were unlighted since they had nothing to do at this stage, and neither had Warm Dormitories Nine and Ten or Medical Eleven unless something went badly wrong.

". . . thirty-three . . . thirty-two . . . thirty-one," the voice from Gunroom Control was saying. "Thirty seconds and primary and backup lasers on automatic. Shield firing aperture synchronized. Committed to first detonation, dear God protect us all . . ."

"Central Control One," the captain's voice broke in calmly, "This is not the time for prayer, Father. The right time is either before or in thanksgiving following the successful conclusion of the event, not during it. Proceed with your countdown."

Nolan had nothing but sympathy for the gunroom priest and wished that he himself had someone to pray to at a time like this. But the most that he could do was hope very hard that the Redmen charged with the design and building of the as-yet-untested shield assembly had known what they were doing, and that the scientists of Cathay had been accurate in their estimate of the energy about to be released when the light pressure from four tightly focused laser guns converted a tiny globule of deuterium into a nuclear fusion explosion just aft of the blast shield, because he did not believe in the Great Spirit Manitou, or Buddha either.

". . . seven . . . six . . . five . . ."

Nolan turned his head quickly to look at Dervla, to find that she was looking at him in a manner that he could only describe as clinical. He smiled uncertainly and returned his attention to the displays just as the countdown reached zero.

The picture being relayed from the ground station flared into a sudden, dazzling whiteness. And in spite of the main ship structure's being in the shadow of thc blast shield, even the black sky beyond the direct vision panel seemed to lighten momentarily to a misty gray as the gas particles and dust motes floating in the vacuum of near-Earth space were illuminated by the tiny sun that had come briefly into being astern.

There was a sudden but very gentle shock, so gentle that Nolan barely felt the pressure of the padding against his back, as the force of the explosion overcame the tremendous inertia of the ship to move it forward. And as the shock was transmitted through the fabric of the vessel, there was a sound like a soft metallic sigh as a structure that had been assembled in orbit for the first time experienced thrust and weight and independent motion.

The screen showing the ground viewpoint had cleared but for a small hailstorm of interference caused by the recent detonation, and the ship status displays remained empty of warning lights.

"Central Control One," said the captain. "The blast shield is holding. There are no system malfunctions, no structural deformation, no detectable loss of air, no crew injuries reported. Gunroom Three, you will proceed to second detonation. You have the count."

A third firing cycle followed the second, which was also free of any structural or human incidents, and by then the fusion detonations aft had become, if not an accepted part of life, at least a matter of much less concern.

"Control One," said the captain. "I want synchronized firing from all four guns, timed to give five detonations per second for a duration of fifteen minutes. Human monitoring backup on each system. When you are ready, Gunroom Control."

Because it was almost impossible to separate five gentle pushes of one-tenth gravity per second, the pressure against Nolan's back became soft and continuous. The ship status display remained clear of warning lights, and Nolan gave a great sigh of relief, then, afraid that it might be taken as a sign of human weakness, he changed it to a clearing of the throat.

"I had assumed that a few single detonations would be enough to test the system," he said thoughtfully. "But I can see the sense in going quickly to maximum design allowance because, if something goes badly wrong, it is better if it happens when Earth is still close enough to help us."

"It seems as close as it ever was," said Dervla. She pointed toward the direct vision panel where the bright, flat curve of the planetary horizon was creeping into view over the forward edge. They were above the north polar wastes, moving south toward the far-flung Empire of Cathay on a slow, outward spiral that was taking them farther from Earth. The ground station that had them in sight was in daylight so that the picture it transmitted was of a spidery, white stick insect with a tiny pulsing sun at its tail seen through a bright fog. She went on, "Fortunately for all concerned we had nothing to do this time, but they will have to do it all again in reverse to return us to our original orbit. We might not be as lucky then."

"I don't think so," said Nolan.

"Such trust you have," said Dervla, "in the behavior of men and machines."

"I didn't mean that . . ." Nolan began, when there was an interruption from the speaker.

"Central Control One," said the captain, in a voice that was calm but no longer impersonal, "secure Gunroom Control Three and stand down. The post-test structural inspection can wait until the beginning of the next watch. This test is terminated and, judging by present indications, with complete success. All duty officers stand down. Thank you, Fathers."

There was a moment of silence, broken by the voice of one of the medical orderlies. Hesitantly, he said, "Father Sanchez, Warm Dormitory Nine. I have three nonurgent casualties, of too minor a nature to interrupt the test or inconvenience the—"

"Medical Eleven," Dervla broke in sharply. "Please specify injuries and how they were sustained. Do you require assistance at the scene?"

"No, Healer," Father Sanchez replied. "There are two cases of motion sickness with nausea and regurgitation suffered during the second firing. One case of probable dislocated shoulder sustained as a result of changing bunks to avoid the pollution. All three are conscious and ambulatory. I'm bringing them to you now."

"Thank you, Father," said Dervla, switching off the sender, then to Nolan, "Ye Gods! Motion sickness under one-tenth G—an elevator accelerates faster than that. Still, I expect the excitement of the moment was a contributing factor, and it might have been much worse. Then, what *did* you mean?"

"What . . . ?" began Nolan uncertainly, then he remembered their interrupted conversation and went on, "I meant that you might be wrong about us returning to our original orbit. We expended a lot of energy during this test, and doubling it just to return to where we were would be wasteful, especially if the only reason was to keep us within easy range of the Earth shuttle. The monsignor was right; I am grateful to him for refusing me that leave."

Below them the Sea of Cathay filled the direct vision panel, its deep, blue-green expanse marred by the curling white tentacles of a typhoon.

"In Cathay there is a saying that even the longest of journeys begins with the first step," he said quietly. "I think we've already taken it."

Chapter 17

As yet they were being held by the invisible bonds of gravity to the mother planet, but every time they completed another orbit over the north and south poles their distance increased and that unfelt grip had lessened. But physical contact was maintained by shuttles operating at the limits of their endurance, and bringing chemical fuel to top up the massive reservoir needed by the landers, important cold sleepers whose caskets would travel in the crew stacks, or written messages that could not be entrusted to the normal communication channels. But even these visits were becoming increasingly infrequent, and the end of both the gravitic and physical forms of contact came to an end two weeks later with the announcement from Central Control that at the conclusion of a most meticulous and exhaustive postdetonation structural inspection, no fault or weakness had been found in the fabric of the ship and that for the next twenty-four hours thrust would be continuous.

By that time their distance was such that the night-darkened hemisphere of the planet below them filled all but the corners of the square viewing panel. He could make out the irregular, bright smudges of the cities of the Westland seaboard where the sun had set, and those of Hibernia and the western coasts of Europe and Africa which were still in the darkness that preceded dawn, separated by the black and featureless Great North and South Oceans. Many, many millions of people in those cities, towns, and single, isolated dwellings, from those too young to know what they were seeing to the very old whose vision and capacity to understand were beginning to fade, would be looking up at them. They would be watching the small and incredibly expensive fireworks display of tiny, closely spaced sunbursts that was lighting up their night sky, and from the lowest of the lowborn up to the Ard-Rioghan herself, their eyes and thoughts would be on the ship. Nolan did not know what they were feeling, but he hoped that it was pride.

The period of sustained thrust was accomplished without mechanical failure or human mishap, and by then the moderate dimensions of Dervla's viewport were able to encompass the tiny, bright semicircles that were the southern hemispheres of the Earth and Moon. The ship was breaking free of its two-million-miles-distant mother planet and was curving into a long, flat trajectory that would take it below the ecliptic and ultimately out of the Solar System, for the sun of their New World was a not very prominent stellar object in Earth's southern skies. And so it was that the only bonds now holding them to the home world were their memories and the equally insubstantial communication channel.

Healers Dervla and Nolan continued to alternate on watch, twelve hours on, twelve off. They had no calls on their professional services, and the crew's self-imposed vow of silence ensured that there were no social calls either. Sometimes Dervla would decide to spend a part of her off-duty time in the adjoining medical treatment room in an attempt, she said, to relieve the pangs of conversational starvation, and if Nolan was wakeful he would go in and try to talk to her. But she was never easy to talk to, and if it seemed that the conversation might shift from professional to personal subjects, she would not speak at all—until one day Dervla informed him that she was not averse to listening to Healer Nolan talking about himself, especially if she was able to acquire information additional to that contained in his crew dossier.

"My only intention," Dervla said in a very serious voice, "is to increase my understanding of the personality responsible for the surgical work of my department, here and in the colony, and not merely to satisfy personal curiosity."

"I understand," said Nolan. "But you are beginning to sound like another Healer of the Mind, except that the monsignor has a—"

"Comparing me with Monsignor O'Riordan is not a compliment, professional or otherwise," said Dervla sharply. "If you prefer not to discuss nondepartmental matters with me, then you are not obliged to do so."

"I was about to say," Nolan resumed quietly, "that the monsignor can sometimes slip some very unsettling questions into an otherwise pleasant conversation, so I am glad indeed that you are unlike him."

For a long moment Dervla stared at him in silence, then she said, "It seems, Healer Nolan, that there is a little of the Healer of the Mind in all of us, because you have just inserted a polite warning against any attempt at playing tricks with your mind."

He inclined his head but did not speak. It was obvious that she was greatly displeased with Monsignor O'Riordan, and Nolan had the feeling that he could learn more by keeping silent than by asking questions.

"The monsignor is a pleasant table companion," she went on, with an edge of anger still apparent in her voice. "He is cultured, informed, witty, stimulating, and . . . and he recently made a suggestion that was most disagreeable to me. It was that too much talking, especially if it is about old friends or incidents at Tara, might be psychologically undesirable in our present situation, when we should be looking forward to our future lives rather than dwelling mentally in the past. I told him that speaking of past events and mutual acquaintances was neither a sin nor a dangerous aberration of the mind, but he laughed and said that it was merely a suggestion. Since then, however, our table conversation has become increasingly constrained and concerned only with ship matters, and now my invitations to dine with His Eminence are rare indeed."

"I understand," said Nolan.

"It shames me that you do understand," she said. Her color deepened, but her eyes did not waver from his face as she went on, "Doubtless you are thinking that, forbidden the opportunity of gossiping with the cardinal about the intrigues of the Imperial Court, I have been driven in desperation to seek conversation with one whose subordinate position precludes a refusal. You will also be thinking that this is far from complimentary to yourself. What else are you thinking, Healer, and will you speak of it?"

Nolan did not reply at once, because she was being unusually honest with him considering his subordinate rank, and clearly the answer was important to her.

He said, "I am thinking that you certainly cannot be compared with the monsignor. Among other things you lack the subtlety which sometimes leaves one wondering whether he is a friend or an enemy. I am accustomed to superiors saying uncomplimentary things to me, and my response is to profit by such criticism if it is warranted and ignore it if it is not. I also think that you must be desperate indeed, or your expectations unreasonably high, if you think that I can converse in the manner of the highborn of the Imperial Court. And while the subject of myself is one on which I can speak with complete authority, it is likely that your disappointment while listening to me will be as great as the boredom of silence."

"Come, come, Healer," said Dervla. "Modesty in large doses can be just as nauseating as boastfulness. You are expected to teach, so presumably you have the ability to make the lessons interesting. And, by all accounts, you lead an exciting life. The incidents on Brendan's Island and your circus act on the shield support when you rescued—"

"Sometimes I speak or act without thinking," Nolan said quickly, "and the excitement comes while trying to avoid the consequences of my own stupidity. The potentialities for drama are lessened when, as is more usual, I take time to think before acting."

"Relieved I am to hear it," said Dervla. "But I would hear more."

Nolan sighed and said, "After the death of my parents, who were well-respected in our city, I was accepted for training in Reykjavík's House of Sorrows before moving to Caledonia and then Gaul for the hypothermia work that would be necessary if I was to have any chance of winning a place on the ship. There is little of interest to tell about my training, apart from the periods of irresponsible behavior indulged in by the students who, although predominantly female, could be quite unruly. Discipline was lax by your Order of Orla standards, although the females invariably followed the Hibernian tradition of training as physicians while the men were allowed to become surgeons, if they could ensure that their professional behavior was exemplary and their nonprofessional escapades were minor and unreported."

"From all that I have read about your Order of Orla," he went on with a small, apologetic smile, "it is clear that my medical training was completely unlike your own, which demands a single-minded dedication to healing from the age of ten, and the pursuance of a physical and spiritual regimen so strict that it allows for no human weaknesses. You had no opportunities for relaxation and forgetting studies and examinations, no time for unruly behavior, or playing the cruder, anatomical practical jokes or, indeed, for any fun at all . . ."

"How little you know, Healer," said Dervla, and suddenly she smiled. "But I must resist the temptation to reminisce. We are talking about you . . ."

It surprised him that the time passed so quickly and pleasantly, but the reason was that the conversation that developed had become far from one-sided and, as often as not, the questions she asked Nolan gave him as much information about her as she learned from him. And there were times when, without warning or any cause that he could find in the preceding conversation, her manner would change suddenly from that of a friend and professional equal to the cool condescension of the superior officer, and then change back just as quickly. He could not help feeling that there was some great anger in her, controlled but always close to the surface, and he was glad that it was not directed at himself.

The strange idea came to him—strange because it was the first time that he had thought of Dervla as being a woman—that the fact of being the only unfrozen female on the ship might be worrying her. But with the exceptions of himself and a few of the lander pilots, the crew were ecclesiastics and sworn to a lifetime of celibacy, and the idea that Dervla might be thinking that she had anything to fear from him made Nolan smile.

"What amuses you, Healer?" she said, using again the voice of a superior officer. Clearly it was not a time for speaking the truth.

"I was thinking," said Nolan quickly, rubbing his fingers loudly across his chin, "that it lacks a few moments of my breakfast and of your evening meal, and that I have missed my six hours' sleep without realizing their loss. If you will excuse me, I am hungry and must make myself more presentable for the refectory deck."

For a moment Dervla regarded him closely, and he reminded himself that at Tara she had probably become adept at detecting the lie behind a diplomatic nicety, and he expected her to tell him so. Instead, she said "Our next meal will be delayed by at least one hour, I have been told, and I'm expecting the announcement to be made momentarily. You will certainly have to make yourself presentable, in full dress uniform and without the exercise harness. The captain is to address the assembled ship's crew."

"Everyone?" asked Nolan in surprise. "What about . . . ?"

"Everyone," she repeated, "including the duty officers. I am not privy to the details, but His Eminence considers this address to be too important for it to be delivered other than face to face. The ship will be allowed to run itself for a few hours. After all, we are expecting it to do so for five hundred years. Your position will be on the platform beside me, one pace to my left. And please, Healer, if there should be discussion afterwards, let others ask the awkward questions."

A large area of deck and one of the raised component inspection platforms had been cleared for them in the hanger of Lander Dock Seven. The captain, flanked by Healer Dervla and Monsignor O'Riordan, was already on the platform and standing to one side of a large projection screen. Nolan went at once to his assigned position feeling thankful that he was not the last officer to arrive. The earth-brown cloak of Dervla and the monsignor's scarlet cassock were the only touches of color amid the stark black and silver of the ceremonial uniforms and the gray, metal shadows of the landers all around them.

This was a very important occasion and everyone present knew it and was standing rigidly to attention, held lightly to the deck by the magnets of their boots. While it required no effort to stand in the weightless condition, it was very difficult to remain perfectly upright. With no downward pull to balance them, the leg muscles pulled with unequal tension and had to be corrected every few minutes. Not only were the men swaying gently from side to side but their fine, ankle-length cloaks were floating out in untidy folds and bundles. For an important ceremonial occasion, he thought wryly, gravity was required in both senses of the word.

Dervla saw his smile and frowned at him. The captain was about to speak.

"Monsignor, Reverend Fathers, Respected Healers," he began formally. "All of you know without having to be reminded that we are setting out on a voyage unique in the annals of history, and that it is a journey from which there is no return. But as with any long journey, before the departure come the farewells . . ."

At his signal the screen lit with the famous picture of the Great Tower of Tara and at its foot the untidy sprawl of the Imperial City of Atha Cliath, in places glittering with high, new structures and in others tawdry with the old. A muted fanfare sounded and suddenly their High-Queen and Empress, the Seventh Maeve, was regarding them.

She was dressed in the same archaic costume that she had worn during her reception for *Aisling Gheal*'s officers, and the words and her manner of speaking them were so similar that the same feelings of high excitement and pride stirred again the hairs at the back of his scalp. But then he detected a change in both her manner and her words.

It was as if she was speaking to them in confidence and hinting at matters which, for diplomatic and political reasons, she was not making plain. Nolan could not unravel her meaning at first, but it was clear that the assembled clerics had no such difficulty. Then slowly it became obvious to him that she considered *Aisling Gheal* to be a ship whose primary purpose was to be about the business of God and Hibernia.

He had heard it said that her more liberal statements, which were needed from time to time to oil the machinery of the Empire, were produced by those very senior prelates of the Imperial Civil Service who were her advisers. But now, on this unique and, to her, highly emotional occasion, she was displaying her own true feelings in the knowledge that her listeners were no longer in a position to betray her confidence.

The second message was from the most senior of Westland's Paramount Chiefs, the physically frail, incredibly aged, and immeasurably powerful Silver Elk. His words were wise and gentle, as those of a great-grandparent speaking to the grandchildren of which he is especially proud, and, even though his people had done more than any other nation save Hibernia to make *Aisling Gheal* a success, there was no slightest hint of partisan feeling in them. Nolan was sorry that his message was so short.

Before the third message could begin, there was an interruption. Monsignor O'Riordan cleared his throat gently, smiled, and said, "If I might make an observation, Your Eminence. We have listened to the words of our High-Queen and the great Silver Elk, and we know that the Celestial Emperors of Cathay and Nippon will also praise and thank us and wish us well. Every ruler, perhaps every single person on Earth who has reached the age of reason, would wish us well if they had the chance to speak and we the time to listen. But there are only a limited number of ways to say farewell, and I am sure that even the most egotistical and praise-hungry among us would tire of listening to such repetition. There will be ample opportunity later for anyone who wishes it to hear these messages. They have only to ask . . ."

And after speaking those words to them, Nolan thought cynically, nobody will want to ask.

"But now, Your Eminence," he concluded with another gentle smile, "I am sure that we would all like to hear the more important reasons for your calling this meeting."

Looking stern and impassive, the cardinal-captain regarded the monsignor for a moment in silence, and Nolan had the feeling that a frown was not very far from his face.

"Very well, Monsignor," said the cardinal in a voice that had in it all the icy calm of a frozen lake. But when he turned again to face his officers an immediate thaw was apparent.

"This is an especially proud moment for all of us," he said. "A proud moment and a sad one, because the mightiest rulers of all the nations of Earth are wishing us well and calling down the blessings of all the gods they believe in on our great enterprise, and at the same time they are reminding us of the home and friends we are leaving.

"Cutting short these well-wishings," he went on, "may seem to many of you to be an act of needless cruelty. But I have been assured that it is a psychological necessity, that all emotional ties with Earth should be severed sooner rather than later. In this unique situation it is indeed kinder to be cruel. Monsignor."

The monsignor smiled the gentlest of smiles, and said, "It seems that I am earning a reputation for being the kindest and most cruel of prelates. Some of you may feel that I have already earned it, by refusing surface leave to officers whose duties would have permitted it. But let me assure all of you that my kindnesses, or cruelties, toward you have scarcely begun."

He turned his head to look toward Dervla and Nolan before returning his attention to the officers. He did not smile and there was no gentleness in his voice as he went on, "I have already spoken to some of you on this matter and made suggestions. Now I am giving orders, not advice. Henceforth you will accustom yourselves to the idea that you are no longer of Earth, and you must believe in this idea until you can accept it as you do your own name. His Eminence has already said it, but I shall say it again. There are very good psychological, as well as ship-related operational, reasons why the process should begin at once.

"To this end," he continued, "there will be a general tightening of discipline, an increasing emphasis on and orientation toward individual crew self-reliance, and concentration on the purpose for which we are all here. To aid this process and engender in you the proper state of mind, farspeaker traffic between the ship and Earth will be reduced to a minimum, and then it will deal only with the technical and scientific aspects of the project rather than personal matters. Messages of a personal nature will be politely ignored and will not be relayed to the individual concerned. Similarly, farseer broadcasts including news coverage will not be relayed. With the exception of those required by the astrogation department, all direct vision ports throughout the ship will be covered. This measure is being taken to reinforce the fact that *Aisling Gheal* is the only world there is until we reach the new one.

"In all such matters of self-discipline," he said, with a glance toward Dervla, "senior officers and department heads are expected to set an example."

There was still no trace of a smile on the priest-psychologist's round, pink face as he went on: "No doubt a few of you will feel homesick, or suffer related emotional problems, and I stand ready at all times to assist and advise. But I expect such difficulties to be minor and easily controlled, because our dedication to the success of Project Aisling Gheal is total, as is our vocation to the priesthood. Naturally, the one benighted unbeliever among us lacks the support of this spiritual discipline, but I believe that his enthusiasm for the project comes close to equaling our own."

The monsignor paused for a moment, but Dervla frowned at Nolan to be silent.

"Since the time that you passed the psychological testing and were accepted for this project," he resumed, "you have known that every officer among you, regardless of rank or specialty, is required to assume watch-keeping responsibilities at least three times during the course of the voyage. During those periods you will be all alone, the only warm, thinking human being in a ship filled with hyperrefrigerated sleepers. It is for this reason that you must begin at once to develop the habits of solitude and silence during off-duty periods, or while performing duties which do not in themselves require verbal communication.

"The psychological advantages of this prior preparation will be obvious to you," he continued, "but I realize that acquiring the habit of silence will be harder for some than others, and I am here to help with whatever form of spiritual encouragement or physical chastisement that seems necessary. You will feel lonely at times, terribly lonely, each and every one of you. But you must learn to accept and adapt to it, for to do otherwise is to risk destroying the whole project. Be warned, therefore, a watch-keeper must not resuscitate a fellow officer except for reasons of the direst operational necessity. If the unthinkable were to happen and one of you harmed a fellow officer or colonist simply to relieve his loneliness, we are empowered to exact punishment up to and including the ultimate excommunication."

There was absolute silence in the lander dock, for ultimate excommunication was the ecclesiastics' term for a summary execution.

Then suddenly the monsignor was smiling again.

"And now," he went on, "we shall discuss the watch-keepers themselves, and the further kindnesses I have planned for them . . ."

Chapter 18

IT had been calculated that the voyage would take five hundred and eight years and fifteen days, but the additional time needed to land the colonists was impossible to estimate with accuracy until their arrival in orbit around the New World. To the colonists it would seem that no time at all had passed from the moment they climbed into their cold sleep caskets on Earth until they were thawed, one hundred at a time, prior to boarding the landers that would take them down to their new home. But to the ship's officers, depending on their positions on the watch-keeping roster, between six and eight years would have elapsed.

The reason for this was that the entire ship's crew was needed for the initial acceleration and insertion into interstellar orbit, and for the subsequent deceleration into the target system. In order to conserve their precious biological time for the work that would follow landfall, and to ensure that they would still be young and physically capable of performing their duties, it had been decided that only one watch-keeping officer would be warm and awake at any given time. He would stand watch from the moment the timer in his cold sleep casket awakened him until, two long and lonely years later, he returned to it for another two centuries of cold sleep, upon which his relief would be warmed.

Having accelerated to her tremendous interstellar velocity, *Aisling Gheal* would coast between the stars with all but a few lighting, heating, and sensor circuits shut down. In that condition there was very little within the ship that could go wrong. The solitary officer on duty would have only a few instruments to observe and check for any minor course deviation, and then only at the beginning and end of his watch. Watch-keepers who were not themselves astrogators had been giving training sufficient for the performance of this simple task.

In the unlikely event of a ship-threatening emergency occurring, thc officer on watch would initiate the revival of the senior officer whose specialty was best suited to dealing with the emergency, and only if absolutely necessary would they then decide whether the captain or other officers needed to be awakened to deal with it.

"I do not believe," Monsignor O'Riordan went on, "that this great undertaking will be placed in jeopardy by a failure in any of its mechanical components. And having come to know and understand all of you very well, neither do I believe that the human components will prove untrustworthy. But it would be remiss of me not to consider the possibility of such failures, and to guard against their occurrence by providing special training for those few who might, but in all likelihood will not need it."

He was being careful not to look at anyone directly, but Nolan was as sure as it was possible to be that the ship's subordinate Healer would be among the chosen few.

"In addition to the habits of silence and solitude," the monsignor continued, "these few will be physically separated from and have no opportunity to speak to other ship's officers for the length of time which I judge to be necessary. During this period they will not be closely confined, but they will inhabit quarters in a section of the ship distant enough for the movements and, I sincerely trust, infrequent voices of the other officers to be unheard. They will maintain themselves at the peak of physical fitness by wearing the exercise harness during every waking moment.

"As a preparation for watch-keeping duty," he went on, "they are forbidden to wander about the outer hull. For should an officer of the watch become detached or injured while outside, there would be nobody warm and awake to rescue him. The food and water supplies will be adequate for a lengthy period of confinement, but the actual quantity should not be taken as a guide to the length of the exercise, since the surplus can be returned to stores if it is terminated early, or replenished as necessary if the stay is extended. Unlike normal watch keeping, during this exercise there will be no books or games to pass the time. The subject will have to depend on his own mental resources for recreation, amusement, and, I sincerely hope, for serious, constructive thought."

The monsignor paused, and this time it was a lengthy one, because he seemed to be looking at every single officer and devoting several seconds to each. Finally he half-turned to look directly at Nolan.

"My son," he said, smiling, "we Healers of the Mind have the ability to know when a patient, or indeed another Healer, is wanting to speak. The imposition of silence does not take effect until the end of this meeting, so if you have questions, observations, or comments, constructive or otherwise, please speak. It is probable that you will be speaking for a number of your fellow officers."

Nolan looked at Dervla in case she wanted to speak, but the small movement of her head might equally have been a nod of encouragement or a warning to be careful.

"The first question," said Nolan, "is regarding the position of these isolated areas. The ship is big, but not so large that your selectees can be isolated from all physical and sound contact with the crew and each other, and certainly not in the crew module. This leaves the colonist modules, which have to be kept cold for obvious reasons, and are barely habitable for a warm person. They will also require structural modifications if they are to be further compartmentalized into cells.

"Or it may be," he went on, "that you intend the number of selectees to be small and their periods in solitude short, so that they can be rotated through the available accommodation. Since we have a year before we all go cold and the first watch-keeping officer takes over—"

"Please, Healer," said the monsignor gently, "ask your questions without making unwarranted assumptions, or trying to answer them for yourself. The selectees will be housed in the colonist modules as you have said, but there will be no structural modifications. They will be informed of the limits of their confinement, and very generous limits they will be, and trusted not to exceed them. A combination of strenuous exercise and insulated clothing will keep them warm, particularly before going to sleep. Perhaps this will make them feel more appreciative of the warmth and comfort provided when they take their turn on watch.

"Other matters raised by your question I shall be dealing with in a few moments," he added. "You have another question?"

He had, but Nolan wished that he had been given time to think about that first, partial answer before asking others. Hesitantly, he said, "The reason for the solitary two-year watches were explained to us during basic training, as was the thinking behind the tests designed to ensure that we, as individuals, could be emotionally stable if not happy for extended periods with our own company. Many, many times have we been told to prepare ourselves for these watches, but I wonder if we have thought deeply enough about what the results might be to the officer concerned. I have thought about it, but to be honest I remain uncertain of the cumulative effect of—"

Monsignor O'Riordan was holding up a hand. He said, "Your honesty does you credit, my son. But now it seems that you are trying to open a debate, Healer, rather than ask a question. Please make your point quickly."

Nolan took a deep breath, and tried to keep the irritation he felt from affecting his voice as he said, "Quickly, then. The two-year watches will be separated by close on two centuries of cold sleep. But the officer concerned will be aware of no such separation. Apart from the moments prior to cooling and following his warming, and the insertions that might have been made in the log of the watch, no time will have passed for him.

"His solitary watch will last, not for two years, but six."

Everyone was watching him, including the captain. The monsignor smiled and said, "What is the question, Healer? Or perhaps you have an answer?"

This time Nolan shook his head without trying to hide his irritation. "No. Perhaps I am restating and explaining the question because I consider it important that we know exactly what to expect and do not try to fool ourselves. An answer might be to waken several officers between watches, so that the officers going on and coming off watch will have a short period, a few days or weeks depending on the emotional state of the watch-keeping officer concerned, of conversation and encouragement of friends to look forward to, or back on. Another answer might be to have two or more watch-keepers warm at the same time, but with overlapping watches.

"The disadvantages," Nolan went on, "are that both suggestions would be costly in crew biological time. We would all be much older when we arrived in the target system. With the second one there would be the risk of the lengthy period together causing friction between the shared watch-keepers, it being a truism that a person is much more likely to fight with others than with himself. So the solitary-watch-keeper idea is probably best and provided the officer is fully prepared for . . ."

O'Riordan was raising his hand again. He said, "The problem could not have been more concisely stated had I done so myself. And it is reassuring to know that the project's crew philosophy has the guarded approval of our junior Healer. But now I would like to continue."

He turned to face the assembled officers again, and said firmly, "The original project plan, a plan which must have been designed for public consumption rather than for practical use, called for the entire crew to remain warm for the period of one year from leaving Earth orbit, during which *Aisling Gheal* would be accelerated to interstellar cruising velocity, the ship's structure and systems tested, and the final course corrections made. At the end of that year the officers would throw a great big self-congratulatory ceilidh for themselves, followed by the mass cooling of all crewmembers with the exception of the officer of the watch. Without my having to point out its obvious flaws, you must already have realized that the original plan is criminally wasteful of our biological time, our internal power, and our consumables, all of which should and must be conserved for use in any contingency that may arise at the end of the voyage. As well, the waking presence of the entire ship's crew, the majority of whom will have little to do except watch a few of their fellow officers at work while at the same time maintaining strict silence, places an unacceptable strain on everyone concerned. The saying about Satan and idle hands is particularly apt in this situation."

The smile had gone from his face again and the voice was scornful as he went on. "So it should come as no surprise to you when I say that there will be no precooling celebrations of any kind, just as there will be no listening to repetitious and unnecessary farewells from Earth, for such things are only for the juvenile and emotionally insecure, of which, I am sure, there are none among you. We are fortunate in having the solid pillar of our Faith to support us, and the glorious mission of spreading mankind and the rich culture and traditions of Hibernia and that same Faith to a fresh, new, and untainted world. We no longer have need of the weak and temporary crutches that are of Earth and the past.

"For us of *Aisling Gheal*, the Bright Vision, there is only the future."

The cardinal-captain's features remained impassive and unreadable, Nolan saw, and Dervla's lips pressed tightly together in what could have been disapproval or the effort of remaining silent. The other officers had their eyes on O'Riordan, and with few exceptions those eyes were shining with a light that made Nolan feel a sudden unease.

They had the look of men being harangued before battle, except that these were warriors who had no need of it, because they were already fanatically loyal and devoted to their cause. He reminded himself that they were priests, followers of the Christus, preachers of a faith that held gentleness, forgiveness, and kindness to be important above all else, and that they could inflict no hurt on anyone. But his unease remained.

Perhaps it was O'Riordan himself who worried him. The monsignor was said to possess one of the finest theological minds in the Empire and to be a skilled debater in his subject, but none had ever accused him of being a fanatic or a bigot. Yet Nolan had heard him tell the crew that their mission was to spread the traditions of Hibernia, not even the Hibernian Empire, and their faith to the New World. It might be that in the excitement of the moment his language had been less precise than was usual or, with Earth left behind them forever, he might no longer consider his Earthly reputation of importance. But among the colonists there were men and woman of Westland, of Cathay, Nippon, and many other nations who subscribed to different faiths and traditions and with beliefs that were equally hard-held, and who would resist conversion. This was not the way that the saintly but unsainted Brendan would have wanted this voyage to go.

His feeling was not one of unease, Nolan thought as O'Riordan began speaking again, but the beginnings of dread.

The monsignor was saying, "All crew-members whose specialties are not required for this stage of the flight, all of the lander pilots and their technical support, for example, as well as presently redundant officers in all specialties, are to be cooled with the minimum of delay. This will be done, with certain exceptions, within a matter of a few months rather than a year. The exceptions will include two communications officers, and the minimum number of astrogators and engineers needed for final course corrections and to monitor the performance of the main drive. And, of course, there will be the few I consider to be in need of additional psychological preparation for watch-keeping.

"This drastic reduction in manning levels will mean longer duty for those left warm," he continued. "Sixteen hours on duty and eight off, or perhaps eighteen on and six off. But after all, there will be nothing else for these officers to do, for they will speak only when their duties require it and remain silent and rest at all other times. The duty crew will work hard knowing that the majority of their fellow officers are in cold sleep, and that the sooner we can all go cold the shorter the voyage will seem. We will still be in farspeaker range of Earth and will doubtless receive many messages, but, apart from acknowledging them and reporting that all is well with us, we will not waste time on unnecessary dialogue. Do you fully understand all that I'm saying to you?

"We are no longer of Earth."

There were nods and murmurings of assent from all over the lander deck, and the beginnings of a cheer which O'Riordan silenced with a gently raised hand in a gesture that was almost a benediction. The gentleness had returned to his voice as he said,

"Of course you understand me. But now I must ask the heads of department to consider how best these major reductions in manning levels may be achieved, and submit to me as soon as possible the names of those to be cooled. When you begin the process you will be surprised at how many of our officers can be done without.

"Temporarily, I hasten to add," he said, and laughed gently. "For example, with a drastically reduced crew we might consider the necessity for two Healers remaining warm."

He paused for a moment, and it was plain that he was waiting for some kind of reaction from the senior Healer. Dervla was at the very top of her profession, deservedly proud of her position and accomplishments, and would not take kindly to a mere Healer of the Mind telling her what she should do. Nolan himself was expecting something in the nature of a verbal explosion, and was pleased for her when it did not come. Instead she spoke quietly, but in a voice so chill that it might have come, had such a thing been possible, from the mouth of a cold sleeper.

"I disagree, Monsignor," she said. "If the ship is to be operated by a skeleton crew, working extended watches with minimum rest between, it is probable that the number of accidents and injuries would increase, and the presence of two Healers would be an advantage."

The monsignor smiled gently at her and said, "I shall, of course, give due consideration to the professional advice of one who was once Healer to the High-Queen. Thank you. Your Eminence, is there more that you would say to us?"

O'Riordan had left little for the captain to say, and while he was saying it and dismissing the men, Nolan was too busy watching Dervla to pay much attention to him. Her face was dark now, with anger and embarrassment, but she did not speak until Monsignor O'Riordan had followed the captain from the lander dock and they were alone.

"I did not need such a public reminder," she said angrily, "that my power and prestige and the influence I had at Court, that I earned after many years of study and self-discipline and that is a professional achievement of which I am justifiably proud, has been left behind on Earth. I know this to be so without his reminders. And why is he in such a hurry to cool everyone? Surely we could talk among ourselves a little longer, about our past lives as well as our future hopes, without endangering the project. And cutting us off from farspeaker contact with Earth, was that really necessary? He gives reasons, but are there other reasons that he does not give?"

Nolan did not reply. He was remembering Cathay and the walk to the College of Lensmakers and Father Quinn telling him, very seriously, that in spite of his feelings about Cathay-Nippon history and his technical qualifications, he was first and forever a priest. Nolan was beginning to understand what those words had meant.

''If you have decided to impose the monsignor's vow of silence on yourself,'' Dervla raged at him suddenly, ''shake your bloody head or something!''

Nolan shook his head. ''I'm sorry, my mind was elsewhere for the moment. I have the feeling, from listening to Maeve's farewell message, that something is happening. But I don't know why it was necessary to keep it from us, or if there is anything else that is being kept from us. And with the monsignor imposing his silence on everyone, I don't know how we can ever find out.''

They began their slow, sliding walk back to the medical department. Dervla's face had returned to its normal color and she seemed less angry, but she did not speak. Perhaps there was something more than O'Riordan's bad manners worrying her.

Nolan said, ''Don't worry too much about being prematurely cooled. I am certain to be one of the officers the monsignor casts into solitary confinement, so they will need to keep you warm until after my release.''

''Warm,'' she said with a bitter edge to her voice, ''and silent. An oozing pox on him. Why must he forbid normal social conversation? His reasons aren't strong enough. At least talking to you was better than nothing.''

''You are too kind, Healer Dervla,'' said Nolan.

She laughed suddenly and added, ''A lot better.''

Chapter 19

DURING the first few moments of his solitary confinement Nolan was sure that the sheer heat of his anger would be more than enough to keep him warm for as long as his sentence should last, especially since it caused him to work against the exercise harness with a totally unnecessary expenditure of energy to relieve his feelings. But gradually his anger toward the monsignor cooled, and the perspiration covering his body began to feel even colder in spite of the heavy, insulated coveralls.

It was colder in the livestock and seed storage module than in any other air-filled section of the ship, because there it was whole compartments with their contents rather than individual caskets that were refrigerated, and the icy metal deck and wall surfaces sucked away his body heat whenever he touched one of them for more than a few moments.

Nolan could not be precise about periods of time because, at O'Riordan's suggestion, his watch had been left with his other personal possessions in the medical department. The monsignor had insisted that his period of enforced solitude, the duration of which had yet to be determined, would seem very much longer if he was able to measure and fret himself needlessly over the slow passage of the hours and the days. Instead he was urged to strive first for inner composure and acceptance of his solitude by considering it as a simple rehearsal for the watch-keeping duty to come, while at the same time exercising his body with the restraining harness and his mind with the recollection in detail of everything he had been taught and would eventually teach. How quickly the time passed, the monsignor had told him with one of his gentle, infuriating smiles, would depend on how constructively or otherwise he used the brain that the God he professed not to believe in had given him.

The only advantage of not being able to measure the passage of time was that he did not feel obliged to wash himself or his undergarment either regularly or frequently, but only when the smell coming from both of them became obtrusive. The process was performed as quickly as possible in one of the crew bathing cabinets that had been moved aft for his use. The unit's heating system had been disconnected for three reasons, O'Riordan had told him genially: so that he would not be tempted to spend too much time in the comfort of the warm water, or risk an ague through returning to his normal cool environment with opened pores, and, on the positive side, it was well known that cold baths improved the character.

The bathing was accomplished with a sponge, a hard bar of soap which smelled even more strongly, albeit in a different way, than did he himself, and a breathing mask to keep him from drowning in the shapeless, ever-changing masses and streamers of icy water that crawled and slapped weightlessly over his body. Washing the undergarment took longer, and by the time the cabinet had been pumped dry and the icy gale that was designed to remove the surplus moisture from his body had died away, the cold, clean spare garment, coveralls, and exercise harness felt sinfully warm and comfortable by comparison. He would then anchor his feet to the deck and whirl the newly washed garment around his head or slap it against a convenient bulkhead to rid it of any remaining traces of dampness—on the first occasion, he had omitted this important step and found ice crystals in his clean undergarment—until it was dry and his teeth had stopped chattering.

The intervals between periods of continuous thrust became shorter and fewer. Nolan wondered why His Eminence was so impatient to reach interstellar cruise velocity, and whether he was being foolhardy or simply displaying his confidence in a propulsion system that had now been operationally tested to his complete satisfaction. Knowing the scientific reputation of the cardinal-captain, Nolan decided that it must be the latter, and felt reassured.

In this, the most afterly inhabited module of the ship, the sounds made by the detonations on the blast shield were transmitted through the fabric of the vessel as a quiet metallic pounding that continued for many hours or days at a time. When the periods of thrust and sleep overlapped, Nolan sandwiched himself between the two heavily padded layers of his weightless hammock and wrapped his cowl tightly around his ears until hunger or the slow seepage of cold into his warm cocoon drove him to eat or exercise.

Only once did the gentle acceleration cause serious trouble, and that was when he had been searching the barnlike interior of a storage compartment for anything resembling a direct vision panel. What he found, centered on the vast outer wall more than fifty yards above deck level, was a flat rectangular projection to which someone had taped an animal loading-sequence and location chart. The cold had affected the adhesive so that when he touched the corner of the sheet while checking his weightless drift against the wall, the chart rolled itself up suddenly to reveal a transparent panel. Through it he could make out the dim outlines of the module's animal resuscitation and transfer lock, and an outer seal containing another small direct vision port.

He was able to see outside the ship.

But his external view was something less than panoramic. The tiny window showed only a length of lander docking rail, and above this short and dimly lit strip of metal horizon a few stars were shining.

Entering the chamber and moving closer to the port would give him a much better view, naturally, but the operation of the lock mechanism would show on the control deck's instruments and someone, perhaps even the monsignor, would come aft to investigate.

Apart from astrogation officers during the performance of their duties, everyone had been ordered not to look outside the ship. Nolan still considered it to be a petty and unreasonable order of questionable psychological value and, even if he had thought otherwise, looking at that tiny circle of sky would be at most a venial offense. Besides, being alone and an unbeliever, he was under no moral obligation to confess his secret transgressions to O'Riordan or anyone else.

Nolan was floating weightless and at right angles to the panel, with his head thrown back while he rotated himself slowly about his vertical axis, in an attempt to find a viewpoint that would make the few stars he could see resemble part of a known constellation, when thrust was applied and he began to drift slowly toward the deck. He began to laugh silently, then stopped because he was no longer falling so slowly. There was nothing on the smooth expanse of wall that he could use to check his fall, and he was still trying vainly to twist himself around so as to land catlike on hands and knees when the deck came up and hit the back of his head.

He was fortunate in that the folds of the cowl, which he had pulled back almost to the nape of his neck while he had been looking through the viewport, were thick enough to prevent him from cracking his skull. As it was, he lost the ability to see and think for a time, and when consciousness returned slowly it was with the feeling that he was still in a particularly strange and unpleasant dream, and for a few moments he had difficulty remembering where he was.

There was a pounding inside his skull that seemed to be much louder than the sounds that were coming from the blast shield, and he felt as though he were being pressed gently against a block of ice while he looked up through the strands of a gigantic and overfilled spider's web. The bodies of the victims were encircled by padded body belts and leg cuffs from which radiated the thin, immensely strong strands of rope anchoring them to attachment points all over the deck, walls, and the distant ceiling. The cables began to vibrate slowly as thrust was canceled and the icy pressure on his back eased, and the paired bodies of the horses and cattle, the sheep and pigs and donkeys, and the smaller domesticated animals began bobbing and twisting as if to the music of a dance that only he could hear. One of them seemed to be watching him with wide-open, frozen eyes. He shivered with more than the cold as he remembered that these were not the paralyzed victims of some gargantuan spider but the cold sleeping occupants of an interstellar ark.

He rolled awkwardly onto his hands and knees and, gripping a nearby cable to steady himself, placed his boot magnets against the deck. For a moment he thought the effort would cause his head to explode, but the pain diminished quickly to a steady, throbbing ache as he slowly retraced his steps to the hammock.

For a long time he lay shivering and nursing his throbbing head or pitting muscle against muscle in an attempt to bring some warmth back to his body. It was possible that he had been unconscious for only a few minutes, which meant that his concussion would not be as serious as it felt. In fact, the level of discomfort had lessened: he was beginning to feel warm and almost comfortable and ready for sleep.

But casualties who had suffered head injuries severe enough to result in unconsciousness, however temporary, were advised against sleeping too soon after receiving them lest they become comatose. Within arm's reach of his hammock there was a far-speaker set which was for use only in emergencies. He knew that his proper course of action would be to report his injury to Control One, who would immediately inform Healer Dervla, who would want to examine him. His report would also have to include the details of where and what he had been doing when the accident occurred. Thinking about Dervla's caustic verbal reaction to his probably insignificant bump on the head was bad enough, but submitting himself to the more gentle, chiding lecture from the monsignor on the necessity for obeying orders, even one as tiresome and seemingly unimportant as not looking out windows, would be much worse.

Nolan was still trying to resolve the problem when he wakened an unguessable time later, feeling rested, refreshed, and very much better.

A long time passed. Even for one who had lost all sense of duration and for whom minutes could sometimes feel like hours, he still knew that a long time had passed. He had been careful not to overeat, but his store of food had been replenished many times while he slept so that his period of solitude and silence would remain unbroken. He considered flouting another regulation by allowing his hair to grow, and in effect estimating the length of elapsed time by the length of his beard. He might even have continued to obey the rules concerning hygiene and general neatness of person by keeping a record of the number of times he needed to shave. However, much as Nolan disliked agreeing with any of the monsignor's suggestions, he decided that he would be happier not knowing how long his stay here would last.

Many, many times he slept, wakened, and performed the routines necessary to maintain his body in optimum physical condition and to exercise his mind. But, strangely, the exercising of his mind and memory became the most important and time-consuming activity, which continued even when he was undergoing the periodic torture of a bath.

In pre-Christian times any Druid hoping to achieve the higher adept levels was tested by immersion in the waters of a cold mountain spring while he recited, without the alteration or omission of the slightest phrase or detail, an epic poem of bloody battle and individual exploits that took many hours to complete. Or he recounted the histories and geneology of the principal tuaths and clans of Hibernia, Cymri, and Caledonia, or the names and positions and times of rising and setting of the stars and planets that were needed for planting and harvesting crops and to help mariners establish their positions while sailing beyond sight of land. The persons of these senior Druids were held to be inviolate, so that they could travel freely without let or hindrance, and certain of the more cynical historians suggested that the fruits of such a savagely effective memory training enabled them, should the need arise and the reward be sufficiently generous, to provide timely and accurate intelligence regarding the numbers and dispositions of an opponent's army.

It was during and after one of his cold baths that Nolan liked to recall incidents that were pleasantly warm as well as historically significant, in preparation for that future time when he would be teaching the colonists' children, as well as to help him ignore the present cold. He did not speak the material aloud, because the farspeaker could be switched on from Control, and he had been told that talking to himself would also be considered an infringement of the rule of silence.

The warmest and most pleasant episode was the epoch-making—although no one considered it of any significance at the time—visit of Aidan to Alexandria in the second century before the birth of the Christus. Aidan the Enlightened, or Aidan the Accursed, depending on which side one had chosen in the War of the Heroes that was to follow, was a much-traveled scholar and philosopher with a lively mind who did not scorn at turning a profit from the knowledge he might acquire.

In Egypt at that time it was the custom for the Pharaoh to provide important visitors—and Aidan had been neither reticent nor completely factual while describing his own importance—with accommodation, servants, and a pension suited to their station, together with invitations to the Court functions and entertainments.

On these occasions the usual diplomatic games would be played, with the visitor being wined and dined in congenial company and encouraged to tell of his homeland and its High-King, the lands and cities he had visited and the dress, customs, and achievements of the people he had met during his long and no doubt epic journey to the Court of the Seventh Pharaoh. His lightest word would be examined for content of a commercial or military nature likely to be of use to the merchant princes and the generals who were present, while at the same time the visitor would be trying to extract the same kind of information from his hosts. In this game neither the visitor nor his hosts were expected to tell the complete truth, but due allowance was made for the obvious fabrications and misdirections, just as a high level of exaggeration in the related exploits was accepted for no other reason than that it made the tales more entertaining.

As a visitor Aidan was popular as a teller of tales but disappointing as a source of commercial and military intelligence. Whenever he had imbibed too freely of the dark and deceptively strong wines of Egypt, which was nearly every evening, he would relate shocking and highly scandalous gossip concerning the unrecorded activities of his High-King and other members of the Court at Tara—tales of a kind which, had they been told about the family and friends or the person of their God-King and Pharaoh, would have cost the teller his head.

But from Aidan they never seemed to learn anything useful, anything that was not already known, because he did not know or even display other than the polite curiosity that was required by good manners about matters which they considered all-important. And the reason given for this large area of ignorance in an otherwise intelligent, urbane, and cultured personage was that Aiden professed to be a scholar and philosopher, a seeker after knowledge for its own sake, who had no interest in the coarser pursuits of martial conquest and the acquisition of wealth. Although there were several ladies of the Court who would have been pleased to broaden his education, he seemed to have only three abiding interests: the sampling to excess of the local wines, consorting with others of a similar turn of mind to himself, and browsing in the greatest library in the known world, where he was most likely to find these intelligent but impractical people.

Aidan was such a simple, friendly, outgoing man that not one of the jaded and cynical sophisticates of the Court ever suspected that he was better at playing their games than they were themselves.

More than any of the other personages that he met in Alexandria, Aidan favored the company of a philosopher and scientist and writer of many learned works on mathematics and physics, whose name was Hero. There had been many meetings and philosophical debates and much scholarly bragging between these two, but only at the one that was destined to have such far-reaching effects on subsequent Hibernian history had the circumstances and conversation between the two been remembered and recorded for posterity.

On that particular occasion they had still been suffering from their different excesses of the previous evening so that, instead of exercising their minds by conversing on the rarefied subjects of philosophy and mathematics, Hero sought to rest his aching head with the less mentally demanding work of demonstrating and discussing the operating principles of his aeolipile.

It was a strange device that consisted of an enclosed three-legged kettle with two copper pipes projecting from the top. The pipes were bent inward at right angles to penetrate and support a small copper globe so that it was free to rotate horizontally. Protruding from two diametrically opposed points along the globe's vertical axis were two shorter and finer pieces of pipe, which were also bent at right angles so that the open ends faced in opposite directions.

When one of the slaves kindled a fire under the kettle, the water it contained boiled and the steam passed upward through the two supporting pipes and into the globe, where it found its way out through the small angled spigots.

For a short time the aeolipile did nothing but hiss and puff tiny clouds of steam until, slowly at first, the globe began to rotate in the direction opposite to the strengthening jets of steam coming from the spigots. Within a few moments the globe was spinning rapidly and the whole device was obscured by a hot, wet, self-generated fog. It continued to spin so until the water inside the kettle had boiled away.

Aidan had been greatly impressed by the demonstration but, embarrassed by the praise, Hero had dismissed his device as being of no importance.

It represented nothing more than a very simple experiment designed to show that heat could be converted into rotary motion, Hero said, insisting that the thing had no uses whatsoever other than as an interesting toy for the Pharaoh—a toy that his God-King had viewed once and, doubtless because of the smoke and steam and the noise like the hissing of angry serpents it produced, then seemingly forgotten. Aidan continued praising Hero's ingenuity, and suggested ways that the principles it embodied could be put to use. But Hero had dismissed these suggestions, saying that his slaves could perform the work much more efficiently, cheaply, and without unpleasantly affecting the home environment, and he would much prefer to have Aidan's views on some recently uncovered scrolls reputed to have once been in the private collection of the First Ptolemy.

Aidan returned with Hero to the library, but not before he had obtained permission to make a sketch of the aeolipile device in the hope, he explained, that his own High-King would find it an amusing toy.

And thus it was that Aidan the Enlightened, or the Accursed, brought to Hibernia the knowledge of a device that embodied the first, simple principles of steam-generated power, jet propulsion, and the beginnings of a technology that was to lead ultimately to the starship *Aisling Gheal*.

Nolan shivered as the imagined hot, dry air and sinfully comfortable life at the Pharaoh's Court faded from his mind. *It is only a hero*, he said silently to himself, as he often did when the sheer size and complexity of the ship began to trouble him, *just an overgrown and outrageously expensive hero . . .*

But he knew that the shiver of awe that he felt would not respond to bodily warming, no matter how hard he exercised.

He became aware of a dark figure watching him from the other end of the corridor that had become a frigid, narrow home to him. It moved closer and passed below a lighting strip and he saw that it was Dervla. Only the eyes were visible behind the partially open cowl, but he knew that it was the senior Healer because she alone of all the crew was entitled to wear coveralls and a cowl of earthen brown. He stopped exercising and turned to face her.

Immediately she opened her cowl and raised a finger quickly to her lips, then gestured for him to resume his exercises.

She continued to watch him for a few moments, then she smiled, raised a hand in farewell, and was gone. The silence and the solitude to which Nolan thought he had grown accustomed became suddenly more intense. He was still trying to think of a reason for Dervla's brief and silent visit when he retired to his hammock.

She had directed him to be silent and to continue exercising, and had closely observed the process, he recalled, so that she could be in no doubt that he was physically fit and mentally in control. Had it been otherwise, his movements would have been restricted and he would have started babbling at her as soon as she appeared. And she had not spoken to him, so the purpose could not have been a professional consultation too sensitive to be entrusted to the farspeaker or a passing on of instructions.

It was not that they had gossiped or talked continually at every meeting, far from it. And at the approach of the monsignor or another officer they had quickly changed the topic of conversation to some aspect of the postlanding medical problems. But they knew that they were making more verbal noise than the rest of the crew put together, and that O'Riordan was displeased with them. She had apologized to him on several occasions, although with Dervla it was often difficult to tell an apology from a criticism, by saying that if she as his superior had not insisted on talking to him, he would not have felt obliged to talk back and thereby sentence himself to the monsignor's equivalent of Limbo. But a stay in Limbo, no matter how long it might be, was not supposed to last forever.

The fusion drive had been silent since Dervla's visit. The time passed slowly and silently, and Nolan passed the time with silent recollections of the history lessons he would someday give, of his medical and spasaire training, of the Imperial reception and the people he had come to know since then. There was the Ionadacht Ciaran, the Princess Ulechitzl, Chief Wanachtee and his squaw, Golden Rain, who, like the young Heir Apparent of Cathay, had been brought on board secretly, and all of whom had influenced him in various ways into promising them his personal protection until they reached the New World.

His protection was a commodity that they had seemed to value much more highly than he did himself.

And he recalled those who were not in the ship with him: the Seventh Maeve; the incredibly frail but all-powerful Silver Elk; and Hseng Hwa, whose rank and reasons for approaching Nolan were still a mystery to him even though his memory had been sharpened by the solitude and complete silence to such a keen edge that he could clearly recall every word that had been spoken, as well as the smallest gesture and change of expression that had accompanied them.

But recently the silence had become less than complete.

The sounds were faint and distant, like an intermittent metallic whisper composed of tappings and scratchings, with long periods of silence between, as if the ship had become infested with some spacegoing species of metal-hungry rodent. So faint were the sounds that whenever he was exercising, the soft abrasion of his cowl against hair and chin was even louder.

At first he decided that it was due simply to the cold, that the ship had by this time traveled far enough from the sun for the individual components of the vast structure to contract, and complain, as they sought for a lower-temperature equilibrium. Such microscopic contractions would have been allowed for in the design and were nothing he should worry about, but that explanation did not entirely satisfy him. If the sounds had been due solely to a gradual loss of heat, they should have been continuous. Instead, they stopped and started with, so far as he could judge without his watch, regular and much shorter periods of complete silence separating them. He wondered if the sounds were man-made, by members of the crew who were working steadily on some task with pauses for meals and changes of shift.

His curiosity about those half-heard sounds grew until he could think of little else. In the hope of hearing more clearly and perhaps identifying them, he tried pulling back the cowl and pressing his ear tightly against the corridor wall.

The sounds being conducted through the intervening structure of the ship were slightly clearer but no less confusing, and the metal surface of the corridor wall was so cold that it required a mighty effort of will to keep his ear in contact with it. After a very few moments of listening he firmly replaced his warm cowl and began giving himself some good advice and insisting that he take it.

His earlier fall in the storage compartment had been an accident, and he had been lucky to escape with a mild concussion. But the medical results of this foolishness, a potentially serious ear condition caused by localized hypothermia, would be entirely his own stupid fault. Was it worth risking partial deafness just to have his curiosity increased rather than satisfied?

Most decidedly it was not.

More time passed. He tried to exercise his mind with subjects other than the faint noises reaching him from a distant part of the ship, and finally he succeeded—until the sounds stopped and his curiosity regarding what they could have been returned to plague him anew.

But the deeper silence lasted for only three of his waking periods, and he was just awakening to a fourth by the gentle pressure of continuous thrust and the loud and utterly strange sound of a voice coming from his farspeaker.

"Healer Nolan, report to the control deck at once," it said briskly, then a moment later, "Please respond, Healer Nolan. You have permission to speak."

I have almost forgotten how, Nolan thought. He cleared his throat and said, "Nolan. Is there a medical emergency, and can you give me the details, please?"

"There is no emergency, Healer," the voice replied. "Leave your hammock and farspeaker where they are for the time being. The monsignor would like to see you in Control One without delay."

"Coming," said Nolan.

An urgent summons like this could mean anything, and he did not know what surprise was in store for him other than that if it came from the monsignor it would most likely be an unpleasant one. Surprisingly, he was completely wrong.

"I'm very pleased to see you looking so well, my son," said the monsignor, smiling as he looked up from the internal farspeaker panel that he was sharing with Father Quinn, and pointing toward the position normally occupied by the captain. "I'm sorry, but I must be impolite and ignore you for a few moments. Please take the seat of the mighty; His Eminence has gone cold and is not likely to object. Besides, you haven't been able to see the stars for a long time, so you should enjoy the view."

That was not strictly true, but Nolan had the feeling that this was not the time to tell the monsignor he was wrong. He said, "Thank you, sir."

Nolan was surprised to see that the three of them had the darkened control deck to themselves. The conversations on the farspeaker were too muted for him to hear every word, but that did not matter because it was enough that there were two other people nearby and that they were talking together or to other officers scattered about the ship. The realization that he was no longer alone caused the starfield framed in the forward viewpanel to mist over, and the image of the Sun in the stern viewscreen to become a tiny incandescent blur. He blinked his eyes rapidly, and when he could see clearly again, O'Riordan and Father Quinn had unstrapped and were standing face to face, their boot magnets scraping quietly against the deck.

The monsignor raised his right hand in benediction, and while the other priest bowed his head, he said, "May the good God that we all love and serve, and who watches over all of us, guard and cherish you in your long sleep, Father."

The other priest left without speaking and the monsignor turned to face Nolan. He stared down at him for a long moment, then laughed softly.

"We have been listening on your farspeaker at irregular intervals, my son," he said gently, "and we find you guilty of a minor infringement of the rule of silence. Do you know that your snoring is a truly diabolical sound that shreds the nerves of anyone unfortunate enough to be listening to it? However, since the offense was unintended, nothing more will be said of it. Regrettably, a few of our officers, lander pilots, and nonclerics, of course, offended more grievously and their character defects will ensure their absence from the watch-keeping roster. But in truth you, my son, have passed the tests of silence and solitude in quite exemplary fashion, and I am impressed with the high degree of emotional stability and self-control that you have displayed over the past fourteen weeks.

"Especially during the visit Dervla made to you," he went on. "She insisted on seeing that you were physically and mentally fit for duty before she would agree to be cooled. I was sure that you would not be able to stop yourself from saying something, if only a few words of greeting, and it was gratifying to be proved wrong. Altogether your behavior was such that I do not foresee any serious problems arising for you in the years to come. But did you encounter any difficulties that were not apparent to us, or incidents which might be of interest to me as a psychologist? Any nightmares, any continuing pathological aversion to leaving the warmth of your hammock, any visual or aural hallucinations? It would severely undermine my faith if our benighted unbeliever turned out to be a moral superman."

He paused for a moment, then added gently, "You are no longer bound by the rule of silence, Healer Nolan. That particular exercise in self-control is no longer necessary in your case."

"Thank you, Monsignor O'Riordan," Nolan said.

He was surprised and greatly pleased by such a compliment from a renowned Healer of the Mind and a senior officer. He realized then that it was the first time he had called the monsignor anything other than "sir," but if the little priest noticed it he gave no sign. But an inner voice was warning him to be careful, reminding him that a man disarmed, whether by flattery or force, was not in a position of strength.

This was not the time to mention his accident in the livestock compartment, or his restricted view of the stars, or the strange, faint noises he had heard.

"There were no nightmares or dreams that I was able to recall on waking," he said in his clinical, Healer's voice. "There was no way of measuring the passage of time, but I spent most of it in the hammock because that was the most comfortable place to be, especially after food or exercise when the body temperature was elevated. I had waking dreams of being in tropical countries, or other hot places, or nice, warm wards in Houses of Sorrow, and when I recalled the history lessons I am to teach, my favorite was the meeting of Aidan and Hero in Alexandria. But at all times I knew that I was alone.

"There were no hallucinations," he went on. "I heard nothing but the noises from the blast shield and the sound of my own breathing, and saw no other person until the visit of Healer Dervla. I'm surprised she cooled herself, leaving the crew without a Healer in attendance, before my return."

"The final course correction has been made," said the monsignor, "and there are very few officers left warm. Far too few to warrant the continued wastage of the biological time of a medical authority of the eminence of Healer Dervla. Had a serious accident occurred, we would have called on you for help. But now the officers remaining warm grow fewer with every hour that passes, and we no longer have need of a Healer. That is the reason why—''

"You would like me to go cold?'' said Nolan, trying hard to keep the disappointment he felt from showing in his voice. He had been looking forward to having people about him again, and to talking medicine, the only subject she seemed able to discuss comfortably, with Dervla. This time his omission of the other's title was deliberate as he went on, "But I'm still curious to know what has been happening in my absence. Is there time to tell me before I go cold?''

"There is ample time,'' said the monsignor, "for me to summarize.''

O'Riordan looked at him for a long moment, then he laughed and said gently, "The ship is on course for the target star. Acceleration will be maintained until interstellar cruising velocity has been reached, when the fusion drive will be closed down automatically and the empty deuterium tanks jettisoned. Earth and the Empire were informed of this before farspeaker contact was severed. There is nothing they can say to us now that can make any difference to what is to happen. Because of the early coolings, some changes in the standing orders for the officers of the watch, and in the watch-keeping roster itself, have become necessary.

"It has been decided,'' he went on quietly, but in a voice that was much too firm to be described as gentle, "to forbid all movement on the outer hull to watch-keepers, who may grow bored with the interior of the crew module and wish for a change of scenery. As a Healer you will appreciate the necessity for this order?''

Nolan dipped his head slightly in agreement, and the monsignor went on. "Spacesuits will still be available for emergencies, but the storage racks have been fitted with timers which, when read in conjunction with the watch-keeping roster, will enable the user to be identified. The officer who contravenes this order and draws a spacesuit without a very good operational reason for doing so will, at the end of the voyage, be severely disciplined. You will remember that, Healer?''

"Yes, sir.''

"The other change is not an order,'' the monsignor went on, "for the simple reason that there is no way of enforcing it or detecting an infringement without filling the ship with internal sensors and giving the impression, which would be psychologically undesirable, that we do not trust some of our own officers. Instead, we are strongly advising our watch-keepers to remain within the control and crew modules at all times. They will find it much more comfortable that way because we have now decided to withdraw lighting as well as heating from the aft connecting corridors, and will not restore them until we arrive in the target system."

"As well," he continued, "the ship has been well built, but as the years pass there will be a gradual loss of atmosphere from the colonists' modules. This will not affect the sleepers in their sealed caskets, but it would seriously inconvenience anyone walking among them without a spacesuit. Module pressure will only be restored prior to boarding the landers."

There would certainly be more comfort for the watch-keepers in the heated and well-lit control and crew modules, Nolan thought, and the idea of allowing the remaining warmth of the aft modules to dissipate into space was a good one since, in the event of a colonist casket losing power and one of the cold sleepers going into a premature and lethal thaw, the already-low ambient temperature might allow time for the malfunction to be corrected before tissue damage became irreversible. But plunging more than nine-tenths of the ship into centuries of darkness, to Nolan's mind, was most decidedly not a good idea.

The heat from the lighting fixtures was negligible, as was the power drain on the ship's reactor. And without adequate lighting it would be next to impossible to check on the condition of individual colonists . . .

"That is all that there is a need to tell you, Healer," the monsignor went on before Nolan could voice his objections, "except that in one very important respect you have been more fortunate than the rest of us. You have already undergone a lengthy period of solitude and silence, and have adapted to it very well. For that reason it would be a great unkindness to continue talking to you, since it would simply reaccustom you to the companionship and conversation of another person, myself. As yet you have not grasped what I have been trying to tell you, so I shall make it short and very simple. I am about to go cold, the last of your fellow officers to do so. But do not be concerned because I have every confidence in you."

Once again the monsignor smiled, then in a quiet and very formal voice he said, "Healer Nolan, you will stand the first watch."

Chapter 20

NOLAN did not believe that he could ever grow tired of the splendor that stretched to infinity all around him, or of the view aft which showed the Sun, small but still too bright to be considered as one of the stars. From the ship's position far below the plane of the ecliptic he should have had a plain view of the Solar System, but the stern camera was unable to resolve any of the minor planets, so that he could see neither the world they had come from nor the one that was their destination. But the external inspection cameras showing the awesome structures and the dizzying perspectives of the ship itself brought him pictures that were a constant reminder of where he was and what he was doing there, and the steadily increasing velocity and distance figures on the watch-keeper's panel gave a more accurate if less spectacular corroboration.

On the three hundred and eighty-second day of his watch the empty deuterium reservoirs were discarded and, half an hour later when they had fallen too far astern for there to be any possibility of a future collision, the fusion engine shut down. At that precise instant—the figure was increasing with every second that passed—the ship had traveled more than 305,000 million miles from Earth and was coasting away from the Solar System at a velocity of one-tenth lightspeed.

Every day after waking he would watch the myriad tiny and incredibly distant nuclear furnaces that were moving slowly and silently past the ship. It might be that decades would pass, perhaps centuries, before their motion would be perceptible to human eyes, but the silent stars were going by because the ship had begun its long voyage between them.

He told himself over and over again that he would never grow tired of that magnificent scenery, but even the sense of wonder might become dulled by too much stimulation, and he was becoming afraid that if he did not turn his mental eye inward he would ultimately weary of the sight of creation itself.

Because there was no Monsignor O'Riordan to tell him what he should or should not do, he fell into a routine of doing exactly what the other would have told him to do—a routine that required a major effort of will to change because it comprised a series of habits that were entirely laudable and were in danger of making of him a healthy automaton of flesh and blood. He had to try very hard to keep his mind flexible, at least, by continually forcing a change of mental subject.

Nolan ate, slept, exercised, and talked endlessly to himself or held long conversations, during which he contributed both sides of the dialogue, with absent crew-members. Often he would call up the watch-keeping roster and choose a name and location at random, then he would go to that casket and stare down at the features of the silent cold sleeper and talk to him for hours on end, asking questions and supplying answers based on the kind of personality a man with that kind of face should possess.

Once he visited the casket of the officer who would relieve him, to discuss some of the problems Nolan was encountering during his own watch, and the ways he had tried to circumvent them. But even allowing for the facial stiffening due to the hypothermia, the other man's features seemed to reflect a personality that was reserved and not at all friendly, and the conversation became quite angry before Nolan apologized for his bad manners and withdrew.

Sometimes Nolan wondered if he was still sane, but consoled himself with the thought that he *knew* the men were in cold sleep and were not, therefore, talking back to him, so that his degree of insanity was still minor. All the same, it might be better if he reduced the number of his imaginary conversations, if for no other reason than that the constant talking was becoming painful to his throat.

He had been careful to avoid visiting the caskets of Dervla and the monsignor because he did not understand their personalities well enough to be able to put words into their frozen mouths, and in the senior Healer's case he would not have wanted to do so because he felt that it would have been an unwarranted albeit secret violation of her privacy. But he thought about both of them, of the two personalities that could not have been more diametrically opposed, of their conversations with him and their words and manner toward others in his hearing. Dervla the direct, the forthright, the outspoken, and often the caustic; and the soft-voiced, gentle-mannered, considerate yet equally inflexible Monsignor O'Riordan. He thought about them long and often.

His memory had become very good indeed, but the memories themselves grew more and more troublesome, in their different ways, in direct proportion to the accuracy of his recollection.

For reasons that he did not understand, he was missing the presence of Healer Dervla more than that of any other officer on the ship, and the monsignor least of all. Yet in the beginning Dervla's manner toward him had been, if not actively unpleasant, then one of angry toleration and impatience with a Healer whose sex made him automatically her professional inferior. She had given the impression that she considered him to be a great, lumbering, uncultured performing bear whose company she would not have tolerated if the monsignor had allowed anyone else to talk to her. Since the incident on the blast shield support, when she had discovered that he was also a medically proficient, acrobatic performing bear, her manner toward him had thawed somewhat, but she would talk only about their work and not themselves or, more accurately, about herself.

There was nothing that she had said or done that would make him want to remember her more than anyone else in the crew. Could the reason be that he was simply reacting to the fact that she had been the only still-warm female on the ship?

He thought about the tall, lean, manlike body, the red hair, and the thick, untended eyebrows. He pictured again the young, stern features that had never known cosmetics, and the gray-blue eyes that never looked away. Most of all he remembered the Druidic severity and single-minded dedication of the training she had undergone since early childhood, and he thought, *Surely not.*

There was a strange restlessness growing in him that was driving him toward thoughts and actions that he knew to be stupid, and that he was excusing his stupidity by deliberately recalling and exaggerating the importance of promises that at the present stage of the voyage he was unable to keep.

In particular Nolan was remembering his promises to Hseng Hwa, Wanachtee, Ciaran, and his Aztec Princess whose name was as difficult to pronounce silently as it was aloud, all of whom he had given his word to protect and cherish during their long cold sleep. If he was to take the monsignor's advice and remain on the control deck for the entire watch, he would not even see his charges until the prelanding thawings, and if there were more than the expected number of medical emergencies, not even then. None of the cold sleepers had any way of knowing whether or not he was keeping his promises, but surely that was not an acceptable reason for breaking them. After all, he had given his word.

But was he simply trying to find an excuse for leaving the warmth and comfort of the control deck, and the increasingly troublesome thoughts about Dervla and the remembered conversations with the monsignor that the place had engendered, in the hope that he would find something, anything, else to think about? Or was the explanation even more simple and he was trying to do penance by deliberately subjecting himself to the extreme cold and discomfort of the colonist modules, for what the monsignor would have called a sin of the mind?

Feeling irritated with himself, Nolan struggled into two sets of coveralls and pulled on the thickest gauntlets he could find in preparation for going aft. The idea was ridiculous because he had never really thought of Dervla as being a woman.

He did not know how long he wandered among the caskets in the crew module where slept the ship's officers and those colonists whose families or friends had been sufficiently rich or powerful to influence the berthings on *Aisling Gheal* and to obtain for them the more expensive and dependable crew caskets. On the side of every casket there was a small hinged panel which gave the identity of the sleeper and the current status of the refrigeration system, but the tiny illuminated letters and symbols gave off a light too dim for him to see his watch even if he had been willing to take off a gauntlet to do so. With only the regimented lines of dimly glowing monitor panels relieving the darkness, and having no way of knowing whether it was minutes or hours that were passing, he felt as if he were stealing time from his long watch. Only occasionally did he use his lamp to illuminate one of the cold sleeping faces, and he invariably apologized as if he had been in danger of disturbing the other's rest.

He was able to go directly to the casket of the Ionadacht without hesitation, and was disconcerted to find that Ciaran was one of the rare few who had gone into cold sleep with their eyes open, but the Princess Ulechitzl he was unable to find at all. Either his memory was at fault and he had lost his way in the darkness, or for some reason she was not in her assigned position.

The place where she should have been held a casket with the large transparent panel indicating that its occupant was a man. Nolan could see that the sleeper was pink of skin, well-muscled, and with the fair hair and countenance of a Skandian, a fact that the identity display confirmed, along with the utterly surprising information that it was a basic colonist casket rather than one of the multiple-use type used by the favored colonists who had been assigned to the crew module.

The Princess Ulechitzl and her casket had been moved.

If a simple transposition had been made, she should now be among the Skandian male colonists aft. But why would anyone want to do that? If any cold sleeper had needed to be moved, then he or Dervla should have been called to supervise the operation. The bodies of hypothermia subjects were incredibly brittle and susceptible to irreversible tissue damage if they or their caskets were incorrectly handled. He had not been called out of his enforced solitude for the purpose, so Dervla must have taken charge in his absence, and if that was the case, then she would have made a detailed entry in the medical log giving the clinical or other reasons for the transfer.

Before he did anything else, and that included worrying himself needlessly over a situation that might have a simple explanation, he would go at once to the medical department and find out what those reasons were.

There was no mention of any casket movements in the medical log.

To be absolutely sure that he had not missed anything he replayed the log several times, from the point where the monsignor had taken him out of circulation and Dervla had made a brief note to the effect that she had lost her assistant, until the most recent entry stating that she had been ordered to go cold. Between those two entries she had recorded, in her usual cold, clinical voice, the details of various minor mishaps that had befallen crew members and the treatments that had been carried out. But while taping the first and final entries it seemed to Nolan that Dervla's tone had sounded angry and critical rather than clinical.

Perhaps he was reading too much into the tone of voice of a very proud, strong-willed person who was unused to taking orders. Or had there been another reason for her anger which did not belong in a medical log, and if so, would it give some clue to the disappearance of Ulechitzl?

For the first time since his watch had begun, he went to Dervla's casket and looked down at her, and found her looking up at him.

Knowing her as he did, he should have expected that she would be one of the cold sleepers who insisted on undergoing hypothermia with their eyes open. But for some reason the effect on him was less disquieting than it had been when Ciaran's frozen gaze had been fixed on him. To the contrary, he felt reassured in some strange fashion and found himself wishing with an intensity that surprised him that she was warm and awake—if only to hear her telling him that he was stupid for worrying, because there was a simple explanation for what had happened. But she was cold, her lips moved not, her frozen eyes did not see him, and there was no explanation for what had happened, simple or otherwise.

Unless he was to discover the reason for himself.

"Sleep well," said Nolan awkwardly, then returned slowly to Control.

His first thought was one of caution. It might be better if, rather than disobeying one of the standing orders to watch-keepers and perhaps leaving evidence that he had done so, he logged an excuse for going aft. He could say that he had gone back to retrieve his hammock and other gear so as to tidy up and leave the place as he had found it while the temperature aft was still high enough for him to go there. That way he would have a weak but, he hoped, an acceptable excuse for disobeying orders. The monsignor would be irritated but not as suspicious as he would have been had Nolan remained silent and the transgression had been discovered later. If he left evidence of his visit to the Skandian sleepers, and he would try very hard not to do so, his excuse would be that he had lost his way in the dark.

In Control his first action was to call up the data on module layout and casket disposition so that he could learn the exact location of the Skandian colonists, where, if a simple transposition had been made, he should find Ulechitzl. But the message displayed on-screen made him swear aloud in angry disbelief.

ACCESS FORBIDDEN. THIS INFORMATION WILL NOT BE REQUIRED BY OFFICERS OF THE WATCH UNTIL AFTER TERMINATION OF THE VOYAGE.

It was becoming clear that the monsignor did not want any watch-keeping officer going aft or checking on the colonist modules, and he had made it very difficult for anyone who considered doing so. The reason Nolan had been given was that O'Riordan did not want his officers wandering and losing themselves, and possibly their lives, in the cold and darkness aft. But now he was beginning to wonder whether there were other reasons that had been concealed from him.

He was remembering the strange bumping and scraping noises he had heard after Dervla's visit. Could they have been made by a casket being moved through the ship and making intermittent contact with the corridor walls? And even though Nolan had no means of measuring time just then, he had felt sure that the sounds had continued for several days. Was it possible that more than one casket had been moved?

There was only one way to find out.

Nolan used a word of which his ecclesiastical fellow officers would not have approved. Discovering what had happened to the Princess was his primary concern, and unless he was very lucky, doing so would require a comprehensive search of all the colonist modules and an examination of every casket they contained.

It might take a long time, but with the second year of his watch stretching before him, time was the least of his problems.

Chapter 21

TWO of his first three search attempts had resulted in him nearly losing his way and dying from hypothermia. He was determined that the fourth and any subsequent trip aft would have to be less fraught with danger to himself, although initially the danger would be great.

Nolan ate and slept several times, and strenuously exercised his memories of the layout of the colonist modules, before he finally decided to make the attempt. He dressed carefully and even more warmly than before, then he went to the medical department for the penlight he used for oral and aural examinations, an instrument of greatly restricted range and illumination but whose use would be unlikely to be discovered by the monsignor. His last action before leaving was to look into Dervla's casket.

He watched her for a long time, but did not speak.

The safest and most comfortable method of searching the colonist modules would be to do it wearing a heated and insulated spacesuit fitted with a helmet light. O'Riordan had forbidden access to the crew suits, and Nolan was beginning to suspect that the real reason for doing so was to discourage the kind of search that he, Nolan, was about to undertake.

The crew's air tanks and power cells were stored separately from their suits, and if the suits themselves were not disturbed it was unlikely that the monsignor would bother to check the consumables. But with the Cathay suit, of which O'Riordan had no knowledge, Nolan would be free to travel the length and breadth, or even the exterior as well as the interior, of *Aisling Gheal* at will, and be able to replenish the power cells and air tanks whenever necessary.

The difficulty would lie in finding that suit before he froze to death.

He had torn a strip from a spare cowl and wrapped it around his head so as to protect the eyes, nose, and mouth from the intense cold—he wanted his vision to be as clear as possible when the destination module was reached so that he would have a better chance of reading the casket IDs. In effect he would be wearing a blindfold for the greater part of the journey, and removing it momentarily only when he needed to check on his position. But mostly he would be trusting to faith.

Faith, he thought wryly, in his memory.

A few moments later he had negotiated the familiar territory of the crew module, a section that he did know well enough to travel blindfold, and was falling slowly through the connecting passageway to the first of the colonist accommodations, Module A. His destination was in Module H.

The slow progress was frustrating but necessary, because he had to judge the force of each jump so that a premature contact with an obstruction or corridor junction would be gentle enough not to injure him. The first time that such a soft, glancing contact sent him tumbling and spinning helplessly in the darkness, he panicked, pulled open his cowl, and switched on his tiny, ridiculous light. Then he reminded himself fiercely that it did not matter how much or how often he spun during these intermediary stages, because he would be stopped at the end of the corridor where he could use the light to reorient himself for the next leg of the journey.

But very often the light was useless so far as showing the way was concerned, especially when it illuminated only a few square feet of wall plating or a confusing bundle of multicolored cable runs. He felt much more confident when he simply trusted to his memory and sense of direction and kept his eyes closed.

At the time, Nolan had been angry at his banishment to the ship while the other officers had continued to be acclaimed and entertained on their tour of the major cities of Earth. But now he was grateful beyond words that he had been left on *Aisling Gheal* with little to do but explore.

The massive airtight doors that separated the colonist modules required power to operate, and all but the trickle needed for casket monitoring had been switched off. There was a small personnel hatch set into each door which could be opened manually, but the operating mechanism had contracted and stiffened with the cold so that he had to brace himself against the surrounding structure and grip the frigid handle of the operating lever very tightly before it would move. The result was that by the time he reached what he hoped was Module H, he no longer had any feeling in his hands or feet.

Shivering uncontrollably and with his jaw clenched tightly to keep his teeth from chattering, he launched himself even more slowly into the next stretch of corridor. This time he had to locate the intersection leading to the module's external loading lock. He knew the approximate distance, and by staying close to the wall and using his light briefly to note the size and speed of the individual sections of plating as they drifted past, he was able to close his eyes and count the seconds needed to take him the required distance before opening them again.

The intersection was exactly where he expected to find it. He gripped a nearby cable run to check his fall, then quickly launched himself on the final leg of his journey.

The last time he had come this way it had been as the silent and anonymous escort of the casket containing the Royal Grandson of the Emperor of Cathay. Nolan had been dressed in a fine, beautifully fabricated spacesuit with its sun visor pulled down, and wearing a brassard decorated with ideographs that were meaningless to him.

In a very few moments he would be wearing that suit again.

But when he reached the Cathay colonist stacks it was so cold that the tears froze on his cheeks and clogged his lashes with tiny ice crystals. He rubbed at his eyes, but the blurring remained so that he could neither read the IDs nor distinguish the features of the cold sleepers. The penlight had slipped from his fingers and was spinning slowly beyond arm's reach, illuminating the drifting fog of his breath like a tiny rotating searchlight.

He knew beyond any possibility of doubt that he could never survive the long, dark, and frigid journey back to Control. He had to find that spacesuit or his frozen but not cold sleeping body would be found in this place when the time came for the people all around him to be warmed for landing. He thought of the monsignor shaking his head over him in gentle disapproval, and Dervla feeling angry at his stupidity in disobeying sensible orders, and he cursed himself loudly and at great length.

But swearing through chattering teeth made a sound that was very strange and completely ridiculous, and suddenly he found himself laughing more than he was cursing. He pressed his teeth firmly together and tried to think.

If he could not see, he decided, there were other senses available to him.

Ignoring the penlight, Nolan felt his way quickly and carefully from casket to casket, but he was no longer trying to recognize the boy's face among the cold sleepers or read the IDs. Instead he was concentrating on the storage cabinets under every casket, pulling back the hinged doors and reaching inside to feel among the few personal possessions that the colonists had been allowed to take with them. The boy he was trying to find would have no need of such things because he possessed ultimate authority among the people around him. Anything and everything they owned was his by right if he should want it.

The thick gauntlets and the intense cold had robbed his fingers and hands of all feeling, but he pushed blindly against the contents of the cabinets, trusting his muscles to register the soft resistance of clothing and his ears to identify the quiet sounds of books or framed pictures as he disturbed them. Then in the fifth cabinet that he opened he discovered an object that was large and hard with a wide, circular opening and a hollow interior.

It could only be the neck opening of a spacesuit helmet.

Within a few moments he had drawn out and identified the other two sections of the suit, leaving them hanging close at hand in the darkness. Then, without giving himself time to think, he stripped off his cowl and both sets of coveralls. But the blast of cold that he expected to penetrate the light undergarment like so much gossamer did not come. His body must already be so cold that the additional drop in temperature was scarcely noticeable.

In the weightless condition his efforts to don the suit sent him twisting and spinning slowly in the darkness, because his penlight had become a tiny dimly flashing satellite that had apparently taken up an erratic orbit around him, but its illumination was too faint to show him the helmet which he must have knocked away during his struggle to dress. He swore again and fought to control his growing panic, because he knew that none of the suit's systems would operate until the three sections were complete and properly connected. When his slow tumble brought him against the side of a casket, he steadied himself and tried to think.

He refused to believe that he would die after all he had been through, not because of a ridiculous mishap like this.

Slowly he began moving away from the light, but keeping his eyes on it while at the same time pushing himself from side to side and up and down between the casket stacks. His vision was still blurred by the effects of the cold, but it was good enough to see when an object obscured the light.

He dived slowly toward it, only to run through the soft tangle of clothing he had discarded earlier. But when he repeated the process, the next object to eclipse his penlight was hard and spherical and unmistakably his misplaced helmet.

A few moments later the suit's heating and drying elements were beginning to thaw the surface of his shivering body and clear the breath condensation from the inside of the visor, and the helmet light was showing the rows of caskets with dazzling clarity. Under a few of them, where he had searched hurriedly in the darkness for the spacesuit, there were slowly expanding clumps of the sleepers' clothing and personal possessions drifting from the open storage compartments. He replaced them quickly while he was still sure which objects belonged to which sleeper.

He also placed his cowl and coveralls in the compartment that had held the spacesuit because, sometime before this watch ended, he would have to come back here to replace the suit and make another long, cold return journey in them. But that was a future event that he pushed firmly to the back of his mind.

Now, he thought gratefully, he would be able to continue his search for Ulechitzl's casket, at leisure and in comfort. There was no great urgency for him to do so, because a year of his watch remained, and in her present state of hypothermia nothing could happen to her that had not already happened. But first he would return to the light and warmth of Control and try to thaw out his mind as well as his body in the bathing tank.

Within a day of acquiring the Cathay spacesuit, his search for Ulechitzl was resumed.

He began by going first to the crew module where slept the colonists fortunate enough to have had important or influential friends. He was wondering if the Skandian who had been moved there might himself be a person of importance who had been incorrectly positioned during the loading, so that the later move could have been an attempt to correct the initial mistake. But why, then, was he not in a crew casket?

A close study of the man's features and ID under the strong helmet lighting revealed neither a face that was familiar to Nolan nor a family name well-known on Earth. The personal possessions, which included a small diary and some photographs of him taken with a family that did not appear to be well-blessed with the riches of the world, seemed to be those of a young agricultural student.

The Skandian colonists had been among the first to be moved up to *Aisling Gheal*, and Nolan had not been present during the loading, so they could be anywhere in the ship. And the computer had been instructed not to release such information to the officers of the watch.

Or was it only one watch-keeping officer from whom the information was being hidden?

That was a ridiculous idea, Nolan thought, but the suspicion did not go away, and more and more often it returned as the search proceeded. He had decided that rather than begin by setting out to examine every single casket in turn, he would make a quick, preliminary search during which he would ignore those sections that he knew did not contain Skandians—the Westland and Cathay stacks, for example—and everywhere else make only a random check of one or two IDs in the hope of finding a name that was of Skandian origin. Having found one, he could then concentrate his search for Ulechitzl in that particular area.

In spite of the suit's more than adequate lighting, the search for the Skandian colonists continued for several days with negative results, even though Nolan was sure that he had covered every corridor in the ship and had checked at least one ID in the stacks opening off them. He even searched the livestock compartments in case Ulechitzl had been moved there, but without success.

Several times his quest took him through the corridor where he had spent his enforced period of solitude. He could see the bright scratches on the corridor wall where his equipment had been attached, and the two sections of plumbing that had been abraded by the movement of his hammock straps. Nowhere else in the ship had he seen similar markings.

His earlier suspicion that he had been the only member of the crew to undergo that particular form of self-discipline had become a certainty. But why? Had the monsignor simply wanted to get rid of Nolan by sending him as far aft as was possible because something had been happening forward that he was not supposed to know about? Or, perhaps, had it been something about which as a Healer he would have been expected to object?

But that was nonsense, he told himself firmly. With the exceptions of Dervla and two of the lander pilots, the entire crew were ecclesiastics whose life's vocation and nontechnical training made it impossible for them to knowingly do harm to another human being. There had been occasions in the past when some overly zealous priest or religious group had crossed the borderline into madness and holy murder, but the idea of the highly intelligent and mentally stable officers of the ship doing so in concert was ridiculous. They would have to be engaged on a project that was nonharmful but highly secret. Feeling very confused indeed, Nolan broke off the search and returned to Control to give the matter long and careful thought.

He had discovered the Ulechitzl substitution in the crew module just after his visit to Ciaran's casket, which had not been moved from its original position. Since then he had ignored that module because, apart from a few members of the crew, he had not known the names or casket positions of any of the other officers well enough to know whether other substitutions had taken place. That was something he should establish as early as possible, because the noises he had heard during his banishment aft had continued for many days.

After a thorough search among the noncrew sleepers in Module One, he discovered that twenty-seven of the crew-type caskets had been replaced with those of basic colonist design, and that their occupants had Skandian or other European IDs. His subsequent examination of the caskets containing the ship's officers, including that of Monsigner O'Riordan, showed nothing amiss.

That left the captain, who, as a Prince of the Church and senior officer of the greatest ship ever built, was the only person on board allowed a private cabin in which to sleep either cold or warm, and Nolan hesitated for a long time before entering it. He had the feeling that the cardinal would be another one of those people who cold slept with the eyes open, and that awake or not, His Eminence would somehow know and disapprove of this invasion of his privacy. But his was the only casket in the entire crew module that he had not examined, and the habit of physical and mental neatness that had always plagued him made it important that he complete the process. And so, without giving himself any more time to argue with himself, he entered the captain's cabin.

From the opposite wall the metal casket supports reached toward him like stiff and empty arms. Neither Cardinal-Captain Keon nor his casket was there.

Chapter 22

NOLAN'S first, wild thought was that there had been some kind of mutiny aimed at permanently removing rather than replacing the captain, because this time there was no colonist casket occupying the place of the original. His second and more sensible thought was that he should search the cabin for some indication of why the captain was not there.

It was a spacious cabin, almost as large as the medical treatments room, but rendered small by the number of computer consoles, storage cabinets, and equipment racks growing from the deck, walls, and ceiling, and to Nolan's mind it resembled an engineering laboratory rather than a private accommodation. He found that a few of the cabinets were neatly filled with devices whose purpose was unclear to him, while others had been disturbed or were partially or completely empty. There was no sign of any personal effects.

The captain's hammock was stowed flat against the wall, indicating that it had not seen recent use. The one device that Nolan would have recognized, the fantastically expensive ceramic tube that he had used to splint a pair of fractured legs, was not present. And when he opened the large wall cabinet used to store the captain's personal spacesuit, that, too, was missing.

No monsignor, not even O'Riordan, would dare forbid the use of a spacesuit by a cardinal, no matter how delicately the order was couched. Nolan laughed aloud in sheer relief, because he thought he knew what had happened to the captain now, but he would have to make sure.

As a change from traveling the dark corridors of the colonist modules, he decided on the more interesting and forbidden route along the outer hull. He used one of the manually controlled personnel locks which did not require any power, and whose operation should go undetected.

It was as if he were walking slowly under the stars across a dark gray, ghostly landscape of great, bulbous mountain ranges and gigantic, angular trees lit by the single, dazzling star that was the Sun. It sank behind the distant rim of the blast shield as he continued to move aft, and the other stars brightened and multiplied as the landscape dimmed into invisibility. He had to use the suit light to find his way to the power module.

As he had expected, Nolan found the captain without any difficulty. Normally the power module would have been forbidden to cold sleepers because the level of background radiation might have adversely affected their gene structure, but the cardinal's age and celibacy made such considerations irrelevant.

An equipment storage compartment had been cleared and converted into a combination of living quarters and laboratory. There had been no shutdown of power to this section, so the place was well-lit. He could see the items that had been missing from the captain's cabin forward, including the bulbous ceramic wand and the spacesuit clipped to the walls for ready use. The black hemisphere of a powerful heating unit projected from the ceiling, and there were a few photographs and paintings attached to the small areas of wall that had been left empty. The hammock was also empty but the casket was not. Nolan was relieved to see that His Eminence cold slept with his eyes closed.

Looking down at the stern, powerful, and deeply lined face, Nolan knew that this was a man with the authority to spend his years of watch-keeping exactly as *he* wished, not as the monsignor required the subordinate officers to do. It was obvious that the captain intended passing his watch-keeping time on one or more of the private projects he had mentioned, instead of confining himself to Control, although doubtless he would go forward from time to time to check that his powered-down vessel was still on course and the few systems left operating did not require attention.

But was the sleeping captain aware of what had happened to some of the colonist caskets? Unless there was a conspiracy of some kind involving only a small number of his officers, the answer had to be yes.

For a moment Nolan considered reviving His Eminence so that he could ask for an explanation. But a premature warming, whether of a colonist or of a ship's officer, should only be performed in the direst of emergencies. The satisfaction of his curiosity, he felt sure, was not a sufficiently strong reason.

Nolan sighed and turned away, deciding to take the internal route back to Control. He had no intention of continuing his search for the Skandian colonists until he had eaten and rested, but there was another casket whose occupant and position was known to him, because he had helped place her there.

As he entered the Westland section he was remembering Wanachtee's flight up to *Aisling Gheal* to replace the spoiled body of a Redman with the one containing his young wife. The thought came to him then that he, Nolan, might have been the first to engage in the covert transportation of caskets that had now become so prevalent.

Without hesitation he went to the remembered position. A glance at the casket indicator showed that the hypothermia system was functioning perfectly. But when he looked at the occupant's face he saw the pale skin and racial features of a male Skandian, not those of Golden Rain.

He was so angry and confused that he did not remember the return to Control. What reason could there be for swapping caskets around like this? Why was it that it seemed to be his friends, or, more accurately, those he had been asked to protect, who were affected? Or did that have anything to do with the situation at all?

Was it only the females that he had been asked to protect who were affected? Certainly the Ionadacht, Ciaran, was in his assigned place while Ulechitzl was not. Golden Rain was missing also, but what about her husband, Wanachtee? The Redman chief was a lander pilot, and the number of trained spasaires was still small enough for their names, and those of their wives, should they be married, to be widely known. That being so, it was certain that Wanachtee had concealed his true name, so that it would be difficult to find him without examining the face of every Redman sleeper in the ship.

And why were so many Skandians involved?

Even though he reminded himself many times that there was no urgency about continuing the search, Nolan found that he was eating so hurriedly that he might only have had a few minutes to spare rather than a year. And when he at last composed his weary body for slumber, his sleep was disturbed indeed.

It was as if a recording was playing continuously in his mind, with sequences that were clear and sharp in sound and vision but with abrupt and apparently random changes of scene and subject.

Nolan remembered having had such a dream in the past when as a child he had been suffering from a fever with elevated temperature. But these were not the phantasms of a delirious mind, they were the accurate if disjointed record of incidents that must have been seriously worrying him, and which still worried him when he awakened.

What was the real reason why Ciaran and Wanachtee and, on behalf of the Cathay boy-Prince-Elect, Hseng Hwa approached him? Nolan doubted that it was because of any great personal charm or ability as a Healer. Wanachtee had suggested that the Healer was honest and enthusiastic and, unlike his ecclesiastical colleagues, often spoke without guarding his tongue. But the Redman's words might simply have been the flattery that precedes the asking of a favor. On that occasion he had told the Chief that some people, and that included his friends, tried to use him without realizing that he knew he was being used.

But why had he been chosen for use by such an oddly disparate group of people as an Imperial Guards Captain, an important Redman Chieftain, and what could only be a senior adviser to the Imperial Court of Cathay, and what was he being used *for*? In the cases of Ciaran and Wanachtee, the choice might have been made quickly, as a result of things said and done at first meeting. His success in rescuing himself from that self-created disaster on Brendan's Island must have given the Redmen an exaggerated and completely mistaken impression of his resourcefulness. But in Hseng Hwa's case the choice must have been made long before they had met, because, in a nation where the average male body was small, that spacesuit had been precisely tailored to fit him. Had they all known, or at least suspected, that something would happen to some of the cold sleeping colonists, and that they or their charges might require a special guardian?

But why him?

He was one of the least-respected and most junior officers on the ship, a mere male Healer with all that implied to its Hibernian-born Imperial Citizens, and, if that was not bad enough, a heretical and at times outspoken unbeliever. The idea that he had any special or valuable qualities was ridiculous.

Even though Nolan did not think of himself as a conceited man, that answer did not entirely satisfy him, and many sleepless hours later he dressed and checked the seals and tanks of his suit and prepared to resume the search. But when he was passing the medical department on his way aft, an impulse made him go in and across to Dervla's casket.

His anger was still with him as he glared down at her and demanded, "What is happening here, Healer Dervla? And what do *you* know about it?"

For a long time he looked down into the eyes that seemed to be looking up at him, and for some reason that he did not understand Nolan found himself wanting her to speak, no matter how impatiently or caustically, and tell him that she knew nothing of it. But she could not speak, nor give him the reassurance he needed, except with those calm, frozen eyes.

His search for the Skandian stacks continued with no result other than a further deepening of the mystery. He was finding single Skandian sleepers in the sections containing Nubians, Mesopotamians, and Indonesians and all the caskets were of the single-use colonist type. It seemed that transpositions had been made between the colonist sections as well as with the non-crew sleepers forward. For another reason that he could not understand, the Skandian colonists had been scattered fairly evenly throughout the ship.

Nolan had not been required to lecture on Skandian history because teachers among their own colonists would do so. But he knew that for many centuries before and shortly after the War of the Heroes, their ferocity as warriors had been legendary and they had raided or established settlements on the coasts and islands of western Europe and, it was thought, for a brief period on the New World before the arrival of Brendan. But now the Citizens of the Imperial District of Skandia were in the main practical, hard-working, resourceful, and law-abiding people not noted for any great fervor toward any particular religion, and were otherwise unremarkable. Judging by the number of them he had found in what would be to them foreign stacks, there could be few of them remaining in their original Skandian section.

If there were any left at all.

With that thought a great light dawned in his mind, for now the explanation for him not finding the Skandian section was clear. He had been searching quickly and, he had thought, efficiently by looking at the skin pigmentation or the ID on the casket nearest to the entrance, then moving on if they were of the wrong racial type. Now that he had realized his mistake he would have to change the search pattern.

Nolan found it three hours later—the Skandian section he had been searching for—because the ID check on its first ten sleepers suggested that it held colonists of every nation on Earth save Skandia. His air would last for another hour at least and so, with growing confidence, he continued the search for the crew-type casket that held Ulechitzl.

He found it a few moments later, fully functioning and with the sleeper's face as still and beautiful as a delicately crafted sculpture. He laughed aloud in sheer relief and moved on. There was another to whom he had appointed himself a spacegoing guardian angel.

There were forty sleepers of many different nationalities in the section. All but a few of the caskets were of the multi-use crew type, but none of the people who had been moved from the crew module were familiar to him, and in any case he was looking for the colonist casket holding Golden Rain.

Nolan's tanks were nearly empty and he was wondering if he should open his visor and risk breathing the frigid outside air for the short time needed to complete the search. He had less than twenty caskets to examine and he was becoming impatient and worried in case she had been moved to another section entirely, or something more serious had happened to her. But he did not have to open his visor, because the next casket he examined held Golden Rain.

Its malfunction light glowed like an angry, red eye.

He swore bitterly and sought for the clinical calm that Healers were supposed to maintain in times of crisis. Quickly but with great care he disconnected the power cable and detached the casket from the support brackets, then moved it even more carefully into the module's examination room. But all the while his actions were those of a programmed automaton because he was seeing again this lovely young woman as she had been during that earlier, covert transfer when the ship had still been in Earth orbit, and the way that Wanachtee's eyes had never left that tall, beautifully formed body. At the time he had thought that the sight of her unclothed had aroused in the Redman the stirrings that were normal to any male in that situation. It was only later that he had realized that she was Wanachtee's squaw and that he was regarding her with an intensity of love rather than lust, and he had promised to watch over her.

What words could he say to Wanachtee at journey's end?

A close examination showed that the casket had been roughly or inexpertly handled during the transfer from its previous position. There were several small scratches and dents on the outer casing, but these in themselves should not have caused a failure. The power cable was properly connected and secured, and the thick plastic insulation that protected it showed no sign of damage at any point along its length. Yet the monitor insisted that the power supply to the secondary hypothermia system, the one needed to maintain the contents at optimum temperature, had failed. He had no way of knowing how long ago the failure had occurred, but in spite of the intense cold inside the module, the sleeper's temperature was rising slowly toward the level where tissue damage would occur. Initially the more delicate cell structures of the brain would be affected and subsequently the body as a whole, and the only positive element in the clinical picture was that the very low ambient temperature was delaying the process.

Golden Rain was not yet dead and, theoretically, might still be saved.

His air-supply indicator was glowing red as if in sympathy with the malfunction light, so he reconnected the casket and began a hasty return to Control. On the way he tried as hard to control his baseless feelings of optimism as he had his earlier sorrow and helplessness, because on the surface the problem was insoluble. The fact that he had been given time to think did not mean that he would find the answer.

There would have been no problem at all if the ship had been allowed to carry replacements. But the caskets were tested so thoroughly before and after loading, and they were not supposed to be disturbed in any way for the duration of the voyage, that the possibility of a malfunction was vanishingly small. Besides, competition for colonist places on the ship had been so fierce that *Aisling Gheal* had not been allowed to carry empty caskets to the New World.

For the next three days Nolan wrestled with the problem and the struggle continued during the intervening nights. One possible solution was so simple and tempting that even his waking mind found great difficulty in rejecting it. For reasons he did not understand, the transposition of colonists had become endemic throughout the ship, and this solution would simply involve another transfer—that of Golden Rain's body into the fully functioning casket of a colonist unknown to Nolan and whom he had not specifically promised to watch over, and the other into the faulty one. That solution would trouble Wanachtee as it did Nolan himself, if the Redman ever learned of it, but at least it would not inflict on him the hurt that the death of his beloved squaw would have caused.

And if Golden Rain was already damaged beyond the ability to sustain life, a strong possibility that could only be discounted after a thorough medical examination, that solution would have brought about the needless death of another colonist.

As a Healer he considered himself to be a fairly ethical and civilized being, and so he had to reject that idea. But there was another solution, one with an unknown but very high level of risk to himself, because it would involve the unauthorized warming of a ship's officer. And if the officer he chose had been among those engaged in the covert transposition of caskets, a request for his cooperation in rectifying a malfunction, for which the other man might himself be responsible, then Nolan would be in a very difficult position. The officer might feel it necessary to seek the advice of a superior in the matter and revive the monsignor, in which case Nolan's decision to revive a celibate priest to assist with the physical handling of an unclothed female would be a minor matter compared with what O'Riordan's reaction would be.

The longer he thought about it the more he was convinced of what he must do and to whom, regardless of the consequences. After all, what could the highly moral monsignor or even the cardinal-captain actually do to punish an unbeliever should his breach of regulations be discovered? He knew that the physiological condition of Golden Rain was not an urgent matter, that there was time to think about it for hours or even days. But he also knew that if he did not make the decision now, then he might never do so. And if he could pretend that the whole affair was a Healer-patient relationship in which the treatment and associated conversation was privileged, then it was possible that the monsignor would never learn of what Nolan had done.

You are lying to yourself, he told himself angrily, and you are a complete fool for believing yourself. But by then he was already in the medical department, holding an undergarment and a set of her brown coveralls while his free hand punched the codes for the timer override and immediate revivification.

He watched while the silent, measured explosion of heat brought life again to the body and the open, recently frozen eyes looking up at him began to blink.

Chapter 23

THE cover seal popped open with a loud, derisive sound and Nolan moved back as the casket lid swung up. He did not try to help her detach the freeze pads and body restraints, because the speed and manner in which she performed those actions would indicate whether or not the withdrawal from hypothermia had caused damage to the brain tissues. With relief he saw that her movements were slow but well coordinated as she detached the straps and lifted her weightless body over the edge of the casket. It was then that she saw him, and her opening words made it even more unlikely that there was anything wrong with her mind.

"I expected to be alone when I wakened," she said, frowning. "Why are *you* here?"

"I, that is, there has been a . . ." Nolan began, then fell silent.

It was utterly ridiculous, but for a moment he was unable either to frame a coherent sentence or take his eyes off her. He had heard it said that the weightless condition could do surprising things to and for the female body, but he had not been prepared for a surprise on this scale. He cleared his throat and tried again.

In a voice that was much too stiff and formal, he said, "Please do not be alarmed, Healer. There is nothing about which you, personally, need feel concern. I have the first watch and it is only a year since you were cooled. I have initiated this unscheduled warming because of a medical emergency that has arisen. The case is nonurgent but—"

"It is urgent," Dervla broke in sharply, "that I cover myself. Pass me my clothing, please, and avert your gaze while I dress. You are staring like some callow adolescent at his first sight of an undraped female. Surely, Healer Nolan, at some period in your probably second-rate training in anatomy you must have been confronted with an unclothed female body?"

Nolan turned away. She could not see the embarrassment in his face, but he felt that even his ears were burning as he said, "My apologies, Healer Dervla. And you are quite correct, I have had that experience on a number of occasions. My reason for staring was that I did not expect yours to have such a pleasing . . . for it to be so . . . so well-formed.''

There was a moment of silence that was broken only by the quiet, irregular sighing of fabric against skin, then suddenly she laughed and said, ''Never in my life have I heard a compliment delivered in such an uncomplimentary voice. You may face me now.''

The coverall cowl was still buttoned back so that her hair hung around her head like a copper halo, and the heightened color in her cheeks made her eyes seem a deeper blue. Nolan stared into them, thinking that she could scarcely object to that, and did not speak.

Her color deepened slightly and she said, ''Your surprise, at least, is understandable. Until now you had no way of knowing that those members of the Order of Orla who have need to do so must bind ourselves so that none of the males with whom we make social or professional contact will think of us as anything but sexless Healers. The binding is tight and irksome, and since you are yourself a Healer and are already aware of my guilty secrets, I see no reason for continuing to use it in your presence.''

Nolan was still trying to think of a reply that would not get him into more trouble when she went on: ''Has this shocking revelation rendered you mute, Healer? Speak. What precisely is this nonurgent medical emergency of yours, and how long will it require my staying warm?''

''The background to the case is complicated and will need time to explain,'' he said. ''And I am sorry, the treatment I have in mind will require several days, perhaps as much as a week, to complete.''

''Don't be sorry, then,'' she said, smiling again. ''Together with everything else, my hunger from that damnable two-day fast preceding cooldown has also been preserved intact. My subjective symptoms are those of advanced malnutrition.''

''Food is available from the dispenser in the officer of the watch's cubicle,'' said Nolan, beginning to feel more at ease with the situation. ''While you are treating your symptoms we can discuss the other patient's condition.''

''That can wait,'' she said. ''When I visited you aft I was already fasting, and went cold a few hours later. I want to know everything that has been happening on the ship, and especially the reason why the duty roster was changed to give you first watch.'' Dervla frowned again, but this time in concern rather than anger, and went on, ''That food dispenser is programmed to deliver only enough nutrition in a day to satisfy the requirements of a single watch-keeper. Have you considered that problem, Healer?''

''As we both know,'' Nolan replied, ''it was you yourself who programmed the dispenser to provide a daily ration based on the officer's body mass and prior food consumption. You said then, and I have since come to agree with you, that I am grossly overweight. That problem, too, is nonurgent.''

''A gracious answer, Healer Nolan,'' said Dervla, jumping neatly toward the corridor leading to Control. ''Let us hope that increasing hunger does not cause you to regret it.''

While she was relieving her symptoms with what remained of the day's food ration, Nolan repeated the dialogue between O'Riordan and himself as accurately as he could remember it, but of his subsequent thoughts and activities until his discovery of a female colonist in a malfunctioning casket he said nothing. By then the dispenser was empty and Dervla had moved to the watch-keeper's station to begin calling up the ship status displays.

''According to this,'' she said, tapping the screen, ''no space-suits have been withdrawn from internal stores. You've already told me that suit excursions were forbidden, so what were you doing so far aft without protection? I cannot believe that you were simply wandering about back there, in the cold and dark and wearing only coveralls, and chanced upon this faulty casket. Is this female colonist known to you, or perhaps loved by you? What is there about her that warranted your taking such an insane risk?

''Healer Nolan,'' she ended harshly, ''what are you hiding from me?''

Choosing his words carefully, Nolan said, ''I am hiding events and conversations of a personal, or indeed privileged, nature which took place on Earth. I would prefer not to discuss them with you for the reason that they might involve you needlessly in my own wrongdoing. Otherwise I am hiding only a mystery, much supposition and speculation, and suspicions which may prove to be baseless or simple of explanation. To minimize any future criticism of your action in helping me, it would be best if you provided only the necessary medical assistance and nothing more''

''Healer,'' she said angrily, ''you have succeeded in arousing my curiosity to the extent that I shall not be able to rest, even in cold sleep, without knowing what is in your stupid, noble, or misguided mind. Let me remind you that I am your superior, and that privileged information concerning a patient may be discussed with another Healer engaged on the case, and who is similarly obliged not to reveal it to outsiders. I am waiting.''

Nolan did not reply.

For a long, uncomfortable moment Dervla looked straight into his eyes, then she said, "I have suppositions and suspicions of my own. One of them, which is not, I think, baseless, is that you suspect me of knowing more about your mystery than you do and that I am concealing that knowledge. This is not so. I have hidden nothing from you . . ." She gave a faint smile of embarrassment but did not lower her gaze. ". . . in every sense of the word. What is this great mystery, be it real or fancied, that troubles you? Please speak."

Nolan felt his earlier resolve begin to weaken. He was beginning to think that keeping her in protective ignorance of what he thought might be happening in the ship was not such a good idea, because the combination of intense curiosity and incomplete information might cause her to say or do something that would cause her even more trouble.

Rightly had she reminded him that anything that passed between them regarding a patient—and in the broadest sense every single person in the ship was their patient—was privileged information that could not be revealed to any power, temporal or ecclesiastical. Dervla had also said that she harbored suspicions of her own, suspicions that might support and illuminate his own.

She was drifting laterally above the watch-keeper's position, half-turned toward him and with one hand steadying herself against the edge of the acceleration couch. Weightlessness had caused the loose-fitting coveralls to bulge outward so that they looked like a great, shapeless, bifurcate sack tied tightly in the middle. But suddenly the sharp, recent memory of that long-limbed and beautifully contoured body, a mind picture that no garment however shapeless could conceal, returned to throw his mind into pleasant disarray. He shook his head in self-irritation. This was not the time for thinking such thoughts.

Dervla misunderstood the shake of his head. She said coldly, "Very well, Healer. We shall speak only of our patient."

In a manner that was cool and clinical and in every way the match of Dervla's own, Nolan described the problem of Golden Rain and the method he had devised for solving it. Both the patient and her faulty casket would have to be examined carefully for damage and, to do so effectively, both would have to be brought forward to the medical department where the patient would be resuscitated prior to undergoing an exhaustive clinical examination. Even if it had been functioning properly, her own one-use, colonist casket could not be used since the second half of its cycle would be needed to warm her at journey's end, which was the reason why Dervla's multi-use crew casket would be used to revive her. If the patient was found to be in good condition, she would remain in the department in Dervla's casket until the fault had been remedied, after which she would be transferred back to her own casket and returned to her position aft.

"It would seem," Dervla interrupted at that point, "that the success of your procedure is wholly dependent on the use of my casket, and that any contribution I might make, apart from keeping quiet regarding a secret which you have chosen not to reveal to me anyway, is of secondary importance.

"No matter," she went on before he could reply. "That is a minor, nonphysical wound which will soon heal. But the next part of your procedure will require the use of two spacesuits, whose removal from stores will not remain a secret beyond the period of the present watch. Have you considered that possibility, Healer?"

"Yes," said Nolan, "but I believe the risk is a small one. Only one spacesuit will be needed, and the reason I shall record for drawing it will be a medical emergency requiring simple repairs to a faulty colonist casket aft. No mention will be made of bringing the casket or patient forward for examination, or that you were revived or your casket used at any time. My crew suit will be large for you, but you are tall enough to wear it without inconvenience. I will use another suit, about which the ship's officers know nothing."

"The mystery deepens," said Dervla, then added quickly, "That is purely an observation, Healer, not another vain request for information. Have you also considered the fact that the unscheduled warmings and coolings will register on my casket's monitoring system, and that the information will be available to anyone interested in calling it up?"

"Yes," said Nolan again, "but that possibility, too, is small. I think there would be an aversion, or rather a disinclination, among the ecclesiastics to risk a sin of the mind by taking such a close interest in the only female officer on the ship. Even before this emergency arose, I, who have no priestly vows of celibacy to maintain or fear of sinning with the mind to hamper me, found it difficult to approach you at first."

"I see," said Dervla, and gave a small, puzzled shake of her head. "You had a strong aversion to looking at me or even approaching my casket, but plainly you were able to overcome it and—"

"I do not have an aversion to looking at you . . . !" Nolan began.

"I am aware of that," said Dervla.

"Either then or now," he went on, feeling his face begin to burn. "It was just that I felt that doing so would be an invasion of your privacy even though you would not know of it. I—I felt very lonely and confused and not a little frightened by some of the things that had been happening, and I wanted to talk about them to someone other than myself, someone who would understand me even though they were unable to answer or even hear me."

Dervla was looking at him in an odd way, but she did not speak.

Nolan laughed. It was a strained, awkward sound, he thought, that resembled nothing so much as the barking of a dog. He said, "When you have the watch, you may talk to me if or whenever you wish. I won't mind, and I shall certainly not argue with anything you say."

"Thank you," said Dervla, and shook her head again. "You are a very strange man, Healer Nolan. But now let us tend to our patient."

All the while that he was withdrawing a large-sized suit from stores and recording his reason for needing it, and even when he was helping her check its air tanks and seals, Dervla did not speak. He did not think that she was angry with him; it was simply that her mind seemed to be elsewhere. It was only when he began climbing into his own suit that she broke her silence.

"The decoration, the workmanship," she said in a surprised voice. "Your suit is from Cathay."

"It was a gift," said Nolan, removing the brassard that was still attached to it. "A gift and a disguise."

"It is the equal of the one made for the cardinal," she went on, "and that was built to a higher safety standard only because he expects to spend much of his watch traveling between Control and the power module on a private research project. And there is no necessity to hide that emblem; I have seen one at Tara and know what it represents. You have strange and powerful friends.

"That is another observation, Healer," she added with the faintest of smiles, "not a question."

Nolan placed the brassard in his undergarment pocket. I wish you would tell me what it represents, he said silently, then aloud, "I'm not hiding it, just trying to protect it from accidental damage while we are moving the casket. And I already know about the captain's project aft. He is presently occupying a casket in the power module, with his own spacesuit, food dispenser, and much other equipment by him. He is well, his casket is functioning properly, and according to his timer he will be awakened for his first watch in just over eighty-three years."

It was not until they were moving aft along the main corridor of Module B, their visors sealed against the increasing cold, that she said, "A properly qualified Healer such as myself must, among her many other medical talents, be experienced in dentistry. I thought that experience would prove useful in the present situation, because extracting information from you is like pulling a tooth. But now, it seems, you have spat one out at me."

Nolan laughed, in relief rather than at the humor in her words, because he had finally decided that if he was trusting her with this operation then he must trust her with everything.

"There are many more teeth," he said seriously, "loose and ready to come out when the visor isn't in the way."

They had used much un-Healerlike language and were hot and perspiring freely inside their suits by the time they returned, because the casket, although weightless, possessed mass and inertia and, it seemed, a suicidal mind of its own that was intent on crashing it into every cross-corridor they encountered and damaging itself further. But once inside the medical department, they again became cool and clinical, in their actions if not their words.

"Surface condensation is beginning to form," said Nolan worriedly. "Help me move her to your casket quickly, but with great care. Do not grip the body too tightly, nor allow it to touch any hard surfaces during the transfer. In this condition the tissues are as fragile as spun glass and could be damaged if—"

"You have already told me as much, several times within the hour," said Dervla in an irritated voice. "Please do not remind me of it again."

"I'm sorry, Healer," said Nolan.

Within a few seconds it was done. He positioned the restraints and thaw-pads, closed the lid, and initiated the warming. Only then did he take the time to look at her face.

"And I am sorry," said Dervla in a voice that was almost as cold as the sleeper. "It is obvious that you have a deep and personal concern for this one. She is an exceptionally lovely young woman, and you are to be congratulated."

"Don't be ridiculous!" said Nolan. "She's not my . . ."

He had to stop then, because the frozen copper statue was coming to life. She was moving, the long flawless body was tensing and twitching with the cold of the icy film of condensation that still clung to her, and suddenly she was looking around the sides of the casket.

Nolan lifted up the lid and released her upper-body restraints, then he slipped his arm behind her shoulders and lifted her into a sitting position.

"Don't be afraid," he said in a quiet, reassuring voice. "We are Healers performing one of the routine, random checks on the functioning of the colonist caskets. You are being awakened for a few minutes so that we may do so."

On the other side of the casket, Dervla gave a sigh that might have been of disapproval. Surely the Order of Orla was not averse to telling the odd therapeutic lie?

"I'm—I'm cold," said the girl, and clenched her jaw to keep her teeth from chattering. Her face was only a few inches from his own, and her eyes were very large and soft and dark.

Gently, he said, "Of course you are cold. I'm sorry about that, but I cannot warm you properly, or give you something hot to drink, because that would delay and complicate your recooling. And now I must examine you and at the same time ask you a few questions, to confirm the information that the biosensors are giving me. I'll be as quick as I can. Do you understand what I'm saying?"

She nodded, and he went on, "Are there any areas of your body, large or small, which are painful, numb, or giving itching or burning sensations? Any localized loss of feeling, impairment of vision, headache, diminished mental clarity? Any sensation, or lack of it, which I have not mentioned and which worries you?"

She shook her head.

"That's good," said Nolan. "And now the memory check. Can you describe the place where you lived? I know that it will seem like only moments ago to you, but can you recall exactly the date when you were cooled? Can you remember the names and faces of your friends, and your own name, too, of course? Think about these things and take your time."

But the girl did not need time to think. Promptly, she replied, "I was cooled during the Moon of the Leaping Deer, early in the morning of . . . you paleskins would call it the seventh day of April, fourteen hundred and ninety-one, Anno Domini . . ."

The morning of the same day that she had been taken up to the ship, Nolan thought. Once he had agreed to do that small favor for Silver Elk, Wanachtee had moved fast.

"I can remember the places where I lived both recently and during early childhood," she went on, "and the names and faces of my relatives and friends are clear in my mind, as is my own name which I would prefer not to speak."

"Your name is not important to me," said Nolan, smiling, "so long as I am satisfied regarding your ability to remember it. If you tell me that you can remember all these things, that is good and I believe you."

She returned his smile, then looked down at her uncovered body for a moment before meeting his eyes again. Impishly, she said, "A girl should be allowed to keep something hidden from a man."

Nolan laughed quietly and said, "Not, I hope, from every man. Not from the one who, like you, sleeps in a casket that does not bear his true identity. As a Healer I can find nothing wrong with you, either in mind or body, and must now return you to cold sleep."

"Please wait," she said, and her slender brown fingers were tightly encircling his wrist. "If you know that, you must be Healer Nolan and the one my great-grandfather told me who would be asked to watch over us while we slept. Have you seen my . . . Is he, also, well?"

Nolan could give no such reassurance, because he did not know where in the ship Wanachtee might be, but the probability was high that the other was, indeed, well. Not wanting to worry her needlessly with the exact truth, he gently detached her fingers from his wrist and pressed her back into the casket.

"When you next awaken," he said softly, "it will be many centuries from now, but to the both of you only a moment will have passed. You can ask that question of him yourself."

When she was cold again Nolan continued to look into the casket for a moment. Her face was composed, her eyes closed, but it was the first time that he had seen anyone smiling in their cold sleep. He rubbed at his eyes irritably and looked across at Healer Dervla.

"She is well," he said, "but now we must try to cure the ills afflicting her casket."

Healer Dervla's response was to take a deep breath that she exhaled not at all silently through her nose. Then in a calm, controlled, and entirely clinical voice she said, "Healer Nolan, may all of your hair fall out and your eyes shrivel in their sockets, may a wasting fever turn your lungs to slime, may the manhood of your loins wither and drop off, and may an oozing, suppurating pox cover every single inch of your outsized body, if you do not tell me, now, at once, who is this woman, what secrets do you share, and what the hell is happening on this ship.

"Speak, Healer, ere I succumb to terminal curiosity," she ended fiercely. "Spit me out another tooth!"

Nolan moved to the other casket and began opening the fastenings that kept its internal padding in place. He said, "She is Golden Rain, the recently married squaw of the Redman executive sub-Chief, Wanachtee, who also sleeps somewhere in the ship. She is also greatly beloved by her great-grandfather, the great Chief of Chiefs, Silver Elk, who asked that I perform a small favor for him, that of secretly bringing her, with the help of Wanachtee and a number of Mojave Spaceport personnel, to the ship.

"If you don't mind, Healer Dervla," he added, "I will work as we speak."

While he was making a careful visual inspection of the circuitry that lay under the layers of padding, he went on to relate the effect on Silver Elk of the Coshawnee incident and the relevant conversations and actions of Wanachtee and himself.

"I remember that you were given permission to visit the children of some influential Plains Chief," she said when he had finished speaking. "At the time you were scarcely missed—because there were some difficult financial negotiations in progress, His Eminence told me later. Was it a coincidence that the difficulties were resolved, to the satisfaction of all concerned, on the seventh of April?"

"Probably not," said Nolan.

Dervla made a sound that could have meant anything. She said, "Do I understand correctly? You have been asked to take special care of this Westland woman because she is already married to another colonist, when we both know that all such pairings are expressly forbidden until the colony is established. As well, you have in your possession a brassard that is worn only by those entrusted with the urgent and private business of His Celestial Highness of Cathay. Healer, I would hear more."

In a voice that was louder than would normally be considered mannerly, for the reason that his head and upper body were deep inside the faulty casket, he told her of his lecture in the Imperial College of Lensmakers and the subsequent request by Hseng Hwa that he travel silently, his features hidden by the glare shield and wearing the brassard in plain sight. He had not been told the identity of the person he was to escort, but had learned later that it was a boy-child of the Imperial Family.

". . . And I cannot find a fault in this accursed thing!" Nolan went on angrily as he looked up at her. "But fault there must surely be, and it must be found."

It was plain from Dervla's expression that curiosity rather than the technicalities of cold sleep caskets was uppermost in her mind.

She said, "It seems that you have been requested, or perhaps have chosen to make yourself, personally responsible for the safety of the Heir Apparent of Cathay as well as this lovely and unlawfully married colonist from Westland. Before I ask you why, please answer me this: Are there others of whom you have appointed yourself a special guardian?"

He must have missed the fault during the first and perhaps overly hasty examination, Nolan thought, so he would have to repeat it with more care. He sighed, and said, "There is the Ionadacht, Ciaran, and—"

"Surely not!" said Dervla incredulously. "What need has the Captain of the Imperial Guard for a guardian?"

"And the Princess Ulechitzl," Nolan went on in a firm voice. "I believe now that his concern was for her safety rather than his own. They met for the first time at Maeve's reception at Tara, but it was plain that Ciaran felt very protective toward her, although her own feelings were not so clearly displayed. In any event, his concern seems to have been justified, because her casket was one of many others that were moved aft from the crew module. Fortunately, hers did not develop a fault."

Dervla was silent for a moment, then she said thoughtfully, "Why should she, or indeed any sleeper, be moved during the course of the voyage? I remember this Princess Ulechitzl. A small, beautiful, and very intelligent girl who, in the years ahead, would naturally seek the protection of a large and capable man like Ciaran, or indeed yourself. She is doubly fortunate in having both of you as guardians. And, Healer, my original question remains: Are there any other beautiful young female colonists under your protection?"

Nolan's eyes were on her, but his mind was seeing only the complexities of the last circuit board he had examined. Again she misread his expression.

"It seems, Healer," she said coldly, "that my questions have become an irritation to you. I shall therefore leave you to work without distraction."

"No, please stay," said Nolan quickly. "I need all the nontechnical and moral support that you can give me. And I will gladly answer your questions until there isn't a tooth left in my mouth. But now I must concentrate, because this time I shall be powering up the individual circuits which together make the warming possible, and hope to uncover the fault in this way since the other method has failed. The procedure is risky, however, in that I might accidentally initiate a premature warming sequence and—"

"Risky!" said Dervla fiercely. In a voice of angry concern she went on, "That is no exaggeration. I have learned enough about hibernation anesthesia to know that the radiation needed to warm a cold sleeper is seriously damaging, perhaps even lethal, to a body that is already warm. Please be careful. I need you as a Healer, not a patient."

"There should be enough warning for me to withdraw in time," Nolan said reassuringly. "The risk, if you think about it, is to Golden Rain and the ship."

She was thinking about it, for the scattering of freckles that he had not hitherto noticed were standing out darkly on a face that had grown suddenly pale.

"This is a colonist casket," he went on grimly, "which means that if I cause it to go prematurely into the thaw cycle, its usefulness is ended so far as warming Golden Rain is concerned. She could remain in your casket until journey's end, but that is not a possibility to be given serious consideration by either of us, because you would then have to remain warm in the ship for the rest of your life. That would be a complete waste of a multi-cycle unit, and of your own life and professional knowledge which will undoubtedly be instrumental in saving many lives on the New World. You would have to be a martyr, a selfish and stupid and most irresponsible martyr, to consider doing that. So it would be Golden Rain who would have to live out her life on board, with all the personal tragedy, not to mention the moral difficulties she would cause to a succession of celibate watch-keeping officers."

Dervla laughed suddenly, then said, "I'm sorry, it is not a matter for laughter."

"No," said Nolan, and went on, "out of kindness, and to reduce the level of temptation to our priestly watch-keepers, I would seriously consider reviving Wanachtee as well, so that the two of them could at least live out their lives together on the ship."

Dervla looked at him long and steadily, with an expression he could not read. When she spoke, her words were critical but the tone was not.

"Healer Nolan," she said, "you seriously trouble me. Your heart is too soft. Were you to do anything as stupid and sentimental as that, I have no doubt our priestly colleagues would find it easier to resist the temptation of a married female, but the other forms of disruption might be great indeed. What if, as is highly probable, there are children? And the children have children? *Aisling Gheal* was never designed to be a generation ship. But I assume you have already considered these possibilities?"

"Yes," said Nolan.

"And?" Dervla prompted gently.

"And I must correct the fault in this bloody casket," he replied, "and make no mistakes while I'm doing it."

Dervla gestured toward her own casket and said, "Golden Rain sleeps and there is no great urgency about this repair. Much depends on your skill as a technician rather than a Healer, and it may be that a lengthy pause, to rest, or talk about other matters, would help you to order your thoughts."

"You tempt me sorely," said Nolan, "but I feel that if I do not find this fault soon then I shall never do so. But it is work for the fingers, not the mind, so by all means talk and give me something else to think about."

"I had no intention of tempting you," said Dervla, her face deepening in color. She went on thoughtfully, "The captain once told me that the original intention was to make the unlawful warming of a colonist or crew-member a crime punishable by death. This was during the early days, he said, when the crew as well as the colonists were expected to be in proportion to their natural contributions. It was believed that the loneliness and other psychological pressures of a solitary two-year watch made the threat of the ultimate excommunication the only effective deterrent to would-be offenders. But that would have meant that any watch-keeper might have been called on to execute a colleague. Fortunately, the planners considered this solution to be barbaric and the psychological pressures on each and every crew-member to be unacceptable. That was why Maeve's suggestion that the ship be crewed entirely by technical members of the Imperial Civil Service of Hibernia was adopted after much long and bitter disputation. But it was finally agreed that the ship would indeed be manned exclusively by Hibernian-trained ecclesiastics rather than their brethren of the European Church, some of whom in the past had been inclined toward moral laxity, the excessive acquisition of worldly riches, and much other unpriestly behavior. Hibernia's strict religious training, rigorous, near-Druidic self-disciplines, and uncompromising dedication to the celibate life would enable them to serve as watch-keepers with minimum risk of psychological disorders. Also, as priests, they would be obliged by their calling to mete out such punishment as might become necessary in as nonviolent a fashion as was possible.

"A few nonclerics were included," Dervla went on. "Lander pilots, who were not to be allowed to stand watch, and the members of the medical department who were thought to be psychologically stable and sufficiently dedicated to their own calling to similarly resist the temptations of the flesh. They were also included, His Eminence told me, to help ward off the criticism that *Aisling Gheal* was becoming the private property of the Hibernian Empress."

"The captain," said Nolan in surprise, "spoke of such highly confidential matters to you? Should you be telling me about them?"

"His Eminence," said Dervla, her tone becoming defensive, "has been helpful to me at Tara and on the ship. He is the only other officer on *Aisling Gheal* with whom I could talk freely, and in the present circumstances any misplaced confidences will not get back to the High-Queen. Besides, I spoke only to relieve your mind of one of its problems by reminding you of the form of relatively mild, nonviolent, priestly punishment that awaits you if the work does not go well."

"Thank you," said Nolan. "I meant no offense—"

"Of course you meant no offense!" said Dervla, with a sudden flare of temper. "You never mean to give offense. You seem always to consider the feelings and needs of others to the exclusion of your own. You are a great, fat jelly of a man with no backbone, no mind of his own, and a man who can refuse nothing to anybody. And yet there are times when you seem to lose whatever mind you have, and you speak or act in a fashion that places you, places us, at the most fearful risk. The Coshawnee incident, the rescue on the blast shield support, your use of that ceramic splint, and . . . and Father Quinn told the monsignor who told the cardinal who told me about the lecture in the College of Lensmakers. Highly complimentary to the Order of Orla and myself you were, and I should thank you for that. But if those blackthumbs had succeeded in discrediting you and casting doubt on the already-agreed postlanding medical procedures, the project could have been set back by months or even years. And now you have involved me in this present situation, one that could place the entire project in even greater jeopardy if the Redwoman cannot be cooled. For a big, soft, inoffensive man who is everyone's tool, you can certainly cause havoc out of all proportion to—"

"I'm sorry," said Nolan, feeling his own temper begin to slip, "but what else could I have done?" In an attempt to answer at least one of her accusations he went on, "If I am used, then it is only by those I like or respect or—"

"Your trouble," Dervla broke in angrily, "is that you like people too easily."

"Again, I am sorry," Nolan replied, in a tone that was a total contradiction of the words.

For a moment they glared at each other in silence. Then gradually Dervla's angry expression began to change to one of sympathy and concern.

"Healer Nolan," she said quietly, "it is I who should apologize. This is not the time for recriminations and harsh or hasty words which I, to my shame, have been using for the relief of my own feelings rather than in your support. You have a difficult and delicate task ahead, one that only you can perform, and harsh words from me are not helpful. Once again, I apologize."

A small, cynical part of Nolan's mind wondered whether the apology was truly meant or if it was simply a therapeutic exercise with the purpose of steadying his mind and hands. But as he looked into the clear, warm eyes he had studied so closely and often when she was cold, he felt heartily ashamed of that untrusting group of brain cells, because it was plain that her apology had been both.

When he did not speak for a moment, Dervla said very seriously, "You have already broken, for reasons which you personally consider good and sufficient, several of the strictest regulations governing the behavior of ship's officers. The unlawful use of a spacesuit to travel aft and on the outer hull, the special attention you are giving to certain of the sleepers, and now, the most grievous offense of all, the unscheduled and completely unlawful warming of two cold sleepers.

"I am curious, Healer Nolan, and not a little afraid," she went on. "Is there any ship's regulation so strict and binding that you would never consider breaking it?"

For a very long time they held each other's gaze, neither speaking nor moving, until Nolan looked away again toward the faulty casket.

"Until now," he said softly, "there was only one."

Chapter 24

"MY brain," said Nolan with great vehemence, "is composed of rancid porridge, the mind of an amadan. I am unworthy to be numbered among the members of a sapient race. Great God in Heaven, I am *stupid*!"

Dervla gave him a worried look. "Far be it from me," she said in a neutral voice, "to disagree with the self-diagnosis of another Healer, but is there supporting evidence? What distresses an unbeliever to such an extent that you are driven to call on the Deity? Is your news good or bad?"

"It is good," said Nolan in an embarrassed voice. "But I was so stupid that I don't deserve good news. Nearly four hours of careful, repetitious, and totally unnecessary work that must have aged me by four years . . ."

Time and again he had examined each and every section in the casket's internal circuitry without finding either a break or a faulty component to explain the system failure, he explained, until he was sure that Golden Rain had the most perfect colonist casket in the entire ship. In desperation he had begun looking outside the casket, and at the sealed and supposedly damage-proof power line.

"During the transfer from the crew module," Nolan went on, "the casket must have escaped from them. Before it could collide with anything and damage itself, and without realizing what he was doing, someone must have pulled it up short by grabbing the power cable. Being flexible, the protective insulation stretched without breaking, but not so the wiring inside. I know to within a few inches where the break occurred, and it is a simple matter to splice it and restore the casket to full operation."

He stopped suddenly to give a tremendous, eye-watering yawn and went on, "After that, we can transfer the sleeper from your casket to her own while she is still cold, and return it to its original position. Or rather the position to which, for some mysterious reason, it was moved. Our problem is therefore solved. There need be no more unlawful warmings or the danger of a population explosion on the ship. Her thaw cycle will function normally whenever it is required, and Golden Rain will sleep safely until the end of the voyage and her meeting with Wanachtee, which to her is but a few moments off."

"And I," said Dervla, "will be able to return to my own casket."

"Yes, of course," said Nolan. But it must have been obvious to her that those were not the words he had wanted her to speak.

"You have done very well, Healer," she went on quickly, "and I think that you are much too critical of yourself. There is nothing wrong with your mind, apart from its inability to obey lawful orders, and considering the length of time you have been active without sleep, I would say that your mental shortcomings are due to fatigue rather than stupidity. But that is a condition easily relieved. The splicing can wait for a few more hours, so you should return at once to your hammock and catch up on your sleep."

"You give good advice, Healer," said Nolan, smiling, "but there is still much I must tell you . . ."

He broke off as she raised a hand in the casual, imperious gesture of one who is in the habit of command. "Later there will be time for that, too. And I was not giving advice, Healer. It was an order."

He turned away quickly in an angrily prompt obedience that was in itself an insubordination. Since her warming he had thought that her feelings toward him had softened, but he had been wrong. She was his head of department, a Healer and All-Mother of the Order of Orla, and nothing more. He knew that it was a physiological impossibility, but he could almost believe that the mind and heart inside that splendid body had been permanently and independently frozen into their own form of cold sleep.

As he was leaving, she called softly, "Sleep well, Healer Nolan."

But he was much too angry at first to sleep, and when he did, his dreams were confused and disturbed by visions of a Dervla who was not a cold and unfeeling superior officer, and whose smile was warm and loving and full of concern, and not at all like that of a mother.

Their subsequent conversations were stiff and formal, at least on Nolan's part, for Dervla scarcely spoke at all. While he was describing the sounds he had heard after her visit, his surprise and pleasure at the monsignor's giving him the first watch, and then the discovery that a large number of crew caskets had been transferred aft, his voice and manner were as impersonal as that of a Healer describing a long and involved case history. So long was it that by the time he was finished, they had returned Golden Rain to her place and reconnected her casket.

"Healer Nolan," said Dervla, breaking her long silence at last, "I know nothing of any of this. It is as inexplicable to me as it is to you. I can offer no help."

Which meant that there would be no more reason to delay her cooling, and after the required two-day fast he would again be all alone in the ship.

It was a thought that had not troubled him, until now.

He said quickly, "Have you been privy to any conversations, incidents, or meetings at Tara or on the ship, the content or meaning of which was not completely clear to you? Is there a suspicion in your mind, however tenuous, that something was being concealed? Something that might shed a light, however dim, on this mystery?"

"I'm sorry," she said. "I can recall no such conversations or incidents."

"Is it possible," Nolan went on, "that while you were talking to the captain, he may have let slip something which might—"

"Your persistence is beginning to irritate, Healer," she broke in sharply. "If he did know about it, I'm sure that His Eminence would not be a party to anything dishonorable or unlawful. Our conversations were as those between friends, between troubled friends. My original answer stands."

"My apologies, Healer Dervla," said Nolan, his embarrassment hidden by the suit visor. "Please believe me, I had no wish to pry into a privileged communication."

Suddenly, Dervla laughed. It was altogether the saddest laugh that Nolan had ever heard. She said, "I believe you. But can a conversation between patients be considered privileged?"

Nolan did not reply at once. The sudden revelation that she was seriously troubled about something, as had been the cardinal-captain, was a factor that he had to consider very carefully if he was to help her. He knew that she would not have spoken of it at all had she not wanted to say more. But a blundering, insensitive question at this stage might cause her to become once again the imperious and seemingly impervious Healer Dervla who would say nothing. This was not the time for prying.

Instead, he said, "Where we are now, there is only Module J and the grain and livestock storage compartments between us and the power module. He won't be able to talk to you, naturally, but would you like to visit your friend?"

"Yes," said Dervla.

They arrived in the captain's laboratory and aft living quarters a few minutes later, squinting against the strong light after the darkness of the corridors. Nolan switched on the heater and opened his visor. Tiny clouds of condensation accompanied the words as he spoke.

"There is a minor radiation hazard," he said. "We would have to remain here several months for it to have any genetic effects, but I thought I should remind you."

Dervla opened her own helmet but did not reply. She floated across to the captain's casket and hung there as she stared intently at the calm, frozen face. Nolan followed her, pausing a moment to check the casket monitor before positioning himself beside her.

"He is well," he said.

Dervla's breath puffed out in a sharp, irritated sigh, obscuring her face. She said, "You know, Healer Nolan, we should not be here."

"I know," he said.

"You do *not* know!" she said angrily, nodding toward the cold sleeper. "*We* should not be here. I did not want to travel in this oversized spacegoing collection of scrap metal, and neither did His Eminence!"

"But that . . . that's impossible," Nolan protested, surprise and shock making him forget that it was not good to call one's senior officer a liar. But he need not have worried, because it was obvious that she had decided to talk and nothing was going to stop her.

"Oh, he wanted to go to the New World," she went on angrily, "he was as keen as you are about that. But not now. There were technical reasons which he did not try to explain to me, and he wanted to place a five- or maybe a ten-year hold on the launch. But Maeve told him that the project was beginning to fall apart, that he was the only person with enough scientific and moral standing to hold it together, and that if he did not leave soon then *Aisling Gheal* would end its days as an orbiting factory instead of Earth's first starship. She also reminded him of his age and said that in five or ten years hence he would not be able to survive the journey. She forced him to come, as she did her Court Healer."

While she was speaking, Dervla had never taken her eyes from the cardinal-captain's face. The heater was beginning to take the chill from the room so that her face was no longer wreathed in the fog of breathing. Her voice became quieter and she looked bitterly disappointed rather than angry as she went on. "The things I said to the High-Queen were not moral judgments made because she was nothing but a Royal wanton—they were spoken only out of concern for her continued health. It is the custom that only the highest qualified of my Order should guard the health of the High-Queen. But Maeve wanted another sycophant rather than a Healer of the First Name, and so I was chosen for the unique professional challenge and immeasurably high honor, which I could not refuse without disgrace to my Order, of serving instead the medical needs of Earth's first star colony."

Dervla was quiet for a moment and Nolan, too, remained silent. He was beginning to realize why, on Earth as well as in the ship, she had appeared so often to be angry and withdrawn. He had assumed, mistakenly, that everyone on *Aisling Gheal* was a willing volunteer. She must be a very angry and unhappy Healer who was trying, not always with success, to accept her fate.

"Cardinal Keon learned of Maeve's plan for me before I did," she went on, "and told me of it during his next medical examination. He knew that I enjoyed the life of Court, with its pomp and pageantry and being privy to the intrigues and scandals at the heart of the greatest empire the world had ever known. He knew and sympathized, because, had it not been for that stupid limp, he would have been its High-King. So he tried many times to make Maeve change her mind and send another Healer, one of the many who would have sold their souls for the chance to go in my place. But she would not, and gradually the meetings we had to report his lack of progress became attempts by a great man and a most sympathetic priest to ease my sense of loss, a loss which he himself had been feeling for the whole of his adult life.

"And then," she went on, "we moved to the ship and the monsignor suggested that I was gossiping too much with the cardinal-captain, who was too kindly to forbid it. It might well be that the captain himself thought that it was time for me to stand on my own feet. You would not think it to look at that face, but he was such a kindly and sensitive man, and I miss talking to him."

Dervla looked up again and said, "And now, Healer Nolan, you are doubtless shocked and sickened by this shameful confession of selfishness and cowardice?"

"No!" he said with great vehemence. "You're not a . . . I mean, there are many people, many billions of people, who would disagree with you. They would say that wishing to remain on

Earth shows good sense, displays intelligent self-interest rather than selfishness, but never cowardice!"

Dervla gave a small sigh and said quietly, "Even when you speak in haste, you sometimes use the right words."

"Only when I mean them," said Nolan.

Dervla shook her head, and for a moment she looked again at the still features of the captain, then she said, "I remember too much here. Let us leave this place."

Nolan switched off the heating unit and made a quick visual inspection of the room. Dervla's eyes were staring at something very far away and he thought that she looked the picture of one who badly needed a change of mental subject.

As she was about to seal her helmet, he said suddenly, "Would you like to take the scenic route back along the outer hull? It is much faster than going back through that unlit rabbit warren, and at the very least you will find it an instant cure for claustrophobia."

"Are you trying to humor me, Healer?" Dervla asked sharply, but she did not say no.

Without further speech he led the way to the nearest airlock. Once outside, he detached his boot magnets and drifted away from the hull preparatory to using his suit thrusters. Dervla was still standing crouched beside the lock.

"I was not given the time for full spasaire training," she said.

"What!" said Nolan incredulously. Quickly he jetted down beside her and began reopening the airlock. "Don't worry; you'll be all right if you just stand still—your boot magnets will hold you to the hull. But why didn't you tell me? We'll go back by—"

"By the scenic route," said Dervla firmly.

Only now did he remember how slow and careful she had been while donning the spacesuit, and he had approved because it seemed that she was being safety-conscious. He should insist that they take the internal route back, but he had an idea of how far his insistence would get him.

"You don't have to fly," he said reassuringly. "Just slide your boot magnets along the hull plating. If you come to a structural projection, be sure that one boot remains in contact while you step over it. If the obstruction is large or awkwardly shaped, I shall remain in contact and hold you steady until you are attached again. In the unlikely event that you were to lose contact and drift away, I would go after you and use my suit thrusters to bring you back."

"I heard all about your last space rescue," said Dervla as she took the first slow, sliding step. "I would not want to be brought back with my legs splinted."

"You won't be," said Nolan. "I'm sorry about this, Healer Dervla. I meant only to give you something different to think about, not to risk scaring you out of your wits."

"Your treatment," Dervla replied, after taking a few more steps, "is best described as crude but effective."

"But taking that treatment," said Nolan, "was hardly the act of a coward."

"Neither," said Dervla, and suddenly she laughed, "was it an act of *intelligent* self-interest."

From their position at the stern, the tiny, brilliant Sun was still hidden by the blast shield, so that as their eyes became accustomed to the darkness the stars grew more brilliant and seemed to crowd low above them, outlining the dark curves and angular projections of a metal world that was clear only when their spotlights fell on it.

"I—I have no words," said Dervla in the tone of voice believers use in a cathedral, "it is so beautiful."

With Nolan gripping her upper arm to steady her, Dervla had begun to move quickly and with growing confidence. But he found it difficult to encircle the thick, padded sleeve with his gauntleted fingers and soon moved his grip down to her hand.

He began to remember some of the dreams he had had, dreams that had begun like this with him walking hand-in-hand with a beautiful woman under a sky crowded with stars, and ended as all such dreams end. But in those dreams they had been separated only by the lightest of raiment and the warm and scented air of a summer evening, instead of an instantly lethal vacuum and a mobile life-support system that allowed little more than visual contact. He tightened his grip on her hand, but felt nothing but the back pressure of his own gauntlets.

Dervla must have felt it because she cleared her throat and said, "Is there something you would ask of me, Healer?"

"Yes," said Nolan. He had something to say, but suddenly he was unsure of what exactly it was or how he should go about saying it. And so, in an act of the most abject moral cowardice, he said something else entirely. "Earlier you said that you were a Healer of the First Name. I am not familiar with that term. What does it mean?"

"Oh, that," said Dervla. "From what Father Quinn told me

about your Orla lecture, I thought you knew everything there was to know about us. As you do know, Orla herself refused to be called by her family name. Similarly, the one graduate of the year who displays the highest attainable standards of personal behavior and professional competence in all disciplines, standards which no undertrained male Healer however gifted could ever equal, is called only by her first name. All other Healers, even those eminent in the Order itself, and, of course, all of the lesser-qualified males who call themselves Healers, are addressed or otherwise referred to only by their family names.

"If you were sufficiently curious," she went on, "you could find that my family name appears on the crew roster, as does your own Christian, excuse me, your non-Christian name. You have a proud if common name that is given, for obvious reasons, to one male child in every Hibernian family. But let me remind you that the difference in our levels of professional training is so great that you will always be Healer Nolan to me and I Healer Dervla to you."

"I shall remember," he said.

"Very well," said Dervla. "Is there anything else you would know?"

She had begun to sound angry with him, and Nolan could think of no reason for it other than that his question had reminded her of everything she had left behind at Tara. Or more likely, was she simply reminding him of who and what she was, and answering indirectly the question that he had been too cowardly to ask?

Perhaps he would ask it in a different way.

"There is another question," said Nolan. "I had meant to ask it earlier, during one of our conversations in the department. But the chance was lost because the monsignor must have decided that we were gossiping instead of holding, as we insisted, professional discussions regarding medical treatment on the—"

"We were gossiping, Healer," said Dervla impatiently. "What is your question?"

"—New World," Nolan went on, ignoring the interruption. "I have no clear idea of what you intend. Will I be working with you from the central House of Sorrows, and traveling to outlying areas when required? Or will we be separated with individual responsibilities for our own districts? And if you intend us to be separated, either by time or distance, I need to know how to deal with—"

"That is many questions, Healer," she broke in again.

"And the most important one," Nolan continued, "has to do

with what you have called my lack of proper training. I am a surgeon rather than a physician, but on the New World I will need the kind of knowledge that only you possess, if my patients and myself are to survive. Can you teach me to recognize the difference between vegetation, roots, or plants or berries that are harmless and edible, and those which are toxic and perhaps lethal?"

"God in Heaven!" said Dervla, and halted so suddenly that he was not able to stop before his grip on her hand had pulled her away from the hull. "Do you expect me to teach you the knowledge it took me fifteen years to learn, in a *day*?"

"Of course not," said Nolan. He reached forward with his free hand and gripped her other gauntlet tightly so as to steady her and bring her boots back into contact with metal. "I don't want all of your knowledge. I do not need to know all the unnecessary, polysyllabic Latin names and the medicinal properties of the roots and herbs and molds of Earth. We will not be on Earth. I only need to know how to look at a leaf or a berry that I am seeing for the first time, and be able to tell whether or not it will poison me. Can you teach me how to do that, with a better-than-even chance of my being right?"

"Healer Nolan," she said in a quiet, serious voice, "it is not as easy as you made it sound in Cathay. That ability comes through a combination of experience and a finely tuned instinct, and that, too, needs more than a few hours to impart."

"Perhaps, Healer Dervla," he replied in a tone that matched her own, "you could take more than a few hours to impart it."

His hold on both her hands meant that Dervla was facing him, but they had not traveled far enough forward for the tiny, distant Sun to have risen above the blast shield, and the light from the star-crowded sky was too dim to enable him to read her expression when she spoke.

"Surely," she said, "you aren't suggesting that I spend the remainder of your watch trying to teach you?"

When Nolan did not reply, her voice developed a sarcastic edge as she went on, "No doubt you would find that a more instructive and interesting way of passing your remaining year than living with your own company. But it is in the nature of things that as the days passed you would want more from me than information, and my answer is, as you yourself know that it must be, no. So I shall go cold as soon as the remaining hours of my fast are over."

She detached a gauntleted hand from one of his and turned away to resume the interrupted walk.

Dervla was moving much more confidently, Nolan saw, and they had traveled more than half the distance to Control. Behind them the Sun had risen above the edge of the blast shield, and the dark, metallic landscape around them had begun to reflect dull highlights of a paler gray. They were sliding along one of the four great longitudinal members that ran the length of the ship, and the deep, convex curves of the valley slopes between Modules F and G were below them when next she spoke.

Without preamble she said, "I shall begin by stating some general rules to which there are many and dangerous exceptions. On Earth it is usual for most forms of vegetation to both attract and repel, the first with flowers or berries or fruit for the purpose of reproducing its kind, by attracting pollen-carrying insects, or by dropping its fruit to rot and germinate in the ground, or by ensuring that the fruit is pleasant-tasting so that it will be eaten by animals that will carry the inedible seed stones farther afield. To repel, it will use such stratagems as growing thorns, or poisonous stems, or foul-tasting or stinging leaves, or even use the bitterness of unready fruit to protect itself against overeager eaters until its reproductive mechanism is quite ready."

She did not look at him as she spoke, but stared instead into the sky ahead of them as if each star were a silent and attentive student in a vast lecture theater. She went on, "Plant roots, covered as they are by soil, have little need of defense and are likely to be harmless, or at least less harmful. When examining an unfamiliar plant, especially if the intention is to use it as a possible source of food, it is very important that its natural weapons—that is, its methods of attraction and repulsion—be identified. This is best done by closely observing the immediate environment and noting whether it is dominant or there are other types of vegetation competing with it, and the behavior of the animal and insect life in the area toward it . . ."

Dervla continued talking firmly and clearly, and paying him the compliment of not pausing to ask if he understood everything she was saying. By the time they reached the crew module and were removing their suits, Nolan's head ached with the effort of concentration needed for him to be able to remember and accurately retain every word.

"There is much more I can tell you," said Dervla. She laughed quietly and went on, "But from the look that has just passed across your facc like a heavy raincloud, I would say that it is you who are badly in need of a change of subject. Why don't you visit the food dispenser, alone, since I have no wish to suffer by watching you gorge yourself."

"Are you sure you won't join me?" began Nolan. "With even a little more time I might learn to—"

"I shall not break my fast," Dervla said firmly, "nor delay my cooling."

"Then, I shall remain here with you," said Nolan, "and make the best use I can of our remaining time together. And, of course, I will change the subject."

She gave him a wary look, and said, "To what?"

Nolan smiled, realizing that the meaning of his earlier words might have been misconstrued, then he said very seriously, "To the reason for the transfer aft of those sleepers in the crew module. At present I have no clear idea why it was done, only the wildest of suppositions. But if you were to listen to what little I know or suspect . . . ?"

For many weeks, Nolan told her, he had thought about little else but this mystery. He had begun by accepting that if the transfer had been made for operational reasons, then the crew would have been informed or, if any of them had already been cooled, an entry should have been made informing them of what had happened in the watch-keeper's log. Since this had not been done, he had assumed that the operation was a covert and therefore unlawful one.

It was by no means certain that the entire crew was involved, because the casket transfers had been made by a small number of officers—otherwise the malfunction due to rough handling of Golden Rain's casket would not have occurred. And unless the operation contained elements of mutiny, which seemed unlikely, then it must have been carried out with the knowledge of the senior officers, who included Monsignor O'Riordan and Cardinal-Captain Keon . . .

"And before you rush to his defense by telling me that His Eminence would never lend himself to a dishonorable act of any kind," Nolan went on quickly, "from everything I know or have heard of him, I would agree with you. But he *must* know what is going on in his ship. He must have been told of this secret plan or conspiracy in every detail. He may not have any control over the situation at this stage, and knowing the kind of man he is, the probability is high that he is not in agreement with it."

"You've lost me, Healer," said Dervla.

"When I met Ciaran for the first time, it was at Maeve's reception," he went on, "and he said that Monsignor O'Riordan, rather than the captain, was my real chief. The Ionadacht is a friendly man with a ready wit, so at the time I assumed he was joking. But if his remark was intended to be taken seriously, perhaps he was giving me a friendly warning to be careful of the monsignor without, however, telling me why. As an unbeliever with no clear idea of the inner motivations that drive a priest, much less those with the special qualities of dedication needed for the Imperial Civil Service, I hesitate to describe the monsignor as an arch-villain, or indeed any other kind of bad or criminal person, but I would say with certainty that in all this he is the arch-plotter."

He could see that Dervla was becoming impatient, so he continued quickly, "As the ship's psychologist, second-in-command, and the most senior prelate on board after the cardinal, it is natural to assume that there would be many weighty matters burdening his mind, and equally natural that he would feel the need to share that burden with another, especially if it included his concerns regarding the rights or wrongs of this plot we are trying to fathom. If I read his character aright, he would not want to overburden a junior officer with his self-doubts or transgressions even though that junior ecclesiastic would be equally as capable of acting as his confessor. So it is my theory that he would unburden himself, under the Seal, to the cardinal."

While he was speaking, Dervla's face had grown increasingly stiff and pale with anger. Nolan had a sudden memory of his homeland, the Isle of Fire and Ice, and of a volcano about to erupt.

"Forgive me, Healer Dervla," he said, "for having such a nasty and devious mind."

She shook her head angrily, and said, "You have a mind, Healer Nolan. It is others who are being devious. Wait."

For a long time her gaze remained fixed immovably on his face, but he doubted that she was even seeing him, for it was plain that her eyes were on people and events distant indeed in time and space. Finally she spoke.

"Your theory explains much," she said. "If the monsignor revealed anything about the project, the smallest deviation in plans or problems with the colonists or crew that was not already common knowledge, under the Seal of Confession, then His Eminence could not speak of it. More, he could not by a single word or meaningful silence or facial expression give the smallest hint of the content of what he had learned. Should the matter be brought up or even approached by anyone else, he would be bound to change the subject and avoid speaking of it. It explains why, even at Tara, he would not speak to me of the project except in the most general terms. When I pressed him, he would change the subject, and I had the impression that he was angry, although not with me. Maeve would not answer specific questions, either, even though she was as closely involved with the project as were the cardinal and Monsignor O'Riordan. And now that I recall it, the monsignor, too, seemed averse to discussing anything about the colony with me, its senior Healer.

"He gave the impression that he did not approve of my going," she went on thoughtfully, "possibly because the High-Queen had told him that I was not a volunteer. And my impression of him was that in his own quiet, gentle way the monsignor is a zealot who does not approve of anyone whose enthusiasm is less than his own. But in my case he could not go against the directly expressed wish of his High-Queen.

"As a cleric who was aware of all the Court gossip," she continued, "I would have expected him to approve less of Maeve than of myself. But they seemed to get along very well together, because he had at least four times the number of audiences with her—presumably to discuss the project, since they had no other interests in common—than had His Eminence, whom she avoided whenever possible."

Nolan shook his head vigorously, as if by doing so he could shake an answer from his bemused mind. He said, "Everything you have told me points to the conclusion that long before we left Earth, and perhaps shortly after the project's inception, this conspiracy that so puzzles us now was already known to the monsignor, the cardinal-captain and even the High-Queen. It is very much larger and more complicated than I had first thought. But what are they doing, or trying to do, and to what purpose?"

She made no reply, and her expression of puzzlement must have been the mirror of his own.

After a long silence, he said, "If we were to visit the Skandian section and list the identities of all the sleepers in the transposed caskets, that might give a clue to why they were moved."

Dervla sighed, and said, "Doing that would give me an excuse for staying warm for another few days, and breaking my fast. My stomach is making unruly sounds which you are too polite to mention. But it might also be a waste of time, because the majority of the names would be unknown to us. Until we know what the conspirators' intentions are, there is nothing we can do. And even if we did know, we might not be able to do anything. But while we do not know personally the sleepers who were transferred, we do know the kind of people they are. If they are not leaders in their own particular fields, then they are members of highly placed and influential families . . ."

She broke off as Nolan shook his head again. Dervla's words, he did not know which of her words, had awakened an idea at the back of his mind. He said, "A leader is not easily led."

"What," said Dervla impatiently, "is the significance of that particular profundity?"

"I don't know," he replied unhappily. "But there was something you said that made me wonder . . . Is there anything else you can remember happening at Tara, or later? Any remarks by His Eminence or the monsignor about the project that seemed unimportant at the time, and may still seem so now, which in the light of—"

"Healer Nolan," she said, "you are trying to build a house out of cobwebs."

"I know," he said.

"Very well," she said. "I can recall one interesting, but doubtless insignificant, meeting between the cardinal, the monsignor, and myself in my consulting room at the House of Sorrows, during which your name was mentioned. Monsignor O'Riordan had the earlier appointment, and I had completed his examination while the cardinal was still awaiting his. We were discussing the physical and psychological pressures of watch-keeping, and O'Riordan told me that his original intention had been that the two Healers as well as certain nonecclesiastical officers would not be required to stand watch. After he left us, I was making polite conversation about the project with His Eminence. This was before he discovered that I was a most reluctant volunteer. I said that while I was not myself a Healer of the Mind, it seemed strange to me that the monsignor, who was such a quiet, gentle-mannered, and kindly man, should be the second-in-command of the starship, and I wondered how such a man would survive the experience. It was then that the cardinal said a strange thing in a voice that made me think that it might be some kind of private joke."

Nolan looked a loud, wordless question at her, and she went on, "He said that Monsignor O'Riordan was less interested in survival than in immortality, and that he wanted to be a better Brendan."

A better Brendan, Nolan thought. The analogy was clear, because Brendan the Navigator had been the first Hibernian to cross the Northern Ocean to the New World, and *Aisling Gheal* was about to travel the sea of stars to do the same. But surely the monsignor was setting his sights a little high. *Better* than Brendan indeed!

The idea that had been sleeping at the back of his mind was stirring again, shaking itself and coming out into the light.

"For obvious reasons," Nolan said very seriously, "Brendan is my favorite historical figure, and I have long been a student of his life and times. But I do not understand how Monsignor O'Riordan could ever hope to be better than the best. Brendan, too, was a small and gentle man. He was an enlightened priest and a fearless explorer who, if there was any fault in him, and as an unbeliever you will forgive me for not considering it a fault, it was that he was more statesman than missionary . . ."

He fell silent because all at once his mind was like a sprinter racing for Gold in the Tailllteann Games and his words could not keep pace. But he could see in Dervla's eyes that her mind, too, was racing in the same direction.

"But after decades of observation," she said, "we have detected no smallest sign of intelligent life on the New World. Surely an uninhabited planet is a poor prospect for a missionary?"

Nolan shook his head. "No. It is the unbelievers on the ship, the unbelievers and those who believe in gods different to that of the monsignor, and their descendants, that he wants to convert. The ecclesiastics among the crew are forbidden to marry, and it has been long accepted that they would be the colony's teachers charged with the responsibility of passing on all that is best of Earth's science, culture, and philosophies. I have no doubt that they will teach accurately and well, but I am also sure that there will be a lack of emphasis where the teaching of other religions is concerned. And if the celibate priesthood is to survive, a seminary must be established to train future priests, and they can only come from the already converted among the male children of the colonists. Their aim would be the establishment of a colony and ultimately a world whose population was wholly of the True Faith.

"If you detect a flaw in my theory, Healer Dervla," he ended, "I would be obliged—nay, profoundly grateful—if you could prove me wrong."

It was Dervla's turn to shake her head. She said, "I have no argument for you, Healer Nolan, for I am remembering the speech of Maeve's at the Tara reception. She made a slip of the tongue, from which she recovered very well, when she referred to planting the standard of Hibernia on the New World. I am also remembering the person she was and the life she led. You yourself must know of historical precedents for a ruler who spends his or her entire life in wanton profligacy and excess, who tries to atone for a lifetime of sin, and square the account in the hereafter, by performing some great and glorious act which will be especially pleasing to God by, in this case, making Him a gift of a planet that will in time be entirely populated by His followers."

Nolan made no reply, and her tone became defensive as she went on, "If that is the plan, then the monsignor and the others who are involved are doing a great wrong to the members of other sects. But to a zealot it might not seem to be a wrong. It would be like giving the human race a second chance to live in peace, and to multiply and prosper in a second Garden of Eden!"

"Yes," said Nolan in a voice so grim that it made her look at him uneasily. "And the people who would be most likely to hamper this glorious plan, the unbelievers with minds of their own and the leaders of the racial groups who hold other beliefs, would first be segregated inside the ship, in the Skandian section, and then placed eventually where they could do no harm.

"What does our kind and gentle monsignor intend to do with them?"

Chapter 25

NEITHER of them could say with certainty what the monsignor would do, and in tones that grew louder in direct proportion to their shortening tempers, they argued about it for more than a day. It was Dervla who had the last word for the simple reason that she also had the rank.

"Enough!" she said, raising her hand in the imperious gesture that so irritated him. "Is it likely, from what we know of him, that Monsignor O'Riordan will toss their caskets out of an airlock in midvoyage? It is not. And for the few hours of warm time remaining to me, you will change the subject forthwith or remain silent."

For a few moments Nolan considered choosing the latter option, then his anger cooled and he said, "Very well, I shall change the subject. I think we are agreed that no action can or should be taken until we are orbiting the New World, and before then we will each have to stand three two-year watches, which should be enough time for us to decide on the proper action to take. We are further agreed that our knowledge of the plot must be concealed from the monsignor, and everyone else connected in it, until then. Our best chance of success lies in pretending that—"

"Healer Nolan," said Dervla sharply, "the subject has not changed."

"Healer Dervla," said Nolan firmly, "the subject *has* changed. I am talking now about ensuring your future safety. Please hear me out."

Since the monsignor did not know about the Cathay spacesuit, Nolan went on to explain, it would be best if O'Riordan thought that only one suit, the one used by Dervla, had been needed for the work on Golden Rain's casket. In the watch-keepers' log entry that Nolan would make, he would report that it had been a very simple fault—that, at least, was the truth—which had been remedied without moving the casket. He would say that he had ignored the monsignor's advice about not going aft on this one occasion because he wanted to retrieve the hammock and equipment left behind in the grain storage compartment—he was, after all, a man of tidy habits—and on the way back he had taken a wrong turn and found himself in a casket stack where a malfunction light was burning. It had been too cold to investigate properly at the time and too cold for the sleeper to spoil quickly. He would say that he had thought long and carefully before disobeying the monsignor's order against the use of spacesuits by watch-keeping officers, but had decided that the situation constituted a medical emergency and his duty as a Healer had greater force in this case than a ship's regulation. He had taken a suit and returned to repair the faulty casket.

To answer any later questions regarding the number of air tanks that had been used by Dervla and himself, he would say that he had been worried by the malfunction and had thought it wise to check on a statistically meaningful number of other caskets in case the one failure he had discovered had been due to a design fault, but had found all of the units examined to be functioning properly. He had then returned the suit and he would not contravene the regulation again . . .

"Nor will I," Nolan went on. "Henceforth I shall not even think of leaving Control for any reason. All that remains is for me to return the Cathay suit to its place, using the suit that you have been wearing as protection against the cold, then come back here and return that suit to stores. This can be done in an hour, and after that nobody but ourselves need ever know that you were warmed."

"And by the time you return," said Dervla quietly, "I shall be cold."

"But I meant to stay with you until then," Nolan said quickly. "I don't have to replace the suits right now; that can be done at any time during my watch."

"No," said Dervla. "It should be done quickly, so that you can return to normal watch-keeping as soon as possible."

"But not immediately," he said.

Her eyes were watching him so steadily that he had to force himself not to look away from them. He wondered what he could say and, more importantly, what he would do if she made her strongly worded suggestion a direct order. The use of the captain's incredibly valuable ceramic tube as a splint had not endeared him to His Eminence, and the unauthorized use of a spacesuit would not make the monsignor his friend, and now he was considering disobeying an order of his department head, who would not take kindly to a word or act of disobedience from a mere male. But her eyes were still on his, and he could feel his face growing warmer as he waited for her next words.

Most decidedly, he thought, it was not an enemy that he wanted to make of Healer Dervla.

"As you wish," she said finally. And then, as if to show that she was still in command of the situation, she went on, "But I distrust your certainty that my warming will go undetected. Such overconfidence worries me."

Nolan gave a small, silent sigh of relief and said, "Thank you, Healer Dervla; I shall replace the suits as soon as you are cold. But I did not mean to worry you, or sound overconfident. I am fairly certain, not absolutely certain, of the outcome. It may be that my attempt at therapeutic reassurance was a trifle unsubtle."

"It was," said Dervla.

Nolan felt his face grow warm again. In a serious voice he said, "I am grateful for your assistance with Golden Rain, and for helping me reach some understanding of the monsignor's conspiracy, and most of all for reacting so well to the personal liberties taken as a result of warming you. I will be in trouble with O'Riordan, and, from what I know of you, it may be that you will have some idea that a trouble shared is a trouble halved, but in this case I fear greatly that it would be a trouble doubled. You must not be involved, and I am fairly certain that you won't be."

Her eyes were still on him but she did not speak.

"With the exception of myself," he went on quickly, "the other officers have had only the most rudimentary instruction on hypothermia and the casket systems, and all they are expected to do is conduct a quick, visual check at a distance to see that the malfunction warning is unlit. If an urgent malfunction was to occur, I would be warmed to attend to it. The others have been told repeatedly not to open the systems monitor panel, since an unskilled person doing so might accidentally precipitate a warming. It is highly unlikely, therefore, that anyone would learn from the timer record that your cold sleep had been interrupted. Being religious and morally self-disciplined, I should think that they would be satisfied with only the briefest of looks at your face, lest they be tempted to a sin of the mind.

"It is also unlikely," Nolan went on, "that they would reach such a level of loneliness that they would permit themselves to indulge in long, one-sided conversations with a cold sleeper. And so you can see that no close examination of your casket's monitors will be made, and none but ourselves need ever know that you were awake."

Dervla nodded slowly, and then smiled. She said, "I agree, Healer, it is a virtual certainty. But I suppose it would be senseless to forbid you to indulge in any more such conversations with me, since I would not know whether or not the order was obeyed."

Nolan returned her smile and said, "When you are standing your own watches, Healer Dervla, I would not mind if you felt the need to talk to me."

"Feel the need to . . . !" began Dervla, her face deepening in color. Then with a sarcastic edge to her voice she said, "Tell me, Healer, are you always so chivalrous and unselfish where women are concerned?"

"Only," said Nolan quietly, "the beautiful ones."

"Healer Nolan," said Dervla, with a sudden shake of her head that sent her short hair drifting like a copper mist across one side of her face. "Somehow you manage to sound both selfish and complimentary in the same breath. I think it is time once again to change the subject, hopefully to one that will be of more use on the New World than the ability to string together pretty words."

Nolan continued to watch her. His mind was full of words that he wanted to say, but they did not spill out of his lips. Dervla frowned.

"It is unlike you to be silent for so long," she said, "or to be without questions. Is there more that you would know about the recognition of edible plantlife, and the tests you can make that would not involve your poisoning yourself? Speak, Healer. In the time remaining, is there anything you would ask of me?"

The question he most wanted to ask of her was still hiding like a small, timid animal behind the barricades of his teeth. But other, more devious questions were able to slip through.

"I would like to ask about the colony," said Nolan, still looking at her. "What are your plans, both professional and personal, when it is established?"

"*If* it is established," she said, correcting him sharply. "Another reason for my not wanting to play any part in this project was that I had grave professional doubts regarding its chances of success."

The dark sadness of homesickness, the malady of the mind that was all too often incurable, was on her face. He knew that in a moment she would become angry with him, for no other reason than that anger could sometimes disguise weakness. Quietly, he said, "But now you have a part in the project and, once we have landed, you must agree that it is the most important part. On the New World you, a Healer of the One Name, will be faced with the ultimate professional challenge, one that even your great Orla, the Earthbound Orla herself, did not have to meet."

Dervla's eyes had not left his face while he was talking, and Nolan wondered whether it was strength of mind or her training that enabled her to look at him so long without blinking. He tried very hard to hold his gaze on her, for to look away would signify that he did not mean what he had said, and because her face was far from being an unpleasant sight.

Suddenly she sighed, and when she spoke there was sympathy in her voice, as if it was he rather than she who was troubled. She said, "You are a kindly man, Healer Nolan. You have serious problems of your own to face, yet you speak only the healing words that you know must be said to me, and do not say the words that I think you are wanting to speak. In this, perhaps only in this, you are a coward.

"It is no matter," she went on before he could reply. "But to answer your question, I expect that we shall be working together, with you the subordinate surgeon and I the physician, and making the best use we can of the medically trained among the colonists until the colony is healthy and well established, and the children that will come are old enough to be taught. By that time you will be teaching them history and, under my supervision, the elements of surgery. The ship's officers, too, will be teaching and, we now believe, will already have established a seminary and begun the selection and training of young boys for the priesthood. And by then I shall have my own teaching House of Sorrows in which I shall train the colony's future Healers in the—"

"Female Healers, naturally," said Nolan.

"Female Healers, predominantly," Dervla replied. "You know, or you should know by now if you admit it to yourself, that females have always made the better Healers. In body and mind they are born to the work, and any male with the necessary qualities of sensitivity, sympathy, and empathy for the patient that make a true Healer is, as a general rule, something less than a male . . .

"Your face is becoming suffused with blood," she went on, with a smile that he could only have described as impish. "Please don't give yourself an apoplexy, Healer Nolan. I suppose that somewhere there must be an exception to that rule. But this is an old battle that I have no wish to refight. Have you another question?"

"Yes," he said. "Will you marry?"

Dervla shook her head. She said, "You know that I am a Healer of the Order of Orla. When war or pestilence rages I must be as a tender and loving mother to many men, but to no man a wife. It is the rule."

"I know it," said Nolan. "But will or should the rule continue to apply as it did on Earth? You yourself have said that it has sometimes been broken. On the New World you will be another Orla, far removed from the restrictions and traditions of your Mother House, so who is there to stop you from relaxing a rule which is in direct conflict with the basic purpose of the colony? You do not seem to me to be a person who would worry about what the ecclesiastics would think of it, nor would the pains and problems of birthing and rearing children frighten you. Surely you have thought of being a wife, beloved and honored by one man as well as having the respect of many? And would you not want to be a true mother, to your own children as well as being a mother figure to the rest of the population? Even though you would be busy at times ministering to the needs of others, those children would be fortunate indeed in their mother. If they showed the aptitude, you could instruct them as could no other in the practices and disciplines of your Arts, hopefully the boy-children as well as the girls. Truly now, isn't that what your duty as well as your heart is telling you to do?

"I ask again," Nolan said in a voice that was gentle but in no sense timid. "Will you marry me?"

"No!" she said fiercely, then more softly, "No."

Nolan shook his head. "Your answer is hasty and unconsidered. I will not accept it."

"Healer," she said angrily, "you are being insubordinate and—and . . ."

"And persistent," said Nolan.

It was difficult for him to read Dervla's expression, or to be sure whether it was sorrow or sympathy that she was trying to hide from him as she said, "Truly, Healer, I have had such thoughts as you describe many times, but what you ask is impossible. Not physically impossible, naturally, but impossible nonetheless. Mine is not a religious order, but we are celibate by necessity, not choice, because a man, a knowledgeable and honorable man, would no more think of coupling with one of us than he would of seducing a holy nun. We are not all highborn, but we are superior to all of you. A lifetime of training and self-discipline has made it so, and without false modesty we know it to be so.

"Those few of us," she went on, "who have allowed their emotions to overrule their minds, and have been able to make a pretense of inferiority so that their husbands might be happy, have regretted it. You must understand, Healer Nolan, that except in my obedience to the strictures of civil and Imperial law, I will be subservient to no man, and never in matters of professional—"

"Enough," Nolan said sharply. "I would have no pretenses. I would not want to marry a slave, nor would I be one. If there was to be any enslavement it would be of the emotions of both. Dervla, I would not fear a slavery like that."

"I would," said Dervla.

If she noticed his additional insubordination in using her first name without its title, she made no mention of it.

"I would fear it," she went on, "because, if the other were not my equal, I would feel that it was the most abject surrender of all. I, too, have feelings and emotions, and at times they can be very strong. But at such times I have been trained to ignore or control or direct them only toward the needs of the sick. It is conceivable that for my own selfish, physical pleasures, as well as for the emotional reward I would gain as a result of the pleasure my body could provide for him, I might be tempted to direct these emotions toward one patient for his entire lifetime. But an intelligent patient, and you would certainly be that, would soon detect the dishonesty and become very unhappy with the arrangement. And if you did not, I would have to revise my present high opinion of you."

Before he could reply, she said, "You are a very good Healer, Nolan. You have the dedication, the sensitivity, and many of the qualities which are normally found only in the Order. But you are—"

"Not your equal," Nolan broke in, trying hard to control his anger and disappointment. "But what is equality? We are far indeed from Earth, and Hibernia's Order of Orla. But if by some means I was able to return, and undergo all of your training and field tests and the ancient Druidic disciplines of your Order, and pass the examinations with the highest marks, but in one specialty achieve only a fraction of a mark less than you, would I still be your inferior? Surely no two people can be completely equal. And that being so, how much inequality will you allow me?"

Dervla shook her head, and there was only sympathy in her

voice as she said, "You are a fine man, Healer Nolan, a strong and gentle and in many ways an admirable man. Here in the ship the alchemy that attracts male and female is very strong because there is only one source of attraction. On the New World there will be many women to choose from. I have no doubt that the one you choose will respond to you, because we both know that our female colonists were not drawn from the ranks of the ugly or stupid, and you will soon forget—"

"I will *not* forget," Nolan said fiercely, "and you are talking to me like—like a *patient*!"

Dervla smiled gently and said, "I am talking to you like an unsuccessful suitor, whose fragile, male ego has been sorely wounded by my refusal, and whose spirit lies bruised and bleeding. You are right, Healer Nolan, I am indeed treating you like a patient because that is what you are just now. And I am trying to relieve your distress with the only medicine available to me, that of good advice. Think on it. You have five centuries, or in warm time three long and lonely watches, to consider my words."

For a moment Nolan stared deeply into the eyes that would not look away. Then very seriously he said, "You have the same length of time to consider mine."

"Healer Nolan . . . !" Dervla began angrily, then her eyes moved aside to look past him at the chronometer. Her voice and her expression softened as she said, "I shall be going cold in a few minutes."

Nolan followed her in silence to the medical department and to her casket, then turned away as she began to undress. It was an unnecessary gesture, because his mind held that earlier picture in which nothing was hidden. The weightless tangle of her coveralls drifted across the border of his vision like some misshapen, earth-brown dwarf, and he could hear the quiet, purposeful sounds of the freeze-pads and body restraints being placed in position.

In a voice that was much too stiff and formal, he said, "Healer Dervla, we are already agreed that nothing can or should be done about the conspiracy until we reach the New World, so it is unlikely that any other emergency will occur while you are standing watch. But if one should arise, or if you have need of me for any reason, warm me without hesitation."

"And should a problem arise with you," said Dervla, "I suppose it would be a complete waste of my breath if I were to forbid you to warm me?"

Nolan wished that he did not feel so angry and hurt and confused, and that he could soften the harshness of his voice as he said, "From this moment onward I shall be the very model of a watch-keeping officer. No matter how worried or bored or lonely I become, I shall refrain from all spacesuit excursions aft or outside the hull. And don't worry, Healer Dervla, I would not warm you for any trivial reason. Knowing that you know about the conspiracy, and that I can talk to you about it, or, indeed, anything else I have a mind to when you are in cold sleep, will be enough. But most of all, it is knowing that I can warm you at any time if it becomes absolutely necessary that, if you can follow my amadan's reasoning, will make it unnecessary.

"I will have much to think about on those long watches," he ended, "and so, I hope, will you."

For a moment he thought that Dervla was not going to speak, then she said quietly, "I understand, Healer. My cooldown has been set for thirty seconds."

Nolan turned then and moved closer to her casket. Without speaking he made a quick but careful inspection of the freeze-pads and restraints, trying without success to pretend that the body he touched was that of any one of the thousands of other colonists about to enter cold sleep, until finally he looked at her face. Dervla's eyes were gazing up at him, and so calm and still were they that she might already have been frozen.

He felt a sudden, overwhelming urge to do something that she would doubtless consider to be an act of gross insubordination. He leaned into the casket and kissed her gently on the lips.

"Sleep well," he said.

In the few seconds of warm time remaining to her, Nolan expected a flare of anger, words of biting scorn, or some expression of her displeasure. But instead she closed her eyes, and for a moment it seemed that tiny, weightless tears were squeezing through her eyelids as she spoke.

"I sleep," she said softly, "but my heart waketh."

Chapter 26

As he had expected, it seemed that no subjective time at all had elapsed between the time he had felt the cold explosion of hypothermia at the end of his first watch and this, his first warming to the second. One watch would merge into another with no apparent difference other than that astern the Sun would have become just another star, and there would be many entries after his own in the watch-keeping log. He wondered if one of those watch-keepers had come daily to talk to him as he had to her.

The hunger of his precooling fast had also been preserved intact across the gulfs of time and interstellar distance, but that, at least, was a condition that could be quickly remedied. Automatically he removed the pads and restraints and it was only then, while he was still blinking the icy sleep from his eyes, that he saw that the casket monitor was showing its manual-override light.

Something was wrong, he thought, something must be badly wrong for Dervla to warm him prematurely like this. But, to his shame, he felt eagerness as well as anxiety as the lid opened and he looked around for her.

"Healer Nolan," said a quiet, well-remembered voice. "Dress quickly in your uniform. That visible mark of authority may help you, and should have a calming effect on your colonists during what lies ahead. Bring your other clothing and possessions as well, and your instruments from the treatment room. Quickly."

"Is—is there a medical emergency, sir?" he said urgently. "The extra clothing . . . What has happened?"

The monsignor did not reply, and continued to drift silently just inside the entrance as Nolan dressed quickly. O'Riordan was wearing the black uniform with the short scarlet cape that was the mark of his ecclesiastical rank, and in the weightless condition the cape had lifted up and outward so that it encircled his neck like the bony ruff of some prehistoric beast. It made him look so ridiculous that Nolan wanted to laugh, but the expression of angry impatience darkening the other's normally gentle and smiling face made it clear that this was not the time for laughter.

Cautiously, Nolan said, "Is anything wrong?"

"Oh, yes," the monsignor said quietly. That and nothing else.

When they reached the medical treatments room, Nolan received a shock so severe that he forgot his weightlessness and blundered painfully into the edge of the entrance. The first thing he saw was Dervla's casket, open and empty, as were the equipment and medication racks that covered three walls of the room. Then his eyes went to the direct vision port, uncovered now to reveal a narrow strip of black sky above the flat curve of a planetary horizon, and below it the sunlit dazzle of a cloud blanket that was not thick enough to hide the continental outlines of the New World.

"Quickly," said the monsignor, pointing at two satchels that were clipped to an examination table. "Healer Dervla packed them for you before she went down. Come."

Nolan shook his head violently, as much to clear it as in negation. He said, "I'm not going anywhere until you tell me what has been happening . . . !"

"I have no wish to talk to you, Healer Nolan," the monsignor broke in, "so I shall make this as brief as possible. If you do not come with me now, you will miss the slot for the lander taking the last colonists to the surface, and will spend the rest of your life on the ship with His Eminence—"

"The captain?" said Nolan. "Why is he staying . . . ?"

The monsignor held up one hand. "A simple answer inevitably leads to more complicated questions. I shall talk while we're moving or not at all. Come."

They were in Module A before the monsignor spoke again. He said, "When I discovered what you had done, the watch-keeping schedule had to be revised to ensure that there would be no repetition of your crime. The six watches that were to have been taken by Healer Dervla and yourself were redistributed and, at his own insistence, the cardinal took three of them. He was not a young man to begin with, and the passage of twelve rather than six years, together with the results of an injury sustained in his laboratory aft, which he did not report in the watch-keeping log, has seriously affected him physically. Healer Dervla has said, and with difficulty has convinced His Eminence of the medical fact, that if the prelanding deceleration did not kill him immediately, then the surface gravity would do so within a few weeks. He is now resigned to continuing his researches on the ship while keeping in daily farspeaker contact with the surface."

"I should see him," said Nolan quickly. "His condition may have deteriorated and he may need further—"

"I doubt that he would want to see you," said the monsignor, neither looking back at Nolan nor slowing his movement aft, "after the way you have so grievously and foully dishonored Healer Dervla."

"But I didn't—" Nolan began.

"Spare me the protestations of innocence," said the monsignor angrily, "we have already heard them from Healer Dervla. In defiance of the strictest of the ship's regulations as well as simple moral law, you spent warm time together. The rescheduling of the watch roster was to ensure that there was no repetition of your carnal pleasures. No more need be said.

"And no doubt you will want to know how your sin was discovered," O'Riordan went on. "Well, it would not have been had I not remembered that Healer Dervla had been cooled with her eyes open and noticed, long before she was due to be warmed for her first watch, that they were closed. I was worried, because that should not happen unless there had been a malfunction and thaw of the sleeper. I opened the monitor cover and discovered the unscheduled warming and its duration. You are a bitter disappointment to me, Healer."

Nolan was about to protest again, but he would have been wasting his eloquence on the black-clad stubby legs and slowly flapping red cloak of the monsignor. They were moving from Module D into E, past empty colonist stacks whose open caskets drifted in weightless disarray. He thought he knew where O'Riordan was taking him, and there was much that he wanted to ask, and say, before they arrived.

"Please," he said. "Tell me what has been happening? Where is Healer Dervla now?"

"She was warmed in time to go down with the first colonists to land," said the monsignor, "and she has been there ever since. That was four months ago. The deceleration phase into New World orbit was accomplished without accident or injury among the crew, and the minor mishaps that occurred were treated by Father Sanchez. All but a few of the ship's officers, and the final group of colonists who are about to leave now, are on the surface. As yet there have been no major health problems. But I advise you to forget Healer Dervla. You have dishonored her more than enough."

"But I didn't," Nolan said helplessly, "and neither did she. Do anything dishonorable, that is. Or wrong, or even, to your own way of thinking, sinful. She is a Healer of the First Name, after all. You know that she would not stoop to a lie!"

"I know," said O'Riordan, without so much as turning his head, "nothing."

"But surely—" Nolan began.

"I cannot know," the monsignor went on in a very quiet and very angry voice, "because I am not and never have been Healer Dervla's confessor. Had I been, I would know, but would have been forbidden to speak out, either as to her innocence or guilt. The priest to whom she chose to confess herself is similarly bound."

"Just as the captain's lips were sealed," said Nolan furiously, no longer caring what the monsignor might do to him, "when you confessed your own despicable plot to him. No wonder he wants to stay on the ship. He probably can't stand to be near you. I don't know with certainty what you have planned for those people, but I do know that it is shameful and utterly wrong to—"

"Enough!"

O'Riordan had checked himself so abruptly at a corridor intersection that Nolan blundered into him. While he was disentangling himself and the possessions he had been towing, he had a chance to look closely at the other's round and usually kindly countenance. Only then did he realize how much time had passed and that this was the face of an aging and very angry cherub.

It seemed that the monsignor was reading Nolan's mind, for in a voice of quiet fury he said, "Speak not to me about sin, Healer Nolan, or your warped ideas of right and wrong. I have spent the greater part of four watches, eight long years, thinking about your despicable behavior and considering what should best be done about it. In essence, you were and are a vile contagion, and isolating you and your unfortunate victim in cold sleep was the logical interim step . . ."

"But there was no need—" Nolan began.

"There was an urgent need and well do you know it," said the monsignor, in a quieter and even angrier voice. "You are a bitter disappointment to me. Although an unbeliever, I had great hopes for you, for I judged you to be a good man. Even though you were inclined to impetuousness and overenthusiasm at times, you were strict with yourself and, I thought, moral within your own limits. I had hopes that someday you might even look for God or, as sometimes happens with good but misguided people, God would come looking for you. But I was dreadfully wrong; I was deluding myself with wishes. You are nothing but a lusting animal—less than an animal, because they, at least, are guided only by instinct—who has no place in this company.''

Nolan opened his mouth to protest again, then closed it. For suddenly there was a look in the monsignor's eyes that said more loudly than words that the other would not hear him, or if he heard, would not listen. It was the mad, inspired look of the zealot.

''*Aisling Gheal* is a truly great and a glorious enterprise,'' O'Riordan continued, seeming to look through and past Nolan. ''It is charged with the most sublime and holy mission of carrying the Faith to another world, to populating a new and unspoiled Eden. Although the majority of the officers are not privy to every detail of my plan, we will be responsible for teaching and counseling these colonists and, in time, guiding them onto the true path so that their whole world will be ordered and civilized and holy, as that of an Earth which did not know the Fall . . .''

Now Nolan's suspicions regarding the conspiracy were confirmed, as was the reason for segregating the potentially troublesome colonists, but what was O'Riordan doing to do to them?

''That,'' the monsignor went on fiercely, ''is the plan that you, the willing or unwilling instrument of the Devil himself, like a foul maggot burrowing from within, have tried to corrupt by your lascivious behavior with—''

''You are wrong,'' said Nolan again.

''And you,'' the monsignor went on, with a slow shaking of his head, ''have shown yourself as the would-be destroyer of the glorious work we hope, with God's grace, to accomplish. You are the second serpent that would infest our new Eden.''

The monsignor turned then, and as he resumed the journey aft, he said, ''Willingly would I risk eternal damnation if I could use the Biblical precedent for the treatment of serpents, and crush your head under my heel. But I am too cowardly or, perhaps, too weak in my faith. And I am torn by a moral dilemma. What would be the result if our lives in the new Eden began with the crime of Cain?''

It was a rhetorical question, because O'Riordan continued talking without pause. Nevertheless, it was reassuring to know that the other did not intend to kill anyone. Dervla had been right—at heart, the monsignor was a good man.

''And instead,'' he went on, ''I have been petty and vengeful and selfish. You could have been warmed hours or days earlier, and given more time to adjust to what has been happening. Instead I deliberately caused you confusion and, I hope, some anxiety by giving you only a few minutes. The reason for that, you will by now understand, is that I wanted to see and speak with you for the briefest time possible. Now follow me."

They continued aft in silence until they reached the Skandian section, which, like all the others they had passed, was empty, and turned without pausing into the corridor leading to the module's exit lock. Four officers, one of whom Nolan recognized as Father Quinn, were waiting by the open seal, and beyond it he could see a part of the interior of a lander. From the other side of the lock there came the sound of angry voices speaking in many different tongues.

It was Father Quinn who made the report to Monsignor O'Riordan. So far as he and the other three priests were concerned, it was as if Healer Nolan did not exist.

"Monsignor," he said, speaking loudly enough to be heard above the multilingual storm, "all of the colonists have been strapped in and their possessions stowed and secured. As you can hear, they are confused and complaining about not wakening among their friends. No explanation has been given them other than that there was probably an error during the original loading and that they should remain calm until it can be rectified. A few of the empty seats are packed with additional stores as ordered, and the copilot's position is unoccupied. We are at minus six minutes to launch and ready to seal up."

"Thank you, Father," said the monsignor. He looked at Nolan and pointed silently at the open lock.

Once he was inside the three-quarters-empty lander, Nolan moved quickly forward, trying to ignore the lines of angry faces turned toward him and the even angrier and unintelligible questions they were shouting at a ship's officer whom they expected to have the answers. But he was feeling as angry if a little less confused than they were, and six minutes was not a lot of time for him to reach his position forward and strap in. Besides, he could think of nothing to say to them.

The lander pilot was Brenner, the man whose fight with the bar-servant on Brendan's Island Nolan had tried to interrupt. They had not spoken since then and, if the pilot's lack of expression as he watched the Healer strap in was any indication, he was not going to speak now. Nolan wondered if every single member of the crew intended treating him as a pariah for the rest of his life.

Angrily, he said, "Are you allowed to speak to me, Pilot? Have you anything you want to say?"

"Yes," said Brenner. He shook his head, and the expression on his square, mid-European features did not change as he added, "She would not have been my own choice. Much too bossy."

Nolan felt so relieved by the friendly response that he could not think of a suitable reply, and the pilot went on, "I'm not a cleric, Healer, so ease your mind."

"Thank you," said Nolan. But it seemed that once Brenner had started to talk, there was no stopping him.

"If you are worried about the landing," he went on, "there is no need. I've done the ship-colony round trip scores of times without mishap. The fuel reserves on the ship are very low, so there will be no energy-wasting tail landing. For fuel-economy reasons we will be guided to atmosphere and positioned for entry by *Aisling Gheal*'s computer, then I take over and glide in. There is a natural landing strip close to the main settlement, a long, flat beach where we will come down in good light about an hour before sunset. Appropriate, that, since we will be the last of the landers to use it, at least, until such time as the colony is able to produce more fuel. Maybe my grandchildren will see that day and—"

"I'm sure they will," said Nolan quickly. "But if this is the last trip, what happens to the officers we left on board?"

"Don't worry about them," said Brenner. "They have a smaller vehicle, much less power-hungry than this thing, which they will use to move between the ship and colony for as long as the fuel lasts. I'm sorry, Healer. Undocking maneuver coming up. You'll have to be quiet now."

"Sorry," said Nolan, smiling. "Sometimes I talk too much."

For a moment the couch padding pressed solidly against his back. Unable to take his eyes from the stern viewscreen, Nolan watched as gradually more and more of the ship structure appeared until the whole tremendous vessel hung in the center of the picture, lit sharply from above by sunlight that did not come from the Sun, and more softly from below by an earthlight that was not of Earth. Suddenly he shivered.

The greatest fabrication ever produced by the combined hands and hearts and dreams of men hung clean and sharp against the starry sea it had been built to sail. It looked no older now than the first time he had seen and felt the awful wonder of it, but more than five centuries had passed since then, and the work of the *Aisling Gheal* had been done.

"I don't know if I can give orders to a Healer," said Brenner apologetically, "but when you tire of the view, would you do something for me before we hit atmosphere?"

"Yes, of course," said Nolan.

"Thank you," the pilot went on. "It is the noise aft. All the other colonists were much better behaved on the way down and I don't know what is bothering this bunch, but in about twenty minutes' time the noise will be a distraction I can do without. Healer, will you talk to them?"

"Like a stern father," said Nolan, and loosened his straps.

If Brenner did not know why the colonists were angry, then he could know nothing of the monsignor's reasons for placing them together on the last flight down, and this was not the time to tell him and load him down with yet another distraction. Especially now, when the pilot was concentrating all of his attention on the panel before him and tapping buttons so furiously that he seemed to be intent on knocking them through the top of his console.

It was when he began tapping one finger against his earpiece that Nolan became uneasy.

"Healer, wait," said the pilot suddenly. "I don't know what you were going to say to them, but you will have to change it. We've lost farspeaker contact with *Aisling Gheal*, and the colony. Our equipment is functioning, so it must be their senders that are at fault. But both of them going out at the same time . . . !"

Nolan looked quickly away so that Brenner would not see the fear that must have been showing on his face. *Perhaps the contact was not lost, but deliberately severed at the order of Monsignor O'Riordan.*

"What," said Nolan, then cleared his throat to bring his voice down an octave, "what happens if you don't have contact with the surface?"

"Nothing," said Brenner, pressing more buttons. "But it's nice to have their moral support. I'm checking visually now and it seems . . . Oh, damn that stupid, bloody, cross-eyed apology for an astrogator to *Hell*! He's launched us too late!"

"You're sure?" said Nolan.

"I'm sure," Brenner replied angrily, and used a few Teutonic words whose meaning Nolan could only guess at. "I've done this too many times, and so have the control and guidance officers, to be wrong." He pointed at the tiny whorls and wrinkles of the cloud blanket that was unrolling slowly towards them. "You can *see* we're too high. The sunset line is almost below us and so is the colony. We're heading into the day side and we haven't even touched atmosphere yet. On this trajectory we'll come down on the other side of the bloody continent!''

The pilot was beginning to look the way Nolan felt, and tiny, weightless beads of perspiration were sliding off his face every time he moved his head. Nolan forced himself to be calm, then said quietly, ''Can we orbit and try again?''

''Not enough fuel,'' he replied, attacking his console buttons again. ''And I wouldn't want to try it without computer guidance from the ship, which we haven't got.''

Nolan did not reply. He was remembering that the lander pilot had brought a small disgrace to the project by getting into that fight on Brendan's Island, and he was thinking that Monsignor O'Riordan had a long memory and an even longer list of undesirables who were being banished to live, or possibly to die violently, with the second serpent in a distant corner of the Garden.

''Talk to them now, Healer Nolan,'' said Brenner, looking aside briefly from his console, ''but be back here within twenty minutes. And you can tell them, as gently as you can, that we will be coming down on water.''

Chapter 27

IT was immediately obvious to Nolan that the colonists were already making too much noise for him to have any hope of imposing his authority by shouting louder than they, so he decided to do the opposite. Choosing a row of seats that was filled with stores, and which was close to one of the two female colonists, he anchored himself by pushing his feet under one of the retaining straps and slowly held up both hands.

If they wanted to hear him speak they would have to stop talking. He was surprised how quickly the silence fell.

''Thank you,'' he said quietly, lowering his arms. ''I am Healer Nolan. There is something I must tell you, something much more urgent than answering questions or making excuses for the strange composition of this, the final group of colonists to be landed. That must wait until the persons responsible can be confronted with their error. Regrettably, I may not be able to make myself understood by all of you, so I must ask others to pass on my words.

"I know from our previous meeting that you speak many tongues, my lady," he went on, looking down at the tiny, almost childlike figure in her bulky coveralls, "and I would be most grateful for your assistance."

To an Aztec Princess of the blood Royal he could have said "Your Highness" instead of "my lady," but he had made the form of address polite rather than subservient, because, theoretically at least, all inequalities of rank and breeding had been left behind on Earth. Unlike that of the other colonists, her anger was silent and contained within herself, probably because she considered it beneath her dignity to become one with a noisy, complaining crowd.

"I shall be pleased to help you, Healer Nolan," said Ulechitzl, with a tiny but no-less-regal nod of acquiescence. "But please speak slowly and clearly; your Gaelic has not improved over the past six hundred years."

"Then, I shall speak slowly, clearly, and briefly, my lady," said Nolan. He gave a small smile of encouragement, and went on, "There has been an error in the guidance system that was to position us for landing at the colony, so we will have to come down some distance away, probably on water. Our pilot has much experience, in New World landings as well as past Earth operations, so there is no great cause for concern, but certain precautions must be taken . . ."

His early training had included lectures on the placement of the escape hatches and rapid-evacuation procedures for the one-hundred-passenger, colonist-type lander. He tried to look down at Ulechitzl as unwaveringly as she was looking up at him, and to adopt the quiet, confident manner of the air attendant who had explained the emergency drill for landing in the sea during the flight to Brendan's Island after the Tara reception. He was not lying to her, Nolan told himself firmly, merely expressing his hopes as if they were facts.

". . . So it is important for their own safety that everyone remains strapped securely to their seats until the lander has come to rest," Nolan said firmly. "If we come down on water rather than land, only the topside escape hatches will be opened to retain buoyancy. Will you translate all that for them, please? There is no time for detailed questions or discussion, and they will listen with respect to a lady while a man would be subject to continual interruptions. Now I must move farther aft in search of another and no doubt less able translator."

She ignored his clumsy attempt at flattery and began relaying his message without further comment.

The other translator was Golden Rain.

"I am not pleased to see you here, my lady," he said. "You should have been with your husband by now. I have only a few moments to talk to you, so please listen carefully and do not be afraid. Wanachtee has my promise that I will watch over you . . ."

Unless, he added silently, the guardian and the guarded along with everyone else in the lander hit the land or sea so hard that all promises were catastrophically canceled.

There was enough time before his return to Brenner for him to look briefly into every colonist's face while checking the tightness of their straps, and to give each an encouraging word or a reassuring nod. They were more frightened than angry now, and he could feel their need for the personal word and touch of someone in authority. But Nolan himself was becoming more angry than frightened.

He could understand if not sympathize with O'Riordan's reasons for removing the Princess Ulechitzl from the group of non-Christian Aztec colonists, because she could have been a source of continuing resistance to the monsignor's long-term missionary plans. But Golden Rain, a lovely young squaw who wanted only to be with her husband, had been no such threat. Had O'Riordan discovered her in the position that was supposed to be occupied by a Westland male, and decided that she must be classified as a potential troublemaker for no other reason? Or did the monsignor know all about her and Wanachtee and had done so simply because they had contravened the regulation on married couples?

Of one thing Nolan was certain: The monsignor was not omniscient. The Cathay child, who as the Heir Apparent was a symbol of authority even more potent among his people than Ulechitzl was among hers, was not on the lander. That knowledge was a small satisfaction to him.

As soon as he returned to the control position, Brenner said quickly, "You did that well, Healer. Now take your own advice and strap in tightly. We're about to hit atmosphere."

Nolan did so without speaking, not wanting to distract the pilot from his work. But Brenner, it seemed, was distracted by the voices of others, not his own.

"You can't see very much right now," said the pilot, "because there are only a few breaks in the cloud cover and the sun dazzle isn't helping. Once we're through the clouds, you'll have a few minutes to admire the view. Luckily the ship has given us a course and entry angle that will put us close to one of the designated emergency landing sites just south of the equator."

The near vacuum of the upper atmosphere began buffeting them gently, and then within a very few seconds it seemed that the denser air was trying to shake the descending lander apart. It had not been luck, Nolan told himself. The monsignor was a holy man, a good man, who would not wish to kill anyone deliberately—he would allow God and the professional aptitude of Pilot Brenner to make the final decision regarding their fate.

"That's good," said Nolan. "Have you used this site before now?"

"They are emergency landing sites," Brenner replied, "and until now nobody has been this desperate. Close your eyes to slits or you won't be able to see after we go under the clouds, which will be three minutes from now . . ."

The pilot went on talking as the cloud blanket rushed up at them like an enormous white sheepskin rug with the individual tufts growing larger and clearer every moment. Then suddenly they were through, the dazzle faded to a bright twilight, and when Nolan opened his eyes fully and leaned forward to look about, it seemed that fear had closed his throat.

Brenner interrupted himself to say sharply, "Put your head back in the rest or you'll risk a broken neck when we hit. Is something wrong, Healer?"

"Are—are we off course?" Nolan finally managed to say. "I can't see the ocean."

"Who mentioned the ocean?" said Brenner. "We'll come down on that lake, the pale gray patch you can see between the hills about ten degrees to starboard. Don't worry, it will look much bigger when we get down to it, and at our angle of descent the hills won't be a problem. I'm lining up on it now . . ."

The horizon tilted briefly and became level again, and a series of sharp, irregular bursts of acceleration bounced Nolan against his couch.

". . . I'm using up the remaining fuel," said the pilot. "We want the minimum of flammables aboard during an emergency landing. Our approach is about right, now, and I have two options. Go in as slow as possible holding the nose up, which would mean hitting tail down, and maybe flipping over and breaking up, or going down flat and faster, without deploying the landing gear, and trying to aquaplane in like one of those old flying boats. I favor the latter option."

The lake was spreading out before them, so calm that the hills beyond the far shoreline were reversed as in a dull gray mirror, and he could see individual trees and clumps of bushes whipping past below them.

"You're the pilot," said Nolan.

In his anxiety he must have made the words sound too much like a question, because Brenner said very seriously, "Yes, Healer. There are some people who find me ill-mannered and uncouth as a person, but I'm the best damned lander pilot they've got. We'll need the wipers . . ."

They were diving toward the gray water at an angle that was surely too steep, Nolan thought fearfully, but his mouth was so dry that he could not speak. Then slowly the line of the now not-so-distant shore moved lower until it exactly bisected the forward screen, which flickered with the movement of the high-speed wipers. The water was moving past so rapidly that it seemed as if they were sinking into an unending gray blur.

". . . Leveling off," Brenner was saying. "Nose up a trifle, holding off. Level again. Beginning to sink. Brace yourself . . . !"

Suddenly Nolan was thrown forward against his straps as the deck seemed to come up and hit his feet. What seemed like a solid mass of water slapped against the forward canopy, and he was sure that they had gone under the surface, until he saw the wipers laboring manfully to clear the glass and show a blurred picture of the shoreline. Before he could focus on it he was thrown forward again and the image disappeared in another explosion of spray. There was a third shock followed by several more of diminishing frequency and force, and then there was only a continuous rushing sound, and the canopy remained clear.

". . . Water is funny stuff," Brenner was saying. "Hit it wrong and it's like a brick wall, but in the right circumstances it can be almost frictionless. We're going ashore too fast . . ."

There was a long, grinding crash as the lander plowed onto the grassy bank and, with its speed scarcely diminished, into the trees beyond. The leading edges of the wings cut through them like a scythe until one tree, taller and stronger than its neighbors, tore off one wing. The vehicle gave a metallic screech like some great, wounded animal and slewed sideways, abruptly converting forward motion into lateral motion. The other wing dropped and dug its tip into the soft ground, lifting the entire lander high into the air. Unable to support the weight, that wing, too, collapsed and tore free. For a moment there was the deafening crackle of the smaller trees being snapped off at the roots mingled with the softer sound of splintering branches as the hull continued to roll, until finally these natural shock-absorbers brought it to rest, upside down.

For a time that could have been long or very short, Nolan hung face downward in his straps, looking at the ceiling that was now the floor, and marveling at the fact that he was not only alive but unhurt. A splintered tree limb was projecting through the shattered canopy. He could smell the strange, sharp odor of the sap that was oozing from the raw wood, and see that the leaves it bore were large and dark green and shaped like a white-fringed and serrated diamond. He had to grip the sides of his couch tightly to keep his hands from trembling, because suddenly he knew that he was on a world that was not Earth.

"You—you've stopped talking," he said to Brenner. "Is anything wrong?"

Chapter 28

THERE was the sound of voices aft, a quiet sound that gave no hint of injury or emotional distress. Nolan helped the pilot down from his couch, and then with Brenner following close behind he stepped carefully over the coaming of the upside-down doorway into the colonist compartment. The door itself was hanging loosely by one hinge, and he pulled it free thinking that it would serve as a litter to evacuate the badly injured, but a single glance along the compartment showed that it was not needed.

As he watched, one of the colonists released his lap and chest straps and, losing his one-handed grip on an armrest, dropped headfirst out of his seat. Fortunately for him, one leg caught in a seat support, bringing him up short before he could crack open his head against the buckled metal longerons running the length of the ceiling. Ulechitzl was in the row behind him.

"My lady," said Nolan, in a voice that tried to be both loud and polite, "would you be good enough to tell the people around you to remain in their seats until they can be helped down. There is no danger of fire, so they must be patient until then. Please tell them also that I am a Healer charged with the treatment of any injuries they may suffer, now or in the future, but that my treatment will be less than gentle if their hurts are the result of their own impatience or stupidity."

"Of course, Healer," said Ulechitzl.

Before Nolan could go on, Brenner touched his arm and said quietly, "There is a slight risk of fire from the ruptured control hydraulics. The fluid and vapor it gives off are both flammable—you can smell it all over the ship—but if a fire didn't start when we crashed, it isn't likely to happen now. I thought you should know."

"Thank you," said Nolan. "When all of them are down, suggest firmly that they start moving their possessions and the stores to safety as quickly as possible. I shall try to find a suitable campsite. How far from the lander must it be in case there is a fire?"

"Not far," said Brenner. "It's hydraulic fluid and flammable plastic we're worrying about, not fuel. Anything over two hundred paces away would be fine."

"Good," said Nolan. "Now listen. There are only two females on board, the Aztec I spoke to and further aft a Westlander. They are to be brought down first, not because we are a couple of well-mannered gentlemen or any foolishness like that, but because they are our best means of giving instructions to the others without starting arguments. Be polite, because the Aztec lady is a—"

"I'm always polite to ladies," said Brenner, "especially one who is as beautiful as that."

"Glad I am to hear it," said Nolan, and began moving quickly down the aisle toward Golden Rain.

Without serious mishap more and more colonists were brought down to begin helping to free those around them, and everything seemed to be going well. Nolan opened the two exit hatches and left by the one that was not blocked by fallen branches. Trying not to be distracted by the subtle differences in the shape and color and texture of the surrounding vegetation, he moved quickly to the edge of the lake and looked about him.

The late afternoon sun had broken through the cloud cover so that its bright, golden image danced in the ripples stirred by the gentle breeze that blew fitfully across the lake. To his left the trees and underbrush crowded thickly down to the water's edge, but on the other side he could see a small, flat, grassy area overhung on three sides by tall trees. Above the noises coming from inside the lander he could hear the sound of running water. Nolan walked quickly toward the sound, ceasing to count his steps when the number passed two hundred.

He found himself in a small natural clearing that was divided by a shallow ravine through which ran a stream, so fast-flowing that its origin must have been in the wooded hills above. The lander was still clearly in sight, and three Nubian colonists carrying their personal belongings had left the wreck and were following closely behind him. He told them to leave their packs in the clearing and return to the lander for stores.

He returned in time to halt a procession of colonists who were queuing impatiently to get out while Brenner, flanked by Ulechitzl and Golden Rain, was reminding them that the on-board stores had to be moved outside without delay. An angry argument was developing, but he knew that the anger had its roots in hunger rather than in any serious disagreement. As yet none of them had had a chance to break their Earthly precooldown fast during the four or five hours that must have elapsed between the time they were warmed on the ship and moved onto the lander.

He knew exactly how they felt.

"Your attention, please," said Nolan, reaching out both arms so that his hands rested on each side of the exit hatch, politely but effectively barring their passage. Then he told them about the clearing with its supply of running water and of the necessity of setting up camp there during the few hours of daylight remaining. They could not shelter inside the lander for the first night because of leaks in the control actuator plumbing, which used a fluid with a very low boiling point that gave off the sharp odor which they must already have detected.

While not dangerous when inhaled over short periods, Nolan told them, the effect was cumulative and could result in lung damage if it was breathed continuously over several hours.

Brenner opened his mouth at that point, but closed it again without speaking. Nolan went on slowly, "It is a very penetrating vapor, which is the reason why all stores must be moved without delay to the campsite lest they become contaminated. We are on a world that is completely strange to us, about to face dangers as yet unknown, and as a Healer I must therefore insist that we take no risks that are avoidable. Do you all understand me?''

Brenner moved close to him and said very quietly, ''Healer, you are being overcautious. The vapor is harmless, and unless somebody was stupid enough to drink the fluid itself and—''

''But it is flammable,'' said Nolan in an even quieter voice, ''and if there is the slightest risk of fire, I want this vehicle emptied of people and stores, quickly. While that is being done, I'd like you to think about and collect any portable items of equipment that would be useful. Charts or photographs of the surface, paper, tools, metal struts that could be adapted as digging implements or weapons—that sort of thing. Would you do that at once, please?''

For a moment Brenner looked angry, then he shrugged and said, ''Now that everyone is down safely and the lander has landed for the last time, I suppose you have the rank. At least you're using it politely, like one of the priests.''

As the pilot was turning away, Nolan smiled and said, ''Is that a compliment?''

It soon became clear that Brenner did not want to talk to him, and Nolan returned to the campsite to supervise the placing of the tents and a low, thick barricade of twigs and underbrush that would forbid entry to small creatures or, if a larger animal should try to break through, give an audible warning of its presence. There was also the problem, not an immediate one, of the native fruit-bearing vegetation. Many of the trees and bushes he had seen were heavy with fruit or fat clusters of berries that hung enticingly within easy reach. Whenever he saw colonists looking hungrily at them, he warned them in the strongest possible terms that in spite of its visual attraction, the native plant life was potentially toxic and must not be eaten until the Healer had tested and passed it as being fit for human consumption.

Three times he gave that warning, but on the fourth occasion he was interrupted by Ulechitzl, who said irritably, ''Healer Nolan, as colonists we have all had to undergo long and comprehensive training in woodcraft, which included erecting tents and shelters, lighting fires, and protecting the campsite. Perhaps you have forgotten that many of us were cooled soon after completion of that training, so that in biological time the lessons we learned are only a few days old and very fresh in our memories. As are the warnings against eating any variety of native food until it has been thoroughly tested. That, Healer, is a responsibility that we would not wish to share with you."

In a quieter but equally firm voice she went on, "You worry about us unnecessarily, Healer Nolan. Perhaps there is more useful assistance you might give to the other officer in the lander."

Nolan looked at the purposeful activity going on all around him. The sun was setting behind the trees so that only the hills on the opposite side of the lake were bathed in its deep, orange light. It was the kind of illumination, he thought as he turned to leave, that could make anyone's face appear flushed with embarrassment.

He found the pilot kneeling on the underside of the overturned lander and with tools and a portable light beside him. Brenner had peeled back three sections of plating that had already been loosened by the crash and was in the process of withdrawing a length of copper piping from the space under the passenger deck. Nolan had to grab one end hastily to keep it from jabbing him in the face.

"Healer, I'm glad you're here," Brenner said before Nolan could speak. "This is taking longer than expected, and I was about to call you for help. Would you mind pulling out some of the passenger-seat cushions, five or six should be enough, and bringing them up here? Place them in a line running fore and aft with this pipe lying on top of them so that the cushions will insulate it from the hull metal. In a moment I'll pass up a cable with the last few inches stripped of insulation. Wrap the bare wire tightly around the pipe, making sure that neither the pipe nor the bare wire is grounded against the hull. Do you understand what I'm trying to do?"

Before Nolan could answer, Brenner slid down the buckled hull to ground level, then went on, "That was not good for my nice uniform pants. I'm going inside now to check the other connections. From the position of the sun I'd say that in less than two hours *Aisling Gheal* will be overhead. There was too much cloud cover for it to have observed our landing, or should I say our controlled crash, during its previous orbit. Our long-range antenna was integral with the structure of the wings we lost on the way in. But that length of piping should do the job, considering the high sensitivity of the ship's receivers, and it is sure to be listening out for us. We have to let them know that we've landed safely without casualties and, of course, ask what they will be doing about a rescue . . ."

Remembering the monsignor's parting words to him a few hours earlier, Nolan thought that the answer to that question was nothing. But this was not the time to tell Brenner of O'Riordan's intentions toward them. At the same time he did not want the pilot to become too optimistic.

"But we can't be sure that—" Nolan began.

"No, not completely sure," Brenner said, speaking loudly because he had moved inside the lander. "But don't sound so pessimistic, Healer. That antenna should work fine, the farspeaker is undamaged so far as I can see, and my only worry is the cracked casing of its power cell, which could be discharging itself. That's why we have to hurry. Healer, what does an unbeliever do if he's asked to pray?"

Nolan treated it as a rhetorical question, and he did not speak again until the jury-rigged antenna was connected and lying on its long bed of cushions and he had returned to the pilots' position. In spite of the unnatural ventilation holes everywhere, the acrid smell of escaping hydraulic fluid was worse than he remembered, and some of it had collected in pools along the ceiling.

Brenner was on his knees dismantling what had been an overhead communications panel. The lamp clipped to his chest gave his features a demoniacal look as he said, "That pile of junk behind me is the odds and ends you asked me to collect, plus a lot of inspection paperwork and notepads that might help us if we have trouble lighting a fire sometime. There are no maps or surface photographs. This is tricky work which isn't in my specialty, so you can begin moving that stuff to the camp if you like. On the way back, look for the ship. By now it should be visible above the hills at the other side of the lake."

"The cloud is thickening in that direction," said Nolan, bending to choose his first load, "but the sky directly above us is clear."

"It doesn't matter," said Brenner in the impatient voice of one whose mind was on other things. "We don't have to see them to make them hear us."

It had grown so dim under the trees that the single campfire within the circle of tents was giving more light than the darkening sky. By the time Nolan was returning for the third load, it was so dark that he had only the yellow reflections of Brenner's flashlight on the edges of the open hatch to guide him.

When he was less than twenty paces from the lander, the hatch opening was lit for an instant by a bright, blue light. He heard Brenner cursing until the sharp, loud pop of a gas explosion cut him short. It was followed rapidly by other explosions that were softer but continuous, and from all over the wreck tiny flares of igniting gas were bursting like angry, exploding ghosts through its opened seams.

Nolan began to run, because all at once there was much more light than he needed.

In the few moments it took him to recnter the lander, the gas explosions had become less frequent and the small pools of hydraulic fluid were covered by low, flickering blue flames. Although not particularly hot or dangerous in themselves, the burning fluid had ignited the ceiling trim panels and some discarded plastic foam cushions which had begun to burn furiously and give off dense black smoke that made it very difficult to see or breathe without coughing. Brenner was no longer at the farspeaker panel.

Nolan was beginning to search for a probably unconscious and asphyxiated pilot, and keeping his face low so as to avoid the worst of the smoke, when a pair of legs appeared suddenly beside him and the unmistakable shape of a suit helmet was pushed into his hand.

"Take this," said Brenner, his voice harsh with the effort not to cough. "Be careful with it and— What the blazes are you doing? Don't put it on, get *out*!"

"G gas mask," said Nolan angrily. "I thought—"

"Don't be bloody stupid," the pilot broke in. "No air hose or seals. Outside, dammit. I'll be right behind you."

By the time he was able to see and breathe again, they were well clear of the wreck. Nolan followed the pilot, who was now carrying the helmet in one hand and the upper section of a spacesuit in the other. Abruptly he stopped and turned around.

"This is far enough," said Brenner. "There won't be an explosion, Healer, just a fire. But it was stupid of—"

"Pilot Brenner," Nolan broke in angrily. "I do not like being called stupid. When you gave me that helmet I assumed that you had one, too, and that they were for protection against the smoke. With the visor closed and the uniform collar pulled up to seal the base, it could have served as a short-duration gas mask. And if you consider me stupid, what am I to think about an officer who stays inside a burning lander and risks killing himself by smoke inhalation to retrieve a spacesuit, no, *half* a spacesuit! What possible use have we for it here?"

Fire was showing through every opened seam of the lander, and the underbrush, too, was beginning to burn. Brenner's eyes glittered red in the reflected light, but when he spoke, his voice had no anger in it.

He said, "The helmet and upper suit section contain a farspeaker, antenna, and power cell. It is a built-in unit which will need time, great care, and many hours of daylight to disassemble and reconstruct. It has a very limited range, but with luck the ship's receivers will be able to detect it although we will not be able to hear their reply."

"Oh," said Nolan, then added, "I spoke without thinking. I'm sorry."

For an instant Brenner's teeth showed bright red in the fire's light. "And I, too, speak without thinking when I am angry. Especially when I am angry with myself. I had been about to say that it was stupid of me to try to repair the farspeaker in near-darkness. But I was afraid that if I waited until tomorrow, the damaged cell might discharge and leave me without power. Instead there was full power and a short circuit that ignited . . . But you saw what happened. And now I will have to apologize to these people and tell them that my impatience and clumsiness destroyed the lander.

"I can hear them coming to find out what happened," he went on in a voice full of shame and misery, "so it will have to be now."

"No," said Nolan firmly. He put a hand on Brenner's shoulder and gave it a reassuring squeeze. "For the next few minutes you must be silent. This will require a mighty effort of will from you, but you will not say a word."

Brenner shrugged off the hand and said angrily, "Healer, don't be—"

"Stupid?" said Nolan. "Hardly. No man chosen to be an officer of the ship can be stupid, nor should he ever do anything which requires a public apology. These people look up to us for . . . I have no time to explain further, they're almost here. I will talk, Pilot, you will not."

Golden Rain, who had shown herself more surefooted in the dark, was first to arrive. Nolan smiled reassuringly at her but would not answer any questions until the others were present. The lander was well ablaze now, as were the trees and underbrush all around it. But he could hear the vegetation hissing rather than crackling as it burned, indicating that it was green and damp and would soon burn itself out. At least they would not have a forest fire on their first night.

When the colonists had gathered around Brenner and himself, Nolan held both hands high until there was silence. Then he allowed one to fall while the other, its index finger extended, pointed toward a gap in the clouds where shone the bright, man-made star that was *Aisling Gheal.*

In a calm, clear voice he said, "Pilot Brenner and I have set fire to the empty lander so as to inform the ship, which is presently overhead, of our position. What they will do to help us, and what we must do to help ourselves, are matters which we must consider very seriously, but not until tomorrow.

"Tonight," he went on, "we should think only of our safe arrival on a new world, and of celebrating the successful completion of the longest and most glorious journey ever to be undertaken by mankind. Let us forget for this night the problems which will beset us before we can rejoin our friends. We are all tired and hungry and, I am sure, joyful at the happy end to this epic voyage, so let us celebrate with a feast that we will remember for the rest of our lives.

"We have even," he ended, laughing, "provided you with a festive bonfire . . ."

For a long time Brenner remained silently beside him while the others returned to the camp, then the pilot said, "To the ship, that fire could just as easily signify that we had crashed and burned with no survivors. I mean no disrespect, Healer, but do you ever tell people the truth?"

"We will light more fires in different positions," Nolan replied, "and no doubt devise other ways of letting the ship know that we're alive."

Not that the information would make any difference to O'Riordan, who was concerned only to rid his garden of this innocent but potentially troublesome nest of serpents. He had to force himself to laugh

"Of course I tell the truth," he said, very truthfully, "but there are times when it is better for everyone if I do not tell all of it. And now, have you any strong objection to sharing a tent with me?"

The pilot laughed in return and said, "To be truthful, Healer, you would be my third choice. But the ladies are unlikely to choose me. Of course not."

It was a wild and at times very noisy celebration which, in spite of the total absence of alcohol, was continuing far into the night. When the tents had been pitched, the cooking fires lit, and the supplies identified, they had begun to overeat in shameless fashion and had become increasingly uninhibited. Ulechitzl and Golden Rain had excused themselves early and had made a tactical withdrawal to their shared tent.

As the night wore on, the sight and the occasional acrid smell of the lander burning itself out seemed to make them increasingly aware of how very lucky they were to be alive. And so it was natural that as individuals and racial groups they tried to express their gratitude to the man responsible for bringing them down safely, using the only currency available to them by insisting that Brenner sit with them and share their food. So much so that when Nolan pushed his way through the well-wishers to speak to him, the pilot was almost comatose with a surfeit of food and not a little inebriated by the congenial company.

"Enjoy yourself while you can," he told the pilot very quietly, "food rationing starts in the morning. And while you are all eating yourselves sick, your self-sacrificing Healer will stand watch for what remains of the night."

Obviously his voice had been too low for Brenner to hear him because the pilot said happily, "Sit yourself down, Healer. It's a shame I wasn't able to save some of that hydraulic fluid. They tell me it goes down very well with fruit juice."

He refused Brenner's invitation with a shake of the head, and with the camp and its revelers at his back he walked slowly toward the edge of the lake. There were important decisions he would have to make before morning and as a result many changes would occur, not least those involving himself.

In the past Nolan had found it difficult to be secretive, or even to feel any pleasure or superiority in the deliberate witholding of information for no other reason than that those about him were not privy to it. He had always been a good listener, but an even better talker, and for that reason had been entrusted with few secrets other than those covered by professional privilege, because he was in the habit of saying exactly what was in his mind. It was a shortcoming that had irritated many people, while others, he had come lately to realize, had made use of it.

Could he rid himself of the stupid habit of telling everything to everyone? Could he learn quickly to be secretive and silent, or even develop an ability to talk more while saying less? He had already made a start by witholding part of the truth from Brenner, but could he really learn how to use people instead of allowing them to use him? And, more importantly, could he do it without them knowing that it was being done?

The answer was that he would have to do all those things, because the alternative was too terrible to contemplate.

He tried to imagine what would happen if he decided to be completely honest with them. Or if, in a moment of anger or weakness, he was overcome by the desire to share a secret too great to be borne by him alone, and told them about the monsignor's conspiracy. If he were to tell them they were all people whom O'Riordan considered potentially disruptive elements to be excluded forever from the pure and sinless future colony of which the monsignor dreamed, and whose signals for help would be ignored because they were on no account to be rescued, what then? The initial reactions would be of shock, confusion, and helpless fury that would be directed toward all of the ecclesiastics in the colony.

There were many historical precedents that showed the binding power of a common hatred between individuals and racial or religious groups who otherwise had nothing in common, but as a unifying force it lacked stability and permanence. In the present situation hatred and helplessness could quickly degenerate into despair, disintegration, and the early death of the entire group. It would be much better to lie and try to give them hope rather than hatred, no matter how baseless and forlorn that hope might be.

The thought also came to him that if he told them the truth about O'Riordan, and if by some improbable chance a few of them survived to eventually rejoin their friends, their by-then-fanatical hatred and the information they brought back about the plot would disrupt the colony to an extent beyond the worst imaginings of the monsignor.

That was a responsibility he did not want.

The flames from the campfire were dying down and the voices had an increasingly sleepy sound to them. There was no moonlight, because the New World did not have a moon, and the unfamiliar stars that crowded the sky did not give sufficient light to be reflected in the lake, so everything below the horizon was an unrelieved and depthless blackness on which his mind painted dark pictures. Very occasionally he would hear the soft splash of a wavelet against the bank, or perhaps it was some nocturnal fish jumping for the insects that had already taken a few sample bites from the backs of his hands and neck.

He hoped the experience would not kill them, because that might mean that their bites would not kill him.

A sudden, mighty yawn made Nolan's eyes water, but there was too much to think about for him to allow himself to sleep. Feeling his way in the darkness with hands and feet, he moved carefully along the shoreline until he found the mouth of the ravine, then turned inland and walked for a few paces along the bed of the stream until he encountered the camp's perimeter barricade.

He crouched down then, filled his cupped hands with the cold, fast-flowing water, and drank untidily, knowing that this was the first of many risks he must take. It had no taste at all, which was as it should be, and compared very favorably with the recycled water of the ship.

As Nolan was about to straighten up, he put one hand to the ground to steady himself, and felt the palm of his hand bear down on a small, wet, slippery object which collapsed under the pressure. The chances were that it was vegetable rather than animal, but a closer examination would have to wait until daylight. His hand had a faint but not unpleasant smell. He rinsed it thoroughly in the stream before scooping up another handful of water to splash the sleep from his eyes.

It was important that his mind be as clear as possible, because he had a lot more thinking to do.

For a long time he sat facing the unseen lake with his back against a tree, thinking about all the things he must do and not do, and the words he must say and not say. Then *Aisling Gheal*, lit by the sun that would not itself rise for an hour or more, climbed above the distant hills to give the dark waters something bright to reflect. Inevitably his thoughts turned to the ship and that walk with Dervla along the outer hull. He remembered the barely perceptible pressure of her gauntleted hand, the blurred picture of her face behind the helmet visor, the sound of her voice in the suit farspeaker and the things she had told him. Other memories of her came crowding into his mind, sights and sounds that were more pleasant to recall, but he pushed them away. It was her words that he had to remember.

It was very important that he remember every single one of them.

Chapter 29

THEY were spread out in a silent untidy crescent on the thick carpet of greenery that was not grass, facing him as they sat cross-legged or lying supported on their elbows while they waited for him to speak. The midday meal was over, the sun was warm, and they had the look of people enjoying a relaxing holiday. Some of them were talking quietly, even laughing, as they watched him.

Nolan did not return their smiles. In a short time he would have to be very firm with these people, and any prior attempt at ingratiating himself would be construed as weakness.

"I have asked for this meeting for two reasons," he said, speaking slowly and distinctly. "To answer those of your questions that I am able to answer, and to discuss plans for the future. The questions I will not answer are those relating to the mistake on Earth or on the ship which caused you to be separated from your own people, and the reason why our lander was so far off course. Neither Pilot Brenner or myself have answers to those questions, and I will not waste time speculating about those responsible. Instead I shall concentrate on questions relating to our chances of being rescued, our present situation, and our ability to survive it. Is this understood?"

Apparently it was not completely understood, because a few minutes later one of them was wanting to know why he was not at the colony with his friends.

Nolan ignored him and went on firmly, "Before you can calculate our chances of being rescued, you must be given certain facts. They are that with the exception of Pilot Brenner, who has spent the past few months taking colonists and supplies to the surface, we are the last group to be taken out of cold sleep. Ours was the last lander supposedly making its final descent to the colony, where lack of fuel has permanently grounded the other landers. Pilot Brenner tells me that only one space vehicle remains operational, with enough fuel remaining on *Aisling Gheal* to allow it a few trips between the colony and the ship. But it is a small vessel with insufficient capacity either to keep us supplied or to lift us out of here, or even to risk landing on unprepared ground.

"You can see," he said, looking slowly from face to face, "that the chances of that type of rescue are small."

Now they were listening to him without interruption, almost without physical movement.

"The alternative," he went on, "is a surface rescue. The main colony, if they knew we had survived and were continuing to do so, might send out a party to find us. But the colony's facilities for mounting a rescue operation are not much better than our own. They have a helicopter of limited range which is probably short of fuel by now, and a few tracked surface vehicles—slow, awkward things designed for clearing or helping cultivate land, which are too valuable to be risked on an extended journey through mountainous and forested country. It would be faster and easier, but by no means fast or easy, for them to travel on foot.

"If that is their intention," Nolan went on, "and if you want to be reunited with your friends as quickly as possible, then we must meet them halfway."

He paused so as to give them a chance to ask questions, but still they watched him with a silence that made the droning of the insects seem loud.

"At present I have no idea of the distance or the kind of territory we must cross," he continued, "only that we are as far from the colony as it is possible to be while remaining on the same continent. Pilot Brenner will prepare maps and calculate distances as we progress, since he has orbited this world many times and is familiar with—"

". . . The tops of its clouds," said Brenner, but so softly that only the Healer could hear him.

"—Its principal natural features," Nolan went on, ignoring him, "But the first requirement is a list of your names, nations, or Imperial districts of origin, and any special aptitudes you possess that may prove helpful in the days to come. Pilot Brenner has retrieved a suit farspeaker which should enable the ship's more powerful equipment to receive him. We can then pass these names to the ship for onward transmission to the colony. Unfortunately, our contact with the ship will be one-way, since the suit farspeaker is not sensitive enough to receive their reply.

"As well as the names," he continued, "I require as a matter of urgency a list giving details and quantities of all equipment and stores that came down with us. Be particularly accurate in the matter of food supplies.

"We have a very long way to go," Nolan went on, in a tone that he tried to make both stern and encouraging. "The Earth supplies we have with us will last at the normal rate of consumption for only a few weeks. That is why, from this moment on, our food will be strictly rationed, so that I will be given the maximum time in which to discover, test, and provide a native alternative diet. This may be a lengthy process, because every specimen tested must be given a few days for any ill effects to show. And I must warn you again: No matter how hungry you feel in the days to come, on no account must you try to augment your rations with local fruit, berries, or animal life until they have been passed as nontoxic. Do you fully understand all that I have been saying?"

They continued to watch him silently and a few of them nodded their heads, but there was no other response.

"There is much to do," Nolan went on, "and you should arrange among yourselves how best it should be done. If there are problems or disputes, particularly concerning the allocation of food, I will help resolve them. It will come as a great surprise to you to discover how very little food your bodies need to remain healthy and active. We are all anxious to join the colony as quickly as possible, and I would like to break camp here and begin the journey in the early morning of the day after tomorrow."

Several low-voiced conversations started up, some of them in languages foreign to him, others not, but he did not hear his name being mentioned. Still talking, a few of the colonists climbed to their feet and moved away. Others followed, singly and in small groups, including Ulechitzl and Golden Rain.

"Ladies, please wait," he said quickly. "What's wrong with them? I was expecting questions."

They turned and came back to him, and Brenner got quickly to his feet to make a small, polite bow. It was Golden Rain who spoke first.

"It is possible that we misunderstood you, Healer," she said quietly. "You looked and sounded very serious, as does a man with matters of gravity on his mind. I formed the impression that you were giving instructions rather than inviting questions."

"I formed the same impression," said Ulechitzl. "Do you wish us to call them back?"

Nolan shook his head, and then when they left him a few minutes later, he felt pleased and surprised at himself. Without knowing how, precisely, he had apparently made the transition from past subordinate to present superior. But the strongest and the most surprising feeling was one of a sudden loneliness. Impatiently he pushed the feeling to the back of his mind. He had work of his own to do.

With the lid of a food box as a drawing board, and paper supplied by Brenner, he began work on an illustrated catalog of the varieties of local vegetation that might or might not be edible. As a schoolboy he remembered his teacher of fine arts remarking, in a voice that would itself have etched copper plate, that the only time Nolan had been able to draw a circle was when he had been trying to draw an egg. But the illustrations he intended to make were for scientific rather than artistic purposes, and his notes would include information on color and consistency as well as effects on the human metabolism, in case the investigation proved to be the death of him.

Nolan began by retracing his steps of the previous night to the ravine, where in the darkness he had squashed what had felt like an overripe fruit. At the time he had assumed it to be part of a windfall. But daylight showed that assumption to be wrong. The crushed fruit was one of five growing from a thick flexible stem that had been broken off cleanly a few inches above and below the place where they were attached, and there were no trees in the vicinity.

It was possible that they had been blown into the ravine by a high wind, but they were so heavy and thin-skinned that the fall would certainly have damaged them. With the exception of the one Nolan had squashed, none of them showed any sign of bruise or blemish. As well, they had the bleached, yellow-green and swollen look of vegetation that had grown deep underwater, because in the reduced pressure of the air they looked ready to burst.

But if they had grown on the bed of the lake, how had they come to this particular place? The lake was too small for it to produce waves capable of washing the fruit so far up the ravine. He bent closer to examine the stem, and saw that the breaks were not as clean as he had first thought. In both places the stem had been compressed before being snapped off, and he could see a number of small, regular indentations that suggested that the stem have been bitten through rather than broken.

He sat back onto his haunches and looked carefully about him. The theory he favored now was that an amphibious animal of some kind had come ashore to eat the food it had gathered, the ravine being a place where its hungrier or perhaps larger fellows would not disturb it. The creature must have moved up the bed of the stream or along the stones lining either side, because there were no tracks in the soft ground that would have given an indication of its size and shape. But it had been an inquisitive animal, because a section of the perimeter barricade, which Nolan had most certainly not disturbed last night, had been pushed aside where the brushwood had been laid across the stream. Both its curiosity and its hunger had been left unsatisfied when Nolan had come blundering onto the scene in the dark.

He smiled to himself, thinking that he had learned two very important facts. The underwater growth was a food source to at least one native life-form, which made it more likely though not certain that humans would be able to eat it. And the creature concerned was inquisitive, which meant that if it, too, proved edible, it would be easier to trap. Even on this New World, curiosity could still kill a cat, or a something. Or perhaps even an incautious Healer.

Nolan settled himself comfortably on a patch of dry ground and began sketching the first entry in his catalog. Drawing the external view of the fruit showing the attachments to the stem was easy. Cutting through one of the undamaged specimens to obtain a sectional view was more difficult, and messy, but he persisted until satisfied with the result. It showed the specimen to be composed of a thin outer skin that was half-filled with a clear liquid and containing a dense, fibrous mass at its center which in turn contained a cluster of four hard, dark-brown seeds each the size of a pea.

Eating any part of it would not be sensible at this stage, Nolan decided, because if he was to fall ill he would not know whether it was the stream water he had drunk the previous night or the fruit that was responsible. But he could risk tasting the various parts of the growth, provided he spat out and rinsed his mouth thoroughly with water from the stream after every test.

The skin was tasteless, the juice had the strong smell he had noticed the previous night but no taste that he could detect from the few drops on his tongue, and when he bit carefully into the fibrous center he was reminded of pineapple that had been soaked in a very weak solution of vinegar, a taste that was strange but not entirely unpleasant. The single seed that he tried tasted so vile that he could keep it on his tongue for only an instant.

To his drawing of the first specimen he added a note to the effect that the size of the parent plant was unknown as yet, and that its probable method of propagation was to provide an edible center for underwater grazers who would expel the foul-tasting seeds at a distance from the original growth. He left space for the results of later human edibility tests.

He moved inland then, skirting the perimeter of the camp but always remaining within earshot as he continued his search for vegetation that might prove edible. He took samples of fruit of all shapes, colors, and sizes, from a small, hard, and hairy variety that looked like a pink coconut to great, smooth-skinned melon-like objects that shone on the ground like the lanterns of Cathay. He had to be particularly careful lest the object of interest prove to be the New World's equivalent of a hornets' nest. But all the time there was growing in him a wonder at the beauty of this place so intense that it was almost a pain. He made many sketches of everything he found, even to the clumps of ground-growing berries and the leaves that looked as if some small animal had been nibbling at them, but he tasted nothing.

His visitor of the previous night had given him an idea for reducing the number of specimens to be tested for edibility, but it was late in the afternoon before he returned to the lakeside with enough samples to carry out the experiment.

Nolan was concentrating so hard on what he was doing that he did not know of Golden Rain's arrival until she was standing beside him, but he saw at once that she was irritated. Her hair was disordered where it had escaped from the headband, the smooth, coppery skin of her face and neck was beaded with sweat, and it was plain that the combination of recent strenuous activity and the heat-retaining coveralls had affected her temper.

"Healer Nolan," she said in a voicc that somehow managed to sound both respectful and critical, "my apologies for the interruption. The listing of supplies and equipment is all but complete. Some of the men, as you can hear, are breaking off panels from the wreck to use as litters for carrying the heavier items, and Pilot Brenner has drawn a map and would like to discuss it with you before the light fades. We are all very busy, Healer. Why are you . . . ?"

"Throwing things into the water like a small boy?" he finished for her, smiling.

"My young brother and I used to play by a lake in this way," she said, "when we were children. It is not in itself a wrongful activity, but the time is ill-chosen."

"When you were young children," said Nolan, "did you ever play with bows and arrows?"

"Of course," she said impatiently. "And spears, and war hatchets. Children revert easily to our savage past."

"My lady," said Nolan, "do you remember how they were made?"

Golden Rain stared at him for a moment, then she said thoughtfully, "I remember well, Healer."

"Good," he said. "But there is no need to start on that work at once. While you are here, my lady, would you be good enough to help me with this experiment?"

Before she could ask the inevitable question, Nolan pointed to the heap of specimens and small stones lying at his feet, and went on quickly, "The intention is to throw these into the lake, close enough inshore for us to be able to observe them but far enough so that our shadows will not frighten the fish or whatever other underwater creature comes to investigate or, hopefully, eat them. A fruit specimen is easy to throw, but a bunch of berries needs to be wrapped around a stone if it is to carry the distance, and make a large enough splash to signal its arrival. Observe the floating specimens carefully and if they are taken, note the degree of turbulence so that we can estimate the size and strength, or, if it breaks the surface, the shape of the creature responsible.

"My idea is that if the indigenous life-forms find some of the specimens edible," he continued, "so also might we. One problem is that if the metabolism and cell structure of local fauna differs so greatly from ours, both the food and the local eaters of that food might be poisonous, so that both will have to be tested. That is why—"

"We need bows and arrows," Golden Rain said.

"And spears," said Nolan, "and, if possible, fishing nets."

Together they threw the specimens into the lake and stood watching them in silence while they bobbed gently on the water, and then not so gently as unseen mouths attacked them from below and they rolled over and over to display a steady erosion of tiny bites. The damaged specimen of fruit that had been left in the ravine disappeared very quickly, as if it was a particular delicacy, and there was a lot of activity under the floating clusters of berries The other specimens were attracting less attention, and one was being completely ignored.

Golden Rain pointed at the sketches that lay fluttering gently on the ground with stones keeping them from blowing away.

"That pear-shaped fruit with the green and yellow stripes," she said, "the drawing you have listed as fruit specimen five. Judging by its looks it is the most appetizing of all, but they've left it alone."

"Then so shall we," said Nolan. "And my thanks for your help, my lady."

Golden Rain shook her head. He had the feeling that if the

flawless, coppery skin of her face had been capable of registering a blush of embarrassment, it would have been doing so now.

"I am sorry, Healer," she said in a firm voice. "We thought you were playing in the cool of the lakeside like a child while we labored in the heat. We were mistaken."

Nolan inclined his head in acceptance of the apology, then he smiled and said, "Until you go and tell them otherwise, my lady, they will think that I have enticed you into playing the same childish game. While you are doing that, discuss with them the matter of weapons suitable for hunting or trapping of small prey. They may have knowledge in that area which I lack. And please tell Pilot Brenner that I will see him as soon as I have written my notes."

She nodded without speaking and turned away. Nolan returned to his catalog, thinking that he would never make a good leader. He talked and explained too much.

Chapter 30

IT was the afternoon of the third day rather than the morning of the second before they were ready to leave, and the principal reason for the delay had been Nolan himself. He had insisted on trying to solve all the problems and make all the decisions, large or small, on his own. It was only when Ulechitzl and Golden Rain intervened to avert what threatened to become a mutiny that he realized he had been treating the colonists like untutored children instead of the mature and resourceful adults who had won their places of *Aisling Gheal* over the strongest possible competition.

After that incident, Nolan satisfied himself by giving only general instructions and leaving the colonists to carry them out as they would. And now that they were gathered together with the packs and litters at their feet prior to departure, he decided to give them a further rest from his voice by asking Brenner to describe the journey ahead.

"Tell them the truth," he told the pilot very quietly, "but not enough of it to discourage them."

"Impossible," Brenner whispered. "You do it."

Nolan sighed, partly in irritation and partly in relief, because Brenner was not a convincing teller of half truths. Raising his voice, he pointed to the map that was propped against one of the backpacks and went on: "If any of you are too far away to see the drawing clearly, ask me to show it to you later. You have already been told that the landers were not required to carry maps, so this one has been prepared from memory and is the result of visual observations made by Pilot Brenner during orbital or prelanding flights over the continent. For that reason the map is not entirely accurate, which means that the principal topological details must be filled in verbally . . ."

They had landed on Dragonia, the New World's largest single continental landmass, about two hundred miles south of the equator, and had it not been for the trees and surrounding hills, they would have been within sight of its eastern coastline. The continent was close on twelve thousand miles long and more than two thousand at its widest point. It lay diagonally across two hemispheres with its head and tail touching the north and south polar icefields and its vast belly straddling the equator. A range of high mountains ran like a spine from the dragon's neck to its tail, but were lower and more rounded in the equatorial regions, although even there they were high enough to be above the tree line.

Between the north and south temperate zones the land was dotted with lakes, some of which were large enough to be classified as inland seas, suggesting that in the recent past—recent as geologists would measure time—the whole region had been under the ocean. The planet had no axial tilt, no seasonal changes, and the sun would rise and set in the same place every day, so there would be no problems with navigation.

". . . Our present position is here, low on the dragon's back," Nolan went on, "and the main colony is sited on the shore of the bay, just there, in the angle between the foreleg and the beginning of the neck. The distance has been estimated at over two thousand miles, but we may only have to travel half that distance, perhaps more, perhaps less, depending on how quickly a rescue party is sent out to meet us."

He did not tell them that circumventing one of those inland seas would make that distance closer to three thousand miles nor, he hoped, would he ever say to anyone that their rescue was the last thing that Monsignor O'Riordan wanted.

"The sooner you start," he ended, in a tone that was much harsher than he had intended, "the sooner you will meet your friends."

And your future wives, he thought. But it was unnecessary to say that aloud.

A short time later they moved off, chattering like excited schoolchildren and almost running in their eagerness to be away. The first part of the journey would take them around the edge of the lake and over the hills on the other side. In spite of the fact that the men were carrying the stores on litters as well as in their individual backpacks, they were acting as if it could be done in a few hours instead of as many days. Brenner took the lead with Ulechitzl, who, like Golden Rain, was burdened only by her own pack, following a dozen paces behind so that she could relay back any instructions he might have, and Nolan brought up the rear, preceded by Golden Rain for the same reason. Once she hung back to walk beside him for a moment, but she sensed that he did not want to talk and quickly returned to her place.

Nolan was not being impolite, it was just that there was a lot of information that he had to fix in his memory.

There had been forty-three colonists in the lander in addition to Ulechitzl and Golden Rain. They had told him their names and countries of origin, and now he had to remember which names and faces went together. With some of them the differences in skin pigmentation and racial variations in the cast of features were a help, because a pink-faced Skandian with blond hair was unlikely to be called Chen Sung.

Golden Rain and Ulechitzl were the only Westlanders. The three Nubians were also in a minority, as were the four from Cathay. From Europe were the five Teutons and five Skandians, and eleven from the Indian subcontinent and the islands of south-east Asia, while the remaining fifteen came from the fabulously wealthy lands bordering the Red Sea. Their rulers had contributed much to the project, and it was said that if *Aisling Gheal* could have been powered with oil, Mesopotamia would have launched its own starship. Very often these fifteen acted as if they believed the saying implicitly.

Among them there were believers in Muhammad, Buddha, and the Christus as well as a few who, like Nolan himself, professed to having no invisible means of support. Not for the first time he wondered what exactly it was about them that had caused the monsignor to exclude these particular individuals from the main colony. With some of them there had been evidence of strong religious conviction, perhaps even fanaticism. Brenner had been asked to point out the approximate positions of the home system at sunrise and sunset, so that they would be able to bow in the direction of Earth, and Mecca.

It was probably not the religious differences alone that were of concern to O'Riordan, because there were many of those in the main colony. It was more likely to be the fact that this particular group of colonists was strong-willed and self-sufficient to a man, or woman, and they would not be easily influenced or converted by any man, holy or otherwise. Except for the incident of the previous day, they had shown Nolan no sign of disobedience or insubordination, and he had found that they responded more promptly to polite requests than to direct orders.

But then, he thought, most people did that.

On the flight down, the lander had carried less than half its full complement of colonists, but more than its fair share of the lightweight tents, basic agricultural implements, and supplies that would enable them, if they survived the first half year, to become more self-supporting. But the monsignor's generosity in that respect, Nolan felt sure, was intended to immobilize and further isolate his undesirables by making it easier to stay where they were rather than to undertake a long, difficult, and perhaps impossible journey back to the main colony. Nolan had insisted that nothing be left behind, and the result was that everyone was overloaded and slowed to the extent that they would be lucky to travel five miles by nightfall.

Very soon there would be an increasing number of requests to lighten the loads, and Nolan had to think of some very good reasons for refusing them.

They moved inland and away from the cool breezes of the lakeside on a course that was west of northwest, climbing slowly toward the hill Brenner had indicated as their first objective. For a time they followed the course of the stream closely enough to hear it, then they lost it for a while to find it or another just like it again.

Nolan had already told everyone that he had been drinking only the natural water for the past two days, without any ill effects, and he was declaring it safe for general use provided it was drawn from a fast-flowing stream. If taken from a still pool or lake in which insects or microorganisms might be present, it should first be boiled over the campfire. He was in the process of testing specimen one, the fruit he had found abandoned in the ravine, which so far had proven to be pleasant-tasting and harmless except for its tendency to generate wind in the gut. But it was an underwater fruit and they were moving farther from the lake with every step, so he decided to keep his findings secret until another supply became available. Besides, he had eaten all there was.

As they continued climbing, the sun dropped behind the crest of the hill above them, but the reduction in temperature went unnoticed because of the heat generated on the steepening slope. Inside the thick serge of his uniform, Nolan felt that he was cooking slowly in his own body fluids, and the others were sweltering inside their heavy coveralls. But the biting insects were so numerous and persistent that they could not roll up the sleeves or trouser legs, and everyone had pulled the cowls tightly around their faces for added protection.

Gradually the trees thinned out and the underbrush was replaced by a growth like mossy seaweed that squeaked when he walked on it. Sometimes it moved before his feet touched it, as if the broad, fleshy leaves were giving cover to some small animal, and when he investigated a trampled area he found the squashed remains of a small, mouselike creature. He wrapped it in leaves and placed it in his sample box for later sketching and inclusion in the catalog. He saw no other potentially edible specimens of vegetation that were sufficiently different to warrant stopping to collect them.

Close to the top of the hill they approached a clump of trees that were completely new to him, and the sound of loud, disgusted voices from those in the lead gave advance warning of the unpleasantness to come.

Every tree had a thick, short trunk capped by disproportionately small and spherical masses of dense foliage out of which sprouted four long, thin branches that were utterly devoid of bark or leaf. From the tip of every branch there hung, like the beads on an opened necklace, a string of tiny yellow berries. There were four of the branches to every tree, and so slender and flexible were they that they stirred like great blades of grass in the wind and their strings of berries brushed the ground, or touched and became entangled with the strings of adjoining trees. Where this had already happened, the berries closest to the point of contact had grown long thick tails of incredibly fine hair that blew out in the slightest wind, pulling the attached berries free.

Nolan was thinking that this was one plant that did not have to depend on insects or birds for pollenation when the smell reached him. It was a smell redolent of putrefying meat, stale sweat, and every other unpleasant odor that he had ever experienced together with others he had neither the words nor the experience to describe.

He, too, had to walk around those trees.

The wind was behind them as they climbed the rest of the way to the top, and even when they set up camp, the smell of wood smoke could neither hide nor disguise the awful stink of those trees. But it was cool on the hilltop even though it lacked an hour to sunset. The insects that had been plaguing them were gone, hopefully for the night, and the ordinary, nonsmelling greenery was so sparse that they could look far across the country they would be traveling for several days to come. They could also see the sky, which meant that *Aisling Gheal* would be able to see their fires, if anyone on the ship wanted to look.

He pushed that thought out of his mind, and concentrated instead on the dissection and drawing of the mouselike animal while the daylight lasted.

Later that evening he caused great hilarity when he brought the creature's two tiny forelegs to the cooking fire with the request that one be roasted carefully and the other boiled thoroughly in water. Very seriously he explained that for a balanced diet they would need a local source of meat, and that for test purposes these two small limbs were ideal, since between them they contained less animal tissue than that covering the end of his little finger, so that the risk of poisoning himself was minimal. When both were cooked he excused himself, saying that he would dine in private.

Nolan did not suffer any ill effects from the tiny morsels of meat, except for the constant and audible grumbling of his stomach, and during the succeeding four days he tested fruit specimens two and three. Two was a berry that seemed to grow everywhere, although not in profusion. It had a woodish consistency, was palatable but required thorough chewing, and seemed to do no harm after continuous if restricted use over three days. Specimen three had an acid but not unpleasant taste, and a marked laxative effect with accompanying stomach cramps. He had been very badly frightened during the three or four hours it had taken for the symptoms to disappear. But he had not discarded the berries as being completely inedible, because there had been a well-remembered and painful incident when as a boy he had stolen and eaten some unripened apples and suffered similar discomfort as a consequence.

Many times he found the others looking at him as if he were not long for this world.

By the eighth day they had moved into a flat thickly wooded area that was dotted with small pools or swamps over which the insects hung like a dense and droning fog, so much so that any edible life-forms the water might harbor were safe from him. Two days ahead, at their present snaillike progress, lay the slopes of another hill. It was higher and more rounded than the one overlooking the lake, and it lay directly across their course. Brenner's offer to take them around the obstacle was refused by a majority. They preferred using the extra energy needed to climb the hill for the chance to spend one night away from the stifling heat of the lowlands and to see the country that lay ahead.

Several times they came across the patches of thick, mossy leaves that sheltered animal one and the bushes bearing the edible berry, but the others were not yet hungry enough to eat local produce, in spite of Nolan making a further reduction in the Earth-food ration.

Late that evening it began to rain, a torrential downpour that continued without cease until far into the following night. The issue coveralls were as impervious to external moisture as they were to the perspiration of the wearers, so the rain did not bring any relief from the heat, although it was successful in grounding the insects. They camped early, but were unable to light fires and were forced to eat their food uncooked. Water got into some of the dried Earth food as it was being opened, and there were many angry arguments and accusations of carelessness. Normally the wet food would have been thrown away, but by then they were all too hungry to refuse it just because it was sodden.

Nolan did not try to pacify them because he had the feeling that there would be worse to come. It would not be wise to risk diminishing whatever authority he possessed in settling petty squabbles.

When they set off next morning the rain had ceased, but the moisture-laden trees were continuing to dump water on them when they least expected it. Nolan had taken the lead and was keeping all his attention on the swampy ground underfoot, and he did not raise his eyes until the unforgettable stench was all around him. Ulechitzl, who was about twenty paces behind him, made a remark in her own language that sounded derogatory.

Nolan pointed toward the clump of trees, each with their four slender arching branches tipped with strings of berries, and called, "My lady, please pass the word back for Pilot Brenner to take the lead and go around it. There is a test I must make."

"Healer," she said in an angry, incredulous voice, "surely you cannot be thinking of . . . of *eating* anything with such a disgustingly foul smell!"

Nolan opened his mouth to explain his idea and the observations that had led to its formation, then closed it again. If he was wrong, then no other person would know of it, and, he reminded himself, he must learn to break his habit of talking too much.

"It will take some time," he said, beginning to unfasten his pack straps. "The tracks you leave are easily followed. I'll catch up before you reach the hilltop."

Nolan had no wish to risk killing any single tree, so he cut one string of berries from each of three of them. By then the colonists were out of sight but not of hearing. They were all talking loudly about him and his present incomprehensible behavior. He placed the strings of berries, tightly sealed, in his sample box, retaining two of them for experimentation and adding to the catalog. He discovered that the sheen on the bright yellow skin was the result of it being porous and exuding internal juice, and that when he cut one open the stench became more pronounced. Either he was growing accustomed to the smell or his olfactory sensors had collapsed under the assault.

His final actions before leaving were to remove the cloth tied around his head and neck, take off his tunic, and roll up the uniform trousers until they were as high as they would go. The short-sleeved undergarment protected his shoulders from chafing by the pack straps but left his arms uncovered, and with his head and legs bare and with the perspiration allowed to evaporate unhindered, he was able to move more quickly and comfortably then at any time since the trek had started. But deliberately he hung back so as not to catch up with the others too soon.

He needed time to prove the validity of his test.

Golden Rain was at the rear of the line and turning every few moments to look back. As soon as she saw him she came walking back to meet him.

"Healer, are you well?" she said in a worried voice, stopping a full ten paces from him. She sniffed delicately and went on, "Have you been eating anything? If the heat is making you unwell, I will help carry your pack. But please cover your arms and legs or the insects will—"

"The insects," said Nolan, smiling, "will continue to avoid me."

He had intended to be strong and silent and not speak of the test until they had camped for the night, but he was so pleased with the results that he could not contain himself. So he told her of his observation that after their first encounter with the stench trees and while the wind had been blowing from that direction, the night insects had seemed much less numerous, and that around the trees themselves there had been few if any insects. A test had immediately suggested itself, and he had bared his arms, legs, and head and had hung one of the stench-tree fruit around his neck to find out if the insects would still be discouraged from the area. He had tested his theory further by exposing the interior of one that had been slit open, finding that the juice had an even greater effect.

"The smell is, of course, horrendous," Nolan went on excitedly, "but those who cannot accustom themselves to it can block their nostrils while eating. Why not try it for yourself, my lady? A few drops of juice applied to the hair or clothing will repel them."

Nolan watched as she came closer and, with movements that somehow remained balanced and graceful, wriggled out of her pack. She undid the cuff and ankle fastenings of the coveralls and rolled up the legs and sleeves as far as they would go, displaying her long, perfectly formed, spectacular limbs. Then she untied and pulled back the cowl, opened the neck all the way down to her waist, and gave a great, relieved sigh.

"It will repel everything," said Golden Rain, with a laugh that ended as a cough, "and everybody."

As he gave her one of the tiny yellow berries, Nolan said very seriously, "There may come a time when that will be an advantage."

Chapter 31

FROM the top of the second hill they could see a third that was so high and broad at its base that it hid the country beyond. But it, too, lay some thirty degrees north of the point where the sun set and squarely across the course plotted by Brenner. The country between was like a great wooded ocean with many low hills rumpling its surface like smooth dark-green waves, and showing patches of a more intense green, a color that experience had shown to be areas where the trees were rooted in swampland.

The insect repellant was not popular, nor were the handful of colonists who first used it. But then the others, envious of the increased mobility and comfort given by limbs that were open to the air, decided that the smell was preferable to an attack of heat exhaustion. After that the distance traveled in a day showed a significant increase, until they encountered another hazard—a bush that spread its long, thorn-tipped branches below as well as above the muddy surface of the swamp.

The swamp bush had no redeeming features, bearing neither blossom nor berry. Its thorns inflicted deep scratches, which meant that the coveralls had to be rolled down again to protect arms and legs, and the result was that everyone became as hot and uncomfortable as before. Nolan was worried in case the thorns contained a vegetable poison, so every night he insisted on irrigating, with water boiled over the campfire, any of the scratches that seemed to be particularly inflamed. And he further increased his unpopularity by dabbing the adjacent skin with the repellant, not because he thought the juice had medicinal qualities, but to ensure that no disease-bearing insects could come close enough to infect the wounds.

With every sweating and stinking mile their hunger increased and their tempers shortened. Nolan had found and was testing other potentially edible specimens, but as yet he was unwilling to clear them for general consumption. Instead he gave everyone a handful of the specimen-two berries to chew as they walked. It was doubtful if the small thick-skinned berries assuaged hunger, but they certainly kept the jaws too busy to talk. Frequently they passed through areas of the thick-leaved ground plants that sheltered the mouselike animals but, in spite of Nolan's approving them as a food source, there was a unanimous aversion to eating something that so closely resembled Earthly vermin. There was also an increasing aversion to talking or listening to Healer Nolan.

From the scraps of conversation drifting back to him, it was clear that they wanted to elect the pilot as their spokesman, and that they were urging Brenner to side with them against the cold-hearted and aloof Healer. Instead of a strong and silent character, it seemed that Nolan was projecting one that was unfeeling and inaccessible. Something would have to be done about that.

Without knowing what precisely he could say to them, he passed the word forward that he was calling a meeting of all colonists for that evening to discuss their present situation and to answer any questions they might have.

When the time came for him to speak, darkness had fallen and the artificial star that was *Aisling Gheal* hung low in the eastern sky, blazing with a pure, white light that put its natural brethren to shame.

He waited until they had finished eating, even though he knew they had not caten enough to make them feel any more kindly disposed toward him. With his back to the brightest fire so that he could better see their faces, he stood waiting while they sat or lay on the ground facing him. Brenner was sitting among them and watching him without expression. Nolan doubted whether he had the wholehearted support of anyone present, and decided on a course of polite aggression.

"Even though some of your words are unclear to me," he said, "I am Healer enough to understand when you complain constantly of hunger. I, too, feel hunger, although not as sharply as do you, for the reason that I use the available local food while you do not."

If you are unsure of your answers, Nolan thought cynically, start asking questions before they do.

He went on, "Why do you not add bulk and nutrition to your Earth-food ration with specimens one, three, and four? I have tested them for edibility and, except for generating flatulence, they are not harmful in the short term and are likely to remain so.

Why do you not cook specimen one, the berries, with the root vegetable three into a stew with a small piece of animal one for flavoring? The fact that the roots turn blue when they are boiled has no effect on their nutritional value. This is the New World. Why do you not use your ingenuity and forget the color prejudices about food that you learned on Earth?''

This time the reaction that greeted his words was loud and continuous. So long and noisy was it that it took Nolan a few minutes to realize that Ulechitzl was not joining in the questions but arguing on his behalf.

''My lady,'' said Nolan in a polite, firm voice, ''if my meaning is unclear to anyone, please confine yourself to translating my actual words and allow me to argue their merits. I have been able to learn a few sentences of the languages you are using, enough to know that you are elaborating on what I have said. What have you been saying to them, exactly, and they to you?''

Ulechitzl inclined her head to show that she had heard, but she did not reply until she finished what she had been saying to one of the colonists.

''With respect, Healer Nolan,'' she said, ''I am translating arguments which for some reason you seem unwilling to use, and which I deem to be necessary at this time, so I am using them for you.''

Nolan was trying to think of an adequate reply, but she saved him the effort by saying, ''As exactly as I can recall it, when you told us that the local food you had tested was safe to eat, one of them said that you were fooling everyone including yourself. Another said that you looked pale and unwell and that, in spite of your greater girth when we set out, you looked thinner than any of the others. A third said that at ten paces he could hear your belly protesting against the local food, and that the vile stuff would go through us without doing any good, or it would slowly poison us as it was poisoning you.

''I told them,'' she continued before Nolan could speak, ''that if they had observed your actions as closely as your pallor and loss of weight, they would have seen that you have been eating only local food and refusing your share of the Earth stores, and that this might explain your . . . your resounding flatulence. They should also have observed you investigating the body wastes of yourself and others, a totally repugnant procedure to an ordinary person, but one which gives a clear indication of how food is being metabolized. I also told them that it was your duty to keep everyone alive, not poison us, and that as a Healer you deserved our respect. And obedience."

"She told them," said Golden Rain, joining the conversation, "in words that I did not expect from the lips of a highborn and cultured lady of the Westland. But I agree with everything she said."

Nolan did not speak at once, because there was a warmth in him that did not come from the fire at his back, but came instead from the peculiar inner warmth of knowing that he was not entirely without the support of friends. It might have been a trick of the firelight but Brenner, too, seemed to be nodding in agreement.

"You are right, my ladies," he said, smiling at them. "I would not have used those words, but my meaning would have been the same. And now, if there are other questions, I would prefer to answer them for myself."

There was one question that was asked in different words by three different people—a Skandian, a Nubian, and one of the Teutons seated beside Brenner—and they said that they spoke for others. They said that they felt not only the hunger but an increasing weakness because the Healer was forcing them to carry unnecessarily heavy loads, most of which were comprised of the food they so badly needed. If they were to make a journey so long that in the opinion of the majority it could never be completed, they should make it slightly more comfortably by taking some weight from their backs and adding it to their stomachs, instead of increasing the duration of their misery with rationing before they ultimately perished, either from hunger or from the poisonous things that he was trying to make them eat.

Before Nolan could reply, one of the Indies colonists stood up and said gravely, "We must rest, and eat. Sooner rather than later you must let us die with dignity."

This was worse than he had expected, Nolan thought as he stared angrily at the four faces that were staring so intently back at him. He was tired, and hungry, and the latest test specimen seemed to be intent on tying knots of cramp in his descending colon. But he was not yet ready to fold up and die, with dignity or otherwise. He tried to control his anger, because these four represented an unknown number of others and that made the situation even worse. Then another thought came to him.

These were the people, the malcontents, the self-willed and the potential ringleaders of future opposition, that the monsignor had wanted to exclude from the main colony. O'Riordan's information on them was complete, while Nolan knew them only from a few weeks' observation. Could it be that his current problem was due simply to the fact that people who were leaders became used to having unpleasant work done for them instead of learning to do it for themselves?

Some of them, like Golden Rain, the rich and greatly favored granddaughter of the Westland's Paramount Chief, and the one-time Aztec Princess Royal, Ulechitzl, had made the transition very well. The others would have to be encouraged to make it.

Gently, to begin with.

"Lars, K'Laumbiri, Wolfgang, Chen Sung," he began quietly, doubly thankful that he had memorized their names and that they were not difficult to pronounce. "I have no expectation of dying, with dignity or otherwise, and neither should any of you. The journey ahead is long, dangerous, and slow, you know that, but it is not impossible. We have not tried to hide either the distances or the difficulties from you, but the next time you are discussing it with Pilot Brenner, ask him how far we have come rather than the distance still to go. You will find that more encouraging, and the farther we go the more—"

He broke off because Wolfgang was shouting unintelligibly at him. Brenner moved quickly to the side of his countryman and gripped his arm. When the other fell silent, the pilot said apologetically, "He says there is small encouragement when the progress we have made over the past three weeks is canceled. Worse, that the total length of the journey will be increased by us changing course away from the colony. I'm sorry, Healer. I told him of your decision earlier this evening."

"Of course you did," said Nolan furiously, but the anger did not reach his voice. "In case some of you are still unaware of this development, while you were making camp and Pilot Brenner was surveying tomorrow's route, it was discovered that the shores of a very large body of water lie across our west-by-northwest course, and that much of the intervening land showed the colors of swamp vegetation. The decision was taken to divert due north, and to continue in that direction.

"There are two good reasons for this," he continued quickly. "The first is that Pilot Brenner's map shows a large upland area lying in that direction. The intervening ground shelves gently toward it and should, therefore, reduce the incidence of swamps. The second reason is that a northerly diversion will take us more quickly out of this equatorial sweatbox and into the subtemperate zone. The time and distance lost in wading through swamps and around the shores of an inland sea will be regained by us being able to travel with increased speed and comfort.

"And now," he went on, "there is the matter of food for this epic journey . . ."

With many pauses to quell angry outbursts from those who though at first he was avoiding the subject, Nolan began to draw analogies between the main colony and themselves. The principal, perhaps the only, difference was that they were mobile and the main colony was not. In one way they were better supplied than the main colony, because their lander had carried down less than its full complement of colonists and much of the payload discrepancy had been made up with additional stores. He reminded them that the main colony had been functioning for many months while they were still in cold sleep.

It had been functioning very well.

". . . Had that not been so," Nolan continued, looking around at all of them, but with his eyes coming to rest on Brenner, "the pilot would quickly have learned of it, because he was landing new colonists as fast as his vehicle could be turned around. If the colonists had caused trouble by refusing to eat anything but Earth food, he would have been aware of that, too, and spoken of it."

Because he is incapable of keeping his mouth closed about anything, Nolan added silently. Aloud, he went on, "If, instead of being guided in the matter of local food by their own Healer, Dervla, they had begun to eat the seed corns and grains carried across the lightyears and the centuries from Earth, he would certainly have learned of that! But there were no such reports, no talk, and not the slightest hint of a rumor that this most heinous of crimes had been considered, much less committed.

"If you are considering it now," he continued, in a tone that suggested that he owed them an apology for even mentioning the idea, "put it from your minds. You must do as the others are doing, and work hard and live off the fruits of the new land until the first harvest is in, and thereafter for as long as is necessary. The only difference between you is that they have to work and you must walk, and you must also carry your future and that of your descendants with you."

While he was speaking he watched them carefully. Many of those closest to him were looking angry, and the rest were too distant for their expressions to be read in the firelight.

He laughed quietly, in case there were some who could not see his smile, and went on, "Perhaps that last remark is something of an exaggeration. I did not mean to suggest that if we arrived in the main colony, ragged and starving and carrying nothing but a load of personal miseries, that they would not be pleased to see us. Nor would they make us any less welcome, nor hesitate to feed and shelter us. But were we to arrive bearing our allocation of seed grains, unbroken and uneaten, that would be much, much better because it would tell them, far better than any powers of eloquence could convey, the kind of people who had come among them."

His tone deepened as he continued, "On this world there is no money, no means of buying what you want other than by the barter and exchange of goods and services, and it is likely to remain thus for generations to come. There is, however, a form of negotiable currency that will be accepted, and gladly, by everyone. It is the riches represented by the unbroken seals on the seed containers you carry. This load will be useful, even valuable, to the colony. But there is the seed you carry within you as well as that which now burdens your backs, and the link between the two is closer than you realize.

"Consider."

Even though they were quiet now, Nolan was beginning to worry lest they were simply assembling the arguments that would demolish his, but the voice he used was firm and confident.

"Our principal reason for going to the colony is to find wives," he said, then dipped his head in a small bow toward Ulechitzl and Golden Rain, "and husbands. For colonists of a new world, the choice of a mate is very important. Doubtless you have your individual, and very personal, preferences regarding the kind of person with whom you want to spend the rest of your lives, those who will work by your sides, and who will love and comfort you and be the mothers and fathers of your children. But remember, the preferences of those you would have as your mates are equally important, to them, and on a colony world the requirements for a husband will be high.

"The as-yet-unattached females of the colony will be seeking husbands," he continued, "but husbands who are strong in mind as well as in body. They will want men who are adaptable, self-controlled, resourceful, and worthy of respect. Men who will not run from responsibility or collapse like a whimpering child if a crop falls short of expectations, or some other calamity threatens. They will be waiting and anxious to see who and how many of us have survived the landing, and they will be welcoming. But if we should arrive without our seed containers, as helpless objects of their pity and with nothing to offer but tales of woe and excuses, impress them we will not.

"That is why we must bend our minds toward that which awaits us at the end of this journey," he said very seriously, "and away from the heat and hunger, the stench and the scratches, that plague its beginning. If we can do that, I believe that we will impress them as no other member of the colony has done.

"Please think about what I have said."

They began to talk quietly among themselves, too quietly and much too quickly for Nolan to understand their words. Then suddenly the man beside Brenner said something in a loud, guttural voice that made the pilot burst into laughter. For a moment Nolan was so furious with the stupid insensitivity of the man that he wanted to go for him with teeth, fists, and feet.

"Pilot Brenner," he said harshly, "this is not a matter for laughter."

"Ease your mind, Healer," said the pilot quietly. "Most of the people here will try to do, and think, as you suggest. They will try very hard. But one of them has said that his future wife might not be impressed by a husband who eats mice."

Nolan gave a long, silent sigh of relief, and for a moment he felt so light that he could have been back on the ship in the weightless condition.

"By the time Wolfgang marries her," he said gravely, "she might be eating mice, too."

Chapter 32

FOR eleven days they traveled across the flat country that lay to the north, through jungle so thick that it hid all sight of the high ground ahead, the inland sea to the west, and even, for long periods every day, the sun. The areas of swampland had become smaller and less numerous and the hilltops fewer still.

Very often their nightly campsites were on thickly wooded hummocks that gave no clear view of the following day's journey, which was the reason why Brenner was given the lead position every day with the Healer close beside him. If the pilot lost his bearings, Nolan wanted to know about it before too much time and distance were wasted.

He was walking beside the pilot with Golden Rain twenty paces behind them when they moved onto what seemed to be a very extensive carpet of the low-growing plants favored by the mice. There were still many colonists who would not eat the mice, but enough of them did to make this area an important find. He made the prearranged sign that meant that the column should come to a silent halt, which Golden Rain relayed to the others before moving quickly forward to join Brenner and Nolan. She did so in time to see what the other two were already seeing—that the come-lately colonists of Earth were not the only creatures who preyed on the mice.

There were three of them, each covered with brown and green mottled skin or short fur that blended with the background vegetation and made it difficult to be precise about their shape until one of them moved to the attack. Then it could be seen that the body was round and fat, in size and shape like that of a young pig, and standing on four short and disproportionately thin legs. There the pig resemblance ended, because from the shoulders there grew a long, flexible neck that tapered to a tiny, conical head, while from the rear projected a tail that was twice the neck's length, highly mobile, but, unlike the neck, it widened to terminate as a large, flat, and fleshy oval that was less than an inch thick. As Nolan watched it became plain that the tail was the animal's principal natural weapon.

The creature's method of hunting was to pick its way slowly and silently on its pipestem legs among the ground vegetation until it saw a bunch of leaves that moved. Still quietly and carefully the creature turned away from its prey, raising its tail high and turning its head to the rear so as to keep the area in view. Then suddenly the tail came swinging down like a fleshy flyswatter; it turned and pushed its pointed head under the flattened leaves to come up with a stunned or dead mouse between its teeth.

Nolan had been thinking that it was much better equipped for catching mice than the colonists, whose narrow, heavy, and at times overly enthusiastic feet not only killed their prey but destroyed it utterly, when beside him he saw Golden Rain notching an arrow to her bow.

She brought one of the creatures down with her second shot. By then Brenner had dropped his pack and gone after one of the survivors, making the kind of noises that were attributed to Golden Rain's ancestors. The thin, short legs made the creature slow on its feet, and the pilot caught it by its tail and smashed its head against a tree trunk. Nolan immobilized the third one by jumping on its tail and cracking the skull with his staff.

That day they had made camp early so that the Healer could skin, dissect, and prepare drawings of the creature that he called animal specimen two, and that everyone else called a "thumper," for his catalog. Following the removal of entrails and other suspect material, he had followed the usual test procedure by cutting off two sections and cleaning them thoroughly before requesting that one be roasted and the other boiled to remove harmful bacteria.

It was then that the trouble started.

In vain did Nolan explain to them that as a food source animal two was as yet an unknown quantity. Examination of the stomach contents had revealed vegetable matter along with partly digested mouse, so that the creature was an omnivore like themselves.

But the fact that the human beings had eaten mice without ill effects, and that the twos also ate them as a regular part of their diet, was a strong indication, but by no means a certainty, that the larger creatures were also safe to eat. He reminded them that the initial test sample should be large enough for the results to be meaningful, but small enough for any toxic material present not to be lethal. If the test material was harmful or potentially lethal, the stomach would probably reject it within the first hour. If it remained for two to four hours while giving continuous, acute discomfort, vomiting, or diarrhea, it would be classified as inedible. And if it remained for four hours or more without any serious symptoms until it had passed through the digestive and waste-elimination systems, only then would it be considered safe to eat. Finally he warned them that the odor of the test specimen was not an important datum in the test.

No matter how appetizing it smelled while it was being cooked.

In spite of all his warnings, more than half of them insisted on helping him test the specimen, so much so that when *Aisling Gheal* showed briefly through the branches overhead, there was little remaining of the three animals save their skins, and Golden Rain said that those she wanted to use to make long moccasins that would give better protection against thorn bushes than her coveralls.

Before he went to sleep that night, Nolan attached two strips of the thumper's hide to his arm, one with the fur facing outward and the other facing in, so that he could test for skin allergies.

In the seven weeks that followed, they continued northward over steadily rising ground ahead with the inland sea to westward. The store of Earth food had long since gone, and in spite of everyone having adapted to living off the countryside, they were constantly hungry, but not weak from hunger. When the surface conditions allowed it, they walked in a line abreast, making a wide sweep forward in search of the groves that harbored the thumpers' mice. Many of them carried the wooden spears they had fashioned, or the bows and arrows they had made to Golden Rain's directions. A few of them had become more proficient in their use than was she herself. She had also taught them how to make the long thumper-hide boots, because by then the legs of everyone's coveralls were in ribbons.

Nolan had long since packed away his uniform, saying that everyone should know who and what he was by now. He refused to reduce his load by throwing it away, nor would he allow Brenner to discard his uniform, because, he told the pilot, that would give a bad example to the others and there might come a time when they themselves would need this reminder of who and what they were. And so it was that the two ship's officers dressed as did the colonists in hide boots, kilts, and the sleeveless leather waistcoats that left the arms free while protecting the shoulders and backs against chafing by the pack straps, and became indistinguishable from everyone else.

Except for Ulechitzl and Golden Rain, that was. They insisted on cutting fringes at appropriate places, and stitching on designs of dried berries, and somehow managed to add style to the crude garments. They, at least, fastened the fronts of their waistcoats with hide thongs, but not always high or tightly enough. More and more often he caught the other men looking at them, and just as often he found that he was looking at them himself.

Oh yes, he thought worriedly, they were all hungry but very healthy.

When Brenner finally completed the delicate task of removing the farspeaker from the spacesuit upper section, Nolan picked up that load as well. The helmet was bulky rather than heavy, but he did not mind, because he had a use for it when next they reached a large body of water.

Every few days Nolan was able to add to his list of edible roots and berries, but to be palatable the majority of them had to be boiled or stewed with the meat of animal specimen two. So popular was the thumper meat that they tried to catch every animal they found.

But the meat-supply problem was complicated by the fact that the groves that sheltered the mouselike ones did not always contain twos. That was why, when the colonists were advancing in a wide line abreast, the one who first discovered a likely two feeding place would climb the nearest tree so that he could look above the surrounding undergrowth into the grove to see whether thumpers were present. If there were none, and the colonists were not hungry enough to hunt mice, he would climb down and move forward again. If thumpers were present he would signal the fact quietly to those on either side, and the line would curve forward to encircle the area and then close in. The thumpers who survived the arrows and spears rarely escaped the feet.

Nolan suggested that they capture and keep a few of the thumpers alive, to be taken with them as a source of fresh meat when they were traveling through areas where the creatures were scarce. As well, the observation of their eating habits would give him more information on local plant life that might also be edible to humans.

The first serious accident happened while Brenner, excited at having discovered a grove with at least twenty thumpers in it, was climbing down from his vantage point. Apparently he had been gripping a thin upper branch and jumping onto a lower and stronger one when both branches had snapped off short, and he had fallen ten feet to the ground on his head, shoulder, and arm. His calls for help went unheard because the others were too excited by their record catch to hear anything but their own self-congratulations, and by the time Nolan noticed the pilot's absence and found him, Brenner was unconscious.

As Nolan slipped from the role of jungle hunter to that of Healer, his first feelings were of surprise and relief. This was the first serious casualty their party had suffered, and the injuries sustained from a fall of that distance could have been much worse. The indications were that in an effort to protect his head while falling, Brenner had raised his right arm. He had succeeded in that Nolan could feel only a large temporal edema that was still swelling, and no signs of a depressed fracture. In spite of Brenner's being deeply unconscious, Nolan was pleased to see that both of the pupils were reacting to light.

But in protecting his head Brenner had dislocated his right shoulder, broken both the radius and ulna on the right arm, and cracked two ribs just below the armpit. The fractures were clean and uncomplicated and the bleeding from a few surface abrasions minimal.

Subdued now and no longer trying to tell Nolan of the results of the hunt, the others gathered around while he worked. The Healer paused long enough to tell them that they would not be traveling farther that day and to make camp by the stream they had crossed a few hundred paces back, and that he needed a litter. Ulechitzl and Wolfgang remained to assist him.

He was glad that Brenner was unconscious as he relocated the shoulder and reduced the fractures, because there was no anesthetic available and the process would have been painful without one. For splints he used four of the thin straight twigs from the branch that had been the pilot's downfall, because the wood was light, brittle, and easily snapped to the required length. He strapped up the damaged ribs and immobilized the fractured forearm by binding it transversely across the pilot's chest. He thought of applying a wet pad to the bump, but decided against it because it was too hot and humid for there to be any cooling by evaporation. Brenner was still unconscious when they transferred him to the litter, and Wolfgang helped Nolan carry it to the officers' tent, which some helpful colonist had already erected for them.

Laypeople could be sensitive and emotional about apparent cruelty to the sick or injured, so it was only when the pilot and Nolan were alone inside the tent and hidden from sight of the others that the Healer knelt down beside his patient and began slapping him firmly and repeatedly on the face.

After about twenty seconds of it, Brenner opened his eyes and mumbled something in his native tongue which he translated a moment later to, "Bloody hell and damnation, Healer, what are you *doing*?"

Relieved at this verbal evidence of clear thinking, Nolan smiled and said, "I was surrendering to a momentary sadistic impulse. Now listen carefully. You fell from a tree and sustained injuries to your arm, ribs, and shoulder, all of which have been treated. More important and serious, and the reason why I was slapping your face, was the blow to your head. Any cranial injury that results in unconsciousness is potentially serious and now that you are awake you must try to remain conscious until I am satisfied that the blow has not addled your wits. Do you understand what I have been saying to you?"

Brenner nodded, winced, and a grunt of pain escaped between his clenched teeth.

"Moving your head may be uncomfortable just now," said Nolan unnecessarily. "Just answer yes or no. Can you see how many fingers I am holding up?"

The pilot took a deep breath, and winced again. "Yes, three," he replied. "Now my chest hurts, and my arm."

"I know," said Nolan sympathetically, and went on, "Can you remember the exact details of your fall? Can you recall the circumstances and incidents immediately preceding and following it, and your thoughts at those times? Can you remember conversations and events which occurred earlier today, and yesterday?"

There were more questions, to which the answers were invariably yes, and finally Nolan laughed quietly and said, "Your mind seems to be as clear as it ever was, but to make sure I would like you to remain wakeful for at least another two hours. Will you do that for me?"

"I'm not likely to sleep," said Brenner in an aggrieved voice, pausing for breath between every few words. "My arm and shoulder and chest hurt, and my head feels worse than the morning after a night in the beer cellars. Damnation, Healer, why didn't you let me sleep and be comfortable?"

Nolan ignored the question because he had already answered it, and said instead, "You need something else to think about, something of the past or future that will take your mind off the aches and pains of the present. For example, I intend to remain in this camp until you are fit to travel, and then you will be carried on a litter until I am satisfied that you can walk unaided.

"We can stay here for many days," he went on, unable to keep the pleasure and excitement he was feeling from showing in his voice. "That is because the thumpers you found, a small herd of them, have all been either killed or captured. One of them is a gravid female, which opens up the possibility of us breeding our own food herd. But right now the most important thought you should bear in mind is that for the first time since leaving the lander, there is no scarcity of food."

"On top of my other miseries," said Brenner, "now you're making me feel hungry."

"I can relieve that condition," said Nolan, smiling, "as soon as the fires are lit. And while you are waiting, there are other questions I must ask. How is your recollection of the more distant past? Can you detect any obvious blanks in your memories of the ship, your reasons for volunteering for the project, any important incidents from your early childhood? Think back, tell me as much as you can remember, and take your time."

Nolan was no longer worried about the fall having caused structural damage to the pilot's brain, or even a partial amnesia. He was acting now as a Healer of the Mind, and trying to make Brenner forget for a time the pain of his injuries because they both knew that there was no other sure means of relieving it.

He knew, as did everyone else, that the pilot liked the sound of his own voice.

Brenner began by describing his childhood in a large house on the banks of the Rhine, where his family had been vine-growers. Later there had been arguments with his parents and two older sisters about his membership in the local hang-gliding club. It was not a very rich club: the members built and maintained their own machines, and spent their free time slope soaring or racing cross-country, but he had never been able to convince his family that unpowered flight was the safest way to fly.

". . . And in all that time," he continued, "and during the years of flight training that followed, not a single scratch or bruise did I suffer. Until we came here and I fell out of a rotten tree!"

Nolan made a sympathetic sound, then went on thoughtfully, "In fact, Pilot, the tree was not rotten. I examined it while they were making your litter." He pointed to Brenner's splintered arm. "The branches are long and straight and look strong enough, but the wood is very light and breaks easily, much like Earth balsa wood. Your experience of unpowered flight makes me wonder if—"

"You want me to build a glider?" the pilot said in an incredulous voice. He started to laugh, then winced and clutched at his chest with the free hand and cursed instead.

"Not immediately," said Nolan, "and not a hang glider. At the risk of sounding like your parents, I would not want to risk the life of our only navigator. I was thinking of the Cathay multiple-kite system capable of lifting a man. In flat jungle country we need to see where we're going. If there is a swamp ahead, our first sign of it should not be when we're up to our waists in mud."

He stopped before Brenner could reply, because Wolfgang was standing outside the tent. He wanted to know how the pilot was feeling, and if he was allowed food. Nolan allowed the patient to answer for himself, and by the time the Teuton returned a few minutes later with enough for the three of them, Nolan had raised the end of the litter so that Brenner could eat without getting stew on his face.

When they were finished and Nolan was feeling pleasantly distended, he said, "I want to have a closer look at that female thumper and write her into my notes while the light lasts. Stay and talk to him for as long as you like, Wolfgang, but try not to make him laugh."

Nolan was adding to the thumper information in his catalog and bringing the journal he had decided to keep up to date when he saw two of Brenner's countrymen move the litter close to the fire and then, when the smoke made the pilot cough and they knew that it was hurting his chest, return him to the front of his tent. Gradually then, all of the colonists left the fire to sit around the pilot and talk, and laugh, and sing. They sang many songs, solo and in racial groups, and some of the voices were like soft, strong hands that reached in and gripped the heart so tightly that they squeezed out tears. Nolan had thought of Brenner's accident only as it affected him as a Healer, but now he was beginning to see it as an event that had united the colonists, in sympathy, as nothing else could have done. He wondered if he would ever fully understand people.

It was almost dark when he became aware of a hand on his shoulder, and Ulechitzl standing over him.

"My lady," he said.

"Surely you cannot see to write in this light," she said, in a tone that reminded him of a chiding mother. "Why don't you . . . We would like you to join us, Healer Nolan."

He joined them and they made way for him as he checked Brenner's condition, then he sat down beside the litter. Strangely, the talk was not of serious matters, their alien surroundings, the journey ahead, or their chances of surviving it. Nor did they stare interminably into the branches overhead, as was usual every night, in the hope of catching sight of the *Aisling Gheal* making some kind of signal to let them know that it knew they were there. In spite of himself, Nolan felt himself being drawn into this strange fantasy of normality, and he was beginning to feel that he was back once again, a boy at summer camp, stomach filled to bursting, without a care in the world and preparing to sing and talk and tell stories far into the night.

When his turn came to entertain, Nolan had to confess that he could not sing, and there was much laughter and enthusiastic agreement when he demonstrated his inability. Instead he said that he would tell them a story, a story of survival and ultimate victory that was appropriate to their own present, and successful, struggles to survive in this alien land.

The story of Orla.

If the Cathay colonists who were watching him so impassively had been among that earlier audience in the College of Lensmakers, they were, of course, too polite to interrupt him.

It was a longer story by far than any of the others that had been told that night, and he waited for the signs of restlessness and impatience that would tell him that he should break off and continue it at another time. But even though the fires died to lightless ash and the gray of the unseen jungle dawn had begun to dilute the darkness under the trees, there were no interruptions. And when the story was finished they dispersed without speaking to him, but that was because he had pointed to the sleeping Brenner and then raised the same finger to his lips for silence.

He had moved the litter back inside the tent and was laying himself down as quietly as possible when the pilot said, "I'm not sleeping, Healer, just thinking."

"Try to stop thinking," said Nolan quietly, "and maybe you'll go to sleep. Are you comfortable? Do you want me to take you behind the nearest bush?"

"I'm *not* comfortable," Brenner replied angrily. "And no, not yet. Anyway, I'll ask one of the others to take me. You shouldn't have to do that for me. It, it isn't right."

"I agree, it isn't very dignified," said Nolan. "But I won't make a habit of it. There's nothing wrong with your legs, and when I'm sure there is no vertigo and you can walk without falling over, I shall withdraw my services. Besides, the others might not know how to support you properly and would risk undoing my repair work. If or when you want to go, speak up."

As a male trainee Healer in a profession dominated by females, he had been given a large share of the undignified jobs.

When Brenner did not reply, Nolan said, "If the arm is paining you, I can give you something to make you relax enough to—"

"No!" the pilot broke in sharply. "Are you trying to poison me? We were warned not to use Earth drugs. Don't you remember?"

Nolan sighed. Discomfort often made patients irritable and abusive. The proper course was to treat the display as part of the symptomology rather than a personal criticism.

"I remember, Pilot," he said, "because I gave that lecture. It was thought that over a period of many centuries, and in spite of storage in ultralow temperatures, the complex molecular structure of our chemical medications might break down and become ineffective or even dangerous. But this might not apply to vegetable-based, herbal medications, which are much more stable chemically, of the type I can give you now. You will need to swallow, not chew it, because the taste is vile, but Healer Dervla herself has assured me that it should be safe, and effective."

"Should be," said Brenner. Then in an apologetic voice he went on, "Sorry, Healer, I should not have spoken to you as I did. It's just that I've never been sure whether Dervla is more witch than Healer. What will it do to me?"

"It will probably turn you into a frog," said Nolan, "but it will be a sleeping frog."

Brenner gave a small, uncertain laugh, then he took the proffered tablet. But there was no immediate effect, especially on the pilot's tongue.

"I've been thinking about the ladies," he said, after a moment's silence. "So have the others."

Nolan deepened his breathing in a pretense of being asleep, to no avail.

"We were talking about our present situation," the pilot went on, "and another that closely resembled it on Earth. There were fishing communities on tropical islands whose custom it was, when their men were expected to be at sea for a long time, to appoint a woman to travel on each ship for the comfort of the fishermen. These women are not wives, but serve only to preserve harmony among men who are confined together by their work for too long a time. Surely, Healer, the analogy is plain."

"Not to me," said Nolan in a quiet but very firm voice. "The wahines you speak of choose to perform this service. It is their profession. The work is not forced on them, as it would be if the custom was introduced here. Are you considering the use of force, Pilot?"

"No," said Brenner, "persuasion."

Nolan remained silent, knowing that there was more to come.

"Very well, Healer," the pilot went on, in a voice that had become as serious and clinical as Nolan's own. "It seems that first I must persuade you. We are officers of the ship. For that reason alone we are highly respected, you more than I for obvious reasons, because of what we are trying to do. If we were to take—or, if you prefer the word, persuade—Ulechitzl and Golden Rain to be our wives, there would be much envy but no real opposition. The colonists are not stupid. They know that while the ladies remain unattached and potentially available for any one of them, there would be a much greater chance of dissension, jealousy, and ultimately violence breaking out.

"This is a colony world," Brenner continued quickly, "and eventually we will all be expected to take wives. It might as well be sooner rather than later. I do not think there would be much opposition from the ladies, because, as you have already reminded us, the woman of the colony will want mates who are strong, and capable of protecting and providing for them and the children to come. I have a strong preference, but I am willing to defer to you in the matter of first choice and take the other—"

"No."

"No?" said Brenner. "No to which?"

"No," said Nolan firmly, "to both."

"But *why*, for God's sake?" the pilot asked. "I don't understand you. Is it, can it be that . . . I don't want to give offense, but is it something to do with what they say about male Healers being softer and more fem—"

"If you don't want to give offense," said Nolan, "then don't say it. Don't even think it."

There was a long silence during which Nolan tried to decide how much he could tell the pilot about Ulechitzl and Golden Rain, and whether the results of its becoming common knowledge, as it must if he spoke of it to Brenner, would be good or bad. On Earth he had made promises that bound him to actions that he could and could not take, but here on the New World he no longer felt that they bound him to silence.

He told Brenner about Ulechitzl and Golden Rain and the circumstances that led to the promises that had placed them under his personal protection. Although the temptation was great to unburden himself completely to the pilot, he did not speak of the monsignor at all.

"Now I understand your position, Healer," said Brenner, his voice dropping to a conspiratorial whisper. "If Golden Rain is already married to Wanachtee, and Ulechitzl promised to Ciaran, that is why they want to reach the main colony as quickly as possible, and why they will want nothing to do with anyone else. That, and the knowledge that the ladies are under your personal protection, should help cool the ardor of some of the men, myself included, who do not want to live as priests until we reach the colony. But there is no guarantee of their continuing good behavior. The journey is long and many still believe it to be impossible. Without hope, men can become desperate, and you would be witholding from them the two prizes desired by all and which you had refused for yourself. Their anger will be directed at you, and if they were to use force, as seems likely, you would be hopelessly outnumbered. Healer, what then?"

"Then," said Nolan quietly, "there would be a large number of injured colonists and a Healer who was either dead or too badly injured to treat them. The number of casualties would be large because I would not expect to stand alone.''

''No,'' said Brenner, ''in this I would be with you.''

There was a long pause, then Brenner went on thoughtfully, ''And there are the ladies who have become as fast and strong as they are beautiful, and who would fight like tigers. The odds against us would be further reduced, Healer, and I should be able to convince my countrymen to stand with us. With luck there would be argument but no violence.''

Nolan's sudden feeling of gratitude for the pilot's support, as well as the knowledge that the support would be increased thereby, forced him to say more.

''There is another problem I might have to solve, Pilot,'' he said carefully. ''My promises were made to Wanachtee and Ciaran, and while Golden Rain knows of the promise made to her husband to protect her, Ulechitzl knows nothing of the similar one exacted by Ciaran. Wanachtee and Golden Rain are espoused, but the situation between Ciaran and Ulechitzl is more uncertain, and based on only an hour's observation of them together at the reception in Tara. It may be that her feeling for him is less strong than his for her. Or it might be that he, fearing that we are all dead, will marry another colonist. Naturally, I have not spoken to her of this possibility, nor of my promise to Ciaran.

''I must continue trying to keep her safe,'' he went on. ''But do I have the right to extend my protection to an area where it might not be wanted? Can you appreciate my difficulty?''

''Yes, Healer,'' said Brenner in a voice that was happy and excited and bore no trace of pain. ''Yes, indeed.''

''And your solution?' asked Nolan.

Without hesitation, Brenner said, ''You should not protect her if she does not want to be protected, if she wishes the responsibility for her future protection to pass to another man. I am thinking of a man other than Ciaran, a man, let us suppose, like myself. No, healer, let us *not* suppose that. It would be a man very like myself, because she is the one that disturbs my days and delights my sleep, and I want to—''

''No doubt,'' Nolan broke in gently. ''But, Pilot, she may not feel as strongly about you. She is the only woman among us without attachment, so you have chosen when there is no choice. The choosing must wait until we reach thc main colony, when there will be a wider choice. And I have told you who she is, or was. It was agreed that all Earthly titles, no matter how lofty, would have no meaning here. But she was an Aztec Princess Royal, a highly intelligent and cultured lady indeed, and Ciaran was the *Ionadacht na Garda* to Macve herself. Ulechitzl is not a simple maid to be swept off her feet by a uniform, even if it is that of an officer of the starship."

"You do not dissuade me, Healer," said Brenner. "Rather, you have given me a challenge, and hope. When there is hope of a great reward, a man can be very patient. While he is exercising that patience he has the chance to show himself in many ways to be superior to another man, even a onetime Captain of the Imperial Guard, so that when we reach the main colony she will make the right choice."

"Ulechitzl is fortunate indeed," said Nolan. "She now has two protectors for the journey rather than one."

"Yes," the pilot replied. He sounded almost embarrassed as he went on, "I would not want . . . I mean, she would not be greatly impressed by me as a man if I was to protect her and allow harm to befall Golden Rain. I, we, should guard them both."

"Good," said Nolan, in a relieved voice. "That is what I wanted to hear from you." He yawned suddenly. "And now that your problems of the heart are resolved, is your arm comfortable? Are you ready to sleep?"

"Yes, it must be," the pilot replied in a surprised voice. "My mind is on other things and the arm troubles me hardly at all. But I have two more questions for you, and before you answer let me assure you that I will not speak of this matter, nor will I name the lady or repeat the rumors concerning both of you that I heard on the ship. That much, at least, I owe you. But please tell me, Healer, is it a problem of the heart that is the real reason why you are driving yourself, and the rest of us, into making this well-nigh-hopeless journey? And will your problem, too, be resolved if we reach the main colony?"

By telling the pilot all about Ulechitzl and promising nothing, he had converted a potential enemy into a staunch ally. He did not think it was a time for avoiding questions, especially when it was clear that Brenner had already guessed the answers.

"To your first question, yes," Nolan replied. "To the second, I don't know."

There was a long silence that was broken by the pilot, who said awkwardly, "We will reach the main colony somehow, never fear. And you will resolve your own problem, successfully, I'm sure. It is not likely that she would choose anyone else, because

I hear that people like her are forbidden to marry . . . That is, they don't usually . . . But I'm sure you would be able to convince her that . . ."

Brenner floundered helplessly and became silent, and Nolan smiled sadly to himself at the realization that the pilot was trying to offer encouragement, trying in his own way to be a Healer of the Mind. The fact that the attempt was less than successful detracted nothing from the effort. And he was still trying.

Brenner went on, "The majority of the colonists believe that you will take them to the colony. After today's find of thumpers, the rest have fewer doubts. They all, not just a majority, hold you in high regard. They remember the food testing, how badly you were affected in the early days, and how you fussed over them like a mother hen or snapped like a sheepdog at the heels of the laggards. But they say you are withdrawn, solitary, reserved, difficult to approach. They would know more about you, Healer, and would like to call you friend."

Before Nolan could think of a reply, Brenner went on quickly, "Healer, in what we shall all have to face together, the distinction between a colonist and an officer of the ship has become unimportant. You know and call all of them by their Christian names, or forenames, as does a friend or parent, but to them you are Healer Nolan. We would like to learn more of you, to reduce the distance you keep between us. It would be a small beginning, but we would like to call you by your first name."

It would, indeed, be a small beginning and a very large temptation, Nolan thought. The temptation to relax and be among friends who would share his uncertainties, the temptation to seek help with difficult decisions and, ultimately, to reduce his authority. And if they were to be told his given name, they might use it at the wrong time and before the wrong person. The matter was private and professional, and he could not risk such an embarrassment. He could not allow Dervla to think that he had been guilty of such presumption.

She had told him that he was not and never would be a Healer of the First Name.

"Pilot," said Nolan, "go to sleep."

Brenner sighed but said nothing more, and soon his breathing became slow and regular. Nolan, too, tried to compose himself for slumber, but he could hear the tethered thumpers rooting about in the undergrowth and occasionally the sudden, muffled slap of them exercising their tails. And worse than any other distraction were the mind pictures and thoughts and words of Healer Dervla.

Dervla as she had been rising like some flawless Greek sculpture from her cold sleep casket, and shapeless in her spacesuit as she had walked with him outside the ship under the stars, and, word for word, their conversations and their arguments about the monsignor's conspiracy and her dedication to her Order. He was hearing again her words to him, spoken gently and seriously and even sorrowfully, but words of rejection nonetheless. And he felt again the brief touching of their lips and her final words to him before she had gone into cold sleep. There had been no time to ask if those few words were a negation of everything that she had said before. Or was he deluding himself as he was deluding all the others into hoping for the impossible?

His mind gave him no rest as again and again he went over their conversations together, trying to find more inspired words and telling arguments that would make her change her mind. And gradually it seemed that he had found the right words, for her arguments were stilled, and when he kissed her it seemed that there was much more than a few seconds remaining before cooldown, because she was loosening the casket restraints and reaching up to put her arms tightly around him, and in her eyes there was nothing whatever of rejection.

From what transpired then, Nolan knew beyond any doubt that he slept.

Chapter 33

THEY carried Brenner for three days before he was able to convince the Healer that he could walk without doing further damage to his fractured arm. Nolan did not require much convincing, because by then the gravid female in their herd had produced five thumper cubs who were unable to move at anything like a human walking pace, so the pilot's litter was pressed into service as a cub transporter.

That lasted for only a day because the cubs would not stay on the litter unless tightly restrained, and this caused them to complain loudly, loudly for a creature weighing scarcely two pounds, and their piteous bleatings so agitated the mother and the other adult thumpers that they became unmanageable. That evening the consensus of opinion, based on factors more emotional than practical, was that neither the mother nor her young should be eaten and should instead be left in the grove of mice that was nearby.

This was done, but within a few minutes the female was following them, plainly unwilling to leave the herd, which must have included her mate, and with the five cubs clinging happily to her long, wide tail.

They were traveling through an area where the thumpers seemed to be everywhere, frequently wandering into the camp at night. It was while Nolan was writing them up in his journal that the reason for their behavior became suddenly plain to him. He felt stupid for not seeing it from the beginning.

Their thumper herd with its single large female was a matriarchy.

It was necessary only to attach a waist harness, and with a rope tied onto each flank, two men could drive or drag her along between them. The others followed, foraging for food as they came or taking it in turn to carry the young ones on their tails. Sometimes the males disappeared for hours at a time, which meant that they had sensed the presence of a mouse grove nearby, but they always returned with one of them carrying a tail full of slain mice for their queen. Whenever the thumpers encountered another herd, there was great agitation on both sides with neither showing any inclination to join each other. The result was that the colonists began to think of their herd as domesticated and, even though there was additional hunting effort involved, they preferred to kill only the strangers.

With the increasing availability of thumper pelts, the solution to the problem of the hanging thorns became obvious. And so it was that the hide kilts of the men were gradually replaced by trousers, although never as well-fitting or as neatly stitched as those of Golden Rain and Ulechitzl, and their waistcoats lengthened, covered more of the body, and grew long sleeves.

The garments were hot and uncomfortable, especially when one of the sudden, heavy rainstorms passed over or when the hot, moist wind blew through the trees from the north, south, or east and penetrated to ground level like the uneven breath of some great invisible dragon. At times the jungle was so thoroughly rain-soaked that the fires could not be lit and, because of the

Healer's dire warnings about the dangers of eating uncooked meat, they had to be satisfied with the local edible vegetation. But they had ceased complaining about such discomforts to Nolan or each other. Instead they sang as they marched and in the evening told stories or tried to learn each others' languages.

But when the west wind blew, whether or not it was accompanied by rain, it was as if everyone had taken a happy drug, because it had crossed and been cooled by the waters of a great inland sea so that it seemed almost cold by comparison. They had not caught sight of that sea for more than seven weeks, but the west wind told them that it was not far off.

They were still traveling due north and with the distant colony on their left flank. Sixty-eight days after landing they were scarcely two hundred miles closer to their destination. This was information that Nolan and the pilot kept to themselves.

Brenner's arm had mended well and he was becoming increasingly eager to build and fly three vertically linked kites which together would be capable of lifting an observer. The Cathay colonists said that the frameworks could be built using thin straight branches of the light wood notched and bound together with the strands that hung from the stench-trees. The strands were sticky enough to make a secure and self-adhesive joint, and the frames could be covered with tent fabric. After all, they said, the original idea was the Healer's own.

Nolan refused permission, saying that the project would have to wait until they came to a lake where, in the event of a mishap, the landing on water would be less damaging to the observer. He also insisted that the kite design should be such that the tent fabric could be used afterward for its original purpose, because they still needed tents more than information.

The pilot was trying very hard to impress Ulechitzl, but that was another thought that Nolan kept to himself.

They came on the lake five days later. The water was fringed with floating vegetation and so shallow that in places it was almost a swamp, but wide enough for the wind blowing across it to be both cooling and strong enough to lift a kite. The frameworks and bracing struts had been cut and prepared many days earlier, the wood being light and easily carried, so the assembly and testing of the first kite began as soon as they made camp.

Nolan did not have to make camp, because Brenner, anxious to display his confidence in the project, had publicly offered the use of their tent fabric to cover two of the three kites. Instead he spent the time exploring the lake, wading in waist deep at times and using the spacesuit helmet with visor closed to look below the surface. It was not as effective as a glass-bottomed bucket, but it sufficed to show him many fish, some almost twice the length of his hand, and other nonswimming bottom dwellers nibbling at the thumper hide covering his legs. They were very easy to catch, although one of them stung him so that his wrist itched for many hours afterward. He was unable to see any of the pleasant-tasting fruit specimen one that he had found by the lake on the evening of the landing, and he decided that this lake was too shallow to grow it.

Back on shore Nolan reported that the lake held fish or mud crawlers that were large enough to eat and not large enough to eat the fishermen, but that they should not waste time trying to catch them until he had established which if any of the varieties were edible. They were all too busy watching the kite builders to pay much attention to him.

Nolan brought his catch to the thumpers and fed the different specimens to them one by one. Those they refused he threw back into the lake, and the one that they accepted, even so far as offering it to their queen, he dissected, drew, and described in his catalog as fish specimen one. It was becoming a law of nature to him that anything a thumper would eat would not be seriously harmful to humans, although it might not necessarily be palatable to them. Lastly he cut off a few pieces suitable for cooking and waited for the fires to be lit.

By nightfall the first kite had been built and tested successfully, and construction of the other two was well advanced. When *Aisling Gheal* appeared from behind a cloud, the first they had seen of it for many weeks, there was a sudden, spontáneous cheer. It was inevitable that they spent the rest of the evening telling and translating stories of the legendary Sung Hsi-Sen, philosopher, inventor, and Mandarin of the Flamingo Rank, whose senior slave had flown for the first time in his master's man-carrying steerable glider; and of the great Plains Chieftain Noisy Bird, whose proper name was remembered only by a few historians, who had added a lightweight hero to a larger glider and given mankind powered flight.

With great delicacy they forebore mentioning a fact known to all of them, that both Hsi-Sen's slave and the first Redmen to fly like an eagle had eventually crashed to their deaths.

By the late afternoon of the following day the three kites and Pilot Brenner were ready to fly, but the launch was delayed by a serious disagreement among the ground crew. The problem was theological rather than physical. It seemed that in Cathay the flying of kites had a deep, religious significance, which was the reason why each one had been decorated with ideographs painted with the dark red juice of the fruit-specimen-five berry.

The kites were ready to fly, the ground crew insisted, but the pilot was not, and would not be allowed to until his forehead was similarly decorated.

"This is stupid," said Brenner angrily. "I know what they want to do and the reason for it. But the juice spreads and stains, and will need weeks of washing to remove. I'm going to end up looking like a . . . a Redman!"

Ulechitzl smiled at him and said, "In what you are about to do, the more Gods you have on your side the better. May the wind god, Ehecatl, also bear you aloft."

When finally he submitted to the painting, his face was almost as red as the dye.

The trees overhanging the lakeside caused the wind to gust and eddy uncertainly, so that the first kite was the most difficult to fly. Once it was out and over the lake where the wind held steady, it rose high above the treetops, pulling the second and then the third kite after it. Brenner was attached by an abbreviated harness to the third kite, but two of the ground crew were gripping an arm each to hold him down. There was much incomprehensible shouting of instructions, or it might have been prayers, then suddenly Brenner was pulled aloft to a height more than twice that of the treetops. He hung suspended in his harness, twisting slowly one way and then the other, while the three stepped kites above him seemed scarcely to move.

They watched him for several minutes while he shouted and pointed to the northwest, but the people on the ground were making too much noise for him to be heard.

Then without warning the wind that had been in the west died away, only to gust suddenly and more strongly from the north. The supporting kites jerked and twisted erratically and moved out of line, and the framework of the second collapsed suddenly so that the detached fabric fluttered like an untidy flag between the first and third.

Brenner, his weight too much for the remaining two kites, was losing height rapidly. With desperate haste the ground crew was trying to pull him in, because the wind was blowing him just as rapidly toward the trees. They saw him loosen his harness to be ready to jump while he was over the lake, but he was still very high and the water at the lake's edge was shallow and might not cushion his fall. For a moment they watched him swing in the loose harness so that when he let go, he was able to rotate and fall, arms and legs outspread, onto his back.

There was a tremendous slap against the water and an explosion of droplets. By the time Nolan reached him, a few seconds after Ulechitzl but before the others, Brenner was standing waist deep, bespattered with mud, spluttering and coughing.

"Pilot," said Ulechitzl, "are you hurt?"

"No, my lady," said Brenner, coughing again. "I am well."

"How often must I tell you, Pilot Brenner," said Nolan, his intense relief bringing him close to anger, "not to drink stagnant water."

It must have been a case of fortune favoring the brave, Nolan thought, because a whole day had passed and the pilot showed no ill effects from his involuntary drink of lake water. With Brenner taking the lead they were moving again, the lightwood frames dismantled and packed, their fabric returned to mundane use as tents, and even the young thumpers seemed to be infected with the general eagerness to travel, because they were leaving the adults' tails for hours at a time to walk on their own tiny feet.

During his few comments aloft Brenner had concentrated his observations on an arc covering west to north, since all other directions were of no interest to them. He said that they seemed to be on a plateau, because, at a distance which he estimated to be three days' march to westward, the roof of the jungle was close to the horizon and sharply outlined against the distant, hazy blue of the inland sea. About six days' march to the northwest lay a small mountain peak with a high shoulder running east, both so high that nothing could be seen beyond them. The upper slopes of the mountain and ridge were covered only by grass and low bushes. From that peak they would be able to see in every direction for fifty miles.

And much farther, the pilot insisted, if the Healer would allow him to build and fly his own kite.

Nolan avoided making an answer, but on the way to the peak he observed Brenner spending a lot of time with the Cathay colonists, who, whenever their path took them past a lightwood tree, added to their packs branches and lengths and thicknesses that did not appear suitable for use on a conventional kite.

The slope before them grew steeper until, early on the sixth day since Brenner's flight and the seventy-fourth day from the landing, they climbed above the tree line. They were able to look the way they had come, across the endless green carpet that was broken only by the widely scattered blue holes and patches of discoloration that were the lakes and swamps. To westward they could look down on a glittering sea that stretched unbroken to the horizon, but all else was hidden by the peak and the long grassy ridge above them. The sky was free of the smallest blemish of cloud, a cool breeze was trying hard to reduce the fiery enthusiasm of the sun, and everything seemed so clear and sharp and freshly minted that Nolan found himself wishing that he could sing.

When the peak was only a few minutes away, Nolan insisted that Brenner should be the first to the top, and he smiled inwardly when the pilot asked Ulechitzl to accompany him. He watched them begin an undignified scramble up the slope, frequently going onto all fours when they gripped handfuls of grass to help them climb faster, to stand at last on the summit outlined against the deep blue sky. But they neither pointed nor turned to wave nor, it seemed, did they talk to each other, and when they were joined by Nolan and the others, the reason was plain.

On its north-facing slope the peak and connecting ridge formed a great headland overlooking a wide inlet or river estuary that ran eastward and directly across their path. Both shores of the inlet were edged with rocks or narrow strips of sandy beach and, further inland, by wide, flat stretches of yellow-brown which he thought might be salt marshes. The inlet widened, narrowed, and widened again before curving southward to disappear behind some distant hills, and the whole land area to the east was mottled with the distinctive green and swamp-growing trees.

As yet not a single one of them had spoken. Nolan wished that they would complain or curse or in some fashion give spoken vent to their anger and disappointment as he himself wanted to do. But instead they were silent and thoughtful and kept their hurt buried deep like a cancer, and that could be dangerous indeed.

"We will go no farther this day," he said calmly. "Pilot Brenner, when it is convenient, there is much to discuss and decide upon."

It was not the pilot's fault that he did not arrive until an hour later, the delay being caused by the large number of colonists wanting his ear rather than the Healer's. And when he did meet Nolan outside their tent, Ulechitzl and Golden Rain insisted on joining them, saying that the results of their deliberations should be made known to the others without delay.

Not wanting to start an argument before anything had been decided, Nolan agreed. It was a time for listening and saying nothing.

"Healer," said Brenner, when it was plain that Nolan was not going to speak first, "from this peak we can see about eight days' march to the east along the south bank of the inlet, although dragging ourselves through the intervening swamps and marshlands could greatly extend that time. What is worse, we would be moving blindly in a direction opposite to where we wanted to go, and without any certainty as to how far we would have to travel before we could turn northwest again toward the colony. The feeling of our people is very strong on this point. A majority, including three of us here, do not want to move until they know where exactly they are going. There is a smaller number, not yet a majority and not including we three, who feel that they should not move at all. They say that they now know enough, thanks to you, to be able to live off the land, and that they should settle here and forget your hopeless plan of reaching the colony."

"With respect, Healer," he went on, "we should not make any decisions until we have gathered enough information to make them soundly. This can only be done by making a high-altitude survey of the surrounding territory, and for that I need to build a glider."

Nolan regarded him for a long moment, then said quietly, "Can I stop your building a glider?"

Brenner looked uncomfortable and did not answer the question. Instead, he said, "Don't be concerned for me, Healer, there is little risk involved. This would not be a kite flying at treetop height above a lake. It would be carefully built, trimmed, and tested, and I will not trust myself to it unless I am completely satisfied that it is safe to do so. And the conditions on the peak and along the ridge are perfect for slope-soaring. Healer, there may never be a better chance to see where we're going."

Nolan bowed to the inevitable, but with reluctance. He said, "Your injured arm, will it inconvenience you?"

Brenner smiled and shook his head.

"Very well, Pilot," said Nolan. "Watching a glider being built will give your majority, and minority, something else to think about. Will we lose our tent again?"

Before Brenner could reply, Ulechitzl said, "Healer, if the pilot reports the circuitous route eastwards to be too long or impassable, and the minority who wish to settle here becomes a majority, what then?"

"Then the majority can do as it wishes," said Nolan in a quiet but very firm voice. "This is neither a democracy nor a military dictatorship. Naturally, I would advise them against making such a stupid decision, because the settlement they would establish here would have no future beyond the lifetimes of its members, who would die childless."

Nolan paused for a moment to stare closely into the faces of Ulechitzl and Golden Rain, then went on, "Unless one of you wished to emulate a thumper queen, for only such an arrangement would ensure the absence of sexual jealousy and the violent destabilization that would follow. It would not be an easy existence for the queen concerned, and I would advise against it, too, for medical and psychological reasons.

"But to return to the original question—" he said before they could respond. "If they wish it, your majority may stay here while we four who have, I believe, very strong reasons for wanting to do so, will proceed to the colony accompanied by anyone else of like mind."

"But . . . but would you leave all those people," said Ulechitzl in an incredulous voice, "without the services of their Healer?"

It was a question that Nolan had asked himself many times without being able to find the answer, so he did not try to answer it now. Instead, he said, "There is an additional option to traveling east or settling here. We can save time, distance, and effort by going north across the inlet. Your majority and minority should be given that possibility to consider as well."

"But, Healer," said Golden Rain, speaking for the first time, "we are not boatmakers."

"No, my lady," said Nolan. "But two weeks ago I would not have said that we were aircraft builders, either. I think you will find that the children in us who made the bows and arrows will also remember how to build rafts."

She smiled but did not speak. Brenner half rose onto one knee, plainly anxious to make full use of the remaining light while Ulechitzl was wearing the dissatisfied expression of one who is about to start an argument. It was time, Nolan decided, to end this meeting.

"If you will excuse me," he said, tapping the book that was lying on the ground beside him, and preparing to use boredom as his weapon to drive them away, "I have found a completely new specimen to add to my catalog. It is a small fruit resembling a pale-blue hairy apple that may grow, in these equatorial latitudes, only in the high mountain grasslands. The thumpers eat it without hesitation, and now it is my turn.

"But is it not strange," he went on, in the voice of an enthusiast warming to his subject, "that none of the vegetation here uses protective coloration, or tries to camouflage itself in any way, especially from above? I am led to the conclusion that apart from a few species of insect, there are no flying creatures on this planet."

They were all on their feet and about to leave by then. As Ulechitzl was turning away, she looked at Brenner and said, "You are wrong, Healer. There is one."

Nolan smiled but did not reply, and Brenner's face grew red with embarrassment and pleasure at what seemed to be the first compliment he had received from her.

Four days later Nolan felt a dreadful certainty that their only flying creature was about to render himself prematurely extinct.

The contraption strapped to the pilot's shoulders looked too large, too complicated, and much too fragile in its construction ever to leave the ground even though, in the interests of saving weight, Brenner's arms and legs were bare. As he faced into the fresh northerly breeze that was blowing up the slope toward him, the pilot's expression was serious but unafraid. The four kite-makers were supporting the wing struts and holding the fluttering glider steady into the wind. Brenner shrugged his shoulders in the harness and felt for the position of the footrests behind his hips and checked his grip on the bar that controlled the wing camber, his only means of directional control. Nolan was sure that at any moment the impossibly fragile structure would collapse, break up, and blow away.

Suddenly the wings were no longer being supported and Brenner was walking forward. Then he broke into a slow, careful run down the slope, and within twenty paces his feet were no longer swishing through the grass and he was floating away from the ground. Still descending and remaining within fifty feet of the slope, even when clumps of trees replaced the grass, the glider grew smaller and smaller below them until it moved out and above the waters of the inlet. There it made several gentle turns to port and starboard before curving back toward them.

Ulechitzl moved across the slope to join Nolan. With her eyes still on the glider, she said, "The intention was to remain fairly close to the ground, in case of a wing failure similar to that on the kite, until the overall stability and flight characteristics were established. After that will come the slope-soaring to achieve maximum altitude. So far the flight is as he intended it."

Nolan was well aware of Brenner's intentions, having argued about them with the pilot far into the previous night. But the calmness of the voice combined with the anxiety in Ulechitzl's expression suggested that this was a time to pretend ignorance, and confidence.

"I have no doubt about it, my lady," he said.

The glider made a wide, sweeping turn that again brought it close to the lower slopes, and they were able to look down on the wing decoration lit by the morning sun before it sailed eastward along the ridge, steadily gaining height in the updraft. When it returned to fly past them again, it was level with the top of the peak, and by the third pass they were beginning to lose sight of it in the glare of the sun. When next it passed above them it turned outward in the direction of the opposite shore of the inlet.

For a moment Nolan wondered angrily if Brenner was going to attempt to overfly the opposite shore. But no, the pilot was heading outward and losing height rapidly while executing a wide, sweeping turn. A few moments his glider was floating gracefully into a stall close to the ground, and Brenner was walking under it instead of flying.

Ulechitzl and Nolan were the first to reach him. While they were helping him out of the harness, his teeth were chattering so badly that he could scarcely speak.

"I didn't believe such a thing was possible on this world," he said plaintively, "but I'm *cold*."

Chapter 34

THE altitude of what had already become known as Brenner's Peak, together with the additional height he had been able to achieve with the glider, had given the pilot a view in all directions of well over one hundred miles. Beyond the low hills to the east the inlet narrowed to become a slow-flowing river that twisted and turned and frequently doubled back on itself, linking together many small lakes and swamps as it meandered across a great, flat expanse of jungle that stretched unbroken to the horizon. Northward, the picture was entirely different.

On the other side of the estuary the high ground concealed a stretch of coastline that was bordered by low hills and a land surface covered as much by grass as by jungle. And even better was the news that Brenner had been able to see, at a distance of ten days' march or less, the distant coastline curving toward the northwest in the direction they wanted to go.

The majority were immediately in favor of building rafts and the minority, if there was one, spoke not a word.

At the foot of the headland there was a small cove with a narrow strip of sandy beach, and during the descent Nolan tried very hard to recall everything he knew about raft-building, only to discover that he knew nothing at all. When he tried to hint at the totality of his ignorance to Golden Rain she laughed, saying that a Healer was not expected to have knowledge of that subject, but that their training courses had taught them how to use local materials to build homes and outbuildings for themselves, and that a raft was little more than one side of a house.

Her words brought great relief to Nolan, even though he knew the problem was not quite as simple as that.

The prototype broke up as the result of wave action as soon as it left the sheltered waters of the cove. In the days that followed, modifications were made and gradually the failures became less spectacular until they ceased to occur entirely and construction began on three more rafts.

Neither the time nor the hard work seemed important because they had dry ground, a cooling wind, ready access to structural materials, plenty of food, and a more than adequate supply of enthusiasm.

Nolan's presence was not required, except to remove slivers occasionally from a woodworker's hand or deal with like minor injuries, and so he took to exploring the bed of the cove and the inlet beyond as far as his safety line, which was just over three hundred paces in length, would allow. He used a raft that he had made himself, a crude structure comprising three lightwood logs lashed together with a cross-member and outriggers to give lateral stability, and the helmet rescued from Brenner's spacesuit. He was able to catch three different varieties of fish, two of which proved edible and were added to his catalog.

As a rest from lying facedown and staring into the dark-green tangle of the seabed, he sometimes turned onto his back to watch Brenner enjoying himself. The glider flights had become a matter of daily routine, with the pilot launching and landing himself unassisted from the lower slopes and cruising back and forth above the raft builders, ostensibly for the purpose of spotting lightwood trees or wild thumper herds, or climbing on the updrafts until he reached a height two or three times that achieved on his first flight, an altitude that enabled him to overfly the opposite shore and return with height to spare.

The shortest distance to the other side was six miles due north, Brenner reported, but there were rocks close to the surface all along that stretch of shoreline. From the air he could not be more precise about their depth, and there was no tidal activity to reveal them or cover them safely, so there was a serious danger of the rocks damaging the rafts and drowning the thumpers. He suggested making a fifteen-degree diversion to the northwest, which would take them past the headland opposite and enable them to land in a sandy cove less than two miles further up the coast.

Nolan examined the hand-drawn map that Brenner had produced and reminded him, perhaps unnecessarily, that he was the navigator.

No longer did Brenner object to having his forehead decorated before every flight. On Earth, Nolan thought, he would have worn a set of golden wings on his tunic with the same degree of pride.

By the time they set out, their original raft configuration had been changed from an awkward and unwieldy square to a long, cross-braced rectangle. There was a minimum number of ten colonists to every raft, five on each side charged with propelling them through the shallows with long shaven branches or, in deeper water, with oars. A larger oar fastened loosely to the stern acted as a rudder, and a short mast and crosstree carrying a reefed section of tenting was mounted forward to take advantage of a favorable wind. In addition, three of the rafts carried stores, including Brenner's partly dismantled glider, and the fourth bore the thumpers.

Loading the thumpers was the most difficult job of the day because of their rabid fear of the water. Every one of them, including the well-grown cubs, had to be carried by two men through the shallows and onto their raft. There they huddled in a line along the center of the deck, clinging to the logs and each other and not making a move in any direction that would bring them closer to the edge. Nolan felt very sorry for them, and in the absence of any local sedative medication he fed them with an extra ration of mice.

For the crossing he had ordered that the rafts be loosely roped together in case one should start breaking up, when it could be pulled in and its crew and supplies transferred to adjacent rafts.

Nolan and Golden Rain were on the first raft to be poled out of the shelter of the cove, followed by Brenner and Ulechitzl, and the one with only its crew and the thumpers on board, the most lightly laden of the four, brought up the rear as the designated rescue craft.

When they began to pole and then row themselves out of the cove, it was midmorning on the 102d day since the landing, and the time had been chosen so that the temperature difference between sea and land surfaces would be minimal as would, they hoped, be the winds. The sky above and around them was cloudless, the waves were low and gentle, and the sea was like deep-blue rippled glass, broken only by the measured dipping and raising of the oars. All the signs pointed to a smooth and uneventful crossing.

Gradually the strip of beach grew small behind them and, the unaided human eye being an imprecise instrument of measurement at best, the other shore seemed no larger. Nolan looked at the untidy flotilla strung out astern, saw nothing amiss, and put on the spacesuit helmet.

He did not know how long he spent staring at the sea bottom as it crept past below him. It was as if he were the observer in an airship that was drifting over a landscape of sea-green forests in which nothing moved except the shoals of fish that flew through the thick, green air like flocks of silent, wingless birds. Then he felt the hand of the oarsman kneeling nearest to him gripping his shoulder and shaking it insistently, and reluctantly Nolan lifted his head out of the water.

Brenner was shouting something at him, the words muffled by the helmet, and pointing astern.

The beach had shrunk to a thin yellow line drawn between the green lower slopes and a sea whose mirror surface was being pulled into wrinkles by a wind that had yet to reach the rafts, and the reason for the agitation of both the sea and Brenner was plain. The headland and peak were outlined by a great pile of cloud that was dazzling white on top but which had a base of leaden gray. As he watched, a line of shadow began to slide down and across the upper slopes, followed by the paler gray curtain of a rain squall.

"Raise your sail, Healer," Brenner was shouting. "Make the wind work for you."

Nolan waved an acknowledgment, and with the help of the two forward oarsmen he lifted the crosstree and sail into position. By then the breeze had freshened, the sail was taut and quivering, and the low mast was bending in an alarming fashion. He used two of their poles as makeshift braces, propping them solidly to the bows at deck level and to the middle of the crosstree, and the mast ceased its shaking.

Nolan would not be unduly worried over the loss of his mast, which would be a temporary inconvenience. But if the sail were to blow away, someone would suffer the continuing inconvenience of being without a tent.

They were so close to the wooded headland on the other shore that he could see individual branches on the trees and, clearer and even closer, the rocks that projected like a line of uneven, rotting teeth beyond the point.

Nolan called for the attention of his rowers and pointed at the rocks, then swung his arm in an arc to the northwest. A glance astern showed Brenner and the other crews doing the same. The breeze was freshening and it seemed that only a few moments went by before they were slipping past the headland and drawing level with the cove on the other side that was their destination.

Feeling excited and very pleased with himself, Nolan gave orders for the oarsmen on the port side to row forward and those on the starboard in reverse. While the raft was swinging ponderously onto its new heading, he began taking down the sail so as to reduce wind resistance. The breeze that had been moving them forward was now broadside on, and he did not want to drift too far past the beach and be faced with a long, hard row against the wind to reach it.

His raft had completed its turn and the oarsmen were rowing forward together in the new direction when the rain squall reached them, and with it a sudden increase in the wind strength. Within moments the raft was pitching and rolling alarmingly, and small waves were splashing over the feet of the starboard-side rowers. The other rafts, their sails still in place, were just beginning to change course and were being blown past him. Brenner was pointing toward the north and shouting something, but his words were muffled by the sound of the heavy rain lashing against the deck.

"Turn north," Golden Rain shouted. "He says to raise your sail again, that it's safer to run before the wind."

For a moment he wondered whether her hearing was more acute than his or she had the ability to read lips. "Very well, my lady, I'll pass it on. But I had not realized that our pilot and navigator was an experienced sailor as well."

She seemed to be thoroughly enjoying the whole situation,

because suddenly she laughed and said, "No, Healer. He is not a sailor, but the Skandians are on his raft and some of them are sure to be—"

Loudly enough to be heard above the wind and rain, there came the sound of splintering wood, and the deck jerked sideways under their feet. Golden Rain and Nolan were knocked onto their hands and knees. On the starboard side the oarsmen fell inboard, and those on the port side tumbled into the water. Three of them had been able to hold onto the side and were scrambling back on board, but the other two were struggling in the roughening sea and drifting away.

Cursing himself because he knew without looking what had happened, Nolan grasped one of the two poles remaining after he had braced the mast, and extended it quickly toward the man who was farthest away, so quickly that he came within inches of cracking the other's skull. Without needing to be told, Golden Rain held out the remaining pole to the second man. They were both pulled back on board, coughing and spluttering but not complaining of any hurts. Within a few moments the rowers were back in their positions, turning the raft back onto its original heading. Only when the sail had been raised again did Nolan go to the stern to view the damage.

When they had been wallowing helplessly broadside to the wind and the pilot's raft had gone sailing past, in the excitement of the moment Nolan had forgotten to untie the line connecting his raft to Brenner's. The rope had not been one of the uncertain products of their attempts at weaving the stench-tree vines: it had been tried and tested and brought with them from Earth, and it had not broken. Neither was there any sign of damage to its attachment point on the bow of the pilot's raft, but the cross-member bracing the stern of Nolan's raft and the rudder oar fastened to it had been torn away.

The shock had caused the logs in that area to spread apart by a few inches, but the cross-members amidships seemed to be holding them firm. Occasionally a larger-than-usual wave would break over the stern and wet the aft oarsmen's feet, but the rain was soaking everyone anyway. The sail forward was pulling well and steadying them, keeping the wind squarely astern so that their pitching and rolling was held to a minimum, and any tendency to yaw could be controlled by the rowers.

The rain squall passed ahead of them and the sea changed from gray to deep blue again as the sun was uncovered by the hurrying clouds, but the wind strength was increasing. The beach where they had intended to land was hidden by a low, projecting headland behind them, and the entire coastline abreast and ahead seemed to be composed of a long, uneven cliff with partly submerged rockfalls at its base. He could hear Brenner shouting instructions to the two rafts close behind him, but the wind blew his words away. That did not matter, because he could see men on all three rafts interrupt their rowing to shorten sail and untie the connecting lines. Plainly Brenner did not want to endanger the masts in the freshening wind or risk another accident like that which had befallen Nolan's raft.

Nolan knew that he, too, should shorten sail, but another inspection of the damaged stern made him have second thoughts. The logs there had splayed out until the gaps between them were six inches in places and wave action was making them move independently of each other. He did not know how long it would take for the constant movement to loosen them from the midship bindings, or how long before his crew would be in the water clinging to a collection of single logs instead of kneeling on a raft.

In this situation, he decided, safety lay in speed.

Gradually they began to close on the three rafts ahead, which were staying together and trying to maintain their line-ahead formation. The wind had become more erratic now, and the poles bracing their masthead were bending and vibrating like one of Golden Rain's bows with every strong gust. As he began to draw level with them, Nolan had his rowers steer close enough for him to be able to talk to Brenner.

He pointed to his full sail and pole-braced mast and shouted, "Pilot Brenner, I have damage to the stern and the logs there are beginning to open out. There is no immediate danger, but I want to stay ahead of you so that if we do start to break up, you can rescue us without having to row upwind. If I lower my sail you'll know we're in trouble."

"I understand, Healer," Brenner replied, and raised his arm in a gesture that was something between a wave and a salute.

The uneven cliffs gave way to a lower wooded coastline, but there were still too many rocks projecting from the shallows and the wind was too strong for them to risk landing. Three times they came on narrow, sheltered inlets with sandy or pebbled beaches, but by the time they saw them the raft was abreast of the opening and it was too late to change course, and the other rafts were half a mile astern and too distant to be told of the discoveries.

It was a situation he should have foreseen, Nolan told himself, and decided to talk to Brenner about long-distance visual signaling.

Their stern continued to hold together, but on both sides of the raft the outboard logs were beginning to twist under the feet and knees of the oarsmen, making it more difficult to row. They did not complain, however, and a few of them had breath enough to spare from their exertions to sing as they rowed.

About five miles along the coast he could see another headland jutting westward by about twenty degrees across their present course. So tall was it that Brenner had been unable to see what lay immediately behind it. Nolan raised his arm to point to the northwest and the oarsmen brought the raft round onto the new heading, which would clear the headland by a comfortable margin. No longer with the breeze squarely behind it, the sail began to flap and spill wind, but it was still pulling strongly.

He turned to go aft, intending to check once again on the condition of the stern, and saw a picture that made him use words that were quite unseemly for mixed company.

"I missed that, Healer," said Golden Rain diplomatically. "What did you say?"

Nolan pointed wordlessly astern. The three rafts were no longer in line-ahead formation, no longer under reefed sails, and no longer half a mile away. They were sailing in close line abreast, their mastheads braced with poles as was Nolan's, and they had closed to just beyond hailing distance. He could clearly see Ulechitzl and Brenner standing together in the bows, steadying themselves with their hands on the bracing poles, and smiling.

Ulechitzl waved and Golden Rain waved back.

Nolan opened his mouth to say more angry words, for if one of the rafts was to lose its mast and fall behind, the rescue would be difficult and dangerous for all concerned. Brenner should have considered that possibility instead of trying to impress Ulechitzl. But Nolan had to remind himself that it was wrong, and very prejudicious to future good relations, to be openly critical of a fellow officer.

"Now," he said irritably, "we're in a bloody boat race!"

He had not meant the remark to be taken seriously, but Golden Rain laughed, and all of the men nodded enthusiastically and smiled in Nolan's direction, and the tempo of the singing and rowing increased.

The wind held steady from the south and their stern also held itself together, albeit with less steadiness, and they were still holding their lead over the other rafts as the headland began to loom like some great, crouching, and petrified beast over the starboard bow. But it was large, not close, and the rocks spreading out from its base and tearing the sea to milky shreds were at a safe distance.

As they began to round the headland they could see another that was about two miles further north. This one was smaller than the one they were passing, grass-covered at its top and with thickly forested lower slopes. Nolan was wondering if they could find a place to land nearby or if they would have to sail on, when suddenly a wide, sheltered bay opened up before them, stretching between the two headlands like a great green gold-edged crescent.

The entire length of the beach was clear of rocks. They could land safely anywhere.

His men cheered and waved their oars, as did the others a few moments later when they saw what the first raft was seeing. Nolan pointed to the north end of the beach where it ran to the base of the other headland, because he knew that was the place Brenner would find most suitable for glider operations.

They reached the beach less than two raft lengths before the others, and the shock of the bows striking the sand made the stern logs open out like a great, uncovered fan. There was much laughter and self-congratulation among the crews, in which Nolan did not join. He wanted to unload the stores and thumpers and glider parts and set up camp without delay, because he had serious matters to discuss with them. More than anything else he wanted to talk to them about the rafts, and ask for any suggestions they might have for rendering them stronger, more seaworthy, and stable in rough seas and, if it was possible, for making them capable of holding a course in a not entirely-favorable wind. He did not think there would be any opposition to what he wanted to do. Where the advantages of sailing were concerned, they had only to look at the western sky to convince themselves.

The sun was still high above the horizon and needing at least three hours before it would set. In one long afternoon they had sailed and rowed a distance that would have taken at least five days of travel by land.

Chapter 35

"THIS morning," the pilot reported in a quiet, impersonal voice that tried vainly to conceal his pride and excitement, "I reached an altitude in excess of four thousand feet, the highest achieved by the glider so far. Visibility was good, except to the northwest where there is a very deep low-pressure system moving this way. That entire stretch of horizon is bubbling with thunderheads. Depending on whether it tracks north or south of us, there are likely to be very strong winds that will either blow us out to sea or back onto the shore which, for the next thirty miles north of here, is too rocky for a safe landing."

The pilot was becoming as good at weather prediction as he was at mapmaking. And it was plain from his expression that Brenner was eager to say more.

"To the north the coastline becomes progressively uneven," Brenner resumed, "with many deep inlets alternating with rocky headlands that project far to westward, and beaches such as this one are rare. However, as we already know, there is an overall curvature toward the northwest. In that direction, right at the limit of my visibility, there is land. Eventually we will have to travel to that shore, and I would suggest that we go to it directly rather than hugging a very inhospitable coast.

"The rafts will have to be made more seaworthy," he went on, "but the saving of time otherwise wasted in circumnavigating the coast will be great. Until the weather improves we have nothing better to do but work on the rafts; and the journey should take no more than three days."

I could not have argued the case better myself, thought Nolan, and said nothing while they gradually convinced themselves that that was what they had really wanted to do all along.

And so it was that on the morning of A.L. 142, the 142d day after landing, they again put to sea, this time in three larger craft which, apart from a few of the original deck logs, had nothing in common with the four earlier rafts. These three were longer, more strongly braced and with pointed bows to ease passage through the water, and with sterns raised to keep any high following waves from running the length of the deck. The thwarts were also raised by the thickness of two logs, and notched between them so as to accommodate the longer oars that were being used galley fashion, by rowers who were seated in comparative comfort and pulling rather than kneeling and having to lift and rotate their upper bodies with every stroke. There was even a rudimentary keel and rudder on each raft, but the most obvious difference was the addition of a strongly braced mast amidships carrying a fore-and-aft rigged sail to augment the square sail in the bows.

They were the three most unlovely craft that Nolan had ever seen, looking as if they had been put together by a child who could not make up his mind whether he wanted a Viking longboat or an old-time Cathay fishing craft—which, considering the people responsible for the design, was understandable. But they had been tried and well tested during the three weeks of unsettled weather that had followed their arrival in the bay, and they continued to prove themselves in all respects seaworthy.

The wind was favorable but inconstant. When it dropped, which was frequently, they maintained progress under slack sails with the oars, so that by the end of the first day they wanted only to eat their cold food and sleep. With the coast they had left visible only as an uneven blue line astern, and a layer of high cloud concealing the stars, the rafts were roped loosely together in case they should separate in a darkness so absolute that there was no way to distinguish sea from sky. Brenner and Nolan, who had not been rowing, divided the night watch.

Next morning the wind freshened and veered southerly, blowing diagonally across their sterns and making the rafts heel over to starboard. In a drill already well practiced after the previous landfall, the crews moved to line the port side so that their weight would balance and stabilize the rafts and enable the new sails to be used to maximum effect. The water was foaming past them with a speed that could never have been achieved with oars. By sunset the wind had died and their destination was no more than three hours of rowing away.

"Close up and rope together," Nolan called to the other rafts. "We will go no further tonight. You can see that the shore has one small beach and the rest is cliffs. I don't want to risk us drifting onto rocks in the darkness. We will land after first light tomorrow."

As soon as Brenner's raft came alongside, the pilot jumped

aboard and came close to Nolan, so close that his words would not be heard by anyone else.

"Healer," he said, "I am deeply embarrassed. I have made a major navigational error. This is not the promised northwest coast but another headland, and beyond it the horizon is empty."

"I had noticed that myself," Nolan replied softly. "But I also notice that you do not appear to be unduly worried by your mistake. Why?"

"I expect to verify everything I tell you after tomorrow's observation flight," Brenner replied. "But, Healer, considering the distance and direction we have traveled these past two days, and the configuration of the land ahead, I am quite certain that this headland is but the point of a very large peninsula and that it is too prominent a feature to go unnoticed on even the smallest maps and planetary photographs. How clearly can you remember those early pictures of the New World?"

Even before his acceptance for Project Aisling Gheal, Nolan had studied those photographs before going to bed, like an adolescent with his first pictures of undraped females, and dreamed of them afterward. They had been composites, taken at various times and overlaid so that the entire land surface appeared to be cloudless. He remembered the dragon shape, the projecting forearm where the colony would be sited, and the large and small inland seas and lakes that decorated its side and stomach with patches and stipplings of dark blue. The answer was yes, very clearly, but the pilot could not wait for his reply.

"When we were on our landing approach," Brenner went on, "I had a glimpse through the clouds of an inland sea below us. There were waves which, to be visible at that altitude, could not have been generated on a lake. We were past it and over forests so quickly that I assumed it to be the smaller inland sea to the east. But that sea does not contain a natural feature like this peninsula. The larger sea, some two hundred miles westward of where I thought we were, has just such a feature projecting from midway on its east coast. Healer, do you realize what this means?"

Again, Nolan was not given the chance to reply.

"It means that when we set out, we were some three hundred miles closer to the colony than we had thought," Brenner went on, in a voice that was no longer quiet, "and add to that the distance we have come since then. We can, of course, round this headland and follow the coast eastward, north, and then west until we reach the nearest point to the colony to disembark. Alternatively, we can continue northwest by sea until we reach that same point, very much sooner. By sea, Healer, it is just over five hundred miles. And when we touch land we will be halfway home!''

A great quiet fell when the pilot finished speaking, and the three crews had moved as close to the two officers as the raft structures would allow. Nolan had been watching Brenner's face closely, but his mind was racing too far ahead of his tongue for any words to come.

''Healer,'' said Brenner, in a voice almost of pleading, ''based on their showing over the past days at sea, I'm sure everyone will favor taking the direct route.''

''May I remind you again, Pilot Brenner, that this is not a democracy,'' he said gravely. ''But in this instance, I completely agree with the majority.''

The initial flood of enthusiasm waned slightly, but only because it had to be converted into hard work. The rafts were further strengthened and modified. Low weather shelters that would not catch the wind were rigged, and provision was made for collecting rainwater for drinking. Nolan advised carrying as much fruit and edible roots as possible, because they would be less prone to spoiling, and augmenting their diet with freshly caught fish. There was a continuing aversion to eating any member of their first thumper herd.

It was while they were laying in the food supply for the voyage that he was able to make an interesting addition to his notes. The ''wild'' thumpers that had been brought in alive and were able successfully to run the gauntlet of the domesticated thumpers' tails and mate with the queen thereafter acquired the herd scent and were accepted as members. It was a natural guard against inbreeding, Nolan thought admiringly, but what pleased him more was the knowledge that their herd could be increased in numbers without having to wait until the cubs were mature.

As the time for leaving drew nearer, there was a growing insistence among the crews that their craft had become something more than mere rafts, that they should be given proper ships' names, and that Nolan should name them.

He waited until the morning of A.L. 183, the date of their departure, to speak. Quietly and very simply he told them that they were about to undertake a voyage that was certain to find a permanent place in the history of the colony and that even though its like had been accomplished many times on Earth, what they were about to do on this world would go straight into legend. For that reason the names that their ships would bear should also be legendary.

They would be called *Sea Dragon, Sinead,* and *White Heron,* the names of the ships of Brendan the Navigator.

He had chosen his own ship to be named *Sea Dragon*, Nolan told them with the faintest of smiles, not because it had a great, smoke-belching hero in its belly, but because it had a sandpit in its bow for the cooking fire.

A few hours after they sailed, the wind died, forcing them to depend on the oars alone, and for the next three days they crawled like great, ten-legged insects across a sheet of dark blue glass. It was as if the land was reluctant to let them go, for every morning it was there and seeming to be only a little more distant than on the morning before. But on the fourth day the wind rose and strengthened from the south almost to gale force, and they were all kept too busy trimming and sailing their craft to see the coast disappear.

As the days passed, they developed work habits that were much too varied to be described as routine. When the wind was with them they sailed, when it was completely unfavorable they took down the sails and rowed, as they did when there was no wind at all. In the middle hours of the day they rested and tried to shelter themselves from the heat, or escape it by going over the side to submerge themselves in water that was comparatively cool, and to fish. The fish seemed to be attracted by the three strange wooden monsters floating on the surface. Some of them were large enough to make a meal for six people, and many paid for their curiosity on the point of a wooden spear.

At night they told stories or sang or, at Nolan's suggestion, continued teaching their languages to each other. When it was calm at night they roped the ships together and left one man on watch. So as not to waste time, if the night winds were moderate and favorable they ran before them on shortened foresails, with a man at each rudder holding course and calling out to the others to avoid becoming separated in the darkness. But when rain or a heavy overcast hid the sun and the marker stars, they drifted, doing nothing but fish and complain to their Healer because he remained so irritatingly optimistic. Once they were forced to drift in enforced idleness for three days, and they told each other in Nolan's hearing that if he told them one more time that all this had happened before, there would be a bloody mutiny.

It was just before dusk on A.L. 207, more than three weeks since they had sighted land, and a day that had been gray and sunless and without direction, that the storm struck. With the wind came a stinging curtain of rain so thick that the rafts lost sight of each other even before the daylight faded, and waves that within a few moments were high enough to break over the raised sterns. They had no choice but to run before the wind, because if once they drifted broadside to those waves they would be overturned instantly and be lost. All they could do was cling to the solidity of their craft and hope that they would remain solid throughout the night.

By morning the storm had abated to a stiff breeze, although a heavy overcast remained, and it seemed that they had the ocean all to themselves.

Nolan began to take stock.

None of the crew had been washed over the side, nor had any of their gravely diminished food store been lost. The rainwater they had been trying to collect in the tops of their weather shelters was so contaminated by the salty, wind-driven spray as to be close to undrinkable, and the fresh water they had brought with them in thumper-skin gourds, possibly because of impurities in the containers, had long since gone bad. Fortunately, the storm damage to the structures could be repaired while they were waiting for the sun to show itself and enable them to set a course. Only a few men were needed for the repairs. The others he advised to catch up on their lost sleep.

"My lady," he said to Golden Rain, "would you mind going up to the stern and standing lookout?"

She had the keenest vision of anyone on board, and he did not have to tell her what she was looking for. But many hours passed before she found it.

"Healer!" she called suddenly, pointing ahead and about thirty degrees to starboard. There was uncertainty in her voice as she went on, "I see something. I think it might be a bird."

Nolan moved quickly aft to stand beside her and sight along her pointing arm and finger.

At first he could see nothing, but soon his straining eyes resolved a tiny speck that was almost touching the waves. It did look like a bird, he thought, an oddly shaped bird that was tiny with distance, hanging strangely still, and seemingly only a fraction of an inch above the horizon. If there were birds on this world, this was the first he had seen. Nolan laughed aloud in sheer relief and set course toward it.

Imperceptibly the strange bird climbed higher above the horizon and grew larger, but long before *Sinead* appeared below it, he knew what Brenner had done. In an attempt to make his ship visible over a greater distance, the pilot had assembled his glider and trimmed it to fly unmanned as a kite at the limit of the available cordage. His idea had worked very well, because, as his *Sea Dragon* was closing with *Sinead*, Nolan could see *White Heron* coming over the horizon on a converging course.

Two of the adult male thumpers had been lost over the side, there was minor structural damage that was already being repaired, and there were no crew casualties except for a few bruises that were not, the sufferers insisted, serious enough to warrant the Healer transferring from his own ship. The flotilla was together again, and even though they had no precise idea of their position or the distance they had yet to travel, everyone had begun to feel invincible.

Next morning the sun rose into a cloudless sky above an ocean unwrinkled by the slightest hint of a breeze, and it was the same on the days that followed. They rowed only in the cool of the early morning and late evening, until they became too weakened by hunger and thirst even to make the attempt. Only two of the male thumpers, their queen, and the cubs remained, and they would soon have to be killed and eaten before the animals themselves died of starvation. The daily catch of fish was reducing, either because the coordination of eye and muscle in the fishermen was deteriorating or their prey was learning caution. Even the rainwater contaminated by the salt spray was running short. They lay on the decks under opened weather shelters or huddled in the shadows of the sails, too tired to talk or even to listen to Nolan trying to tell them that Brendan's crews had survived much worse.

Usually they liked to listen to him telling the story of Brendan's epic voyage and its aftermath, for the ending of that tale was known to everyone, but they were no longer sure how their own story would end.

"Healer," said Brenner, during one of the early morning meetings preceding the untying of the rafts, "we've been becalmed for fifteen days and I don't know where we are. That storm could have blown us back the way we came, or to any part of this stupid ocean. If only we had a magnetic compass—"

"And if only," Nolan broke in gently, "this stupid world had a magnetic pole."

". . . or there was a nice, stiff breeze," the pilot went on, seeming not to have heard him. "Just for an hour, maybe two, that's all I ask. Then I could . . ."

Brenner fell silent, and Nolan was too tired to ask what he could do. Far too many people were leaving sentences unfinished these days. It was probably the heat.

The breeze that Brenner had wished for sprang up in the early afternoon of the following day, and with it came broken cloud and a scattering of heavy rain showers. Immediately they raised sails and set courses to the northwest.

All except *Sinead*.

Brenner's vessel was dead in the water, sails furled, and was already beginning to fall behind its sister ships. But there was great activity apparent on deck, and with the distance increasing by the moment it took some time before Nolan realized what he was seeing. The crew who were not assembling the glider were rowing into the wind.

Sinead was hidden by a sudden rain squall. Swearing angrily to himself, Nolan ordered *White Heron* and his own ship to shorten sail in case the laggard fell too far behind. As yet there was no need for the glider to be flown, because all three ships were clearly in sight of each other, so what was in the pilot's mind?

As soon as the rain blew past he saw what was in the pilot's mind. The glider was aloft, bobbing erratically on the end of about fifty yards of line. Several times it lost height in the uncertain wind to swoop seemingly to within inches of the waves before rising again, and Brenner was flying it.

The wind above the surface must have been stronger, because the glider gained stability with height until all of the line was paid out. Then suddenly the line was detached and the glider was flying free. By the time Nolan was able to take his eyes off it long enough to look astern, *Sinead* was under full sail and closing the distance between them.

He was sure that Brenner would have to come down before long, because here there were no slopes from which he could soar. But the pilot seemed to be finding updrafts, possibly air rising from a sea heated by the intense sunlight of the morning, or upcurrents associated with the squalls, and he was gaining rather than losing height.

Nolan began to worry then in case the pilot was blown away by one of those squalls and lost, but his mind was soon put to rest on that score. The skies cleared, the wind dropped, and slowly, patiently, and seemingly inch by inch, Brenner continued to climb and circle and shamelessly disport himself for the remainder of the afternoon.

The sun was within a few minutes of touching the sea and the ships had drawn together for the night when he came swooping down in a wide, graceful spiral. Nolan thought caustically that Brenner must have decided against attempting a night flight, at least on this occasion, but he would probably try it at some future time if he thought that it would impress Ulechitzl. He watched the pilot come in low, skimming the waves and holding off as he lost speed, to flare out alongside *Sinead*'s stern, meaning, no doubt, to drop the glider and himself lightly onto the water. But it did not happen that way.

Perhaps the miscalculation was due to hunger, or muscle cramp in the arms used on the control bar, or simple fatigue after that long flight, but he crashed into the raised stern and tumbled heavily onto the deck.

Nolan was beside him within a few minutes, still dripping from his short swim, to straighten the limbs and begin cutting open the seams of his trousers. He saw that one leg was badly bruised above and below the knee and the other had sustained a fractured tibia and patella. There was a livid bruise on his forehead just above the left eye, and the other injuries were superficial.

He worked in a disapproving silence to reduce and splint the fracture, all the time wanting to tell Brenner that he had brought this anguish on himself by making a dangerous and totally unnecessary flight from sea level just to escape the heat of the day and impress his lady, if she would ever be his lady. But Healers were not supposed to speak such unkind words to their patients, and later he was glad that he had not spoken them.

Instead, he said, "This break will take longer to mend than the first one. Lie still and try to rest."

But Brenner was pushing himself up onto his elbows, his teeth clenching against the pain and a grimace on his face that could only be a smile. He said, "Healer, I did it."

"You did indeed," said Nolan, looking disapprovingly at the splinted leg.

"Not *that*," said Brenner scornfully. He raised an arm and pointed to the single high, red cloud that was all that was left of the sunset. "I made enough height to see it. About forty miles due west. *Land!*"

When the ships were tied together that evening it was inevitable that everyone wanted to hear again the story of Brendan the Navigator.

Chapter 36

WHEN the moment came, it was not as Brendan had foreseen it, but a great, epoch-making anticlimax.

His men were too sick from drinking green water and weakened by hunger for him to risk sending one of them aloft. And the crews of the other two ships, which drifted like gray ghosts in the dissipating morning mist, were probably in even worse condition. There was no smallest breath of wind, and the sails made him think of the days of his novitiate, and of washcloths hanging to dry in the heat of the monastery kitchen when it was raining outside.

Now the moisture beading his forehead was not cool rain, but salt sweat produced by the sun which was burning off the last, insubstantial layers of surface mist, to reveal a thin, irregular line on the horizon which was lighter than the sea and darker than the sky.

Land.

The others had seen it, too. From *White Heron* there came the sound of cheering, although it more closely resembled the noises emanating from a House of Sorrows while battle casualties were being treated, and on *Sinead* someone too weak to cheer was battering the sides of an empty water cask with a marlinspike. Brendan forced his ridiculously weakened body to its feet, his feverish brain to ignore the phantasms it had been conjuring, and his parchment-dry mouth to speak.

"Pass the word to First Officer Malcolm that we have sighted land," he said to one of the desiccated near-corpses collapsed across the helm nearby, "and I would have words with him as soon as he finds it convenient."

The dour and at-times acid-tongued Caledonian would not speak to him at all if it was not convenient, and his reasons for not speaking would be heard all over the ship. As the only man in the crew with knowledge of the healing arts, there had been much for him to do these past few weeks, and there had been many times, while he had been comforting the sick and dying, when he would not have left his work for any reason or person. But now he was climbing onto the deck before Brendan had finished speaking.

"I suppose I must compliment you on the accuracy of your navigation," said Malcolm. "Either that or your special relationship with the maritime saints."

Brendan inclined his head in acknowledgment of the nearest thing to a compliment he was likely to receive from his first officer, and tried to hide his feelings as he stared at the man.

Malcolm was so emaciated that he looked worse than many of his worst patients. His long, fair hair and beard had been cropped short to discourage body vermin, and the skin was stretched so tightly over his mighty frame that it was little more than an outsized skeleton. Only on his young-old face did the unnatural shrinkage stop short, for nothing could erase the lines deep-etched there by the death of his entire family in a clan feud.

"Donal," said Brendan severely, using the other's given name to show that he spoke as a friend rather than as his captain, "I am aware that for the past three weeks we have been desperately short of food, but that is no reason for you to take less than your fair share."

"Malnutrition and its associated mental and physical debilitation," the other replied, "can often give rise to a condition resembling premature senility. Perhaps the captain has forgotten that I gave him physiological reasons for fractionally reducing my own ration because I was of larger than average girth to begin with. Had you a reason for wanting to see me, other than to talk about the size of my long-lost belly?"

Brendan took a deep breath and prayed for patience. He said, "You have responsibility for food stores and rationing. What I must know now is, does enough remain to increase the ration to normal over the next few days so as to enable the crew to work the ship?"

"No," said Malcolm without hesitation. "What I can do is give them a little more than the present allowance, and encouragement of a nonmaterial nature which will, for a limited time, make them feel better than they really are. Sighting land will have had that effect in any case. But as for working the ship normally, the answer is no. What are you expecting them to do?"

Brendan was silent for a moment, considering his problem. The flotilla was becalmed within sight of land and their crews were too weakened by hunger to take advantage of the situation. When the sun rose higher and warmed up the land ahead, the air above it would rise and a gentle onshore breeze would spring up, but the ships were too far from the shore to profit from it. He could send one of the other ships' boats, crewed with comparatively fit seamen, to forage for fresh food and water sufficient to render his crews well again. But there might be reefs lying in wait for their boat, they might not be able to find water or be fit enough to hunt for food, and if this part of the coast was inhabited, misunderstandings might occur.

There were stories told that suggested that he was not the first to visit this land, that the Viking longships might have predated him by several generations, although it was generally accepted that they had not come this far south. But the Norsemen were not renowned for gentleness in their dealings with people. If they had been here before Brendan, the memory of their visit among the natives would be long and bitter.

He wondered if Malcolm could pronounce enough men fit from the crews of all three ships to provide oarsmen for *Sinead*, the smallest of the flotilla, to move her close enough for the onshore wind to fill her sails . . .

"You have not been listening to me," said the first officer angrily, breaking in on his thoughts. "That is a stupid thing to say."

"I wasn't aware that I was saying anything," said Brendan, feeling confused.

"Perhaps you were talking to yourself and I happened to overhear," Malcolm replied. All at once his words were sympathetic and his voice the one he used when talking to very sick men. "But you were not making sense. Why don't you use your heroes?"

His sympathetic tone irritated Brendan more than had the earlier sarcasm. "Of course I thought of using the heroes," he said angrily, "but that would mean seriously weakening the structure of the ship and rendering it unseaworthy in anything but the calmest conditions."

"If you are thinking of the voyage home," Malcolm said in a less sympathetic voice, "your crew are unseaworthy in any weather conditions, and will soon be dead. Perhaps *Sinead* or *White Heron* can donate some of their combustible material—"

"They cannot," Brendan broke in, "for the same reasons."

If there had been any moisture remaining in the other's mouth, it sounded as if it had been reduced to acid as he said, "How very reassuring it must be for a captain to know that he has a safe and seaworthy ship, even though it be manned by corpses. We still have the longboat."

"Burning one's boats," said Brendan, "is not supposed to take place until after, not before, a landing. The only way we could land would be to run aground . . ."

He fell silent, remembering the major cannibalizing of his ship after the southwesterly storm of three weeks ago had blown them nearly two hundred miles off course. His awkward and ungainly *Sea Dragon*, the very first hero-driven vessel to be built by the famed shipwrights of Baelfairste, had sustained more damage to the rigging and superstructure than had any of the other two ships, which had been able to ride over those mountainous seas rather than plunge through them. They had remained with him until his damaged paddle wheels had been repaired, refusing to go on because they were not as sure as Brendan, who was navigating for the flotilla, that there was anywhere to go. And when *Sea Dragon* got under way again, using his two smaller boats to feed the heroes, they had sailed as close as possible lest his ship should break up under him. By the time his mainmast and sails had been repaired, the heroes had eaten up the bulwarks protecting the weather deck and everything else of a nonessential nature that would burn.

Then they were becalmed for twelve days. With the exception of the longboat that would be needed to put a landing party ashore, there was no more wood that he could safely burn, and none of them had enough food or water to stay alive for more than a few days.

"The captains of *Sinead* and *White Heron* are the masters of their own ships," he said thoughtfully, "and I cannot order them to endanger their vessels. You know well that they are firm believers in the Old Ways, although as followers of the Christus they would stop short at taking a life, and they do not hold with wood-burners polluting the seas. But if I was to offer them the possibility of a tow to that distant shore in exchange for wood, and I sacrificed my longboat and other semi-essential structures which the carpenters can replace with growing timber on shore, and asked them to use their smaller longboats for the landing, then they might . . . Are my men strong enough to break wood and feed the heroes' furnace?"

"I have found," Malcolm replied, smiling, "that when people are suffering physical or mental distress, it is easier for them to break things than to make them."

"Donal," said Brendan, smiling in return, "you are a cynic."

* * *

On closer approach the land was revealed as a long, narrow island whose foreshore was either too marshy or unacceptably rocky. Brendan would not risk damaging his ships and Malcolm insisted that the crew-members, severely weakened as they were, would have little resistance to the fevers that bred in swamplands. As a result, it was late afternoon when a small sandy cove opened up on their port side, and he saw the ideal position for beaching his ship. He also, much sooner than he had wanted, had his first brush with the natives.

They were in a long canoe fashioned from a hollowed out log, which was pulling rapidly away from the beach because of the efforts of nine furiously paddling and probably terrified oarsmen. Brendan tried to put himself into their minds as his three ships, one of which was belching large quantities of woodsmoke and sparks, moved slowly into the cove. They had probably never before seen such large vessels, and in their position he, too, would have fled.

They were going to cross his bows well within hailing distance, and as the canoe moved close enough for him to look down into it, he made two discoveries—its stern was filled with an irregular, furry heap of what could only be freshly killed animals, and the crew was armed with bows.

Two of the oarsmen shipped their paddles long enough to loose perhaps a dozen arrows which whispered through the air above his head or clattered harmlessly against the foremast and smoke-stack.

"Ignore them," said Brendan loudly. "Cast off the towing cables, *Sinead* and *White Heron*, and drop anchor." More quietly to his own helmsman, he added, "Take us onto the beach."

So much of *Sea Dragon*'s upper hull, hatch coamings, and superstructure had gone to feed the heroes that even a moderately rough sea would have quickly swamped and sunk her. It was urgent that he beach her before the tide began to ebb and post guards, who would be barely strong enough to hold their cross-bows, on the grounded vessel. The fittest crew-members from the three ships would be dispatched to find water and fresh meat before the light faded.

During the month that followed, the hunting parties brought back a plentiful supply of deer, wildfowl, and, from a small river nearby, fish. Malcolm, after a period of experimentation which on two occasions gave him a severe colic and an even worse temper, identified the fruits and berries that would help cure their scurvy.

The ailing crew-members were restored to health, and the woods beyond the beach rang with the unnatural din of trees being felled and saws and chisels working them into shelters and stockade fencing. *Sea Dragon*'s bunkers were full again with new, green wood and the repairs were well under way.

Brendan and Malcolm had been reviewing progress, as was their wont following the evening meal, when the first officer said suddenly, "You take too many risks, Captain. You should not go wandering unescorted after dark. Whether the excuse is physical or spiritual exercise, and I seriously doubt the latter, because it is too dark to read your Breviary, and not enough light for your God in his bright Heaven to see you doing it."

Malcolm was a good but not a Godly man who professed to believe in nothing but himself, which made him prone to such irreverence.

"There is no risk," Brendan replied, laughing. "I walk by moonlight and am unlikely, therefore, to stumble or fall. There are no large nocturnal animals, and no sign of the return of the natives we surprised on our arrival."

He did not give the true reason for his lonely walks in the darkness, that only in the night could he pretend that the sea and tree-lined shore were not of this new world but were, instead, the rocky shore and forested lower slopes of his beloved mountains in the Kingdom of Mourne and that he, Brendan the Navigator, one of the most widely traveled seafarers of his generation, was homesick.

"I am fairly sure now that the natives come here only to hunt," he went on. "When we arrived they did not flee further along the coast, but headed across the stretch of water which divides us from the mainland. Although we have not explored it fully, their behavior supports my belief that this is an island rather than a peninsula. They are probably convinced by now that their hunting ground is occupied by a fire-breathing sea monster and are keeping well clear of us. And in any case, we know from the tales brought back by travelers to Nubia that ignorant savages do not stir abroad at night because they people the darkness with malevolent spirits. I am quite safe."

Malcolm made a derogatory sound and said, "Perhaps they do not stir abroad at night because they cannot see to hunt, and might run into an unseen obstacle and injure themselves. Perhaps the savages are less ignorant, and certainly less stupid, than is our respected captain."

He was seriously concerned for Brendan's safety, even though his way of expressing that concern left something to be desired.

During his lonely walk that evening, and simply to put the first officer's mind at ease, Brendan remained within the distant sight and the pleasant smell of the cooking fires. The moon was high and bright enough to fade the stars, and to make a wrinkled silver mirror of the sea and a dappled black and gray carpet of the tree-shaded sand on which he walked. Then the scene exploded into light, and for an instant he was aware of pain at the back of his head before all sight and feeling were swallowed by darkness.

Brendan returned to consciousness for a few moments to find himself lying on his side along the bottom of a canoe with natives kneeling astride him and paddling hard. The pitching motion of the craft told him that they were already far from the shore. He was able to see a lower leg, its foot covered by a short boot made from animal skin, a few inches from his face. The smell was terrible and he struggled to raise himself onto an elbow, but the effort brought with it a pain that threatened to burst open his skull, and his mind sank once more into unconsciousness.

Chapter 37

DURING his lengthy period of imprisonment, at no time was Brendan short of food, although many days were to pass before he became hungry enough to eat it. But it was plain from the start that his captors could not make up their minds on how to treat him.

There were days when his feet only would be tied and weighted with logs, and the women who came with the food and water would place it just within his reach and retreat quickly. A native wearing a feathered headdress would come into the small hut of branches, animal skins, and mud that housed the prisoner, to regard him impassively and ask questions that Brendan could not understand. Sometimes this person was accompanied by another, less unemotional native who danced and screamed and waved a staff from which were suspended small bones, seashells, and dried-up, hairy bundles whose origin he did not want to think about. On these occasions it was obvious that they were afraid and were according him a measure of respect.

On other days he would be staked outside the hut like a draft animal, with a long, coarse-fibered rope tied uncomfortably and tightly around his neck, and he would be beaten by the women or older children if he tried to loosen it. On these occasions they showed no respect whatsoever and it was clear to him that they were demonstrating their lack of fear of their strange, pale-skinned prisoner and the fire-breathing sea-god that he served. But respectful or otherwise, Brendan observed their behavior closely, listened, and tried to learn.

He also began to teach.

The first lessons were directed toward the older children who kept watch on him and, through them, the women and old men who remained in the village when the hunters were out. The younger children followed him everywhere, wanting to play all the time in spite of the warnings of the women, and gave him no trouble. It was the older, more imaginative and cruel children who needed to be taught.

When they tried to beat him or goad him to anger, he sat down cross-legged in native fashion and remained impassive until they tired of this unsatisfactory sport. He had already observed that a stoic impassivity in the face of physical or mental pain was accepted behavior among these people, and that those who displayed weakness were accorded little respect. But when they treated him with consideration, they quickly learned that he would perform for them, by doing tricks or making grass animals or wooden models, and that was much more fun for the children as well as being more reassuring to their mothers.

One day he was able to borrow a flint knife to carve a model canoe. That was the turning point in his relations, not only with the children but with everyone else.

It was a more complicated model than those carved by the village ancients as playthings for the children. This canoe had a mast and cross-piece to which was attached a large leaf. The arrangement was top-heavy so that he was forced to add outriggers for stability. He demonstrated while kneeling neck-deep and shivering in a river pool and blowing into the small green sail and using the few words he had been able to learn to explain the advantages. The onlookers of all ages derived much amusement from the demonstration.

Brendan was never sure why they gave him the old canoe that was beginning to rot, whether the reason was that some of them were interested in the idea of a craft that did not need to be paddled, or that from his efforts with the larger canoe they would derive even more entertainment.

The launch took place two weeks later, on a day of gusting, variable wind, from the relatively calm waters of the natural harbor at the river mouth. He was given no help with the project and, because he understood many of their words by then, little if any encouragement. He had changed the square-rigged design to a mast and boom that would enable him, if the leather cords that were holding everything together did their job, to sail into the wind. The sail had been stitched together from animal skins and was heavy, stiff, and barely manageable, and a broad paddle lashed loosely to the stern served as the rudder.

Covertly he scanned the shoreline of the land across the straights, searching for a sight of one of his ships or a windblown blur of smoke which would indicate the position of the expedition's camp, but in vain. If he were able to escape to the other shore, he would have to decide on which direction to take, knowing all the while that he might have taken the wrong one and be traveling away from rather than toward his friends.

Unless, Brendan thought hopefully, they were close enough for the glow of their fires to show at night.

He encountered difficulties with the sail, boom, and rudder singly and all together within the first few minutes, much to the delight of the onlookers. But finally he had the craft moving awkwardly toward the harbor mouth instead of spinning and wallowing in slow circles, and into the choppy waters of the straights. Cautiously he tried out the craft, tacking up and down outside the harbor a few times and finding that she handled like a drunken donkey. It was a surprise when he realized that he was already beyond bow-and-arrow range of the shore.

One of his outrigger logs was loose, the heavy inflexible sail was threatening to tear free, and natives were clustering around two of their canoes and shouting and waving their arms, although they had not yet decided to launch them in pursuit. Brendan knew that he could sail as fast as they could paddle if, as seemed unlikely, his craft held together. But he had to tack back and forth across the wind, while they could paddle into it with small loss of speed and overtake him easily.

Rather than be captured again, or perhaps shot with arrows while trying to resist, the sensible course would be to return while he still appeared to hold the initiative and pretend that his intention had never been to escape.

With the wind astern he sailed through the harbor mouth in fine style and ran onto the sand in front of the largest group of onlookers, then fell into the shallows as the shock collapsed his mast and the boom struck him painfully on the shoulder. He crawled ashore half-drowned, reflecting on the lack of subtlety in the natives' sense of humor.

From that day, however, there was a significant change in their behavior toward him. The rope that had been tied loosely around his neck was shortened to less than an arm's length and not attached to anything. It was as if he had given his word not to escape and, even though he had done no such thing, in some odd fashion he felt more securely bound by that symbolic rope than the one that had earlier tethered him to a tree.

Their curiosity regarding him increased. More importantly, they talked to him at every opportunity and made it plain that they were as keen on having Brendan learn their language as he himself was to learn it. He was moved from the drafty longhouse adjoining the stockade to one close to that of the Chief. It housed the Chief's incredibly ancient mother, his wives, children, and others whose family connection was unclear. He had been given a small area at one end of the longhouse. There was no external entrance, but a screen of hanging animal skins gave adequate if rather smelly privacy.

Before going to sleep at night, when his mind was not filled with the strange words of the Redmen, he would wonder about Malcolm and the other members of the expedition. Were they searching for him or had they given him up for dead? Had they recovered sufficiently to mount a rescue if they did find him? He was beginning to make good progress with his understanding of the Redmen, and he longed to be back among his own people, but he could wait for a few more days.

A week after his abortive attempt to escape, there was a birth in his longhouse and, much to his surprise and embarrassment, he was asked to view the proceedings. He was becoming an adept at controlling his facial expressions, and, in any case, he was less concerned with the birthing itself than with the quality of the medical assistance available to these people. He was surprised to find that it was Kargha, the Redman who had regularly come to scream and rattle bones at him, who had ordered that he be present. But it was two elderly women of the tribe who assisted the mother-to-be with moral support and occasional drinks of some herbal medication while Kargha danced and stamped his feet and waved his staff about to ensure that the proper religious practices for the occasion were performed and the evil spirits driven away.

Judging by the amount of dancing and charm-rattling directly in front of Brendan, it was obvious that he was one of the potentially evil spirits from whom the mother-to-be, Chief Tall Tree's youngest wife, had to be guarded, and Kargha wanted Brendan in plain sight rather than off somewhere working his counterspells in private.

When he was summoned to the Chief's longhouse on the evening following the birth of another healthy son, the medicine man and several of the younger hunters were present, and it quickly became evident that Brendan was to be subjected to a thorough interrogation.

There was a long, strong-smelling pipe, whose bowl was filled with smoldering herbs, which was passed among the company to show that the occasion would be nonviolent. When Brendan had recovered from his fit of coughing they asked him about himself, the reason for leaving his homeland, the number of his tribe, and his status within it. Constrained as he was by his limited knowledge of the language, Brendan did his best to answer simply and truthfully.

"You are a Chief, then?" asked Tall Tree, showing no surprise at the news. "You are the leader of this tribe which has floated across the shining sea?"

"Yes," said Brendan.

One of the Chief's sons asked, "Does your tribe number many hunters, warriors, squaws? Will they try to find you?"

"If they know that I live," Brendan replied, "they will search for me."

It was much more difficult trying to explain that his men were paddlers of the great canoes—the closest he could come to seamen—who could become hunters and warriors whenever it was necessary. His men carried special bows with short arrows and did not need great strength and skill to use them. With a broken arrow he scratched out a picture of a crossbow and bolt on the dry earth before the fire, and he thought that a few of them grasped the principle. But when he said that there were no squaws in his tribe, even the Chief lost his impassivity.

"A Chief," said Tall Tree, inclining his head in the direction of the adjacent longhouse, "should have the comfort of squaws."

He did not have to add that several of the eligible girls of the village, one of his daughters included, had made overtures to

Brendan, all of which had been for some reason refused. Nor did he have to point out that a marriage between one of his daughters and another Chief, albeit a very strange one of as-yet-unknown powers, was desirable in that it would remove the likelihood of war between them.

Brendan seized the chance both to reduce the hostility between Kargha and himself and to remove the constant assaults on his vow of celibacy.

"Many of my men have squaws and children in their home villages," he said solemnly. "But I have willingly foresworn the right to the comfort of a woman in my tent, and to the begetting of children, in return for great knowledge and power and the respect of my tribe. Among my people, and yours, the price to be paid for such knowledge and ability is high."

Kargha looked haughtily pleased with himself. He was not a pleasant man, either as a person or in his habits, and not even the least comely of the village women would open her blanket to him. But now Brendan had given a reason for Kargha's enforced solitude by making a virtue of necessity.

Tall Tree smiled faintly, and said, "What is this knowledge for which you have paid so dearly?"

Brendan decided to simplify matters by omitting his years of priestly training and study, and the restlessness that had made the peace of the monastery a hell to him. He said, "I wanted this knowledge long before I reached manhood, the knowledge and skills that would enable me to find a path over the trackless seas to strange lands and peoples. I wanted the ability to live among those people and learn their ways, and to give them my own knowledge in return, if they wished it.

"There are many strange lands and many, many tribes hunting in them," he went on. "Not all of the tribes have pale skins like mine. Some of the lands are so hot that the sun has burned their skins black, and even the children are born with black skins. In other lands the skins are brown and, although I have not seen it for myself, tales are told of a land far to the east where the skin is yellow. But this is the only land to be discovered where the skin is red."

"Do these tribes speak with each other?" asked Tall Tree. "Do they make war?"

Brendan explained that some of the most powerful tribes were separated by great distances. The dangers of traveling for many moons over stormy seas or in lands filled with fearsome beasts left them without the strength to make war. But they talked together and made peace treaties, and sent great canoes filled with goods to each other—goods that one tribe had in plenty and the other desired, in exchange for goods the second tribe possessed that were wanted by the first tribe.

The idea of trading between distant tribes was difficult for them to grasp.

"The land of the Algonquin has food enough to fill the bellies of our people," said the Chief. "Why should we seek more from distant lands?"

Brendan plunged into a long, difficult explanation of trading between tribes, during which he discovered many things about the Algonquin Nation, of which Tall Tree's people formed a very small part. The total area occupied by the Algonquin Redmen exceeded that of Hibernia herself. Scattered throughout were hundreds of villages, some larger, some smaller, than that ruled by Tall Tree. Holding supreme authority over the village chiefs was Running Bear, the Paramount Chief of the Algonquin Nation. Paramount Chiefs were elected to the position, much as were the High-Kings at Tara, but the physical requirements for the position were not as demanding, because the candidates were usually old, wise, and greatly respected men. Local Chiefs were also elected, but the son of a Chief had advantages over the other candidates. The village Chiefs and their advisers gathered together from time to time before their Paramount Chief, but, in spite of everything that Running Bear could do, the meetings were usually councils of war. War was necessary to prove manhood.

Tall Tree and Kargha were launching into a tale of great exploits in battle by members of their tribe, when Brendan brought them back to the subject of trading—for beautiful silks and furs, or precious, hand-carved ornaments, or rich spices that improved the taste and smell of food.

". . . The goods are not carried in litters or on the backs of squaws," Brendan went on, "but on horses and mules which eat only the grass all around them, and drink water from the rivers—"

"What are horses?" asked Tall Tree.

Brendan likened them to large forest deer without antlers, whose backs were padded with blankets so that goods could be carried on them, or a man could ride on them over long distances at great speed. If the ground was flat and the trees did not grow too thickly, he told them, a messenger on a horse could travel many times faster than one who traveled on foot through the forest or by canoe along the rivers. But still they could not grasp the idea. He swept the ground before him clean of his earlier crossbow sketch and attempted to draw a mounted man.

Brendan had never thought of himself as an artist nor, for that matter, had anyone else. He tried very hard to get the outline and proportions correct, but he felt that the two horses they had brought with them deserved an apology.

He had always liked horses, and Black Seamus was a lovely beast who had been moved to *Sinead* because of his habit of trying to kick a hole in the side of the ship in his attempts to reach his mate, the docile and friendly White Dancer. When their food ran short, the cattle they had also carried had been slaughtered one by one, but no member of his three crews would agree to killing and eating either of the horses, although by then they were so emaciated and their mouths so full of sores that there was no strong temptation to do so. He was finishing his sketch and wondering if Black Seamus and White Dancer—who were a present to the expedition from the stables of the High-King—were still among the living, when Kargha gave a great shout of laughter.

"This is no beast," he cried. "It is a thing dreamed of in a fever, or a picture drawn by children."

"It *is* a beast," Brendan said, angered by the scorn in Kargha's voice even though he knew that the criticism of the drawing was merited. "It is a lovely and useful beast. You speak without knowledge!"

Kargha was glaring at him and gripping his staff in a way that suggested he might use it for physical rather than spiritual exercise. Brendan felt like biting off his tongue. He, a stranger, had called Kargha ignorant, something that no other member of the tribe would dare to do. Never a friend, Brendan was sure that he had made of the medicine man a bitter and unforgiving enemy.

He was searching desperately among his few Algonquin words for an apology when Tall Tree held up his hand.

"Peace," he said. "The day has been long and tiring. The night grows cold, and the smoke of the fire hurts our eyes and beclouds our minds. One last matter must be considered."

He unfolded a beautifully embroidered and decorated sash and laid it on the ground before him. The light glittered off the regular patterns of polished bone beads and tiny seashells which, Brendan had learned, carried its message in the ideographic written language of the Algonquin Nation.

"News of the coming of the pale-skinned strangers was sent to Running Bear," said Tall Tree, in the deep, resonant voice he used when addressing the elders of his tribe, "and these are his words. He has called together a great council of Chiefs in this, our village, at the full of the next moon. Many preparations must be made."

"Yes," said Kargha, no longer angry. It was as if he had received an apology or, perhaps, was already sure of his revenge.

"Only a Chief of the Algonquin Nation may speak before the council of Chiefs," Tall Tree went on, in answer to Brendan's unspoken question. "The stranger is Chief of the Tribe of the Great Canoes, but has no land here. He can be given the land which breeds fevers in its swamps and is rarely hunted by us, the land to which he first came. Should the deliberations of the great council deem otherwise, it will be taken from him or he will make war so that he may keep it. He will be adopted by our Nation, he will be bound by its laws and customs, and he will be given a name befitting an Algonquin Chief."

Tall Tree smiled and went on, "I had thought of naming you Short Arrow, or No-Squaw, but these are not names of respect. A Chief must—"

"A Chief," Kargha broke in quietly, "must first prove that he is a man. That is the law."

For a moment Brendan thought of the things he would like to do to this mean and vengeful man, all of them contrary to the teachings of the Christus. Kargha knew his area of greatest weakness and was attacking it.

As a seafarer, Brendan had much more freedom of action and choice of apparel than the majority of his fellows, but the rules of his Order were nevertheless strict. He could not even imagine how his aged and irascible abbot would react to the news that, for purely political reasons, he had taken to himself one or more Algonquin squaws. Public disgrace, summary unfrocking, and excommunication would be the least he could expect.

Tall Tree regarded the medicine man and said gravely, "If the stranger tells us that among his own people he has proved himself worthy of election to Chief, we will believe that it is so."

Kargha raised his staff high and plunged it into the ground between Brendan and the Chief. The charms hanging from it shivered and rattled for a moment, then were still except for a gentle stirring by the night wind.

"If the pale-skinned stranger is to be a Chief of the Algonquin," said Kargha firmly, "then the tests of fitness must be according to Algonquin law."

Brendan regarded Kargha for a moment while the firelight

played with his face and moved his features into expressions that were not there. If the stranger was not to dishonor himself it was for him to speak.

"The Algonquin Nation does me great honor," Brendan said, because there was nothing else that he could say. "Provided I do not share my blanket with any woman, willingly do I submit to the tests of fitness required by Algonquin law."

The tests took many days and nights to administer. Some of them were childishly easy, because they were given to older men-children, but Kargha was insisting on the strict observance of all the laws. The requirement of exercising, in lieu of traveling, for long periods without food or water was not difficult for someone who had survived the closing weeks of the voyage on *Sea Dragon* and, fortunately, he was required to learn the use of bow and tomahawk without becoming proficient with those weapons. But the later tests were mentally and physically quite difficult.

"Tell me," said Kargha, striking Brendan's naked back lightly with his staff, "of the Kitcki Manitou."

"He is the most powerful of all the Manitous," Brendan replied, allowing no hint of discomfort to show in his voice. "He is the Great Spirit, the father of life who was never created. He is the source of all good things. It was at his direction, and it is in his honor, that the Redmen smoke the pipe of peace."

"There is more," said Kargha.

He tried to change his grip on the branch so as to ease the tightness of the rope binding his wrists, but suddenly the muscles of his arms and shoulders knotted in cramp. He opened his mouth and let the cry of pain move silently past his lips as a quiet breath. This was not, he thought, the ideal way to receive religious instruction.

He had been suspended by the hands and feet from a low branch of a tree close to the water's edge, his rump hanging about waist-height from the ground. At night the wind had been cold and during the day there had been no clouds to cover the burning sun. In theory he was the helpless prey of any wild animal that came along, but this close to the village the risk of being clawed or eaten was small. His naked body had been decorated with daubs of clay where it was not covered by red streaks and patches of juice from a local berry that was sweet enough, it seemed, to attract every biting or stinging insect for miles around.

The purpose of the exercise, according to Kargha, was to sharpen his mind and enable it to absorb knowledge while ignoring physical distractions.

"There is more," Kargha repeated, giving him another whack with his staff.

"The Great Spirit dwells in Heaven," said Brendan obediently. "His is above all other powers. He is master of light and is manifest in the sun. He is the breath of life and, as the winds, he moves everywhere. The Algonquin believe that there is another very important spirit, Michabo, called the Great Hare, who was born on the island of Michilimackinak. Michabo is the father of the race, and made the earth, and invented fishing nets, and created water, fish, and the great deer—"

"Tell me of the Thunder Bird," Kargha broke in.

Brendan paused to flex and ease his arm muscles, but briefly so as to avoid the staff.

"The Thunder Bird is a powerful spirit whose eyes flash lightning and the beating of whose wings is the rolling of thunder," Brendan replied. Then he veered from the subject as he went on, "The paleskins, too, have a Great Spirit, who lives in Heaven and is all-powerful, all-knowing, and omnipresent. We believe that He created everything which exists in the earth, sea, and sky, and He did not allow the smaller works of creation to be given to lesser spirits. There are lesser beings who attend the Great Spirit, and men and women who have performed great deeds, of bravery, of endurance, or of kindness on earth, have been brought to Heaven and are especially loved and honored by Him. We pray to these lesser spirits, because they are beloved by and have influence with the Great Spirit, but we do not worship them. He is called by many names, but there is only one Great Spirit."

To ward off any evil that might befall him as a result of listening to such heresy, Kargha shook his staff. It was a perfunctory gesture.

Brendan knew that he could never grow to like the medicine man, but he had grown to respect him. Kargha was not wantonly cruel, now that the laws and customs of his tribe were being properly observed, and he was both intelligent and intensely curious. This was not the first occasion that the teaching of Algonquin law had progressed to a debate on comparative theology. But both men were fully aware of the difference between the possession of knowledge and faith, and each knew that they would never succeed in converting the other no matter how much they talked.

"How and when does the paleskin talk to his Great Spirit?" asked Kargha, with another protective rattle of his charms. "What sacrifices are necessary? What rituals must he perform?"

While the medicine man had been speaking, Tall Tree had approached them to stand listening silently on the other side of Brendan.

"Rituals and token sacrifices are performed when large numbers of paleskins gather to speak to the Great Spirit," Brendan replied, "but they are not necessary. The Great Spirit hears because He is everywhere. He hears even the words spoken silently in the mind."

"You have spoken to him since sunrise?" asked Kargha, looking slightly worried.

"Yes," said Brendan.

"And what," said Tall Tree, joining the discussion, "do the paleskins ask of him? Does the Great Spirit speak and answer?"

"We ask for many things," said Brendan. "For enough food to eat, for contentment of mind for ourselves or our friends, for the success of our plans, for many things. The Great Spirit does not often speak, but answers with deeds. Sometimes there is no answer, or the deeds are not those which were asked, but other deeds which have better results than those which were asked. There are times when the mind of the Great Spirit is difficult for men to understand."

Kargha and the Chief exchanged looks that suggested that the Redmen, too, shared this difficulty. It was Tall Tree who spoke.

"What did you, stranger, ask for yourself?"

"I asked for guidance during the council of Chiefs," Brendan replied, meaning every word. "I asked that there be friendship between the Redmen and the paleskins. I also asked that my friends would find me, but not until after the council has—" He broke off to look out across the beach and its natural harbor, then added sadly, "One of the requests has been denied."

With her paddles threshing and hull nearly obscured by forward-blowing smoke, *Sea Dragon*, closely followed by *Sinead* and *White Heron*, were moving rapidly around the headland and into the bay. Her paddles stopped turning, but the smoke billowing around her and blowing toward the shore concealed the frantic activity on board all three ships as they lowered sails and dropped anchor just inside the harbor. By the time that the longboats of *White Heron* and *Sinead*, dangerously overloaded with armed men, emerged from the smoke, the Redman shelters and cooking fires around the harbor were deserted.

Tall Tree and Kargha watched impassively as the men splashed ashore, leaving only enough of their number behind to return for more, to come running up the beach. They appeared to be well-fed and healthy, Brendan saw, and very, very angry.

O'Donnell, Master of *Sinead*, flanked by Malcolm, was first to reach his tree. The Chief and Kargha had neither moved nor changed their expressions.

"Captain!" Malcolm burst out. "What have the heathen devils done to you? And they stand here, too busy torturing you to run away like the others. I'll cut out their black hearts . . . !"

"Don't harm them!" said Brendan sharply. Since the untimely arrival of his flotilla, he had been trying desperately to think of a way to avert what promised to be a massacre, and to do it quickly and with the fewest possible words. Urgently, he went on, "Hail the ships. Tell them that no more men are to be landed. You have frightened only the aged net-menders and children . . . Don't touch me, Healer!"

Malcolm stopped, his fingers only a few inches from a patch of livid red on Brendan's shoulder, and his face showed deep concern as he said, "I am no stranger to the sight or touching of an unclothed body, Captain, and even though you are an anointed priest, it is just another body."

Then he sniffed, smiled, and moved back.

Brendan thought that the gift of tongues would be very useful at this moment, because he needed to hold two conversations in two different languages at the same time, but the one with Tall Tree and Kargha was the more important. While it was going on, he was aware of his orders being shouted to the ships. Then the talking was over and Kargha moved closer and struck him sharply on the head.

O'Donnell swore again and struggled to draw his sword, hampered by the double grip of Malcolm's hands on his wrist. Kargha ignored them and raised his staff high, communicating with all the spirits in words spoken too rapidly for Brendan to follow, then lowered it again to administer a congratulatory whack on the rump.

"Peace, Captain," said Brendan quickly, his mind running much faster than his tongue. "I have been most highly honored. In the past few moments it was decided that the last few hours of the initiation ceremony, which should not have ended until noon, could be dispensed with since there was no doubt that I could pass the tests. How are the horses?"

"The *horses*!" O'Donnell shouted. "Here you are, tied up, wounded, and bleeding, and you ask about the horses. They are a lot healthier than you are. Let me cut you down from this bloody—"

"The red stuff," said Malcolm quietly, "does not smell like blood."

"It isn't blood," said Brendan. "And don't free me, the ceremony isn't over. The Redman with the staff is Kargha, a healer of sorts, and the other one is Tall Tree, Chief of this village. I want you to disarm yourselves and lay your weapons, all of your weapons, at the Chief's feet . . ."

There were objections, naturally, not only from O'Donnell and Malcolm. The argument raged for several minutes until Tall Tree spoke sharply and Brendan broke off to reply.

"What were you saying to him?" asked Malcolm when they had finished speaking.

"I told him that you wanted me back among you," Brendan replied gravely, "and that you were all willing to lay down your lives for me. He said that you were brave warriors, but that fighting now would be a great foolishness. I told him that you would do what I asked."

With difficulty he inclined his head toward the trees behind him.

There were many, many Redmen emerging from among the trees, their bows ready but not aimed. Not only were the warriors of the village present, but all those who had escorted their Chiefs to the Great Council. They continued to move from among the trees until every trunk was hidden. There must have been more than two thousand of them.

Before his men could react, four squaws arrived to cut Brendan down and carry him into the sea, where they washed off the clay and berry stains and allowed him to exercise the stiffness from his muscles. Then clean and pink once more, with the sun drying him as he walked, he returned to the Tree of Testing. The fact that he was naked as a newborn babe was one of the embarrassments he had learned to ignore in recent weeks, and he remained impassive while Tall Tree and Kargha helped him into his clothes, which had been freshly washed, dried, and scented with herbs by the Chief's squaws for the dressing ceremony.

His breeches and tunic felt strange to him, the thigh-length sea boots and cape bearing the emblem of his Order an unnecessary encumbrance. His cap had been lost when he had been taken by the Redmen. But he did not need it because on his head they placed a beautiful and imposing headdress of eagle feathers which fell behind his shoulders and past his waist. They spoke the time-honored words of the Inauguration, to which he gave the prescribed replies, and then he turned to face his own people again.

"I told him that you would disarm yourselves if I asked it of you," Brendan resumed calmly, "because I am your Chief."

. . . And many centuries later, on a new world distant indeed from that discovered by Brendan the Navigator, the embers of the open galley fire were giving enough light to show that the eyes of the injured Pilot Brenner were closed.

In a softer voice, Nolan went on, "I am being inconsiderate of my patient and everyone else. We will be faced with a long, hard row tomorrow. The rest of Brendan's story can wait until another time. Tonight we need our sleep."

The crews dispersed quietly to their ships and began settling down for the night. Nolan was about to do the same when the pilot said, "Healer, I cannot sleep. Please stay and talk."

"Your leg pains you," said Nolan gently. "But pain is like hard work: its tensions tire the mind and muscles alike. You do not believe it now, but shortly you will sleep. It helps if you think about something else."

"About Brendan?" said Brenner in a weak voice. "About his shameful treatment by Connair, and the Holy See? That would make me feel worse."

"Not about Brendan," said Nolan. "Think, rather, about what was to befall his first officer, Malcolm the Fair."

He heard the pilot give a long, quiet sigh. Nolan smiled in the darkness and said, "And to remind you of what was to happen, I shall ask the lady Ulechitzl to stand the first watch . . ."

Chapter 38

A FAVORING wind of nearly gale force drove them onto the beach of a wide, sandy bay overlooked by wooded hills and, on the north side, by a high promontory. They quickly recovered their strength after the sea crossing, and the delay in continuing the journey was due to waiting for Pilot Brenner's leg to mend.

The ground inland was too hilly to risk carrying an injured man on a litter, and in the additional weeks of forced idleness the colonists developed lazy habits and talked more and more often of remaining in this pleasant place, with its cooling winds and plentiful supply of wild thumper meat and edible vegetation, to await rescue by the main colony. Nolan ignored the talk, hoping that they would soon become tired of lying about in their tropical paradise, and spent the time adding to his catalog of edible roots and berries.

One of which nearly killed him.

It was a small ground-growing nut with a pale blue, liquid-filled kernel. The kernels were small and the parent plants much too scarce for it to make an addition to the food supply, but it had a sharp and not unpleasant taste and an aroma that was reminiscent of cinnamon, and Nolan had tested it with a view to its being used as a spice to improve the often bland flavor of thumper meat. He had tasted and eaten it in minute quantities over several days without any harmful effect, but before releasing it for general consumption, he had squeezed the liquid content of the kernel onto a piece of freshly roasted thumper meat.

As soon as the liquid touched the hot meat it exploded into a small cloud of vapor which in his surprise he had inhaled. Thereafter Nolan had fallen into a coma from which it had been impossible to rouse him for two days.

Later and more careful tests showed that when eaten raw, the kernel had only a mild soporific effect, probably due to normal detoxification by the human digestive system. But when sufficient heat was applied for the juice to vaporize and be inhaled, so powerful was the effect that Nolan had been unsure whether to classify it as a soporific or a general anesthetic. When administered in measured doses, however, it ensured that the injured Brenner spent no more sleepless nights, and his injuries healed apace.

The pilot had been back on his feet and in the air for a week before Nolan finally insisted that they move on.

Brenner's observations showed that they were on the section of coast nearest to their destination and that they could go no farther by sea. Time and again Nolan reminded everyone that they had traveled more than half the distance to the main colony in less than one Earth year, that even though *Aisling Gheal* had not reacted in any detectable fashion to their many signal fires or to Brenner's now-exhausted suit farspeaker, this did not mean that their presence was unknown to the ship and the other colonists, or that a rescue party of their friends had not been dispatched to meet them. Sooner or later they would have to complete the journey to the colony, and making excuses for remaining in this place was a waste of everyone's time.

It was possible that the captain was too busy with his own scientific concerns, or too aged and physically unwell, to scan the surface night after night for the tiny sparks that were all that the cooking fires would have shown –if he happened to be looking in that area. But it was even more likely that they had all been posted missing presumed dead, and that neither the cardinal-captain nor anyone else was looking for them.

Those thoughts Nolan kept to himself while he encouraged everyone to prepare yet another fiery signal, one that could not be mistaken for any natural occurrence, because it would burn far out on the waters of the bay and would show a direction as well as light. All that was required, he told them, was hard work and the patience to wait for the conditions that would ensure maximum visibility from the orbiting *Aisling Gheal*.

On a night that was calm and cloudless, the three ships, long since emptied of stores and loaded with as much wood and combustible vegetation as they would carry without overturning, were rowed carefully into position. Each fire ship carried a single, lighted torch, carefully guarded so as to avoid a premature ignition, to show its position to the other vessels and those on shore, and crews made up of only the strongest swimmers. The ships took position on two sighting fires that had been lit on the beach, one at the water's edge and another just under the trees, so that *Sea*

Dragon lined up on the shore fires while *Sinead* and *White Dancer* stationed themselves in line abreast six hundred yards astern of her and three hundred yards apart.

When *Aisling Gheal* had climbed high into the western sky and there would be no slightest trace of dayshine to distract the observer on the ship from what was to happen on the night side below him, the signal was given to fire all three ships from bows to sterns. By the time the crews arrived back on the beach, the ships were well ablaze and the bay resembled the aftermath of some old-time sea battle.

When viewed from orbit, however, the three blazing ships would together form a narrow isosceles triangle pointing like a fiery arrowhead toward the main colony. When he learned of this, Nolan thought, the monsignor would be a very worried man.

"It is a great pity, Healer," said Brenner, loudly enough to be heard above the sporadic cheering of the colonists, "that there is insufficient wind to launch the glider. This would be a spectacular sight from the air. And it must be generating enough thermals to take me halfway up to *Aisling Gheal*!"

Nolan did not reply. He knew that they had served their purpose and must be abandoned, but the sight of the burning ships performing their last service made him feel sad.

As if sensing Nolan's mood, Brenner said, "Healer, you are continually telling us that we are doing nothing new, that all this has happened before. We have indeed done many of the things Brendan did, although not always as he did them. He burned only parts of his ships because he expected to return home in them, while we are going on. And nothing lies before us except distance, for up until now we have survived every obstacle this world could place in our way. So smile, Healer, and ease your mind.

"At least," he ended, with an apologetic look at Golden Rain, "we will not have unfriendly natives to contend with."

"Thank God for that," said Nolan. Then, remembering what he was, he added, "Or somebody."

And so it was that on the 271st day after landing, their burned boats still smoking behind them and full of confidence and high spirits, they set out on the second half of the journey to the main colony.

They had forgotten how viciously the insects could bite and how abominable was the smell of the protecting stench-tree bulbs, and as the days went by they grew hungrier because the wild thumpers became harder to find, and angrier because they were continually dragging the domesticated herd and themselves up an unending succession of thickly forested lower slopes of mountains and down into valleys whose swampy floors were carpeted with an even denser growth, when they were not covered by swamps that hummed with an angry, strident fog of insects that were not always discouraged by the stench pods. They were hot and hungry, bitten, stung, and torn by thorn bushes. And no matter how high Brenner flew, he could report no change or improvement in the conditions ahead of them. Then on A.L. 329, when they had closed the distance to the colony by less than two hundred miles, it started to rain.

Many times they had encountered heavy and prolonged rain both on land and at sea, but this was far beyond any previous experience. It roared and rattled off the leaves above them to splash onto the ground like a continuing, erratic waterfall, and it tumbled down the slope past them as if the surrounding underbrush were growing out of a wide, slow-running stream. So heavy was the rain that to try to walk in it brought an immediate fear of drowning. It was impossible to hunt or light fires or do anything but huddle miserably inside tents whose floors were continually awash and shout words that were usually curses at each other. The rain lasted for four days and five nights, then stopped as suddenly as it had started.

They took stock, finding that the seed stores had remained sealed and dry, that two of the thumpers had drowned, that the glider framework was warped and would have to be rebuilt, and that everything and everyone else was sodden in body and spirit. Nolan ordered an immediate move to higher, unwooded ground to enable them to dry out. Then he withdrew some distance, ostensibly to write up his journal but in reality to allow the colonists to talk freely among themselves. He knew what they wanted to talk about, and he needed time to think of an answer before the problem was officially presented to him.

Late that afternoon it came as no surprise that Brenner and the two ladies had been chosen to speak for the others.

"Healer Nolan," the pilot said in an embarrassed voice, "we have been asked to tell you that the majority of the colonists want to return to the Bay of the Burning Boats, where there is food and cool air and a life that is as pleasant as it can be in our particular situation. We are attempting an impossible journey, they say, and if we go on we will all die. They say much more, but that is the gist of it, and they ask you with respect if you will abide by the expressed wishes of the majority?"

"I will not," said Nolan.

"You are not a stupid man, Healer," said Ulechitzl angrily. "It is only a stupid man who will not change his mind. Why not?"

"For the same reasons I discussed with Pilot Brenner a few days after we landed. Has he discussed them with you?"

"I promised not to speak of them to anyone until we reached the colony," said Brenner before she could answer. "It is better if you argue the reasons for yourself."

"And your promise was kept," said Nolan gratefully. "But now, Pilot, I think it would be better if you left us for a moment."

Brenner turned without a word and walked away.

"It seems that the pilot and yourself have been withholding information from us," said Ulechitzl in a quiet, angry voice. "And now you are going to keep information from him. Healer, what else are you hiding?"

Hopefully, thought Nolan, you will never know. Aloud, he said, "Unless you request it, my lady, nothing we say here will be hidden from him. Pilot Brenner is a good man, and I wish to save him needless embarrassment. Is the majority in favor of returning a large one, and does it include the three members of this delegation?"

"It is a small majority overall," said Ulechitzl. "And this in spite of Golden Rain and Pilot Brenner wanting to go on and myself to return. But we three will abide by the majority decision. Will you?"

Nolan shook his head. He said, "No, my lady. Whether it is only one person or a handful or, indeed, all of you who accompany me, I shall go on to the colony."

For a moment Ulechitzl breathed heavily through her delicately formed and beautifully proportioned nose, then she said, "Pilot Brenner told me that I would find it difficult to change your mind. I repeat, Healer, a person who will not change his mind is a stupid person, and you are not stupid. Why behave as if you are?"

He did not reply because it was plainly a rhetorical question.

"We survived the landing," she went on, "and with your help and encouragement we survived on the planet itself. But we will not survive if we continue this journey. You have brought us farther than anyone would have believed possible, but now you are intent on leading us to our deaths. After a lifetime of unquestioning obedience in the Court of Tenochtitlan, no matter how distant in time and space that Court lies today, you must know that I will not be treated like some unthinking foot soldier expected to follow an officer wherever he leads, and neither will the others. In their own nations, they, too, were persons of rank and influence. And intelligence.''

That is why the monsignor abandoned you here, Nolan thought, because you would not blindly follow him, either. He did not speak.

''My apologies, Healer, I was never a good diplomat,'' she resumed in a quieter voice. ''I did not mean to suggest that you were a martinet without feeling. You have led us, by example, and have risked your life while teaching us to live off this land. That is why you cannot be allowed to throw your life away. We need you with us, and we already owe you more than we can ever repay. But if you will give up this senseless and suicidal journey, there is one of us who is able to repay you in ways impossible for the others.

''Do you understand me, Healer?''

Nolan had to close his eyes to shut out the sight of her looking up at him, and of the jacket shrunk by four days of rain to the tightness of a second skin over that tiny, perfect body. But the dark screen that was his closed eyelids was immediately filled with the hot, tactile images of what she was offering him, and he had to open them again.

''I understand you well, my lady,'' he said in an unsteady voice, ''but I will not mate with you.''

For an instant she glared at him, anger darkening to copper the smooth bronze of her face, then she said, ''I see. Could it be that you prefer someone taller and more robustly formed, someone who would bear you tall, strong children like yourselves? I am sorry, Healer. For some reason which she has not disclosed to me, Golden Rain is not disposed to offer herself to you. But if you were to remain with us, you might, in time, find ways of persuading her otherwise. Until then you needs must settle for me.''

Again, Nolan shook his head.

''I do not understand you, Healer,'' she said, curiosity diluting her anger at his refusal. ''You are not an ecclesiastic, not even a believer, so what is there to stop you? Perhaps there is no strong emotional bond between us, other than respect and gratitude on my part, but I know there is physical attraction. The majority feeling is that going on with you will lead eventually to death for all of us, but that if you were to remain with us our continued survival would be assured. I, for one, do not wish to end my days like a desiccated fly tangled in this hellish green web all around us, and this is the only inducement I can offer to ensure that you remain with us and I do not die. If the others benefit, I am pleased for them. But in this my personal feelings are not the primary concern. If you wish, you may consider it the partial discharge of a great debt, or a fee paid for your continuing practice of the healing arts on our behalf. You are not the bumbling, enthusiastic and overgrown boy I met at Tara, Healer, you are a man. I can promise that the arrangement will not be unpleasant for you and . . . , and . . ."

For a moment her eyes lowered until she was looking no higher than Nolan's chest, then rose again to meet his gaze. She might not be a good diplomat, he thought as she spoke, but she was most certainly a bad liar.

". . . It is not," she ended in a voice that was trying to be firm, "an important matter to me."

Nolan was silent for a moment. He wanted to tell this small highborn and intensely desirable woman how unworthy he was of her, and how deeply her words had honored him. But that might have indicated a weakening in his resolve, and he was aware that his resolve was weak enough already. He had to speak quickly.

"My lady," he blurted out, "the matter might be considered important, by Ciaran."

"Ciaran?" she said. "What has . . . ?"

"At the reception in Tara," said Nolan, "he was greatly impressed by you and, I assume, saw himself as your lifelong protector on the New World. I gave him my promise that no harm would come to you until we reached the colony. We have not yet reached the colony, my lady."

"So that is why you would not . . ." Ulechitzl began, then she shook her head and went on. "He is—was—an amusing table companion, as were you, and a personable young man. And, considering his profession, one who would not be afraid of anything on Earth or on any other world. At the time it seemed to me that he would be a good man to have as a friend in what lay ahead, but I did not realize he felt so strongly. Healer, he had no right to involve you without my knowledge or permission."

"Without my knowledge or permission," said Golden Rain, speaking for the first time, "Healer Nolan gave the same promise to my husband, Wanachtee, who awaits me at the main colony. On the ship as well as here, he has kept that promise, and glad I am of it."

"And now," said Ulechitzl, turning to her, "I understand why you will stay only if the Healer stays. Sleeping as we have within inches of each other for a year, I am disappointed that you kept this secret from me. But it changes nothing and I—''

Nolan held up his hand for silence. ''The matter would also be considered important,'' he said firmly, ''by Pilot Brenner.''

Ulechitzl swung around to face him again, but when she spoke her voice sounded ashamed rather than angry as she said, ''It seems that nothing misses you. The arrangement I was offering would have been, and may still be, honored for the reasons I have given, even though the pilot knows nothing of it as yet. But with respect, Healer Nolan, you would not be my first choice as a husband.''

''Or even your second,'' said Nolan gently. ''Both are fine men, my lady. But why not wait until we reach the colony before you choose between them?''

Suddenly she was angry again. ''Healer,'' she said, ''you sing the same stupid song. You are going to reach the main colony, but more likely you will die in the attempt, and why? Because of two promises made long ago and incredibly far away which, in the light of what has happened since, no sane person would blame you for breaking. This is not sensible, not realistic, not even sane. What would a Healer of the Mind think of a man who acts like some stupid, selfless saint, an *unbelieving* saint, for God's sake, who is seeking death before dishonor because of a few words spoken at a time when—''

''No,'' said Golden Rain, interrupting her again. ''You must not speak thus of the Healer. Well do I understand what drives him, and it is not only his promises. He, too, has someone awaiting him at the colony.''

Ulechitzl stared at Golden Rain for a moment, shook her head, and then returned her attention to Nolan.

''It seems that I am stripping away your secrets one by one,'' she said, then curiously, ''Pray describe this . . . this paragon beside whom a woman such as myself is as nothing.''

Before Nolan could reply, Golden Rain said, ''You do not expect a man to speak of this to anyone but the woman herself. She is tall, taller by far than I, and slender and well-formed but strong. She is a paleskin, with hair that is the color of burnished copper. She is fair of face and comely. Her eyes are blue, a changing blue like the sea. At times they had the sure, bold look of a commander of men, at others the softness of a mother. When she was helping lift me from the cold sleep casket to check it, her words and touch were gentle. In my presence he did not call her by name.''

Nolan closed his eyes again, feeling close to anger at Golden Rain for bringing back to him such a clear picture of Dervla, then opened them because Ulechitzl was speaking again.

"Now I understand you better, Healer Nolan," she said in a gentler voice, "but the situation has not changed."

Then I must change it, he thought fiercely, and soon.

"My lady," he said, "Pilot Brenner and myself discussed this situation, and its probable consequences, within a few days of arriving on this world. We decided that regardless of our authority as ship's officers or the respect in which we might be held by the male colonists, the situation would be inherently unstable and must, sooner rather than later, deteriorate into violence. You do not lack intelligence, my lady, and must have considered this probability as well, although our recent setbacks may have blinded you to it.

"Without false modesty," he went on before she could speak, "I know that I am no longer indispensable. You have all learned how to survive on this world and, leaving internal violence aside, will continue to do so. I will go on with whoever will follow me. But if you and Pilot Brenner and the others go back to your idyllic beach and well-stocked sea and forest, violence will not be left aside. Your sire will not be able to protect you from the other bulls and may die trying, and others may die for your favors before the situation stabilizes itself. Forgive my bluntness, but you would find yourself Royal once more, as a thumper queen with an overlarge herd is Royal, and it might not be pleasant for you. You might wish for the death you fear in the forests ahead of us. The only solution is for us all to reach the colony."

He paused so that Ulechitzl could speak, but she did not. Very seriously he said, "If you vote to go back, so also will Pilot Brenner. If you decide to come with me, he will not leave your side. My lady, please reconsider."

Still she did not speak, but Golden Rain said, "I am sorry, Healer Nolan. Even if she were to vote with you, there would still be a majority against us."

Nolan took a deep breath and tried to keep the disappointment he felt from souring his voice as he said, "Very well, it seems that I must try to change a few minds. How large or small is this majority? Who is for me and who against, and who is most likely to be swayed? And I think we should ask the pilot to return to us, since we are not likely to say anything more that might embarrass him."

He saw the sudden look of anxiety on Ulechitzl's face, and he went on, "My lady, I will not speak to him of anything that has passed between us, and neither will Golden Rain, other than that I have been trying very hard to make you change your mind."

"You have not yet succeeded, Healer Nolan," she said, "but for your discretion I am most grateful."

It transpired that the three Nubians were two-to-one in favor of going on, the five Skandians three-to-two against, and there was a similar split among the other races with the exception of the four from Cathay who were solidly against him. Even if he could sway Ulechitzl and Brenner, he would lose by a majority of two.

"Healer," said Ulechitzl, "I am sorry. You cannot win. These people have been making up their minds for many days now, and are unlikely to change them unless . . . Are there any others here that you are charged to protect, and who might be grateful for that protection?"

"Not here, my lady," Nolan replied. "There is a man-child who is, presumably, safe with his friends in the colony and no longer in need of my protection . . ."

. . . But it might be, Nolan added silently, that the child can protect me.

"Healer," said Golden Rain suddenly, "why are you smiling?"

Nolan shook his head because the answer would soon become clear. He pointed down the hill and said, "Pilot Brenner, please ask the Cathay group to meet me under those trees in a few minutes' time. Will you ladies please excuse me while I change?"

They gazed at him openmouthed when he emerged from his tent a few moments later in full ship uniform, with his cape thrown back to reveal the brassard, given to him by Hseng Hwa before riding up with that unnamed boy in the Cathay shuttle, suspended from his neck. It was plain from her expression that Ulechitzl recognized the richly decorated gold brassard for what it was and, although it had come from a dynasty distant in time and space, it was still, Nolan hoped, a potent symbol. For yellow gold was the color of the Imperial Family, and the emblem indicated to all who saw it that its wearer was engaged on the official business of the Emperor and must be offered no let or hindrance of any kind, or refused no material or assistance on his travels in the execution of his duty.

Nolan knew that his face was red, and not from the heat, as he said awkwardly, "The meeting must be private. They might lose face and react adversely if another occidental was present. To, ah, adapt the words spoken by Brendan to his men before Tall Tree so long ago, they will do as I ask because I am their Chief.''

They continued to stare at him in silence until Ulechitzl said gravely, ''Your tunic has become loose at the waist and much too tight across the chest and shoulders. Let me remedy that, Healer, before you wear it again. That service, at least, I may do for you.''

Nolan laughed, and he was still smiling as he strode down the slope and into the trees.

That evening he delayed the count until the ship was high above the horizon, hoping that the sight would remind them of the reason why they had come to this world—to join a colony. But the voting was very close. Even though Ulechitzl and Brenner surprised him by walking to his side of the fire, accompanied by the Cathay group and his other supporters, counting his own vote there was a majority of only three. But it was a majority nonetheless, and they would all be going with him, however reluctantly.

They were dispersing silently to the tents when there came a flare of light so intense that for an instant the hillside and country all around them was bathed as in bright moonlight.

''The ship!'' cried Ulechitzl, pointing to the sky where a tiny, unnatural sun was already fading into an expanding sphere of mist. ''The ship has exploded!''

''No!'' shouted Brenner, loudly so that the others could hear him. ''No, you can still see the ship, or will when your night vision returns. It might be correcting its—''

There was another flare of artificial moonlight and, while it was still fading, another.

''It *isn't* making an orbit correction,'' Brenner shouted again, happily contradicting himself. ''That was a signal, to *us*! It waited for a cloudless night so we would see what was happening. We lit three fire-ships and it answered with three fusion explosions. At last it is telling us that it knows we are here and alive!''

There was a celebration that night, a necessarily brief one, because there was very little to eat and everyone was telling each other that they needed as much rest as possible before starting out next day. And when Nolan slept he began dreaming of Ulechitzl and of the many pleasant ways she found to pay his fees.

But the dream changed until suddenly it was Dervla's eyes that were only inches away from his face, Dervla's warm, writhing body pressing against his, and Dervla's strong, slender limbs wrapped tightly around him. It was the dream he had had many times, so perfect in every detail that it was like a vivid and oft-recalled memory of the future, except that he could not conceive of any future that included the gravity-free interior of the ship. For they were in Dervla's medical treatment room, and Nolan had been trying with one hand to get the bunk retaining strap around them, without success. Their hastily discarded coveralls were performing a weightless adagio dance in the middle of the room and they, too, were twisting and turning, with more urgency and less grace. They were bumping lightly against the ceiling, storage cabinets, and treatment tables, laughing, sometimes swearing at the obstructions, but too intent to break contact and return to the bunk. So sharp and clear was the dream that he could have read Dervla's notes on the wall charts, although he had no wish to do so, and just before they reached their frantic, gasping climax, he awoke in his tent to the sound of Brenner snoring.

Chapter 39

THEY had been journeying for one whole year and it was becoming clearer daily that the colonists hated him to a man. Only the ladies and Brenner remained on his side and they, too, were becoming so angry that the support could no longer be described as friendly. They did not want to listen to him telling stories or trying to talk to them in their own languages or, they made it plain, saying anything at all. They knew only that a year of days had passed and there was no letup to their misery.

Every few miles, there were small deep lakes that were too sheltered from the wind or hills too thickly wooded to allow Brenner to fly, so they had no knowledge of the ground ahead or the positions of the distinctively colored clumps of trees where the wild thumpers hunted their mice. They found thumper glades only when they wandered into them by chance.

The jungle was denser and more thorny than anything they had previously experienced. Several of their thumper herd were scratched so deeply that they bled to death, and Nolan used the incidents to experiment with various leaves and plant juices in the hope of discovering one with healing properties. He discovered two, a rapid coagulant and another that seemed to be a strong analgesic, because, although fully conscious, the thumper did not cry out as the others had done while it was dying.

No longer were there any private conversations, because by then everyone had learned enough of everyone else's language to understand whatever was being said, but they seldom spoke to each other or their Healer. Psychologically it was a very dangerous situation, Nolan knew, for no longer was there any suggestion of stopping and settling where they were, because they knew that they could not survive in this hot and humid and often sunless jungle. Neither did they want to try returning to the cool, idyllic beach and well-stocked forest they had left behind, because of an equal certainty that they could not survive the journey back. So they went on, hating every step of the way, because they could not be as certain of what lay ahead.

Later they were to realize how fortunate they had been in their ignorance.

On the fifteenth day of their second year of travel they encountered something very strange indeed, a track in the hitherto trackless jungle. It ran in an east-westerly direction, curving only to avoid the thicker tree trunks, and it seemed that some large and heavy animals had eaten, broken, or trampled a waist-high tunnel through the dense undergrowth. Underfoot the ground was disturbed, but not recently, because new growth had sprung up to hide any tracks that the animals might have left behind. The air felt cooler than it had been under the trees and there was a faint breeze blowing from west to east, indicating that a lake lay in that direction. Their thumpers, the queen and three well-grown cubs that were all that was left of the original herd, became very agitated and tried to run back into the trees.

"Move west," said Nolan softly. "Be very careful, go quietly, and have your weapons ready. This track was probably made by animals going to drink, animals large enough to prey on the thumpers and, possibly, us. Until we know more about them, their natural weapons and how difficult or easy they are to kill, observe but do not attack them unless they attack you."

"Healer," said Brenner, moving up beside him, "if thumpers eat mice, and these creatures and ourselves eat thumpers, theoretically we should be able to eat them. I'm thinking about the size of my next steak."

"You are not the only one," said Nolan. "But a large wounded animal can cause you damage I cannot repair. Remember that, Pilot, and save your hunger for a while."

Moving on hands and knees where the track ran like a green tunnel through the undergrowth, or walking erect where the branches overhead gave sufficient clearance, they followed the trail until it spread out and disappeared at the edge of a lake.

It was the largest body of water they had encountered in many months, with a steep, sharply defined shoreline rather than a gradual merging into swamp. The wind blowing off it was cool and steady, and the look on the pilot's face told Nolan that the assembly and flight of a new glider was high on Brenner's list of priorities. While that was being done, Nolan suggested, they could rest there for a few days, fish the lake, and hunt for thumpers, but, considering the limited medical facilities available to them, run from anything larger.

"For obvious reasons," he went on, "we will not camp on or too close to this trail, but further along the shore where it can be kept under observation. A brushwood barricade will not stop the trail-makers, so we will camp close to the water's edge and protect ourselves on the landward side within a semicircle of small fires which will be replenished throughout the night. On Earth animals fear fire, and there is no reason to believe that they are different here."

During the three days and nights that followed, none of the strange large animals appeared at the end of their trail. Neither were there any wild thumpers to be found, but the lake was full of edible fish. The colonists began talking to Nolan again, some of them in a fashion that might even be described as friendly.

In the early morning of the fourth day he discovered, lying a few paces from the water's edge, another cluster of the underwater fruit that had been the first entry in his catalog. There were five of them, each as large as small melons, and the taste was as pleasant as he remembered it, but, again, of the timid creature who had abandoned them there was no sign. This fruit, he thought, would be worth a few kindly words after that evening's meal, and if he could discover where they were growing, the colonists' words would be friendly indeed.

Nolan took one of the fishing rafts, three lightwood logs lashed together, an oar, and the spacesuit helmet, and began searching the bottom of the lake. The most comfortable position for viewing the bottom was to lie across the narrow raft with his legs in the water and his shoulders and the hand holding the helmet over his head acting as a counterbalance on the other side.

Only once did he look shoreward, when a sudden burst of shouting signaled the successful lifting of Brenner's glider. The pilot was using a strengthening wind and the surrounding hills to slope-soar for height with the intention of flying around the lake, locating thumper groves and mapping the way ahead. Nolan waved at him, then redirected his attention downward.

Below him the lake bottom continued to shelve, but the sun was directly overhead and through the visor the water looked as clear as air, until increasing depth made of it a twilight mist. Then at the very limit of his visibility he saw it, a small, lumpy carpet of green that was well-defined around its edges and slightly paler than the surrounding growths, and he knew that he was looking down at a large bed of fruit specimen one.

There must have been thousands of them.

The depth and pressure were too great to risk diving, and Nolan was wondering whether it would be possible to devise a method of trawling for them when he saw a dark, indistinct, and vaguely cylindrical object wriggling slowly across the lakebed. As he watched it closely, trying to distinguish details, the cylinder foreshortened to a dark circle, and the circle, its outlines blurred by speed and disturbed water, began to enlarge rapidly. The creature was coming straight up at him.

Gripping the side of the raft Nolan tried frantically to push his head and shoulders out of the water while swinging back his legs. Something large and hard that he did not see bumped against his knees, and for a terrible moment he thought that he was about to suffer a traumatic double amputation. But he was able to twist around until his body was lying lengthwise along the raft, without losing anything but the helmet, which was sinking slowly into the depths.

After lying motionless for a long time, and without putting his face anywhere near the water to see where the creature had gone, Nolan rowed for the shore. He had just met the reason, he was firmly convinced, why his timid amphibian benefactor preferred to eat its fruit on shore.

Nolan reported the incident on the lake that night when Brenner and his Cathay ground crew had joined the others inside the perimeter fires, warning them not to fish beyond the shallows. Brenner said that it might not be necessary to fish at all, because he had seen a thumper grove with a large herd less than two miles away and he could lead them to it. He also reported that the land to the northwest was similar to that already traversed, but that there were color differences in the vegetation covering the hilltops which suggested that they were moving into a temperate zone. They had all crowded nearer to the main fire, the better to see the sketch map that Brenner was passing around, when there came a loud, gurgling, high-pitched scream so alien and terrible in its sound that for an instant they could not move. Then suddenly they were all moving, frantically and in different directions, because the creature was among them.

It was low and heavy and large headed, with four legs and a heavy tail and skin that reflected the firelight like rippled glass. Every time it opened its mouth to make that terrifying sound, they could see the large, even teeth. For some reason it was not selecting targets, but charging about the camp, crashing through bushes and tents and perimeter fires, even scattering the main cooking fire, as if intent on devastating the whole area.

In spite of the frantic evasive action everyone was taking, there was no panic. Within a few seconds the first arrows were striking and bouncing off its thick, smooth hide. Even the spear that was jabbed into its flank was quickly shaken loose without penetrating deeply enough to slow the creature's fast, erratic movement. It turned, charged, stopped dead, or made sudden and apparently random changes of direction, making it a very difficult target in the uncertain light of the scattered and dying fires. Only once did it stop and remain still for too long.

Nolan did not see who it was who lifted a heavy stone high above his head and brought it crashing down onto the creature's skull, but the sound made him feel sick. For an instant the beast's neck and limbs went into violent spasm, then it collapsed heavily to the ground and was still.

"No more," said Nolan harshly as several others found rocks. "Leave enough of the brute for me to examine!"

"Look at the size of its head," said Brenner, allowing his rock to fall to the ground, "and the body and tail. It looks like a cross between a lion and an alligator. But, Healer, you told us that all wild creatures are afraid of fire. This one was—"

"Ignorant," said Nolan, finishing the sentence for him, "and probably curious. On Earth, animals fear fire because they have learned what it can do to them, just as our thumpers have learned. But fire to this creature was a totally new experience from which, unfortunately, it was unable to profit."

They relit the perimeter fires, but Nolan decided to wait until daylight before adding to his catalog the first creature of the New World that was capable of killing a man.

"So that we can rest easier," Nolan went on, "the night watch will be quadrupled, and they will make sure that the perimeter fires burn well and continuously until dawn. Also, in spite of your plans for hunting thumper tomorrow, until I have examined this beast thoroughly enough to devise a method of defending ourselves against it, or killing it before it can kill you, you will not move beyond shouting distance of the camp."

The rest of the night passed without incident, and the whole of the next day Nolan spent dissecting the beast and making notes and sketches for his catalog. He had no distractions, because the colonists made it plain that they found the bloody business much less interesting than he did, for as an anatomist he was being continually surprised.

When the work was completed, he decided to bury the offal and intestines rather than risk attracting any friends of the creature that had earlier attacked his raft by throwing the bloody debris into the lake. By that time it was nearly dark, the fires had been lit, and the colonists were eagerly, and hungrily, awaiting his report.

"My examination of this creature," Nolan began, trying to hide his professional excitement behind a dry lecturing voice, "shows that it is an amphibian. The gill openings on each side of the neck and the lung structure enable it to breathe either air or water. While its teeth are large and fearsome enough, they seem more suited to cropping and chewing rather than to tearing flesh and are, I would say, the teeth of a ruminant rather than a carnivore, an assumption supported by the fact that the digestive mechanism includes three stomachs.

"The creature's four limbs appear disproportionately short in comparison to the length of the body," he went on, "which in mass approximates that of an Earthly cow, and give it the appearance of a shortened, smooth-skinned alligator. The legs are of unequal size and strength, with the rear pair being thick, heavily muscled, and terminating in broad, three-toed, webbed feet. Judging by the weight of the tail, which projects behind the rear legs by half the overall body length, they form the body's point of balance as well as its primary means of locomotion which, considering its amphibian nature, may not be as rapid as last night's combination of surprise and darkness led us to believe. The forelimbs are thinner and longer, with smaller feet that have less webbing between the toes. I would say that their primary purpose is to bring food close to the mouth, or to steady the creature while it is eating from trees."

The unsteady firelight made it difficult to read their expressions, but Nolan thought that his use of words like cow and ruminant and grazing had eased their minds, and he was pleased that he could give them even better tidings.

"Although the head was badly damaged, as you know," he resumed, "it revealed several interesting features. On each side of the skull there is an oval of tightly stretched skin protected, like the eyes, by a raised, bony ridge. These must be the ears, and apart from the mouth, there are no other cranial openings. The creature might not possess a sense of smell, which would explain the scorch damage to its eyes and the inside of its mouth. It would also explain the apparent attack on the camp and the terrible sounds it was making.

"Rather than being a predator," Nolan continued, "I would say that our attacker was a stupid or curious, but very unfortunate, animal who blundered into the camp, burned its eyes, mouth lining, and throat in one of the perimeter fires, and, unable to see and in great pain, charged blindly in all directions in an attempt to escape from a hurt that was new to its experience."

Nolan shook his head, feeling sorry for the creature that could have so easily injured someone, then went on. "The eyes and mouth are its most vulnerable areas, the skin being thick and difficult to penetrate. If its meat is edible and you have to kill one in the future, it would be best to use a strengthened spear and strike upward through the roof of the mouth into the brain. If it proves inedible, then I see no reason to forbid a thumper hunt tomorrow."

Around the fire they were all smiling up at him or shouting approval, and the watch-keepers on the perimeter applauded briefly. But as he was cutting off a complete forelimb for roasting, he thought cynically that he should enjoy his popularity while he could, because soon they would have to resume their trek to the colony and their Healer would become once again a person they would be pleased to hate.

The piece of boiled meat he tried was tough, stringy, and had a strong taste, but roasted it was slightly more palatable. Nolan was laughing and wondering aloud if the consistency was due to the creature being old as well as tough, when he became aware that everyone had stopped talking and was staring toward the edge of the lake. Still chewing and holding the roasted leg in both hands, he turned quickly to see what they were looking at.

Silently and with scarcely a ripple they were emerging from the lake, climbing the bank and moving closer while others were moving beyond the perimeter fires to encircle the camp. He could see that a few of the creatures were smaller than the previous night's visitor, but the majority were much larger. They were holding what looked like stone knives in their three-fingered hands, or large rocks, and he would not have been surprised if the satchels hung from their necks contained more ammunition.

They stopped at a distance of about twenty paces from the fire, and it seemed that hundreds of eyes were reflecting the flickering red light.

Nolan cursed silently but with great fervor, and wished that he was holding in his hands something else, anything else, but that partially eaten forelimb.

Chapter 40

THE creatures did not attack them, and the humans, following a sharp warning from Nolan, did not try to defend themselves prematurely with their puny spears and arrows and even punier muscles. He had been the only one to speak until then, and for a long time it seemed to make him the center of the amphibians' attention. Many three-fingered hands were waved in his direction, or at the disemboweled and partially dismembered carcass at his feet, and he could not tell whether the high-pitched, modulated gobblings being directed at him were expressions of anger, interrogation, or accusation. But if their positions had been reversed, he would not have been in any doubt about the matter.

He stood with his back to the fire, looking at each of the nearest alien faces in turn, and unable to make a sound. At any moment he expected a heavy tail to swing around and knock him to the ground, and for the rocks and stone knives to bludgeon and tear into his body. Then suddenly they turned away from him, and six of them began moving through the camp, looking into the tents, at the tethered thumpers, lifting and dropping cooking utensils, spears, unstrung bows, articles of clothing, and gobbling at each other without pause. With every change of direction they collapsed tents or jostled people with their tails. The damage was considerable but not, Nolan thought, deliberate.

One of their tails swung dangerously close to the fire. Nolan pushed it away, and when its owner gobbled shrilly at him, he thrust the roasted forelimb he was still holding into the fire and withdrew it quickly, then pointed at the charred flesh and to the other's tail. He did this several times before the creature backed away, still making its guttural, gobbling sounds.

Suddenly it swung around and began moving toward the bank, where it disappeared with hardly a splash into the waters of the lake. The other five who had been moving about the camp turned at once and followed it, as did the other amphibians lining the bank.

Beyond the perimeter fires, however, there were more than two hundred of them who remained standing in a semicircle that touched the bank on both sides of the camp. And from the trees behind them came sounds of rustling foliage and the snapping of branches, a noise that continued throughout the night.

By first light the amphibians guarding them had disappeared, although farther inland he could still hear a few of them talking together. Either the colonists had finally gone to sleep or were worrying silently in their tents, so Nolan began to move slowly but not silently past the dead perimeter fires and into the trees.

Before he had gone more than a few paces, the trees and underbrush disappeared and he found himself in a wide, straight, and freshly made trail that stretched for about fifty yards in both directions before turning sharply to continue in the direction of the lakeside. At each corner stood three of the amphibians, positioned so that they could see along all three sides of the trail which now enclosed the entire campsite.

When they saw him, all six guards stopped talking, but they remained motionless until he began crossing the trail toward the trees on the other side, then one of them came running ponderously toward him. It stopped, swung its tail around to bar his way, then used it to push him back the way he had come. He could easily have avoided the creature and run into the trees, but with up to six of them chasing him, Nolan did not think that he could have escaped either the pursuit or serious injury.

To show that he understood the situation he raised one hand, slowly so that it would not be mistaken as a threatening gesture, and retraced his steps to the still-sleeping camp and beyond it to the water's edge. There he pushed out one of the fishing rafts and began paddling slowly and cautiously away from the shore.

Sky reflection prevented Nolan from seeing below the surface, and he had lost the spacesuit helmet, but it seemed that he had the entire lake to himself. There was not a single amphibian to be seen and he was not impeded in any way. After paddling and drifting until sunrise, he turned back, but steered toward the shore about half a mile west of the point where he had set out.

He was moving into the shallows and was only a moment from touching the bank when six blunt amphibian heads broke the water around him and a dozen three-fingered hands gripped the sides of his raft and began pushing it along the shore toward the camp.

There was a small heap of the underwater fruit, more than enough to feed everyone in the camp for a day, lying on the bank when he arrived. He stood looking at it for a long time, wondering. The first time fruit had been left like this, on the evening of the landing more than a year ago, he had assumed that it had been abandoned rather than deliberately placed there. Had they lingered for a few more days on the shores of that lake, would they ever have been allowed to leave it? Had the fruit been a gift, or bait, and what were the implications in either event? After traveling more than half the distance to the colony, would they be allowed to complete the journey? He was also wondering, fearfully and selfishly, what punishment the amphibians would mete out for his act of cannibalism.

But it was not until the colonists had tried vainly to escape and been knocked down or driven back several times by the heavy amphibian tails that Nolan had a chance to speak to all of them at the same time.

"Listen to me," he said in a loud, confident voice, "and think on my words. We have been captured, but we are not necessarily to be killed, for that could have been done very easily last night. While we are forbidden to move inland to hunt thumpers, the lake is open to us for fishing because they have a great advantage over us in water. Also, they have left us a supply of their fruit, which suggests that they do not intend to starve us to death. And consider this: Except for the first one who visited us last night, and who might not have intended to come ashore but was attracted to the camp by curiosity, they wear foot coverings of thumper skin. My guess is that their feet are used primarily for swimming and are susceptible to injury when moving on land.

"So please disabuse yourselves of any idea that they are animals, or even ignorant savages," Nolan went on. "They are tool-using, intelligent beings, perhaps highly intelligent although not technically advanced beings, as is proved by the way they have contained us. And like all intelligent beings they have curiosity, so we must—"

"Healer Nolan," said the Nubian, K'Laumbiri, interrupting him in a voice made harsh with fear, "is it not more likely that they have herded us together, allowing us to fish and giving us fruit, with the intention of fattening us for the kill? To them we must look thin and puny indeed, and they may be hoping to improve our edibility. On Earth there are tribes who are intelligent, but not civilized, who practice cannibalism on . . . I'm sorry, Healer. That was indelicate of me."

Nolan forced himself to smile at the Nubian's sudden embarrassment, and said, "Considering the fact that it was us, or rather I myself, who committed the first act of cannibalism here, it was most indelicate. I do not know with certainty whether or not the creatures eat meat, but their triple stomach and digestive system is more suited to a vegetable diet.

"But as I was about to say," he continued, "if the amphibians are curious about us, it is to our advantage, and may even be the best means of extending our lives, if we increase that curiosity. Without frightening them so much that they would attack us, we should show them that in some respects we are their superiors. For example, since the lake is available to us, I want you to build a large enough raft to enable Pilot Brenner to fly his glider. That should certainly impress them. But we must also keep a few secrets from them, our bows and arrows, for example, and how we make fire. And until we are in a position to escape with the maximum chance of success and minimum danger to all of us, we must at all times be well-behaved and docile captives."

"Healer," said Brenner, "I do not understand you. They are not to know about fire and our weapons, but you want us to show them how to *fly*?"

"I am hoping," said Nolan, "that the only creature to observe the bows in use died shortly thereafter and, for my own sake, that from the condition of the charred limb I was holding, its friends think that it was killed only by the fire, a strange and dangerous magic. The very idea of fire must be a hard one for aquatic creatures to understand, much less put to use, and the concept of aerial flight on a world without birds, and whose creatures never leave the surface, would be even more difficult to grasp."

"Do not be too sure of that, Healer," said Brenner quietly. "A fish is well-used to movement in three dimensions."

Nolan did not have an answer to that, so he went on, "First we must try to understand them, discover what they think we are, and whether it is curiosity alone that made them capture us. I thought of trying to talk to one of the six who investigated the camp, and who appear to be leaders of some kind, with a view to learning a few words of their language. It is a strange language, which seems to be composed mainly of vowel sounds, and seems almost to be sung as much as spoken.

"Perhaps you, Chiang Ku," he went on, looking at one of the Cathay colonists, "would advise me in this matter. When I have identified one of their leaders, that is. At present I am unable to tell one amphibian's face from another."

"I understand, respected Healer," the other replied, his yellow features remaining bland and impassive. "My name is Hsung Toi."

His mistake had not been as funny as all that, Nolan thought as he felt his face burn with embarrassment. But it was the first time since they had left their idyllic bay on the inland sea that he had heard them laughing.

During the year that they had been together, Nolan had gained his knowledge of all the languages spoken by the colonists, and they tried very hard to advise him. But for some reason the amphibian who seemed to be in authority would speak only to the Healer and with all other persons, amphibian and human alike, excluded from the proceedings.

As a result, after many hours of pantomiming and mispronunciation, the first word spoken by the creature to him was "Nolan," and his first word to it was "Allumlel," with the first and third syllables pitched lower than the second. The next words exchanged followed a lengthy period of finger-drawing on a stretch of muddy bank, and they were "Man" and "Ull." Progress after that was slow, but steady.

There was an unusually long period of calm weather, more than two months of it, which kept Brenner's glider firmly attached to its launching raft. When he did fly, there was great excitement, or perhaps agitation, among the watching amphibians, and Allumlel did not visit Nolan that day. But when Brenner flew the following morning, gaining enough height to slope-soar off the surrounding hills, the entire lake was dotted with thousands of amphibian heads watching him. Within minutes of Brenner's return, following a totally unnecessary and exhibitionistic double-S turn and landing on the raft, Allumlel was in the camp wanting to talk to Nolan.

It insisted on talking to him for the rest of the day instead of for the customary two hours, and during the days that followed Nolan was scarcely allowed time to eat. His throat was raw and sore from trying to reproduce sentences that sounded like gurgling, off-key songs, and the alien song-speech seemed to fill his very dreams. But suddenly he discovered that he could distinguish the face of Allumlel from all the others, and that he was beginning to understand what the Eldest of the Six was saying to him more easily than he could the heavily accented words of some of his own Teutons and Nubians and Mesopotamians.

But the intellectual challenge and excitement of communicating with a member of a thinking extra-Solar race, surely the most important and unique experience for any human being, was being diluted by his own personal fear.

Even though the amphibians had not harmed any of their captives so far, Nolan was still uncertain of his own fate at their strong, three-fingered hands. Did they consider him personally responsible for killing as well as eating the first member of their species he had met, and what, ultimately, were they going to do about it?

More than fear, Nolan hated uncertainty.

Allumlel had been questioning him about their tents and the reason why the humans had to shelter themselves from the falling sky water that did no more than soothe dry skin, and had gone on to ask why it was necessary to place their food on the piece of that sun-stuff that he called a fire, when Nolan decided that his fears should no longer be hidden.

"The fire kills the harmful insects that might live within the body," Nolan replied, "and sometimes improves its taste. But fire is a dangerous magic which the Ull people do not need. It can escape and consume whole forests, and the creatures within them, as it does a few twigs. It caused the death of the first Ull to visit us. I am sorry that it died, Allumlel, and for what was done to its body."

Allumlel inclined its head in a gesture that in a human would have suggested polite disbelief. "Magic," it said, "is a word that adult Ull use to children when describing matters which the young find too difficult to understand. You are not speaking to a child,

Nolan, and I am curious about all matters, even those for which I may have no use."

Nolan was still trying to think of a suitable reply when the amphibian went on, "Illamsul was a great and much-respected Ull, but very old and with eyes that could scarcely see. Its mind had become as a child's, with the intense curiosity and impulsiveness of a child. It should not have visited your camp alone. But it did, and died, and you, a stranger whose words show an ignorance of our laws, ate it in part. What you did with the other parts, their burial in the ground, was your responsibility and according to your laws. The body itself is not important.

"The body," said Allumlel, gesturing toward the campsite, "is as an empty tent."

Be careful, Nolan thought. They seemed to be moving into the realms of theology, and that was dangerous ground for even a believer to tread, much more an unbeliever like himself. He said carefully, "I would learn more about your laws and customs so that I will not, in my ignorance, give offense. Is there anything that should have been done about the aged and respected Illamsul that was not done?"

Allumlel bobbed its head in the sign of affirmation it had learned from Nolan, and with one finger traced out a rectangle that was about twenty inches wide and six deep across the skin of its chest.

"This piece of skin should not have been buried, Nolan," it said. "It will be unpleasant for you if you decide to retrieve it now. But the insects of the ground find our skin as difficult to eat as do the small fish of the lake and it, at least, will be undamaged."

"Good," said Nolan. "Tomorrow I shall give it to you."

For a moment Allumlel was so still that Nolan wondered if he had given an even greater offense, but then it said, "If that is what you wish."

Apparently no offense had been taken, and Nolan did not know what else he could have done with the piece of Ull skin. He would discuss this amphibian equivalent of scalp-taking with Golden Rain at the earliest opportunity in the hope that it might increase his understanding of the situation. His strongest feeling was of relief that his unknown act of cannibalism had not been considered a great crime. But he had forgotten that intense relief, like drunkenness or pleasure or any other sudden release of tension, could lead to carelessness of speech.

"I am pleased," he said with great feeling, "that my actions in the matter of Illumsel's death have not offended you. I, ah, had thought that you might wish to eat me."

"Nolan!" said Allumlel, and there was no mistaking the anger in its voice. "You are indeed ignorant of our ways. Your suggestion is improper, impertinent, and shows no consideration for my feelings. You must never ask such—"

"My deepest apologies, Allumlel," said Nolan quickly, wondering what he had said to bring on such an angry reaction, "but I am, indeed, ignorant and intended no offense. From now onward let me answer your questions, and hope to avoid insulting you further."

Allumlel was silent for a long time, then it said, "Nolan, there are times when I forget that you come from far away, that you breathe only air, and that your thoughts and customs are different from ours. I would never speak thus to another Ull, but it seems that this is of great importance to you, and has been troubling your mind, so I shall speak of it to you."

The Eldest of the Six looked at the ground for a moment, making Nolan wonder if it was feeling embarrassment, then went on, "The Ull eat only the things that grow on the land or in the water, so that meat, even the small portions required by the rituals, rests uneasily with us. But when the aged and greatly loved Illamsul died alone among strangers, you, for whatever reason, ate of its flesh and preserved its soul within you. And in the time you have been here, your people have shown us great wonders. There is the man-carrying fish of the air and the raft which, with the help of the winds, moves over the lake faster than we can swim. The worth of your life is a matter for others to judge, to consider well and to decide upon, and it is improper of you to show curiosity or try to influence their deliberations while you are alive."

Allumlel looked up at him again before going on, "For all these reasons, Nolan, when the time comes for you to die, we shall eat a part of you and keep your soul and all its strangeness and knowledge within us. It is also likely that we will eat the one who swims in the air like a fish. The others would not be considered worthy."

It was Nolan's turn to be silent as he tried to assimilate these new revelations, and Allumlel watched him without speaking. It was probable, he thought wildly, that it thinks me struck dumb with gratitude at being granted immortality and is giving me time to regain my composure. He did not have the right words for this situation, and for the first time since leaving the ship he wished that Monsignor O'Riordan was with him to advise on these spiritual matters. To his great relief it was the Eldest who spoke first.

"I have more questions," it said.

"Ask them," said Nolan.

"Three of your people are different from the others," said Allumlel. "Their skins are dark, as dark as those of the Ull. Are they your egg-layers?"

"No," he replied, glad that the Nubians had not overheard the question. "There are many colors of skin among our people."

"So I have seen," said the Eldest. "How many of them are egg-layers, and what are their bodily differences? Are you one of them?"

Allumlel's curiosity and questions were unending, and it was more than willing to answer as well as ask them. But words were not enough for this exchange of information, so they had to spend the following two hours with their feet in the lake while they talked and sketched on the dried mud of the bank the reproductive mechanisms of their respective species. So calm and clinical was the discussion that it might have been talking place between two obstetricians on Earth, and Nolan would have much additional data to add to his catalog pages on the Ull life-form. But he was glad nonetheless that neither Ulechitzl nor Golden Rain came to watch what they were doing.

"It is strange that your young are born without the protection of shells," said the Eldest when they had climbed once again onto dry ground, "like the unintelligent animals of the land. And that you are as the thumpers, with only two young-layers to serve the needs of fourteen threes of men. We Ull mate in pairs, and usually for life."

"As do we," said Nolan excitedly. At last he was being given the chance to move the conversation onto the subject of their capture, and with luck he might be able to find out how long their imprisonment was likely to last. As yet he had not spoken or tried to explain graphically about interstellar flight or the reasons for the presence of the colony, so he tried to keep the words and ideas as simple as possible even though, in the process, he would be forced to tell lies. He continued, "A mistake was made when we came to this place. The mistake caused us to land on the wrong shore, and very far from the place where our friends await us. The two young-bearers have mates in that place, as have the others among us.

"Eldest of the Six," he went on, hoping to flatter Allumlel by the use of its title, "our feelings and needs are those of any Ull in this situation. You must realize that we are anxious to be joined again with our mates. When may we leave you and resume our journey?"

Allumlel looked at him steadily for a long moment, then it said, "Never."

"But . . . but that is not *right*!," Nolan protested angrily.

"It is, however, necessary," said the Eldest. "The Six have deliberated upon this matter long and often, and that is our decision. You will all remain here, and those who try too often to escape will die sooner than the others. You will never leave this place while you live."

Chapter 41

FOR the next few days Nolan talked to the Eldest, but without satisfying its curiosity about any new subject. He thought that Allumlel was intelligent enough to understand, following the news that the humans' imprisonment was to be life-long, that a degree of noncooperation was to be expected. It showed impatience rather than anger and it volunteered more and more information about itself and its people, and its curiosity about all things human was at least the equal of Nolan's regarding the Ull. As a result the barrier to the exchange of information became a temporary one.

He was again talking freely to the Eldest, but with his own people he thought it kinder to dilute the truth.

"We must face the unpleasant fact," he told them at the end of his nightly progress report, "that the amphibians are very reluctant to let us go. On a simpler and perhaps more violent level, their behavior is as ours would have been if members of an extra-Solar race had crash-landed on Earth. They want to know all there is to know about us and, although I have not tried to threaten them in any way, they are afraid of what we or the others of our kind might do to them if we escaped. They will not harm us unless we try to escape, so we will therefore put all thoughts of escape from our minds. Let that be clearly understood by everyone.

"If any of you were to die in an escape attempt," he went on, in a tone that brooked no interruption, "retribution would surely follow in time. It might be in a short or a long time, either through the vengeful and suicidal anger of ourselves or that of our friends, or more likely their descendants, of the colony. That must not be allowed to happen. Unexpectedly, we are being forced to share this world with another intelligent race.

"We must do so in peace."

Nolan stared slowly from face to face, waiting for a response. Their eyes reflected the firelight but their lips remained closed.

"Every night I shall teach you what I have learned of their language," he continued in a gentler voice, "and I want you to practice it among yourselves and with the amphibians. Be friendly toward them, answer their questions, keep them interested in everything about us. Soon I will be ready to tell the Eldest about the ship, the colony, and where we come from. That should give the Council of Six something to think about. As well, I am certain that Allumlel is beginning to sympathize with our position and would have no personal objection to letting us go. For that reason I want to do it a favor. That is why some of you will be allowed into the forest—with an amphibian escort, naturally—to collect lightwood for another and larger glider. The Eldest has expressed the wish to fly."

"Impossible!" said Brenner, his voice almost drowned by the sudden burst of laughter from the others. The pilot ignored them and went into a technical discussion on wing loadings, the greatly increased wingspan and area of lifting surface needed to support a payload three times the weight of a man, not to mention the suicidal stupidity of a being wanting to take to the air in total ignorance of the basic principles of flight. The argument continued for more than two hours before Brenner and the Healer reached a compromise.

Allumlel would fly, but suspended from kites rather than in a glider.

"Before you go to your tents," said Nolan, "let me remind you that we must all work with the intention of making it seem much more profitable, in terms of knowledge and satisfied curiosity, for the Ull to let us go rather than keep us here. Someday, perhaps sooner than you think, we will be leaving this place. But we must talk, not fight, our way out of it."

They were all looking at him and, for some reason, smiling, because their teeth were reflecting the light of the dying fire. It was Golden Rain who laughed softly and broke the silence.

"We were waiting for you to remind us yet again," she said, "that all this had happened before."

Going aloft under three stepped kites had happened before, Nolan told Allumlel reassuringly, to Brenner before the pilot had built his more complicated and unsafe glider. Even so, Brenner had damaged himself on two occasions and had been unable to walk for a long time. Such an accident was unlikely to happen to Allumlel, because it would lift from a raft and fly only above the waters of the lake, and their meager supply of rope would ensure that it did not rise very far. However, if the Eldest wished to reconsider its decision, or perhaps ask a younger and lighter Ull to make the first ascent, Nolan would understand.

"No other Ull is sufficiently damaged in the mind," said Allumlel. "And Eldest is my title, air-breather, not a measure of my age. I am ready."

In spite of the many warnings to move clear, the water around the launching raft was black with amphibian heads large and small. The wind from across the lake was freshening by the moment, and two of the three kites were already aloft and tugging at the third which was being held with difficulty by the Cathay ground crew. Then suddenly they released it and the Eldest was snatched into the air to hang bobbing and swaying at the end of thirty feet of rope.

"Higher!" shouted Allumlel. "Higher!"

"Pay out a little more line," said Nolan quietly, "then tie down your end. I don't want to risk—"

A freak gust of wind jerked the anchor rope and, judging from their involuntary cries of pain, a lot of skin from the hands of the flight crew. So strong was it that the three kites were being pushed almost vertically into the air, and suddenly Allumlel was hanging fifty, sixty, then more than one hundred feet above them and being blown toward the trees. Then just as quickly the wind lessened and, without the anchor rope to stabilize them, the kites lost height rapidly. But not rapidly enough. Instead of dropping into the lake, the Eldest crashed into the side of a tree that overhung the water.

The two upper kites were still in clear air and were tugging at the wreckage of the third in which Allumlel and its harness was entangled, gradually dislodging it from the branches. Nolan dived off the raft and, followed by Brenner and the flight crew, swam furiously toward the place where the Eldest would fall.

With a tremendous splash it dropped more than twenty feet into the water to float, twitching feebly, on its back. Nolan took one look at its injuries, and cursed.

"Bring a raft here and run it aground," he said urgently. "Spread a ground sheet over it and help me lift the patient on board. With wounds like that it should not be dragged up a muddy bank. Boil plenty of water and keep the containers covered while it is cooling. I'll need my surgical pack; at least the sutures are sterile. Quickly."

They had to stand waist deep in the shallows while the Eldest was lifted carefully onto a fishing raft. The amphibians who had been crowding around them had withdrawn, leaving only five of their number behind. Nolan was still unable to recognize their features, but he knew that they were the other members of the Council of Six. He was trying to think of something to say to them when Allumlel spoke.

"I did not know," it said in a voice so quiet that Nolan could barely hear it, "that the gentle water could feel so . . . so *hard*. But, Nolan, I looked down on all of you, and across the tops of the trees to the other lakes."

Before Nolan could reply, one of the Six said, "Stranger, Allumlel's wounds are too many and deep to heal. Put it back into the water. We will take it to the Place of Parting and tell it stories to take its mind from the pain, and comfort it while its blood and its life return to the waters of the lake."

"No!" said Nolan, his voice sharp with the anger of helplessness, and the impending loss of a being whose mind and personality he had grown to admire. Desperately he sought for the right words, knowing that they would not understand him as well as Allumlel. He told them the Eldest would not, or might not, die, because he, Nolan, could repair damaged bodies. He had repaired Brenner after two similar flying accidents and the pilot still lived. The body of the burned Illamsul, he told them, had been opened up and cut into pieces so that he could understand its structure and its workings, and be able to repair the bodies of damaged Ull. He did not know the cadences of the language well enough to express emotion, or to plead, so all he could say was that he wanted a chance to save the life of his friend.

The Councillors stared at him, their expressions unreadable, and made no reply. It was Allumlel who broke the silence. Weakly but so rapidly that Nolan could not understand them, it said a few words and suddenly the five were gone.

"Thank you, Allumlel," said Nolan, wanting to say so much more. He cleared his throat and went on, "For what I have to do, you should be asleep. There are dried leaves and berries which, when eaten in small quantities, put thumpers and humans to sleep, but their effect on an Ull might be harmful. I am sorry, Allumlel, but it is likely that while I am working you will suffer a greater pain."

"Then, we will talk," said the Eldest. "You will tell me what you see, what you are doing, and what is in your mind."

The recent words of the Councillor came back to Nolan. It seemed that the Ull were accustomed to using a form of verbal anesthesia, and talked and told stories to the dying in order to take their minds off the terminal pain. He would have to treat this as he would a lecture on surgical procedure, except that he would be addressing the patient instead of a gallery of students.

He began with a brief description of the type and severity of the injuries before discussing the operative procedure. During the patient's heavy lateral contact with the tree, two branches had snapped off obliquely and the sharp edges of the stumps had inflicted two deep, traumatic incisions running from the left side of the lower chest to the lower abdominal area forward of the legs. Wood splinters were present in each of the wounds, one of them deep enough to show the underlying intestine, which was also damaged. The left forelimb had sustained a simple fracture and a few minor cuts and abrasions, but it was the more serious abdominal injuries that must be given priority.

"How long is it since you have eaten?" asked Nolan. Allumlel replied with another question, and it seemed that pain had made it angry.

"Why do you ask me this?" it said. "Surely you could ask more important questions, or go on telling me what is in your mind, for I cannot see what you are doing. But the answer is that I was so excited by the prospect of flying that I have eaten nothing for more than a day, and I am hungry as well as in pain."

"Good," said Nolan, vastly relieved. He went on, "My reason for asking is this: There is a hollow tube inside you which carries the parts of the food that your body cannot use to the place where you push out this waste material. This material is bad, very harmful if it should escape from the tube, because it contains tiny insects called germs. These insects are too small for you to see, but they can burrow into your flesh and cause it to rot, and the rot would spread through your body and kill you. If you have not eaten for a long time, the rot is less likely to start.

"That is why I am washing out your wounds with water that has been heated over a fire until all the tiny insects in it have been killed," he continued, with no pause in his work. "Then I will close the tear in your waste tube, with fibers that will melt away when the healing is complete, and remove the splinters from the larger wounds and clean them before drawing the edges together with stronger fibers that will not melt but will have to be removed when their work is done. I will then wash and repair your fore-limb, and hold it still between pieces of wood until the broken bone grows together and mends.

"You must move as little as possible until you are completely healed," Nolan went on. "Your wounds must be kept dry, because your blood forms a glue that joins the edges and holds them together while they heal. If you were to walk or swim too soon, the wounds would open or the glue would soften, your blood would leak away, the germs would enter, the rot would start, and you would die. If your body needs to be wetted at times, we will pour water from the lake over your skin. But not in the places where there are wounds, because the lake water is not clean.

"Is there anything more about the treatment that you would like to know?"

"There is," said Allumlel. "Are you always so careful with those you repair?"

Nolan clenched his teeth together very hard, to keep himself from bursting into hysterical laughter. He had no sterile gown or mask or surgical gloves, and he was kneeling in nearly three feet of muddy water with Ulechitzl and Brenner, who were likewise half-submerged, assisting him. It was hardly a suitable environment for major surgery, and it was a moment before he could trust himself to speak.

"Yes," he said.

By the time Nolan had inserted the last suture, the sun was sinking behind the trees on the other side of the lake, the shallows were filled with anxious Ull, and the bank was crowded with silent colonists and five amphibians, no doubt the other members of the Council, standing among them. For the first time since the accident, he realized that all of them were outside the guarded boundary around the camp, and the Ull did not seem to mind.

He was very tired, and even more angry with himself because he did not know what forms of infection would grow within those neatly closed wounds, or if the body, for all its size and strength, would be able to resist it. And he knew nothing about the Ull sensorium other than that his patient had suffered severe and continual pain without complaint. He hoped that its friends were adept or inventive enough to tell it stories that would make it forget its discomfort, but he doubted it. He was wondering if there was anything he could do to help in that respect when he saw Hsung Toi among the watchers, and spoke briefly to him before returning his attention to the patient.

Allumlel was staring at one of the tiny scraps of skin and flesh that Nolan had trimmed from the ragged edges of the larger abdominal wound prior to suturing, and it was obvious what was going through the other's mind. But this was not the time for uncertainties, Nolan decided, because no patient was ever helped by a Healer who expressed doubts or made excuses in advance for a possible failure.

"I would be honored to eat it, friend Allumlel," said Nolan gravely, "but I shall not do so. You are not, nor are you likely to become, an empty tent. Only one more thing needs to be done, and you will be pleased to know that it is not painful."

Hsung Toi returned as he finished speaking and went to work. Allumlel submitted, but not without question.

"You have done many strange things to me, Nolan," it said, "and given even stranger reasons why they were done. My head was not injured, but . . . Is this a treatment that will affect my mind?"

I hope so, Nolan thought fervently.

He pointed at the pictograph on Brenner's forehead and said, "It is not a medical treatment, Allumlel. It is a decoration, but one that is worn only by those who swim in the sky."

Chapter 42

THAT night he lit a fire on the bank so that he could keep watch on Allumlel and gave instructions that he was to be wakened if there was any change in the patient's condition, but he could not sleep. Instead, he talked to his patient during the brief intervals when the other members of the Council of Six were not doing so, and every hour he irrigated the uninjured areas of its body, having discovered that the amphibians slept more comfortably under water. At other times he listened, trying to understand as much as possible of what was being said, even though the beings concerned and the rules and reasons for their behavior were often impossible for him to comprehend. But he made two interesting discoveries: The stories being told were based on incidents in the history of the Ull, and his patient, Allumlel, was an egg-layer.

When Nolan tried to tell a story about mankind, it quickly turned into an argument among the six baffled Councillors and himself as to what he was talking about, and with Allumlel complaining loudly that the effort to understand the meaning of Nolan's words had given it a pain in its head. It did not, he noted, mention its other pains. As a communicator Nolan was disappointed; as a Healer, pleased.

Except for a marked lassitude and slurring of speech, which was probably due to its being awake all night, he could see no change in Allumlel's condition next day, but that in itself meant very little. If infection and consequent inflammation had been present along the suture lines, the skin coloration and thickness would have prevented it from showing itself. Trying not to worry the Eldest unduly, he explained his problem—a total ignorance regarding Ull vital signs—and how best it could be solved. Allumlel suggested that Eolsaa, the Second Eldest, although it was in fact much older than the Eldest and becoming set in its ways, might be prevailed on to volunteer, but that it would not be easy.

It was not too difficult to get Eolsaa to hold the clinical thermometer in its mouth for the necessary few moments without biting or swallowing it, but then came the difficult part. The place where a main artery ran closest to the surface and where the skin was thinnest, making it the best position to measure the pulse and blood pressure, was in the posterior region at the base of the tail, and this was not a place that should be touched by strangers. After much argument and discussion about the clinical detachment and impersonal touchings of human Healers, it was agreed that Nolan would perform this highly embarrassing procedure and take its pulse. But not until everyone not directly concerned, Human and Ull alike, withdrew from sight.

With the vital signs of a normally well Ull as a guide, Nolan checked his patient. The blood pressure, which he could not measure with accuracy in any case, was virtually the same. The pulse was much slower, although the rapid heartbeat in Eolsaa's case could have been due to its embarrassment, but the body temperature was definitely elevated. He told Allumlel that it was normal for the body to warm itself so as to assist the healing process, and that there was nothing to worry about. He tried very hard to believe his own words.

For the next two days the Eldest's temperature remained high, then in the space of a few hours it returned to normal. Allumlel talked with one or more of the Councillors for the greater part of the day, but with Nolan it argued. It wanted to be allowed off the raft before the logs put deep trenches in its side that would last for life. It wanted to swim and walk the lake bottom, and sleep with the comfort of the water pressing down on it. In vain did Nolan explain that if it swam too soon, its wounds would open and its life leak away, that the pressure at the lake bottom might force germs into those unhealed wounds even if they did not open, and they would rot. Allumlel wanted these things and the manner of its asking was not polite.

Clinically, Nolan reminded himself, a quarrelsome patient was a good sign. He relented to the extent of moving the raft into deeper water and allowing the Eldest to immerse itself for a few moments whenever it felt the need, but without making any strenuous movements. It was not allowed to walk on the muddy bank or the lake bottom.

Except for the times when he visited the camp to eat, report progress, and urge everyone to remain patient in their captivity, the other Councillors and himself remained with Allumlel. They exchanged stories that were nothing less than history lessons, and they talked or argued with increasing fluency and greater understanding. It was becoming clear to Nolan that for the first time since the accident, they were no longer expecting his patient to die and, in their own particular fashion, they were grateful to him.

Somehow he had to make the Ull understand that they could show their gratitude in only one way, by setting his people free.

There were times when Allumlel seemed to be in favor of this measure, and argued on Nolan's side, but the other members of the Six were completely against it.

"You tell us of great wonders," said Eolsaa, following one particularly impassioned and, Nolan thought, logically well-supported plea. "You speak of an immense raft pushed on its journey between the stars by small bursting suns, a raft that enclosed its own air and in which your people slept in a coldness so deep that there is nothing to equal it on this world, and out of our respect for you we may not speak aloud our disbelief. And you tell us of lesser wonders, of swimming in the sky, which you have shown to be true, of the ways by which you repair living things, of litters pushed by fire and water, and of growing plants that can be woven into your body coverings, or used to make paper that you cover with the markings that tell your stories without need of words. This is not good knowledge and we would as soon hide it in our minds and tell it not to our young, so that it will be erased from our history. We fear this knowledge, and we fear what it will do to the Ull if your people discover us.

"I say again, Nolan the Healer, your people must not be allowed to leave this place."

The position had not altered in the slightest, but that did not mean Nolan had to be silent on the subject. He had learned that the Ull enjoyed his arguments even when there was no hope of his winning one. They enjoyed talking because it was the only form of shared mental recreation they had, and he was a stranger whose arguments were strange indeed.

Nolan was silent for a moment while he ordered his thoughts, then he said, "When you tell the story of a great event, it changes in the telling because the teller adds or ignores parts of the truth for dramatic effect. This makes it more interesting. But the story of the kites and the glider by which Allumlel and Brenner were able to fly must be changeless, accurate in regard to materials and measurements, and this can only be done by telling them onto paper, if others are to fly in safety—"

"But we do not want to fly," one of the Six broke in.

"Too many of the Ull witnessed it for the story to be forgotten," said Nolan. "Allumlel has flown once and briefly. It, and in time others, will want to fly again. At our main colony you will be given the silent stories that will teach you how to fly in safety, and taught how to grow and weave the grasses to make the light and very strong coverings needed for your gliders, which will have to be much larger than those used by us. Having learned to use them, you will be able to carry stories between your brothers in other lakes, quickly and above the forest instead of walking for many days through it. There are many things that Man can teach you, and learn from you."

"There are many things they could do to us," said the Second Eldest, "if they knew we were here. We respect you, Healer Nolan, but we fear Man."

"But there is no reason to fear us, Eolsaa," said Nolan, wishing that he had a God to pray to for inspiration. "Our numbers in the colony are less than the Ull in this single lake. We hope to have many children in time, but they will never equal the numbers of your own people. My people here wish only to be joined with their own kind. They suffer because of this separation, because the forces of life are as strong in them as they are in the Ull, and it would be a great wrong if their suffering made their minds rot and drove them to act as do the thumpers. The blame would be yours, because there is no reason for what you are doing. Even though in your kindness you allow us to age and die, it is a bad story. It is bad because it will stop the story of the first meeting between Ull and Man, and of what happened as a result, from being told. It is a story that will darken and spoil all the stories you tell among yourselves and to your young in all of your history to come, because it is a story that could have been good."

He paused, waiting for a reaction, but neither the Ull in the water nor the humans on the bank moved or spoke.

He said, "We came to this world with few of our mechanical wonders but much knowledge, wanting to live in peace, and mate, and raise families, and expecting to teach only our own children. We can also teach those of the Ull.

"Children who learn together do not grow up in fear."

This time the silence that followed his words was broken by Allumlel. The Eldest said, "It is your teaching that we fear more than your devices, Healer Nolan. We fear that a rot, like the infection from which you so carefully protected my wounds, would invade our minds and there would be no cure. You do not think or behave or believe as we do. Your teachings might destroy the Ull, or Man, because nothing like this has happened to either of us."

Nolan shook his head. "You are wrong, Eldest Allumlel," he said. "Among Man there are many ways of thinking, many different beliefs. You believe that when the soul of a great Ull is eaten at the time of its death, it is preserved in future generations. Some of us believe that all of us, whether or not we are great and deserving, have souls which live on forever. Others, that a good life will ensure that the soul is born again into the body of a greater person, and that bad behavior will cause it to reappear in the body of some lowly creature, like a fish or an insect. There are many beliefs that are even stranger. Some believe that they do not have a soul or a life after death. There are holders of many of these different beliefs in our camp. Often there are arguments between them, but the beliefs of everyone are respected no matter how strange, and rarely does one believer surrender to the beliefs of another. An intelligent mind thinks long and carefully before it would agree to do such a thing, and although the minds of the Ull are ignorant as yet of our beliefs, they are not stupid.

"You are also wrong," he went on, "in thinking that a meeting like this has not happened before, for in the history of Earth there was just such a meeting, and it was to have results that were great beyond the expectations of those who met . . ."

As he continued, Nolan could see Golden Rain and a few of the other colonists standing or sitting on the bank and smiling at him, because it was a story he liked and had told many times, although never before had they heard it in the language of the Ull. With occasional pauses to explain some of the human terms he had to use, Nolan told of Brendan's long and dangerous journey across a great ocean, and of the storms and sickness and deprivations they suffered. The Ull knew about storms, and hunger and sickness when the Blue Rot covered the underwater fruit that was their prime food source, but the idea of dying of thirst was difficult for a water-dweller to grasp. He went on to tell of Brendan's meeting with the Algonquin, of his trials at their hands, and of his attempt to learn their language and understand their ways. When he reached the place when a rescue party of Brendan's men tried to free him, Nolan stopped. The sun had dropped below the treetops on the other side of the lake.

"The strangers were captured," said Nolan, deliberately not pointing out the analogies because they were plain for the Ull to see, "and if they were not to be killed, they would never be allowed to return home to their loved ones. This, even though their leader, Brendan, had learned and understood many of their ways, and had so gained the respect of his captors that they made him a Chief. But it grows dark, and the rest of the story can wait until tomorrow."

There was a long silence during which Eolsaa lowered its head beneath the surface to make the low, bubbling sounds that the Ull used to communicate over a distance underwater. A short time later a group of them surfaced to place a cluster of fruit specimen one on Nolan's raft and a larger quantity on the bank for the use of the other humans. A kindness or a reward for an interesting story? Nolan was still wondering when Eolsaa spoke again.

"It is our habit to sleep during the hours of darkness," it said, "but a habit can be broken. Nolan, we would hear more.

"Now."

Chapter 43

LIKE a child and a favorite fairy story, Nolan thought, *I know the ending, sad and glorious as it is, but I never tire of listening to it. Or telling it.*

The small size of Tall Tree's village and the large numbers attending the council meant that each Chief was allowed only one adviser, usually an elder of the tribe or its medicine man. Brendan chose Malcolm.

Because of an old knee injury, Malcolm could not sit cross-legged as did the others. Instead he stood tall and straight at Brendan's shoulder, facing the Paramount Chief across the circle of lesser Chiefs, and with a demeanor as grave and impassive as that of Running Bear himself.

The council of Chiefs had many problems to discuss and disputes to settle before the matter of the paleskinned strangers could be placed before them. A raiding party of Iroquois had encroached upon the territory of the Algonquin family, setting fire to the

Chief's longhouse and killing several warriors, and suitable retaliatory action was called for. There was a minor war between two adjoining Algonquin villages over a river valley rich in game, but neither side would sue for peace. A fair exchange in winter food and shelter had to be set for the services of an aged, but still expert, canoe-builder while he trained his successors. Then suddenly they were all talking about him.

It was apparent from the beginning that with the exceptions of Tall Tree and, surprisingly, Kargha, he had no friends. The fact that he was the most junior Chief gave him the right to be present at the council, but it conferred no immunity from harm either for himself or for his people, nor did it give him the right to speak without permission. All that Brendan could do was listen and, as the voices became louder and more vehement, feel glad that his men under guard at the other end of the village did not understand anything of what was being said about them.

The general feeling was that the paleskins were evil, that their weapons and their great canoes were filled with an evil magic, and that they were the servants of the dreadful cannibal Manitou driven from the land by the Great Hare, returned now to exact vengeance. The paleskins should be slain and burned as were diseased animals, their great canoes killed with fire-arrows and sunk in the deepest water so that the evil, fire-breathing spirit who dwelled in the large one should be drowned and forever banished. These things should be done so that the evil Manitou would send no more of his paleskinned servants to trouble the Algonquin.

"What are they saying?" asked Malcolm quietly.

"Nothing of importance," said Brendan, begging silent forgiveness for the well-intentioned lie.

There were other Chiefs in the council who had different if less violent ideas. They were in the minority, but it was an argumentative and patient minority of Chiefs who were younger and of a more practical turn of mind.

The paleskin weapons they had examined and tested were easier to use than the bows and arrows of their own warriors, in that they could be used to arm old men, women, and even children if necessary. This would be an advantage when defending their villages against attack. The long knives of the paleskins were also potent weapons. If more of the paleskins came in their great canoes, the journey would be long and tiring for them. They would be hungry and sick and no match for the Algonquin, who could send against them warriors as numerous as the trees of the forest, and capture their great canoes and the weapons and treasure they carried. Great and powerful and rich indeed would grow the Algonquin, and feared by warriors from the northern wastes to the southern swamps, and by the tribes of the great plains to the west and by the paleskinned invaders from across the Great Water. The evil magic of the paleskins should be used, they said, against the paleskins.

The arguments had raged while the morning sun rose above the treetops until it was high overhead, and at no time had Running Bear spoken a word. Brendan was growing quietly and impassively desperate.

He leaned to the side so that he could speak quietly to Tall Tree, as he had seen other Chiefs do when they wanted private words with their neighbors. He said, "I would like to send men to my great canoes, to bring gifts."

"Gifts!" said Kargha, who had overheard him. "This is not the time for gifts. It may be that the stranger sends them back with orders to flee, so that as many of his warriors as possible will escape us."

Tall Tree said, "Your warriors may not leave us. Give your words to your adviser. My warriors will take him to the great canoes and bring him back with the gifts."

The Chief was no fool, Brendan thought. He said, "Your canoe is too small. Two of my canoes, which must be joined together and paddled by my warriors, will be needed to carry the gifts."

"Then, you will use warriors from your great canoes," said Tall Tree firmly, "not those captured by us."

"What was all that about?" said Malcolm, when Brendan straightened up again. "You sound worried."

"There is no time to tell you," Brendan said in his ship-captain's voice. "Listen carefully, without interruption, and do exactly as I say . . ."

A moment later Malcolm turned and, with Kargha following close behind him, hurried toward the beach. Brendan resumed listening and worrying.

He was no longer sure that he had done the right thing by ordering his men to disarm. Even if they had not succeeded in freeing him, a few of them might have been able to fight their way back to the longboats or swim back to the ships and escape. As it was their fate depended on what he could do and say at this council and on nothing else.

His men had not been tightly bound or harmed in any way, and they ate what and when the Redman ate, but that would make no difference to their fate if the council voted against them today.

They would all die, and he could imagine his brethren at home mourning them, saying Mass for the repose of their souls and, in their ignorance of the truth, marking against his expedition the fateful words "Lost at sea with all hands."

Faintly, he heard the sound of a commotion coming from the direction of the beach. The sounds grew louder and nearer, so that everyone at the council began to hear it and stop talking. Brendan uncrossed his legs and stood up, facing the Paramount Chief. It was possible that what he intended to do was an offense against council protocol, but that was a minor risk under these circumstances.

Loudly and clearly, he said, "I would speak."

"Speak," said Running Bear.

Preceded by Kargha, who was walking backward and rattling his charms at two beasts in whose existence he had disbelieved, and followed by a noisy and excited crowd of children, Malcolm led Seamus Dubh and White Dancer toward the circle of Chiefs, which opened before them. The children were told to go away, but remained at a distance to watch, while Kargha rejoined Tall Tree. Brendan walked slowly into the center of the circle to take the reins of both horses from Malcolm.

They had been meticulously groomed and saddled while the transporting platform was being attached between the two longboats, and Seamus Dubh's coat gleamed almost as brightly as the highly polished and decorated leather and buckles of his harness. In the high, bright sunlight the details of the Dancer were lost in the dazzling whiteness of her coat, and it was plain to see that she was with foal. Surely, thought Brendan proudly, even a Redman who had never seen a horse before could not help but be impressed by the strength and beauty of such beasts.

Without speaking, he let the Dancer's reins fall and swung himself into the saddle of the black, touching his heels gently to flanks.

Seamus leapt forward, already at a gallop before he reached the edge of the circle. The Redmen seated there flung themselves sideways out of his path, but there was no need because he easily cleared what would have been their head height. Just as easily he sailed over the shoulder-high stockade at the edge of the village to land on the cleared ground beyond.

Brendan circled the stockade several times at a gallop, knowing that they could hear the hoofbeats and would know that while there was no Redman in the village who could run fast enough to catch him, he was not going to escape. A few moments later he returned the way he had come, but this time he slowed to a trot and, before reentering the circle, to a sedate walk.

Dismounting, he patted Seamus on the neck and ran his fingers through his mane. The black nuzzled him in the chest and swished his tail in appreciation of the recent exercise, and Brendan turned to face the Paramount Chief once again. Even the children were quiet.

"Speak," said Running Bear.

Brendan was silent for a moment, not so much for dramatic effect but because his Algonquin vocabulary was not yet extensive and he had to choose his words carefully. A great many lives depended on what he was about to say.

"In my land these animals are called horses," he said, resting a hand lightly on the neck of each of the beautiful beasts. "They are the servants and friends of men, and as a mark of respect they are given names by their masters. They can pull litters heavily laden with goods or wounded braves over long distances, and in time of war they carry bowmen and spearmen in great numbers into battle, and the sound of their hooves is like the voice of the Thunder Bird in the time of the summer storms.

"My own Great Chief, Connair, has many, many horses," Brendan went on. "But these two are among the finest he has ever possessed. They have been chosen by him as a gift to the Algonquin.

"Seamus Dubh, the envy and pride of Connair's horse-warriors, is for the Great Chief Running Bear," he said, proffering the reins in turn, "and the beautiful White Dancer is for my first Redman brother, Tall Tree."

Running Bear, who was ancient in years, hobbled forward to hold the reins briefly in acknowledgment of his acceptance of the gift, then returned to his place. Tall Tree was about to do the same when Brendan lightly held his arm before he could let go of the reins.

"Does Tall Tree wish to mount his gift?" asked Brendan. "Shall I advise him in the ways that his horse may be controlled?"

White Dancer, while she could move like the wind, was the most docile and sensible of beasts—she would not do anything to risk her unborn foal. He knew that Tall Tree would be quite safe, but the Redman did not know it.

"Rather," said the Chief in a quiet voice, "would I submit once again to the Tree of Testing."

It was an extraordinarily difficult task to coax Tall Tree into the saddle, but, when he learned how to guide the Dancer at a gentle trot around the inside of the circle, it was even more difficult to make him leave it.

The introduction of the horses had interrupted the deliberations of the council, but Running Bear, silently and without any perceptible change of expression, restored order. Brendan settled back to listen, hoping that he now had two powerful allies in the council. Tall Tree would probably have sided with him, regardless of the gift of White Dancer, but he felt that Running Bear's support would not be bought by any gift, no matter how valuable or unusual. His only hope might lie with the younger chiefs, who cast covetous glances at the animals tethered nearby every time they stamped their hooves or whinnied.

If he was to suggest that more such animals would be forthcoming, should the paleskins be allowed to return unharmed for them, that might make all the difference. He stood up and put the suggestion in a loud, clear voice.

They ignored him because he had been ill-mannered enough to break into a conversation between two more senior Chiefs, but contrived to answer him during the arguments that followed. It was evident that the plight of his captured crewmen and those still on the ships had, if anything, worsened since his introduction of the horses.

Many of the Chiefs were now suggesting that his words about the countless warriors and horses of the paleskin Chief, Connair, were meant to frighten, as the stories told to misbehaving children about evil giants who uprooted trees and used them as spears. The Algonquin Nation was composed of brave warriors, not children, and all of the paleskins and their Great Chief should know this. They would know it when their great canoes and their people did not return. They would know it if other great canoes and the warriors they carried did not return. The Algonquin should have nothing to do with the paleskins.

A frail, incredibly ancient Chief, in a voice surprisingly deep to be coming from such a wisp of a man, put into words what were undoubtedly the feelings of the majority. He said, "If the paleskins are not slain now, and their great canoes broken, they will come again in more and perhaps even greater canoes, and they will darken the sun with their smoke. They will carry with them strange weapons against which our bows and our spears will be powerless, and fiercer and more evil beasts who will tear and eat our warriors instead of meekly allowing them to ride on their backs. They will bring the knowledge of paleskin rites and customs which will destroy the Algonquin or, what is worse, make us their slaves."

The words were driving Brendan close to desperation and despair, and Malcolm, too, suspected that something had gone badly wrong. But there was a small part of Brendan's mind, the part that had been trained and strengthened on the Tree of Testing, that was unaffected by outside influences, be they stinging insects or the fear of death. Calmly and without emotion, it remembered the accounts he had read about the effects of misguided missionary zeal, and it considered the probable consequences, the social disruption, degradation, and even exploitation that might ensue before the Faith was accepted. There were times when Brendan wondered if he had chosen the wrong vocation.

"The paleskins here say they are our friends because they are weak," the frail old Chief ended. "The paleskins who will follow them will be strong and will not be our friends. We slay our enemies. We must slay all paleskins."

There was nobody who spoke in support of the paleskins except Tall Tree and Kargha and gradually the voices around the circle grew silent. Running Bear raised his hand and made the sign that told all those present that they must listen without making any interruption. He pointed at Brendan and for the first time used his Algonquin name.

"We will hear the words of the paleskin Chief, Shining Sea."

There was no necessity for Brendan to stand while he was speaking, but it gave him the chance to ease the stiffness in his crossed legs, and they would assume that it was a paleskin custom to stand on such occasions. But before he began, he spoke quietly to Malcolm.

"I'll tell you what I'm saying to them," he said, "so that you will know what is happening."

There was no necessity to do that, either, but pausing every few minutes to translate would give him more time to think. He was no longer sure, following the hostile reaction of the council, of what he wanted to say.

The best course would be to say what he felt, simply and truthfully.

"The slaying of my people is not a good or a wise thing," he began gravely. "It is not good for them and it is not wise for you. It is not good because we came to you in peace, and you would slay us because of the fear of wrongs we have not done and might never do. You would slay us because you do not want more paleskins to come.''

He translated quickly and saw Malcolm's face grow pale. Until then he had not realized just how much trouble they were in.

''But if you slay us,'' he went on, ''more paleskins will come. They will come because my Great Chief, Connair, will not know how we died. The journey here was long and dangerous. Mighty storms sweep the great sea, pushing up waves that are like steep hills of water, and there are floating islands of ice which could break open even our great canoes. Connair would think that one of these fates befell us, and because of this ignorance more brave paleskins would come, and come again until they learned why they should not come.''

And now, he thought, for the important part. Aloud, he went on, ''All of my people are needed to guide the great canoes on this long and dangerous journey, and if any of them are slain, then your words of warning to Connair will not reach him and, again, more paleskins will come. But if you wish to let Connair know that the words of warning that my people take to him are true, I will remain with you as a hostage, to be slain by you if another great canoe should approach the land of the Algonquin.''

When Malcolm heard the last few words, he said fiercely, ''Have you lost your wits? Are you an amadan entirely? You know as well as I do that you brought us here and we need you to get us back. Damn you, Captain, I never thought you wanted to be a martyr!''

Brendan tried to tell him that the winds for the return journey would be favorable, that Malcolm could navigate almost as well as himself, and that from his knowledge of the Redmen he thought it unlikely that they would ill-treat a hostage who was also a Chief. But as he returned his attention to the council he wondered whether his words were a wish rather than a fact.

''The knowledge of our weapons,'' Brendan continued, ''and of our great canoes which are moved by the winds instead of the strong arms of oarsmen, is yours to learn and use, or to forget. The horses are a most valuable gift from my Great Chief. They are a gift of first meeting. Acceptance means friendship and peace between two great tribes. Refusal is a grave insult, the act of an enemy which could lead to war.

''If you do not want friendship with the paleskins,'' he went on, ''send all my people, and the horses, back to Connair. He will understand your actions much better than any words.''

"Now," said Malcolm, "you're talking sense."

"Many of the Chiefs here have suggested that I might promise to send many more horses in exchange for the freedom of my people," he resumed. "I would not make such a promise, because, if I did so, Connair would say that it was a promise made in fear, the promise of a cowardly Chief, and he would be angry and punish me and not honor such a promise. This is the way of my Great Chief."

"The way of your Great Chief," Malcolm said cynically, "would be to clap you on the back and laugh his bright-red head off."

"There will be no more horses given to the Algonquin," Brendan said, ignoring him, "because there can only be one gift at first meeting. If more horses are wanted, you must give Connair something in exchange."

Surely, he thought, they must understand the principles of exchange and barter. But he was not sure.

He said, "If a warrior has broken his bow and has not the time to make another, he will go to a brother with two bows. If the warrior who needs a bow has two knives, he will offer one knife in exchange for the bow. If the other warrior has no knife, he will agree to the exchange. But if his bow is a very good bow and the knife is not a good knife, he will want other things, arrows, ornaments, cooking pots for his squaw, as well. If there is disagreement about the value of the bow and the knife, their Chief or a wise man of their village will decide what is fair."

"If you want horses," he went on, "you must give the paleskins the things which you have in plenty and which the paleskins do not have, and want. If there is a dispute about the value of these things, then Running Bear, or my own Great Chief, will decide what is valuable and what is not.

"It is not good for brothers to fight each other," he ended gravely, "or for the warriors of the same tribe to fight each other, or for the warriors of tribes who are brothers to fight each other."

Malcolm made a quiet derogatory sound and said, "It is as if the Sermon on the Mount were being given by a merchant from the Levant. Why talk about trading until we're sure that we'll be alive to trade with anyone?"

"I'm talking about possible future trading," Brendan replied quietly, "to make them think that I have no doubt that we have a future together. The smaller concerns conceal the larger. But I don't know what is in their minds."

They could not say anything because their Paramount Chief had forbidden them to interrupt, and for that reason the hoped-for response came from Running Bear himself.

"You are not an Algonquin, Shining Sea," he said reprovingly. "You have been captured by the Algonquin, instructed in our ways, and have passed the tests given to a warrior and Chief, but you are not one of us. You are as a child of a dead enemy, pitied and taken into his slayer's longhouse and cared for by the squaws until manhood. But you are not, and should not say that you are, a brother to the Algonquin."

Brendan took a deep breath and prayed, not for the gift of tongues, but for greater fluency in the one he had so recently learned. Whether it was the truth or a fable which he had always wanted to believe, on the words which he would speak now depended the lives of his entire expedition, and of the others who would follow them.

"I have much knowledge of the different customs and beliefs of the many paleskin tribes," he replied, looking all around the circle to let the other Chiefs know that his reply was not only for Running Bear. "Since I was welcomed into the longhouse of Tall Tree, and was instructed by Kargha and spoke with many other wise men of the village, I have learned many things about the customs and beliefs of the Algonquin. And I have learned that these beliefs and customs and ways of thinking, the respect that is felt for a brave hunter or a great Chief, the need they feel to keep their squaws and their children sheltered and well-fed, and the many other things that are done and felt and thought about, are the same for both paleskin and Algonquin.

"The wise ones among the paleskins teach us that it is wrong to make war," he went on, pausing only to give Malcolm the gist of what he had been saying. "They tell us that killing another warrior in the anger of battle is a brave deed, but that it is more honorable and more worthy of the respect of his people, and much more difficult for him, if he spends his years of strength hunting and providing food and shelter against the winter hunger and storms for his squaws and his children. To kill such a man is a grave wrong. There is sadness among his friends, his squaws will grieve at his loss and for their children who will go hungry and unhappy until, if they live and grow to manhood, they will seek to kill the children of the slayer of their father. It is a great and lasting wrong, the paleskins are taught, to kill other men."

There was a murmuring of voices around the circle of Chiefs, which seemed to indicate a mixture of impatience and surprise that he was not pleading for the lives of his people. Plainly they had not expected words like these from him, and neither had Malcolm.

"This is not the right time for a sermon on brotherly love," he said quietly.

"From Kargha," Brendan went on, "I learned the story of the tribes of the north, who met together in a great council and decided that the Delaware people should be killed to the last man, woman, and child. Then the Great Spirit appeared among them as a bird of shining white, and hung with opened wings above the Great Chief's daughter, and told her that his heart was sad and hidden in a dark cloud because they sought to drink the blood of his firstborn, the family of the Delaware, oldest of his tribes. To appease the anger of the Master of Life and bring joy back to his heart, he told her that the warriors must wash their hands in the blood of a faun, and give presents, and smoke together the great pipe of peace and brotherhood, which would unite all Redmen forever."

Sadly, Brendan continued, "The paleskins, too, have a Great Spirit, who appears as a bird, or a shining cloud, or a burning bush, to warn us when we are about to do a great wrong. Killing and stealing and all kinds of wrongdoing make Him sad, but there are some paleskins who still steal and cheat and make war, just as there are some Redmen who still do these wrong things to their brothers."

Running Bear held up his hand. There was sympathy and a note almost of regret in his voice when he spoke. "Again I remind Shining Sea that he is not our brother."

"From Tall Tree and Kargha," Brendan went on, "I learned of mighty beings and warriors of the past who did great deeds, deeds which brought happiness to their tribes, not the lamentations of war Among the paleskins there are brave warriors, too, who do not make war. They show their bravery by traveling far from their homes, seeking new lands with strange and dangerous and perhaps beautiful beasts, or people whose customs are stranger and even more beautiful, and sometimes these warriors risk the storms of the great seas to find these lands. They fight, not themselves, but the hunger and thirst and sickness and dangers they find, so that they will have more knowledge and become wise and greatly respected among men."

Several times while he was speaking, low-voiced arguments broke out around the circle, which Running Bear stilled with an upraised hand. Malcolm said quietly, "I see what you are trying to do, and if this was a moral debate among civilized people I think you might win it. But you're being too subtle. These people are savages."

"I was also told stories of a great disaster," Brendan went on, "of a great flood which drowned everything and everyone, and of how Michabo, the Great Hare, repopulated the world after this great flood. These stories have been handed down from father to son, and because of this, changes have taken place in the telling, so that the story told now is different from the events which actually happened . . ."

There were loud objections being raised to the idea that the Algonquin mythology might not be wholly accurate, as if Brendan was one of the near-heretical theologians at home who questioned the exact sequence of events and cast of characters in the Garden of Eden.

"The paleskins, too, have their stories of a great flood," he went on quickly. "Unlike Michabo, who remade the earth from a piece of mud brought to him by a muskrat, we are told that a great canoe was built at the directions of the Great Spirit, and that this canoe carried men and women and pairs of all the animals of the world, who survived until the flood drained away and the land rose again out of the waters. The tribes with brown skins, and those in other lands whose skins are black, all tell the age-old tales of a great flood. Like the stories of the Redmen, those told by the men whose skin are black or brown or pale have changed in the telling, but in the heart of the story, the part which tells of the great flood, there has been no change."

He paused and held up one hand, waiting for silence. Then he deepened his voice so that it would carry clearly to every member of the council.

"This," he said solemnly, "is because it is the same story."

They were all watching Brendan now, hearing but not discussing his words. Even Malcolm was silent after he had translated for him. His expression was disapproving, because some of the things his captain was saying verged on the heretical, and there was worse to come.

"There is another story told by my people, a story of a great disaster," he continued in the same measured, solemn voice. "It tells of a time in the past, distant beyond the memory of memories, when the land heaved and trembled and the very mountains were split apart as by mighty war hatchets. Into the great cracks which opened in the land fell the great trees of the forests, the longhouses, even whole villages and the people who dwelt in them were swallowed up by the shaking earth. Then the waters of the sea rushed in to fill these deep, unnatural valleys, and the land sank like a broken canoe. Even the highest mountaintops were covered by the waves of the Great Sea.

"This story, too, has changed with the telling," he went on sadly, "but the tales of a great flood do not change. Many different tribes share the legend of a lost land of order and great beauty, filled with people who were brave in war, noble and forgiving in peace, and wise beyond the imaginings of we who came after them."

He paused for a moment, his voice falling almost to a whisper as he went on, "The land is known to my own people as Hy Braesal, the mighty and beautiful island, and Tir na n'Og, the land of the forever young, or as Atlantis, or the Westland. But all of the legends agree that it did exist and that its tremendous forests and plains, its beautifully built and decorated longhouses, and the vast knowledge and unsurpassed works of art of its people, were buried forever under the Great Sea.

"Many, many of its people died with the sinking land," he said sadly, then proudly, "but not all of them."

"Some of them," he went on fiercely, "were able to escape in the few smaller canoes which had not been wrecked by the heaving land and raging flood. In time they escaped to the lands in the east and south, to settle and intermarry with the tribes they found there, tribes whose skins were pale or dark, and slowly they learned new wisdom and forgot the old, except for the story of the great flood which had buried their native land.

"Until I came among the Redmen," he said, "I had not known that some of our people had escaped to the West, and braved the dangers of the Great Sea to settle here."

Brendan folded his arms slowly and looked around at the faces, still and silent now, that were staring back at him.

"The Great Chief Running Bear is wrong," he said simply. "I am his brother."

Before he could sit down again, the arguments were raging around and across the circle, so fiercely that he had to raise his own voice while translating his last few passages for Malcolm. When he had finished, the other stood staring down at him for a long time before he spoke.

"You argued well for us, Captain," he said. "Very well. I had not suspected that you had such a wide knowledge of mythology or such a devious mind. Without knowing what you were saying at the time, I could tell that you spoke as though you believed your own words. Or . . . or *did* you believe them?"

"I would like to believe them," said Brendan.

Malcolm's expression became concerned as he went on, "Be careful, Captain. It is one thing to tell a few lies in order to get us out of trouble, but marrying the legends of Atlantis with the Biblical flood, well, if your abbot ever gets to hear about it, you'll be lucky to escape excommunication. And claiming that these savages are long-lost members of our family, and offering them our friendship as equals. I don't know how the High-King will take to that. Connair is a proud man, and quick-tempered.

"What are they saying now?" he went on. "Will we be all right? Have you convinced them?"

Brendan listened closely for a few moments, then said, "Almost half of them are on our side, but I don't know how it will go."

"And you have no more stories to tell?" Malcolm asked hopefully.

"No more stories," Brendan replied. "But there is something I can and will say. But be quiet, Running Bear is about to speak."

The loudest sound as the Paramount Chief spoke was the crackling of the wood that had been thrown onto the fire. Running Bear said, "The paleskin Chief pleads well for the lives of the people, and argues wisely. If we do not want many more paleskins to come, we must return all the paleskins unharmed. If we wish to be friends and trade with the paleskins, we must return them unharmed. His tale of the Lost Land, even though he himself does not know that it is true, is one that stirs the heart with sadness and wonder. But are all paleskins as Shining Sea? Will there be enemies as well as friends among them? We are full-grown men and warriors, not children to be moved by stories, and must consider carefully what will happen to the Algonquin Nation if we do what he asks for his people."

"Shining Sea," said Brendan, once again rising to his feet, "asks something for himself."

"Speak," said Running Bear.

"Shining Sea is a Chief among his own people," Brendan said quietly, "and would not live as a prisoner of the Redmen. Shining Sea asks that he be allowed to remain among you, to learn the wisdom of the Redmen and to teach the knowledge of his own people. He asks that he be allowed to travel the hills and forests and rivers of the Algonquin.

"If my people wait among you until the winter storms are past," he went on, "they should be able to return to the homeland in safety. If the paleskins are invited to return, Shining Sea asks that he be allowed to meet them, and tell them that they may not make war on their brothers, or cheat their brothers in trade, and that if injury is done or life is taken, he asks that he meets with the other Chiefs to decide on a fair settlement of the dispute. He asks this because it is not good for brother to war on brother."

The debate was much shorter and less vehement this time, so that he was able to tell Malcolm only what he had said before the Paramount Chief was being helped to his feet, and the crackling of the fire again sounded loud in the silence.

"The paleskins may return unharmed to their lands," said Running Bear. "Shining Sea will be honored among his Algonquin brothers. There will be peace between us."

Chapter 44

SEA Dragon, *White Heron*, and *Sinead* wintered in the harbor of Tall Tree's village and returned safely to Hibernia early in the following summer, loaded down with the gifts of first meeting for the Great Chief and High-King, Connair of the paleskins.

They carried fine furs and soft cured hides, many of which were worked into the beautifully embroidered and beaded clothing that the Redmen wore on important occasions, and delicately carved ornaments of wood and bone and gold. The Redmen considered the soft, yellow metal to be rare and precious but they did not, judging by the quantity they sent to Connair, regard it as highly as did the paleskins. They also carried an even more precious cargo, to the mind of Malcolm, *Sea Dragon*'s new captain, his wife Bright Rainbow, youngest and most comely of the lovely daughters of Running Bear.

Brendan had been deeply worried, both by that overly generous gift of gold and by the surprise wedding which he had performed two weeks before sailing. Gold begat greed and even uglier sins in the minds of some men. The marriage Brendan had performed, much less noisy and colorful than the Algonquin ceremony at which Kargha had officiated, placed serious responsibilities on the couple that he did not think Bright Rainbow fully understood. And he was not sure that she would be happy among strangers. When in a weak moment he confided his worries to Tall Tree, the Chief dismissed them.

"You have said that a generous gift of first meeting confers honor on the giver," Tall Tree said, "and if the Great Chief Connair wants more gold and furs, he will have to send many, many horses and crossbows to the Algonquin. The sea-warrior, Malcolm, spent the winter in the village of Running Bear, as did a few of your no-squaw paleskins who chose to sleep on the ground rather than on your unsteady great canoes, and Bright Rainbow came to know and honor him enough to open her blanket to him in love and obedience. Her fate and her children will be his."

Malcolm was even more reassuring. He said that Bright Rainbow was the most beautiful and gentle colleen that he had ever seen, that she was a Princess of a great nation, and that, considering the treasure that was accompanying her, she would be received by Connair at Tara with honor. When the Court had a chance to meet her, he did not believe that the High-King would be given any choice in the matter. Brendan was not to concern himself about her, or about anything else that happened at home.

During the decade that followed, Bright Rainbow was not only accepted but honored by all who visited Tara or the rebuilt clan home of her husband in Caledonia, while the absent Brendan became very unpopular indeed.

The Redmen would trade only for horses, since they were already copying and building their own crossbows and large sailing canoes and, as a matter of personal prestige, the early horse-owning Chiefs caused paths to be cleared through the forests between their villages so that they could visit each other on horseback. As more and more horses arrived or were born, the paths formed a network for trade and rapid communication all over the Algonquin Nation—especially when Brendan demonstrated the advantages of a wheeled litter over one that was dragged over the ground. As a result, the paleskin Chief Shining Sea was always present within a few hours, or at most days, of the arrival of the trading ships from Hibernia.

The bargains he struck for the furs, gold ornaments, carvings, and pipes which everyone at home were wanting to smoke, together with the cabbagelike weed burned in them, were irritatingly fair. The Redmen, he made it plain, were not to be exploited or taken as slaves as had been the savages of the African coastal jungles.

When a trading fleet from Iberia tried to do just that, Shining Sea was instrumental in organizing the rescue of the captured Redmen. It required the men and ships of the Hibernian traders who had been loading three sailing days to the north, and several thousand warriors who showed that they could fight just as well from the decks and rigging as in their native forest. The land and sea battle that ensued went straight into Algonquin and Hibernian legend.

Many generations were to pass before any but Hibernian ships were welcomed by the Redmen, and only their paleskin brothers from Hibernia were allowed to settle in the lands of the Algonquin or in the great plains to the west. And by then Shining Sea, sometimes called Brendan the Navigator, had traveled widely, learning and teaching as he had wished, so that his name and his wisdom were honored even among the Huron and Iroquois of the plains. When he became too old and frail to ride his horse and wagon, he was unanimously elected Paramount Chief of the Algonquin Nation.

It was Dairmuid, the more far-seeing and intelligent High-King who succeeded the proud and impetuous Connair, who understood Brendan's insistence on treating the Redmen as respected allies rather than as savages to be exploited, and he appreciated the future political and commercial advantages that would accrue, as well as the military assurance that Hibernia need never again fear an invasion from Europe. And when Dairmuid's First Brothers, the Algonquin, were joined by the Hurons of the Great Lakes and the plains-dwelling Iroquois, and later by the many tribal families to the north, south, and even farther west, Hibernia had a monopoly on trade and immigration to the vast, rich, and as-yet-unexplored territories of the Westland; and suddenly Brendan, the renegade monk and semisavage who dared not return home, was on the way to becoming the explorer statesman remembered in the history books.

Dairmuid was the first High-King to undertake the dangerous journey across the great ocean to the new lands, where he traveled widely, impressed the village Chiefs with his great strength, bravery, and wisdom, and underwent the Algonquin rite which made him and his successors brothers of the Redmen for all time. He also, at the culmination of the ceremonies, invited Brendan to come home.

As Shining Sea, Brendan told his High-King regretfully, it

would not be proper for the Paramount Chief to leave his people for any reason, much less for the selfish and personal one that he was still homesick. He also pleaded the frailty of age which would make it unlikely that he would survive the voyage, and Orla, Dairmuid's principal Healer, concurred.

Many honors were conferred on Brendan, the navigator-monk who had single-handedly opened up a new world and ordered its affairs with peace and justice, before this High-King returned to Tara. They were civil, military, and academic, and there was talk of a canonization . . .

"But sainthood," Nolan went on, "which is a rare honor bestowed on those who are unselfish and good in themselves, and who by their words and actions inspire these qualities in others, was withheld in spite of continuing importunings of the Holy See by a succession of High-Kings. Countless thousands of Redmen were converted to his belief in the teachings of the Christus while he lived and traveled among them, but there should have been many times more. It was thought that Brendan lacked missionary zeal, and had too much respect for the beliefs of others to bring what he considered to be the True Faith to them against their will. Or it might have been that too many of the kingdoms of mainland Europe, and especially their merchant princes, never forgave him for forbidding the exploitation of the Redmen."

Nolan stopped then, and gave the Ull sign that his story was finished by gently slapping one palm against the water. The lake was reflecting a mirror image of the dark line of trees on the far shore and a sky whose gray dawn was tinged with pink. Without speaking the five Councillors turned and began swimming slowly away from the shore, to stop when they were too far away for human ears to hear them. Allumlel remained on the raft beside him, also in silence, as were the people who were still lining the bank.

"Your wounds," said Nolan in a voice hoarse from overuse, "are well enough healed for you to join your friends."

"It is unnecessary, Nolan," Allumlel replied, "because they know what my words would be and, although I have vacated my position as Eldest of the Six, I know with less certainty what their words will be. But there are two questions, selfish questions, that I would ask."

Nolan wanted the answers to many questions of his own. Why had Allumlel resigned, or perhaps been discharged, from its position? Had his words made any difference to the situation? And what did Allumlel think would be the words of the council? He continued looking across the lake where there were only four amphibian heads showing above the water. But a fifth head, Eolsaa's, and then another reappeared as he watched.

"Ask them," he said.

"With respect, Healer," said Allumlel, "please speak the truth rather than a kindly story that you would tell to a being soon to die. Will my wounds heal so that I will be well enough to walk the long trails between the lakes, and climb hills, and swim down to gather the deep fruit?"

A selfish question indeed, Nolan thought, but of the kind that every Healer expected from a convalescent patient He said, "In truth, Allumlel, you are healed. Had a rot invaded your wounds it would have killed you long since. Your strength is returning and soon you will be able to walk, climb, and dive as you desire, and mate and lay children if that is what you wish . . ."

He stopped because the Councillors were returning and swimming so rapidly that a broad triangle of disturbed water spread like a rippling fan in their wake. It was Eolsaa who swam closest to the raft to place the object by Nolan's hand. It was a limp, wet cylinder of Ull hide joined and decorated along its edges with stitching of some bright yellow fiber.

"I speak as the newly chosen Eldest of the Six," said Eolsaa, "and with the full agreement of the Council and our people of these waters. This band has been made to fit your forelimb, Healer Nolan, and it is already yours by right. In the time ahead you will wear it so that all the Ull you meet, on the trails and in the lakes you travel on the journey to your colony, will know that you have eaten and carry within you the soul of the great Illamsul, and that you are deserving of their respect, their assistance, and their obedience . . ."

There was more, but the shouting and cheering of the colonists on the bank made it impossible to hear, and the Six left while everyone was still trying to shake his hand or slap his back, and the sun was well risen before they returned to the camp and their long-delayed rest. He was so relieved and happy that it was difficult to feel regret about anything, but he considered Allumlel his friend, and for some reason he had caused it to lose its position as Eldest of the Six, and he should offer his apologies, and sympathy.

"My second question is this," said Allumlel, before Nolan could speak. "May I come with you? I would like to learn more stories, of the kind that must be marked on paper, from you and other humans, so that I can fly again. And . . . and I would like to see a horse."

Chapter 45

INSTEAD of having to push and hack their way through the dense, tropical forests, they were able to use the network of covered trails that linked together the populated lakes that spread across the belly of the dragon and up to the mountainous subtropical region that lay to the northwest. Had the giant Cathay telescope or the orbiting ship been able to see those hidden pathways, Nolan thought, the observers would not have been so quick to assume that the New World was uninhabited. But using them made their progress during the second half of the journey much faster than any of them would have believed possible.

But there were many lakes where, after the first cautious overtures of friendship by Allumlel and himself, they were delayed for many days. The local Six, and often the whole amphibian community, wanted to hear the story of the first meeting between Ull and Human, and they always asked for demonstrations of Brenner swimming in the air. And if the home lake was large enough to classify as a small inland sea, the sailing rafts that the humans built were guided and escorted to the opening of the correct trail on the other shore. When this happened, Nolan would not allow the rafts to be burned after use as a signal to the ship, but left them for the adult Ull to study and their young to play on.

There were other lakes—a very few of them, fortunately—that they were forced to cross in great haste. In those places the communities were small, fearful of hearing new stories, and their hostility was barely held in check by the words of Allumlel or the armband that Nolan wore.

"I am sorry, Nolan," said Allumlel after one such encounter, "that the story of the Ull has some dark and shameful words in it. I hoped that we would not meet these Ull, whose minds and habits are little better than our great, stupid brothers of the oceans who will kill and eat anything they meet, whether it has a mind and soul or is nothing but an unreasoning animal. Such behavior distresses me, whether it is in an Ull or a Human."

It was not the first time that one of Allumlel's apologies had turned into a criticism, and Nolan had found it best to answer in the same way.

"And I, too, am sorry," he said, "that you have seen our people eating thumper meat. You are shocked and disgusted that we eat and therefore give another life to a lowly creature without a soul. Like you, we do not believe that the thumpers have souls. But if they did, and if we were to save ourselves from dying of hunger by eating them, they would be giving life to us and it would be only fair that we should give them another life in return. The eating of meat does not sicken us as it does you, and this has caused us not to behave or believe as you do. What we do is not good or bad, it is different. Your mind will have to open many new trails before you can accept this difference."

"Nolan," said Allumlel, "your people have too many trails in their minds, too many goods and bads. I have overheard them argue, and some of them have tried to explain their different beliefs, about your great teachers Buddha, Muhammad, and the Christus. All of them tell stories that are good, but they are all different. My mind is trying to open new trails, but it cannot travel them all at the same time. You would not do or speak anything that is bad. I must know what is good, and which is the right trail. So I ask you, Nolan, what must I do? What am I to believe?"

Nolan continued walking in silence for a moment, bent forward from the waist so that his head would clear the roof of the trail. It should be a philosopher and theologian like the monsignor answering those questions rather than an unbelieving Healer, but he would have to try.

"First you must listen carefully to all stories including your own," said Nolan, "and decide which is the one you want to believe or, if they are not the same story, the one you believe to be right. That is what the humans do. But sometimes a mind can be soft and easily shaped so that its thinking can be changed by other minds and directed into wrong trails. When you decide, you must be sure that the decision is yours and not another's."

Allumlel did not reply, and Nolan went on, "I told you the story of how Brendan's paleskins became the brothers of the Algonquin. The story I did not tell you, because to intelligent beings some words do not need to be spoken, was that all creatures who walk not the single trail of animal instinct, but think instead about the strangeness of the minds they have within themselves, and of the meaning of the world without, they also are brothers. The brotherhood of thinking beings, regardless of their shape or size or planet or origin, is a good story that changed your mind, for if it had not, you would be swimming the waters of your home lake instead of journeying beside me. But it, too, is a story whose goodness you must decide for yourself, because humans, myself included, are not always good, or bad. Some of us can do a great good or an even greater wrong without the intention of doing either."

"I do not understand you, Healer," said Allumlel.

For a few moments Nolan walked on in silence. Reaching the main colony had now become an expected future event rather than a forlorn hope. The only uncertainty was the monsignor's reaction to the arrival of the Healer and the other undesirables that O'Riordan had tried so hard to exclude from his Garden of Eden. After the delay at Allumlel's lake, the ship would have reported that the party of survivors were on the move again. But O'Riordan did not know how many had survived, or that Nolan had told them nothing about the others' plan to abandon them on the other side of the planet, or that they had made contact with a native intelligent race that outnumbered the colonists by many thousands to one. There were no Ull in the area of the colony, Allumlel had told him, although the ocean shore might contain numbers of the large, unthinking brothers that it would be better not to meet.

The monsignor must be a very worried and angry man by now, and even though he was a good and holy man, he might also be angry enough to use violent means to abate the imagined threat to his glorious new Eden.

And if the meeting between Nolan's group and the monsignor was violent and involved Allumlel, the threat to the colony would not be an imaginary one. Before then he would have to prepare his Ull friend for a meeting with a different kind of human thinking.

"Then, I will try to explain," he went on, "how a word or act can be neither good nor bad and still bring about great events. On Earth the so-called Gift of First Meeting was an invention of Brendan's, but it became the accepted form of civilized behavior thereafter because it brought about the formation of the Hibernian-Westland Empire. More recently, and I hope this hitherto-untold part of the story does not shock and disgust you, I did not know what I was doing when I ate the flesh of Illamsul. I was testing another possible source of food for my people. A great good came of it, but the act itself was without that intention. It was a sheer accident."

Without slowing its pace, Allumlel swung its head around to look at him. It said, "We of the Six guessed that some such thought was in your mind, which is the reason why you were restrained and a number of us wanted your deaths. But I do not believe you. If an event occurs, whether it is large, small, good, or bad, it cannot be an accident.

"I will understand if you have difficulty with this concept, Healer," it went on, "because your friends tell me that you would not care if your flesh went uneaten, because you are an unbeliever."

Next, Nolan thought, it will want to debate predestination and free will. But then another thought came to him: If Allumlel and the monsignor were ever to meet and talk, their mind trails might not be so divergent that in time they could not be made to converge.

There were many philosophical and religious debates in the days that followed, but rarely did they involve their unbelieving Healer. Instead Allumlel and the others argued with enthusiasm and great subtlety and often in voices loud enough to suggest the prelude to a riot, although they never came to blows. Nolan was glad of the distraction, because it gave them all, and Allumlel in particular, something to think about other than their increasing hunger.

The inhabited lakes grew fewer and the trails between them longer, less traveled, and badly overgrown until there came a day when they were once again in trackless forest. With no regular supply of the underwater fruit, they had to go back to eating anything they could find. Gradually Allumlel became accustomed to the abhorrent sight of humans eating thumper meat, but for itself there was only the edible growths listed in Nolan's catalog and a few others that it knew about already. As they continued northwest the forests thinned, the hills became higher and steeper, and there was a welcome drop in temperature.

By the time they reached the coast and those without the advantage of Brenner's aerial viewpoint saw for the first time the thin gray line of the mountainous peninsula that formed the lower forelimb of the dragon, fifty-two days short of two full years had elapsed since the landing. But on the other side of those distant mountains lay the colony, and their impatience to move on was like a growing insanity.

Their first idea was to build oceangoing rafts and sail there directly, but Allumlel objected strongly, saying that it had no desire to be eaten and have its soul transferred to one of the stupid large brothers. Politely, they ignored it, and when the first of three rafts had been built and was floating at anchor in a sheltered inlet, two of the large stupid brothers, who were similar in shape but five times as massive as the Ull, came to investigate it. Allumlel insisted that they were small and quite young specimens, and being playful rather than deliberately hostile, but in the space of five long breaths they had reduced the raft to its component parts. The journey continued overland.

Twenty-three days later, while they were climbing the lower slopes of the mountain whose summit would give them their first sight of the colony, Allumlel became immobilized and insisted on being left behind. There had been no rain for six days, and the Ull, whose species was accustomed to spending at least their hours of sleep in water, was in great pain. The combination of walking and climbing, exercises practiced only in moderation by the Ull, together with surface dehydration, had caused its thick and normally flexible hide to harden and crack open, and any attempt at movement made the fissures bleed. But Allumlel's gesture of self-sacrifice was being politely ignored until they knew the Healer's thoughts on the problem.

"As you can see," Nolan told them, "the patient is in urgent need of a moderately large and continuing supply of water for external use. We have two options. The first is to do as Allumlel suggests and press on to the colony as quickly as possible and ask for their help. Traveling there on foot would be too slow to save the patient, even if they use ground vehicles or the helicopter to reach here quickly. But if Brenner and the ground crew were to climb to the peak and launch the glider, much time would be saved. The colony would be at extreme range, but from previous operations with the lander, the pilot remembers many intervening hills whose updrafts he has the skill to use, and by flying he could take the message to them in a matter of hours rather than days. The second option . . ."

"Respected Healer," said Hsung Toi, in a polite but very firm voice, "this problem with our friend Allumlel has been discussed among us and agreement has been reached. For reasons which they must soon explain to us, the colony authorities have not helped us thus far. We would prefer to take the last few steps of this great journey without any help from them, and enter the colony together."

He looked at Allumlel so that there would be no doubt about his meaning, and added, "All of us, together."

"I understand," said Nolan, and smiled to show that his feelings if not his next words were with Hsung Toi. "But the patient will not be helped by your pride. I was about to say that the second option is to split you into two groups, the smaller to launch Brenner from the peak and the larger to go back to the nearest source of water. From this altitude we can see two mountain pools and a small river, all within a day's travel. If you sleep rough, take only bows, hunting spears, and the water bags, without the tents and stores to slow you down, you could be back here by the forenoon of the day after tomorrow. I can only guess at the colony's reaction time to Brenner's message, so it is possible that you could make one or more round trips before any other help arrives."

They would think that he wanted them to carry weapons to add to the supply of wild thumper meat, and if the monsignor reacted well, they need never know the other reason.

He went on, "The patient's condition is unique to the memories of the Ull, because no other member of its race has placed itself at such grave risk. I had considered asking you to bring back thick branches as well as the water, with the intention of making a litter strong enough to carry it to the nearest pool. But the continuing dry weather has caused a rapid deterioration in its condition so that any movement, much less a long and unsteady journey down the mountainside, would be lethal."

He looked at them all in turn, then said, "Without endangering your own physical condition or your ability to travel quickly, I would like you to leave behind as much water as you can spare for the patient. I will remain with Allumlel. The rest of you should leave without delay."

The donations of water had been generous enough to enable Nolan to test a new idea for treating Allumlel's dehydration. He began by opening out their largest and least damaged tent and spreading it flat on the ground, and very carefully and gently he helped Allumlel move into the center of it. Then he wetted down the worst-affected areas of the patient's body and quickly folded the surplus material across its back in both directions before the water droplets could evaporate in a loose cylinder of tent plastic that was tied at each end to keep any water from escaping along the sloping ground. Except for a narrow opening that allowed it to breathe, the patient was totally enclosed by a moisture trap that kept its skin wet, but hot.

"I feel like a thumper in one of your cooking pots," said Allumlel, "but my skin feels more comfortable. I am grateful, Healer. How much of your drinking water remains?"

"Enough," said Nolan. He had always believed that lying to a patient was an important part of the treatment.

He remained with Allumlel talking, in the manner of an Ull intent on relieving a friend's distress, until the sun had set and the cool of the night made the patient comfortable enough to sleep. The campfire of the water party glittered like a tiny amethyst in the blackness of the valley, and on the peak above there was a larger fire that seemed to be out of control. A spark blown onto vegetation that had not had rain for six days was the probable cause.

Or perhaps Brenner was remembering Padraig, the saint who had lighted his hilltop bonfire earlier than the one on Tara, to proclaim to the people that the Christus was greater than any High-King. The High-King concerned had not been greatly pleased with Padraig afterward although not, perhaps, as displeased as O'Riordan would be with this visible evidence that what he regarded as Nolan's party of serpents was on the very doorstep of his new Eden.

Nolan watched the blaze until the fire was either blown or beaten out, trying to put himself into O'Riordan's mind. If the ship had been reporting their progress, by now the little priest must be a frightened and uncertain man, even though a few moments' conversation would be enough to dispel both the fear and uncertainty. But he might refuse to listen to or even meet the leader of the serpents so soon to invade his Garden and, without knowing either their minds or their numbers, he might try the Biblical expedient of crushing their heads before anyone had a chance to speak.

The pilot and the others should have been warned to expect the unexpected when they reached the colony, Nolan thought, but what could he have said without revealing the monsignor's entire conspiracy and thereby converting their long-delayed homecoming into the beginnings of a civil war? And if violence was to be done to Allumlel or its new Human friends, in particular the one who had eaten the flesh of Illamsul, the Ull would eventually learn of it and the colony itself would not long survive their anger.

Only a few words from him would be needed to avert that disaster, Nolan thought bitterly, if he was only given the chance to speak them.

But the monsignor, Nolan told himself firmly, was an intelligent man, and a good and kindly man. No matter how strong and single-minded he was in his priestly beliefs, a good man should not be capable of committing such an evil deed. Surely the sectarian massacres and excesses of religious violence practiced by the overzealous followers of the gentle Christus belonged to the past.

He was still trying to convince himself of that, and beginning to worry about the even more uncertain meeting with Dervla, when he became aware that the mountainside around him was lit by the dull, monochrome light of dawn. And Brenner must have launched at first light, because his glider was circling the peak and climbing into sunlight.

The sun was high and burning down out of a sky that seemed to have forgotten the very existence of clouds, and the following day seemed even hotter. Nolan had been dividing his time between reading from the account he had written of their two-year journey, with particular emphasis on the Ull incidents, and from his catalog. The patient's condition had been worsening both physically and psychologically, and he had been trying to arouse Allumlel's interest in the internal anatomy of its race, with particular emphasis on the Human practice of healing and surgical repair, when it interrupted him.

"An Ull who is distressed," said Allumlel in a weak voice, "can often sense distress in others. Is this so among Humans?"

Nolan sprinkled the last few droplets of the water over the patient's back and quickly replaced its covers, but Allumlel spoke again before he could reply.

"I have seen your people grow more excited and pleased with the prospect of joining friends and mating as the end of their journey comes nearer," it went on, "while you appear to become less pleased. It is as if you expected a great unpleasantness. Healer, is this a story that can be told? Is it a trouble that can be shared?"

Nolan's first impulse was to say no, because to tell Allumlel anything about the monsignor's behavior and intentions regarding the travelers was out of the question. But the patient's obvious concern kept him silent.

"I would prefer to spend the time that remains to me learning more about your mind," Allumlel went on, "rather than of the disgusting contents of my body. Are you troubled by thoughts of the mate you are so shortly to meet?"

"Yes," said Nolan in great surprise. For a moment he wondered if the other's race was telepathic, then he decided that it was more likely to be the simple empathy that developed between two people who had come to know each other very well. He went on, "A leader must never appear weak or uncertain before his followers. I remind you of this because I am sure that you will have time, a very long time, to hear and tell many stories. But this one can be told to you but not the others."

This is insane, he thought. I am treating this creature like a Healer of the Mind, or a confessor!

Allumlel made a low, bubbling sound that could have been expressive of sympathy, encouragement, or simply its own pain, then it said, "Is this a story of unfaithfulness? After all that has happened, does the mate who awaits no longer please, and you would prefer another who—"

"I am not yet mated," Nolan broke in, "nor, as you must have learned by now, are all but one of the others. To my shame I lied to the Six about that."

"I am glad, Healer," Allumlel replied, "for lying is a small shame compared with unfaithfulness to a mate. Is it that you have chosen a mate, but are afraid lest your egg-layer thinks you dead by now and has joined with another?"

"No," said Nolan, in a voice full of misery. "It is a Healer like myself, but not like myself. She is greater, more skilled, and with much more knowledge of healing than I. Because of this she has said that a mating between us would be a bad thing. My uncertainty and expected hurt is not that she would join with another, but that she might not join with me."

"If it is a greater Healer than you," said Allumlel, "then your egg-layer is great beyond my capacity for belief. Among the Ull such uncertainties before mating are common, but differing levels of knowledge and skill between the two would not figure largely in the resolution of the problem. There are much more important qualities I would look for in a mate, qualities which you, Nolan, possess in abundance, and, had you been of my race, willingly would I have carried your eggs."

"Thank you, Allumlel," said Nolan, and laughed in spite of his cracked lips. "Among the Humans, patients often feel that way about their Healers, and the Healers are forbidden to take advantage of what is only simple gratitude. But I am greatly complimented, nonetheless."

Allumlel made another low, bubbling sound and said, "Alas, I am rejected. But all that you tell me makes me wonder whether your egg-layer is as intelligent as you think. Explain its reasoning to me. What great deeds has it done that it should consider itself to be greater than you?"

"She was the personal physician of the High-Queen," said Nolan, feeling pride as well as misery as he spoke the words. "She is an Adept of the Order of Orla, a Heâler of the First Name . . ."

He had to explain at great length before Allumlel was able to understand the significance of those words, but the whole day stretched before them and his talking was the only comfort that he could offer his patient. His lips felt like the dry, cracked bark of a tree and his words were slurred by a tongue that was almost as stiff and dry as his lips. He spoke only of Dervla and the things they had said and done together on the ship and, much as he wanted to unburden himself on the subject, he deliberately avoided all reference to their deductions regarding the monsignor. The water was gone and what little moisture that remained inside the patient's covers was slowly being forced out as vapor by the intense heat, and it was doubtful whether Allumlel would survive much past midday. He could have said whatever he wished in the knowledge that it would go no further, but it would be unkind to burden the last thoughts of a dying mind with such matters.

Instead he continued talking about Dervla because that was what he most wanted to do, and Allumlel was the first person with whom he had felt able to talk about her. Using the Ull speech as much as he was able, Nolan tried to describe their visit to the cold sleeping captain in his laboratory aft, the slow walk back to the Control module along the outer hull of the tremendous ship, and Dervla's attempt to teach him the methods of identifying and testing edible vegetation, knowledge that had enabled his people to survive the two years since their forced landing. Almost word for word he recounted their conversation, his pleading, and her sympathetic but steadfast refusal after he had asked her to mate with him. And he told of their last moment together, of what he had done and she had said before the cold sleep casket had closed on her.

". . . It is likely that her final words to me were spoken in a moment of weakness," Nolan went on, "and she has had a long time to remember her earlier and less emotional words, and to reconsider. But there is an uncertainty, a tiny chance that she has not reconsidered and is waiting for me, and it was that small hope that brought me across half a world. But soon I will see her and there will be only a certainty and—and I am afraid."

There was a sudden movement inside Allumlel's covers. A three-fingered hand appeared in the breathing opening, enlarging it so that the amphibian's head could come through. When it spoke, the voice was little more than a bubbling whisper, but the words were well-formed and clear.

"This is a good story," it said. "To an egg-layer like myself, it is a better story than any other that you could have spoken, and I thank you for it. But now, friend Nolan, you must stop talking."

"I'm sorry," said Nolan, "am I tiring you?"

"You are making it difficult for me to hear," Allumlel replied. "There is a strange noise, like the slapping of a hand against water, but sharper-sounding. Do you hear it?"

"No," said Nolan, and then, "Yes. Yes, now I do."

Chapter 46

IT had been a sound familiar on Earth and it grew rapidly in volume until the helicopter came clattering around the shoulder of the mountain to swing in a tight circle and land about two hundred yards below the camp. The downdraft stirred the grass and made the tents flutter until the landing skids accommodated themselves to the sloping ground and the power was switched off.

Before the rotors had slowed their spinning there were figures jumping to the ground. As he was running down to meet them, Nolan counted ten men. Nine of them were dressed in long, belted tunics and cowls of undyed linen with small black crosses stitched to the chest, and eight of them were armed with the lightweight hunting crossbows that had been brought from Earth, carried at the ready, while the ninth wore a sidearm. The last man was wearing tight-fitting trousers and a fringed vest of animal hide with a bow slung across his shoulder and a water bag on his back, so that at first sight he could have been mistaken for one of Nolan's party. But only two of his people had copper-bronze skin like that, and neither of them were men.

Nolan laughed aloud in sheer relief. The dreaded first meeting would be with friends.

But Wanachtee ran past him without speaking. Eight of the others followed him, spreading out and surrounding the camp while the Redman searched the tents. The one who remained walked up to Nolan, head held high and body erect but relaxed, as if the mountainside was a parade ground and his regiment awaited inspection.

"Ciaran!" said Nolan. "It is good to see you again."

"Healer Nolan," said Ciaran, without either smiling or taking his outstretched hand. "This is not pleasant for me, so listen carefully and do exactly as I say. You are not to approach or speak to Wanachtee or my men for any reason, nor are your survivors to speak among themselves where the guards might overhear them. We may speak together, very briefly, on this one occasion so that your position can be made clear to you. Until a final decision has been taken on how best to counter the threat to the colony's survival that you represent, you will remain in your camp. I am instructed to tell you that any attempt to break quarantine will be met with ultimate force. Healer, you must listen carefully to my words, and believe them."

"Quarantine?" said Nolan quietly. "But we carry no infection, physical, political, or psychological. The monsignor has nothing to fear from us. And Dervla. Is she well, or has she, too, been quarantined?"

"Healer Dervla has quarantined herself," Ciaran replied. "She speaks to her patients and trainees, rarely to other colonists, and never, except indirectly, to the ecclesiastics. She would not endanger the stability of the whole colony by voicing her knowledge of the monsignor's plan, to which I and a few others have always been privy. She never speaks of Healer Nolan, and you should be ashamed even to speak her name after what happened on the ship . . ."

"Surely you mean," said Nolan angrily, "after what O'Riordan *thinks* happened on the ship. We did nothing of which either of us should feel ashamed, and there is no proof that—"

Ciaran held up a hand. "The monsignor warned me that you were good at talking your way out of trouble. Healer Nolan, I am sorry, and disappointed, that you have acted as you did, for I began by thinking highly of you when we met at Tara. But now I have nothing more to say to you."

Nolan took a deep breath, trying to both control his anger and choose the right words, then quickly and quietly he said, "But I have something to say to you. I will speak quietly, and briefly, because Wanachtee is coming back and will be here soon, and I must not embarrass you. So you will listen carefully, and believe. My people, including Pilot Brenner, think that our forced landing on the other side of the continent was such a major error that it could only have been caused by a malfunction. I have encouraged them in that belief because, like Healer Dervla, I would not take the responsibility for saying or doing anything to endanger the peace of the colony. I tell you again, the monsignor has nothing to fear from us . . ."

Wanachtee's arrival made him break off. The words were for Ciaran but his eyes did not leave Nolan's face as he spoke.

"Brother Ciaran," he said, his face as impassive as always, but there was disbelief and something akin to awe in his voice, "the tents are empty. The only living things are animals with flat tails, and their young. I found nothing but cooking pans, tools, empty litters, and—and *seed* bags! A large number of them with their seals unbroken . . . Healer Nolan? I didn't recognize you at first. You are brown enough to pass as a Redman, a *thin* Redman! It is a great joy to see you well." The sudden, crushing grip of his hand around Nolan's was the most pleasant of all pains. "But, Healer, you thirst."

Wanachtee unslung the water bag from his shoulder and held it out, and Nolan thanked him and took it but did not drink. Ciaran's lips were pressed tightly together, his face reflecting anger and confusion. The evident friendship of Wanachtee and Nolan was a complication he had not foreseen. It was a time, Nolan thought, to exploit any advantage.

He was still holding his catalog and the report of the journey in his other hand. He let the water bag fall to the ground and said, "Ciaran, I have made a catalog of the local flora and fauna with particular emphasis on the edible varieties. No doubt Healer Dervla has already duplicated this work, and to better effect, but I would be obliged if you would give it to her."

Ciaran hesitated for a moment, then took the thick, loosely bound catalog in one hand, the hand that he would not need for his sidearm.

"There is also my report of the journey," Nolan went on. "It covers the incidents and problems encountered from the forced landing two years ago until now, and includes our first and subsequent contacts with the native intelligent race and details of their political and social structures, supplied by one of them who travels with us."

It was obvious from their faces that as yet the colony knew nothing of the Ull, and that Ciaran was disbelieving every word he said. Nolan knew that his next move would be dangerous, but he did not think that Ciaran would dare to use ultimate force against him, not before Wanachtee. Nolan was an honorary Redman Chief and Wanachtee was his friend. If Ciaran tried to use his sidearm, it might not be Nolan who died.

With an apparent change of subject, Nolan went on, "Ciaran, at Tara you had my promise that I would watch over the then-Princess Ulechitzl and guard her from harm until she reached the colony. Unknown to you I gave the same promise to Wanachtee, in circumstances that were contrary to regulations at the time, regarding Golden Rain. I do not know the strength of your feeling for the lady Ulechitzl, especially now that you are studying for the priesthood, but at that time Golden Rain was Wanachtee's new wife.

"It is for that reason," he continued, holding out the report to the Redman, "that Wanachtee has prior claim to know what happened to his squaw and should read it first. Then yourself, and the monsignor, and whoever else is interested. That is only fair, don't you agree?"

Ciaran's face was pale, his features frozen in indecision. He knew what the Healer was trying to do, for if Wanachtee read that report, others would learn of it, and the monsignor would not be able to suppress it. But for some reason Wanachtee, his face even more impassive than usual, was not taking it from Nolan's outstretched hand.

In the two years that had passed, the Healer wondered, had Wanachtee given up his wife for lost? Had he taken another squaw, and thought that the report would reopen an old and deep wound? Nolan continued to hold out the report, not knowing what more he could say and afraid to take his eyes off the Redman. But at the edge of his vision, on the lower slope of the mountain, there was movement, and at that moment Wanachtee spoke.

"Healer Nolan," he said, in a voice that could have been coming from a man on the rack, "I will read your report. But first tell me what happened to Golden Rain."

"Wanachtee," Nolan replied, using his free hand to point down the mountainside, "she will tell you herself."

They must have been running ever since they had seen the helicopter land above them. They moved silently because they were saving their breath for the long, climbing run, but they waved their bows and spears in greeting and their smiles could be seen from a long way off. Golden Rain had seen Wanachtee running to join her and was far in the lead.

"Ciaran," said Nolan quietly, "listen and believe me. They know nothing of O'Riordan's plot and are glad only to be back among their own people. But they are strong, their minds are keen, and their reactions fast, because they have survived much. So tell your men to lower their arms. If there is a battle, Ciaran, the monsignor will be in real trouble, because you would certainly lose it."

"Indeed we would," said Ciaran without hesitation. He raised his arm and gave a complicated hand signal to his men, who shouldered their crossbows. Then he gave a long sigh, and went on, "Healer Nolan, I don't care what happened between Dervla and yourself. These things happen or, in your case, they may not have happened. I wanted to believe everything you told me, and now I do believe it. And, Healer, I am truly glad to see you safe and well."

"And I, you," said Nolan, and bent to lift the water bag from the ground. "This is for my patient. Come, now, and let me introduce you. Bear in mind that it understands nearly every word that you say."

But there was little opportunity for speech, because no sooner had Nolan removed Allumlel's covers and thoroughly irrigated its body than his people arrived and began asking questions or answering Ciaran's questions. He satisfied himself by taking a long drink of tepid water that was his first in two days, and listening to them.

As had befitted a Guards Captain of the Imperial Court, Ciaran was a diplomat as well as a soldier. His answers were true, so far as they went, and completely acceptable. Nolan could have hoped for nothing better.

Ciaran said that the colony authorities had lost track of Nolan's people after the cardinal-captain had detonated the three fusion devices midway through their journey. A problem had developed with the external vision sensors, which he had been attempting to modify so that they would give him a clearer view of the party's progress, and His Eminence, who was ailing and completely alone on the ship, had been too unwell to go onto the outer hull to effect repairs. As a result, the fire on the peak two nights ago had been the first signal they had received since then.

Monsignor O'Riordan had not known how many of them had survived the crash and, believing it impossible that any of them could complete that incredible journey, had kept the news of their survival to a few close advisers, explaining the triple detonation at the ship as an orbit correction. The monsignor thought that telling the others that some had survived, but would die anyway, would be bad for morale. At that time the situation in the colony was already desperate enough, and to introduce more despair would have benefited no one.

There had been severe food shortages. The first seed plantings had been overrun by competing native plants and the harvest was less than half of that expected. Serious disturbances had followed, with many, although fortunately nonfatal, casualties, because the people were so hungry that they cared not what they ate. The plantings that had not failed and the remaining seed grain and farm animals had to be placed under guard, and Ciaran, with his previous military experience, was given responsibility for protecting them as well as for regulating the grosser forms of misbehavior.

". . . But now my guards have been reduced in number," Ciaran went on, "because we have had two rich harvests this year and the colony is out of danger. But the credit for that belongs to Healer Dervla, who forced us to exist on local food and shamed us into accepting a year of near-starvation."

For a moment they all seemed to be looking at Nolan. It was Hsung Toi who said, "Healers have a fondness for doing that."

Ciaran smiled, but before he could go on, Ulechitzl moved closer and his smile disappeared. It was plain that the words he had for her would not come easy to him.

"My lady," he said quickly, not giving her a chance to speak, "I fear that I may have gravely embarrassed you. Long before that reception at Tara I knew that I was coming here and that I would study for the priesthood. But I kept my intentions secret, because my past career in the Imperial Guard and early reputation among the ladies of the Court would have given rise to much incredulity and amusement from those who did not know what was in my heart and mind. At Tara I liked and admired you for what you were about to do, but I was afraid that you would be ill suited to the rough colonial life. I am sorry if my intentions were misconstrued. I only wanted to protect you as a friend, and for Healer Nolan to watch over you until you arrived in the colony. That is why I extracted a promise from the Healer to . . ."

He stopped speaking because Ulechitzl was holding up her hand.

"Thank you," she said, "it was well for all of us that you did. But my question is not about you, Ciaran, but Pilot Brenner. What news is there of him, and is he safe?"

Ciaran's relief could almost be felt. He smiled, and said quickly, "I have not spoken to him, my lady. It seems that he could not reach the main settlement but was able to land on an outlying farm in the Cathay area, and they relayed his message to us and, it would appear, everyone else. It was Wanachtee, who has much influence in the colony, who brought us the message and insisted on coming along. Until now I did not know why."

He looked at Wanachtee and Golden Rain, who were seeing and hearing only each other, and went on, "Before we could reach him, Pilot Brenner asked the Cathay farmers to help him relaunch, telling them that he wished to return here as quickly as possible. When we saw Pilot Brenner he was slope-soaring on the other side of this mountain, in no apparent difficulty, and he should be back here before dark."

For a long moment he looked into Ulechitzl's eyes and at the evident relief on her face, then he smiled again and said, "Pilot Brenner is a brave and resourceful man, my lady, and it seems that you are no longer in need of my protection. My congratulations to you both."

There were many more questions from the colonists, and from Allumlel. The first generous dousing with water had made it feel much better, and no further treatment was necessary because the clouds, white-topped and bulbous with bases of leaden gray, that had spread almost unnoticed over the peak, were dropping their heavy loads of rain. Ciaran's men began running for the shelter of their helicopter, and the onetime Guards Captain and present seminarian said that he, too, must leave.

There was much he had to report to the monsignor, Ciaran said, and the colony would want to celebrate the arrival of their lost sheep in fitting style, and would need time for the preparations. The female colonists who were as yet unmarried—a condition, he was now sure, that would not last much longer—were with Healer Dervla at the colony's House of Sorrows, where the medical training she was giving them left them little time to fret. He offered to fly Nolan and his immobilized patient there, where it could have the attention of two Healers and the best treatment available, and to take Golden Rain and Wanachtee back to the Redmen's enclave. He did not seem surprised when both offers were politely refused.

Allumlel told him, in a voice that strengthened with every moment that passed, that if the rain continued all night, it would be able to race the Humans to the peak in the morning. Golden Rain said that she wished to end the journey as it had begun, on foot and in the company of Healer Nolan and her friends, and Wanachtee agreed that it was proper that she do so.

They embraced then, briefly and fiercely, while the rain bounced unheeded from their heads and shoulders. Nolan watched them, feeling both pleased for them and envious, until they released each other with great reluctance and Wanachtee followed the others to the helicopter.

As it took off, Ciaran remained standing in the open loading door. He raised his free hand in a strange gesture that began as a priestly benediction and changed suddenly into a rigid military salute.

The last mile of their journey seemed to be lined by every member of the colony, all of them shouting and applauding or, in the case of the many babes in arms, waving pudgy hands at the direction of a parent or crying because the noise had frightened them. Everyone and everything was being cheered.

They cheered Ulechitzl and Golden Rain, they cheered the men in their thumper-hide clothing, freshly washed for the occasion and worn with the pride of a uniform of an elite corps, which in a sense it was, and they cheered Brenner in his ship coveralls and his decorated forehead, and the ground crew who followed him carrying the dismantled glider. They shouted with surprise and pointed at the litters containing the seed bags, and at the four adult thumpers with cubs on their tails who followed their queen dutifully in line, and at their first sight of Allumlel they went wild. When it stopped to inspect the second White Dancer and its foal which Ciaran had brought to show it, they cheered. And when it stopped to point and ask questions about the space vehicles they passed, all but one of them sealed up until the time when colony technology would catch up with them, the noise made the answers impossible to hear.

Nolan stopped only once, to bow gravely to the young man, once a member of the Imperial Family and now dressed in the linen of a working colonist, whose cold sleeping body he had escorted from Cathay to the ship. When he did that, the customary reserve of the young man's face was forgotten.

But they always began by cheering Nolan because he was in the lead, the first of the party that they saw, and, he had to admit to himself, he was a sight worth seeing.

Once again his boots were glittering like obsidian in the bright sunlight, and his ship officer's uniform, thanks to the careful needlework and cleaning by Ulechitzl and Golden Rain, was perfect in fit and as immaculate in appearance as it had been the first time he had worn it at Tara. But then he had not been wearing the narrow, single-feathered headband of an honorary Redman Chief encircling his dress beret, and the silver-edged cloak thrown back from the shoulders had shown only his insignia of rank rather than the jeweled gold brassard of a trusted messenger of the Imperial Family of Cathay. Neither had there been a wide band of amphibian hide encircling his upper arm, to show that within him lived the soul of a great and well-loved being and that, on this world, Healer Nolan had respect and authority among the Ull.

Perhaps he was making a ridiculous spectacle of himself, Nolan thought as he walked with a measured and unhurried tread, unsmiling and looking neither to left nor right, toward the officers who were waiting outside the entrance to the ecclesiastical compound. But this was no show of self-aggrandizement, even though he was vain enough to be enjoying the sensation. It was a deliberately calculated demonstration aimed at showing Monsignor O'Riordan that Healer Nolan and his people were never again to be used for anyone's purpose but their own, and that anything said to belittle them or the incredible feat that they had accomplished would be totally disbelieved by everyone in the colony.

The monsignor, Ciaran, and Healer Dervla were waiting outside the entrance. Like Nolan, Dervla had had no reason to wear her dress uniform in the two years since the landing, and she made the scuffed and stained uniforms of the priests seem like vagabonds' rags by comparison. She stood as straight and proud as the High-Queen, her eyes a brighter blue in her deeply tanned face, and her hair had grown long again, as it had been at Tara when he had first seen her, and rolled in soft, red-gold waves to her waist. Unable to take his eyes from her, Nolan marched to within two paces of the monsignor before halting the column with an upraised hand. But she turned quickly without speaking and strode toward the end of the line, the earth-brown cloak of an Adept of the Order of Orla sweeping the ground behind her.

Nolan looked down at the monsignor, so angry and disappointed that he could not trust himself to speak. O'Riordan, less rounded in the body and more lined in the face, smiled benignly up at him, and waited.

"Healer Dervla checked the fitness of all the colonists as soon as possible after landing," Ciaran explained. "I told her it would be unnecessary in this case, but she insisted and, well . . ."

He broke off to join the lengthening silence.

Nolan could hear her coming closer, speaking quietly and clinically to everyone in turn as she moved slowly along the line toward him. When she came to Allumlel, who was beside Nolan, she went down on both knees and requested permission to examine its surgical scars, after which she questioned it closely about impaired mobility, abdominal discomfort after sudden movement, or difficulty with the elimination of wastes, exactly as she would have done had it been a human patient. It answered her but said that Healer Nolan had already asked these questions many times, and she said that she had no doubt that he had. Then suddenly she was standing up and facing him.

"They are well," she said, in a voice tinged with wonder and disbelief. "You have cared for them, found food for them, kept them together over two thousand miles, and you made them, *all* of them, survive."

He had forgotten how very tall she was, Nolan thought, as he stared down, only an inch down, into the face that he had thought he would never see again. But everything else he was remembering, and so clearly in sight, sound, and touch, that he felt himself sway forward onto the balls of his feet, fists clenched and the muscles of his arms aching with the effort of not reaching out to her.

It was as if he were watching again as she rose like a splendid, weightless Venus from her cold sleep casket, and when she was helping him resuscitate Golden Rain, and while they were walking the ship's outer hull. And too well was he remembering the words she had spoken, the gentle, compassionate but firm words that had made the dream that had delighted his sleep and tortured his waking moments with self-doubt over the past two years a dream that could never come true. He knew that she was aware of his feelings for her, of the awful need that was in him, and probably of every single thought that was in his mind. She could do that because her whole life had been dedicated to healing, and to caring for and comforting those she could not heal. But there was a softness in her eyes that he had not seen before, as if she was close to tears because she was already feeling with him the pain and sorrow that another refusal would bring. For she was who she was, Dervla the unattainable, a Healer of the First Name.

There was too much that he wanted to tell her, and he would be telling her only what she already knew, so instead he inclined his head in the smallest and stiffest of bows.

"Healer Dervla," he said.

Without taking her eyes from his, she stepped close to him.

"Healer Brendan," she said.

What happened then was not the result of any conscious decision on his part, and there was a tiny part of his mind that fought to remain aloof and observant. It observed the scandalized expression of Monsignor O'Riordan, and the smile that Ciaran was making no attempt to hide. It heard his people cheering more loudly than any of the others, and Allumlel saying that the Ull required privacy for their courtship rites, and Brenner laughing and telling someone that if they pressed themselves any closer together they would be standing back to back. Then that cool, detached portion of his mind surrendered to join the rest in the sheer joy of the moment.

Chapter 47

ALTHOUGH he did not know it at the time, when they finally released each other, the separation that followed was to last for nearly three weeks. It was a matter of circumstances rather than choice, with the monsignor gently reminding Healer Brendan—Nolan still felt embarrassment as well as pride at the use of his first name—of his responsibilities, and Healer Dervla reminding herself of her own. It was intensely frustrating for both of them, but on the one occasion that he was able to speak to her alone at the House of Sorrows, she had smiled and told him to be patient, and said that their condition was serious but that the symptoms, which were identical in both cases, would be treated long before they could prove terminal.

His every waking moment, including the times supposedly reserved for meals, was spent talking to the monsignor or his principal advisers or Allumlel, and frequently all of them together. O'Riordan wanted him to expand on the report he had given to Wanachtee, with particular emphasis on the lake-dwelling Ull, and although the clerics were learning to speak the other's language as quickly as they could, Nolan was always present to reduce the possibility of misunderstanding when the monsignor was questioning Allumlel, or it was visiting the colonists' homes or being escorted to the still water under the fishing jetty where it submerged for sleep, or when it paid one of several visits to the House of Sorrows.

As an egg-layer, Allumlel explained, it was very interested in the birthing of Humans, and that seemed to be the principal activity taking place there. Dervla was pleased to see them both, but of necessity the discussions between the two Healers had to be professional rather than personal.

Although he would have been welcome in any home, Nolan chose to spend his nights in the lodge of Wanachtee and Golden Rain, except on the evening that Brenner and Ulechitzl held their wedding celebration, when he was totally immobilized by a fermentation of unspecified local vegetation brewed by the colonists.

And then came the morning when Ciaran, looking serious and not at all happy with himself, told him that the monsignor wanted to see both Healers immediately after breakfast.

The genial smile that the monsignor had displayed at the entrance had completely disappeared by the time he showed them into his large, Spartan office with its glassless windows, trestle desk, and handmade chairs. O'Riordan placed two of the chairs for them, which they moved closer together, before taking his own seat. He was looking at Nolan when he spoke.

"Healer," he said, in the manner of one who is anxious to be rid of a necessary unpleasantness, "it is better, and will certainly be faster, if I explain the position to you rather than have Healer Dervla try to tell you what she thinks is in my mind. But first I must offer you, both of you, my apologies."

Neither his voice nor his expression were apologetic.

He went on, "Both of you have remained silent regarding your suspicions about me, knowing that to voice them would lead to the destabilization and ultimately the destruction of the colony. Healer Dervla joined the project against her will. She never wanted to come here and she is willing to leave us given half a chance, for her life here has not been pleasant over the past two years.

"You, Healer No—" He broke off and corrected himself, "You, Healer Brendan, are a living legend. Not only have you brought your people safely half across the world, you have made friendly contact with a highly intelligent race which outnumbers us many thousands to one. Yet their style of life and the lack of dexterity in those three-fingered hands make us believe that they will be slow to develop technology. Judging by your friend Allumlel, they are an intensely curious people, philosophical and even spiritual in that they yearn to believe in an afterlife. They thirst for knowledge and willingly will we teach them, and in time, perhaps in a long time, because they are very intelligent and argue well, we will guide them toward the True Faith."

He took a deep breath, and when he continued, there was just the hint of an apology in his voice. "Healer, I am truly ashamed, and can only comfort myself with the thought that out of the great wrong I did by sending your lander off course came an even greater good. For now you have indeed shamed me by returning good for bad, by presenting me with the greatest challenge that a missionary priest has ever been asked to face, the conversion of an entire world.

"But I must do it without interference," he said, and now there was no hint of apology in his voice, "and without the constant threat of betrayal by you. Neither of you have spoken out against me or, I am sure, do you intend to in the future, and I am grateful for your discretion. But there will come a time when you grow old, and forgetful, and the words you would not dream of speaking now will slip out. Or there will be the temptation to impart your secret to your offspring, and our great work will be compromised.

"You have become a powerful man, Healer Brendan," he went on. "A man who can say and do no wrong. If I were to give instructions that were unpopular, even though they will be in the best interests of everyone in the colony, the colonists would immediately run to you to have my orders countermanded or diluted in some fashion. Even if we were in agreement, the colony cannot have divided leadership and remain stable. That is why both of you must leave the colony without further delay."

O'Riordan raised a pudgy hand to silence Nolan's protest, and with the other lifted three thick, loosely bound files one by one onto the desktop. He recognized Dervla's small, neat script on one of them; the other two were his catalog and the report of the journey.

"Healer Dervla," he went on, "has not been happy here and, to the great benefit of everyone in the colony, has been living only for her work. But now that work is done—she has schooled her people well in the healing arts as they apply to this world—and she has already agreed to leave. In fact, had you been a few weeks later in arriving, you would not have seen her again."

"I would have followed," said Nolan firmly, "no matter where you sent her."

"The walking distance would have been too great," said the monsignor, with the thinnest of smiles, "even for you. She is returning to *Aisling Gheal.*"

Before Nolan could speak, he went on quickly, "Interruptions with questions that I fully intend to answer are a waste of time. I realize that you have too much influence among the colonists to be sent away against your will. There is always the possibility that you would not go, and, now that you are alive and well and not dead as she believed, that she would forget her promise to His Eminence and remain here with you. But I believe that I am a good enough Healer of the Mind to predict with accuracy that she will not break her promise to the cardinal, and that you will not be separated from her. Or perhaps, Healer, you are going to surprise me again?

"You are not," said the monsignor, looking at Dervla and back again to Nolan. He continued, "Apart from ensuring your continued silence, which is a reason known only to ourselves and a very few of my priests, the published reason will be that the cardinal-captain is suffering from a heart condition that requires the attention of both a physician and a surgeon for an unspecified length of time . . ."

"And somehow," said Nolan furiously, "you will misdirect our vehicle as you did the lander, and we will die in space or burn up in atmos—"

"No," said O'Riordan sharply. "I want you far from me, Healers, but I would not deliberately cause your deaths, and two such misdirections would be difficult to explain.

"We do not have the facilities for a launch or a landing at night," he went on, "so you will lift off in a little over two hours from now. One of my priests will fly you up, since it would be a great unkindness to ask Pilot Brenner to leave his new wife to do so. Because there is insufficient fuel for a lander, we will use the smaller reconnaissance vehicle which can take six people and, because only three will be on board, a moderate payload. This will comprise colony food to supplement the supply which remains in the ship, as well as local specimens of flora and fauna that Healer Dervla has already selected for preservation in the crew caskets, various important documentation, and an associated photographic record of the colony while it was being established including, naturally, pictures of Allumlel."

He pushed the three files on the desktop toward them, and continued, "For reasons which will become obvious, these are the original documents. Healer Dervla's medical journal and your catalog have been hand-copied, but there was less urgency about copying your record of the journey since Allumlel and the rest of your people remember it well, and retell it constantly and with much less understatement and self-effacement than the original writer."

The monsignor's voice was shaking with emotion as he said proudly, "Later it will be made known that we do not have sufficient fuel to send the vehicle back for you, and then they will be told the third and most important reason for your nonreturn. That you are to carry back to Earth, and to the man or woman who has succeeded to the Chair of the High-King at Tara, the news and the proof that Project Aisling Gheal has accomplished its mission, and that mankind has established a colony on the world of another sun."

There was a sudden tingling at the back of Nolan's neck, of the kind he felt while hearing great music, or when he was being affected by an object of great beauty or, he thought cynically, while listening to a great orator.

"I am not one of the ship's technical officers," he said quietly, "but with only three people instead of a full crew, and the fusion propulsion tanks depleted, even with functioning cold sleep caskets, I . . . I think that the cardinal is a very old man who has the childish dreams that sometimes affect the old, and you should not have made this ridiculous suggestion to him."

O'Riordan shook his head. In a very serious voice he said, "It was not my suggestion. Fuel for one round trip in the smaller vehicle was being held in reserve against the time when His Eminence would go to his reward, after which his remains would have been brought down to the colony for burial, together with anything else useful and portable that remained on board, before the ship was directed to crash safely into the ocean rather than allow the orbit to decay naturally and risk it coming down in an area which we now know to be populated. The cardinal is aware of the Ull development and wishes to remove the future temptation of using the ship to cow the natives into submission. In this I am entirely in agreement with him. Our only weapons against the Ull must be argument and good example."

The monsignor's expression softened. He said gently, "Healer, there is one of the cardinal's dreams that could come true. You may not have realized it, but the very-high-ranking career ecclesiastics in the scientific and technical confraternities are seldom able to practice the simple priestly duties of a pastor. His Eminence, just once before he dies, would like to administer the Sacrament of Matrimony.''

Another reminder, Nolan thought cynically, of all that I would be missing if I refuse, and stay here.

He was so angry that he could not decide whether he despised the monsignor for what he was doing more than he admired the way that he had maneuvered Dervla and himself into accepting what was little more than a mutual suicide pact delayed, at best, by a few months. And yet O'Riordan was a good man, a kindly, nonviolent, and highly dedicated priest who was doing what he considered to be the right thing for the future preservation and the moral health of his flock. For the first time since the monsignor had begun speaking, Nolan turned to look at Dervla.

She was looking at him and smiling. She did not seem to be unhappy about the situation.

''The cardinal has always been my friend,'' she said in a voice of quiet reassurance. ''For a long time he was the only friend I had at Tara and on the ship, and he would not knowingly place me at risk. He is a man of many dreams, Brendan. One of them brought us to this world, and another might take us home again.''

Chapter 48

NOLAN had difficulty in recognizing Cardinal Keon for the tall, lean, and well-muscled man that he had been. Extreme age combined with the degenerative processes of prolonged weightlessness had made of his body little more than a skeleton hung loosely with skin, and had given him a face that looked tiny and shrunken because of the thick, white, and self-barbered hair that surrounded it. But the eyes still retained the brightness of youth, and one faculty that the captain had certainly not lost was the habit of command.

"There is no need to remind me of how weak I am," he said, "or that I would be unable to pull on and off my coveralls if we were not in zero gravity. Had it not been for the zero gravity I would not have been able to spend long weeks making the gun-room modifications that enabled me to reply to your fire-ship signal. There is much to do on the outer hull and, since I am unable to put on my own spacesuit, you must dress and accompany me outside, and work to my direction when physical effort is needed. Until that work is completed I am not about to allow a medical witch or a knife man, highly qualified or well-intentioned though you both may be, to dull my mind with sleep or hack a bloody path through my upper thorax. Or, to put it in language more acceptable to the present company, there will be no massive, medicated rest or surgical intervention."

Dervla looked down at the wasted and fragile body that was strapped loosely to the examination table, and smiled. She said, "Your Eminence, if you intend to refuse the treatment we prescribe, one wonders what two Healers of the First Name are doing here?"

"You are talking to me," said the captain, his voice losing its firmness as he looked from one to the other. "After far too many years talking to myself that is the best thing you can do for me. Let us return to Control and continue with the same treatment."

A few moments later they were in the darkened Control module, lying on the three couches that faced the direct vision panel, talking and watching while the planetary surface unrolled below them and the continent that had taken two years to cross slipped past in as many hours. The captain had begun by apologizing for not keeping track of Healer Brendan's people. He had seen the lander fire and had assumed that it had crashed and burned with no survivors. The later and smaller campfires had indicated that at least a few of them were alive, but it was not until the arrowhead of three fire-ships had been lit that he realized that many had survived and they had covered half the distance to the colony. He had knocked out his vision sensors trying to increase their resolution and left the ship blind. Monsignor O'Riordan had been told the news, but had decided to keep it a secret, because the colonists had been existing at subsistence level and had troubles enough of their own.

Dervla joined in at that point to say that psychologically, it would have been better to tell her patients, in that case the starving colonists, about people who were in even worse trouble than themselves, but, then, she disagreed with everything the monsignor said and did. As she went on speaking, Nolan learned for the first time the details of that near-catastrophic first year of the colony's existence which, as most harrowing events do in retrospect, had their moments of humor. He lightened the conversation further by talking about the insect-repelling stench bulbs, and Brenner's glider, the meeting with the Ull and Allumlel's near-disastrous ascent suspended from three kites. But by then the ship was well into its second orbit since they had begun the treatment and, after nearly six hours of talking, the captain was looking very tired.

"I had strange dreams down there," Nolan went on, deciding to bring the conversation around as gently as possible to the subject of sleep, with the strong implication that the cardinal was badly in need of some. Looking across at Dervla and choosing his words carefully, he went on, "In the circumstances the subject of the dream was not unusual, but the surroundings were. At a time when there was no hope or even intention of anyone rejoining the ship, I kept dreaming that I was back on board, invariably in the medical department, and always in my bunk."

Dervla smiled and said, "What does it mean when a man dreams he is *sleeping*? And speaking of bunks, Your Eminence, don't you think it's time you retired to yours?"

"Time," said the captain, "which is something that I have come to understand better than most, plays games with the sleeping mind. Perhaps an event of great importance to Healer Brendan will take place in the medical department at some future time although I have, of course, no idea of what it might be. But he did not say that he was sleeping."

He laughed gently and, ignoring the sudden reddening of Dervla's face, went on, "Before the hints that I go to my bunk begin to verge on the insubordinate, there is something that I would dearly like to do, provided there are no strong nonreligious objections from anyone, before we retire. Please unstrap and move around to face me . . ."

Beyond the direct vision panel the stars shone bright and clear above the red-gold band of the sunset terminator, and in the darkened control module the banks of indicator lights burned around them like rows of candles with unwavering flames whose colors glowed like pieces of a broken rainbow, when Padair, Cardinal-Captain Keon, using a ring that had been in his family for many generations, joined in solemn wedlock one Brendan Joseph Nolan and Dervla Eimar O'Duigenan, Healers of the First Name whose last names were now the same. Then, with arms so frail that their touch was like that of a bird's wing, he embraced them as would a fond parent rather than as a priest, and left them.

Dervla was curious about the dreams he had mentioned, especially when he said that they had always been about her, and she confessed shyly to having many just like them. But very soon their lips were too busy for speech and they quickly decided that it was much better to demonstrate rather than describe. And once again, as in the dreams, the medical department was turning unheeded around them while the lovely, firm contours of her body moved against his in one long, gentle, and incredibly passionate caress. His last coherent words before the first explosion of ecstasy overwhelmed his mind were to tell her that his dreams had not been like this, because it always ended before they reached the nice part by his waking up.

It was a long time later that she sighed and, still holding him to her, said that from then on, when they had finished with what he so unpoetically referred to as the nice part, they would go to sleep instead of waking up.

They slept well and often during the six weeks that followed, because the captain, although responding well to what he referred to as the talking treatment, tired quickly and needed so much rest that he made few demands on their time other than to ask their help in dressing him for the sensor-repair work on the outer hull or the daily trip along the frigid corridors of the empty colonist module to his laboratory aft. Even when they were not working to his direction, one or both of them stayed with him during his every waking moment and took turns to check on his condition when he was asleep.

The intensive verbal treatment was working well, and it was clear that both Dervla and the captain were enjoying it, as did Nolan himself. He became privy to events at Tara that were in turn scandalous, shocking, and highly amusing, and to quite a few state secrets that lost nothing by being five centuries out of date. But the increasing animation in the captain's manner and speech and the evident pleasure he was taking in their company could not conceal the fact that he was an incredibly old and physically weakened man who, for his own good, should be reminded of his frailty.

Dervla and himself had completed a minor piece of rewiring under the captain's supervision when Nolan said, "Sir, we are seriously worried about your ability to survive the acceleration of departure, which you have said will be rapid. You ignore our advice regarding the admittedly risky cardiac surgery, or the construction of a special acceleration cocoon. Had your bone structure and cardiovascular system not been affected by protracted weightlessness through your inability to use the exercise harness, or if only you had been a little younger . . ."

"Healer," said the Captain impatiently, "you are still trying to apologize for causing me to stand those extra watches because Dervla and yourself were awake together and presumably committing large numbers of mortal sins. At least, that was the monsignor's presumption, not mine. The truth is that if you two had not given me an excuse for standing those extra watches, I would have had to find another that gave me the time needed to complete my theoretical work. Devising and testing a whole new system of mathematics is not accomplished overnight.

"In any event," he went on, "we have insufficient working fluid to accelerate us to interstellar cruising velocity, and there will be no fusion detonations astern of the blast shield, and no need to concern yourselves about the effect of sudden bursts of acceleration on me, because, theoretically, acceleration should be negligible over a distance that is measured in inches."

Nolan felt Dervla's fingers gripping his arm, and he knew that she was having the same thoughts that troubled his own mind. He said, "I don't understand you, sir. Can you explain, simply, what you intend to do?"

The captain laughed suddenly and said, "Healers, your diagnoses of senile dementia are written plainly on both your faces. And no, two decades of advanced theoretical work with Hseng Hwa on Earth—you remember Hseng Hwa, who thought highly enough of you to ask a favor and give you the spacesuit you're wearing?—together with my later work on the ship, cannot be explained simply. But I will try, even though the explanation may reinforce rather than allay your suspicions regarding my mental competence.

"We will travel," he said, and pointed to the white ceramic tube that was held immobile in the center laboratory by a web of power conduits and tightly stretched steel cables, "in that."

"But, sir," Nolan protested, "that is just . . . I remember you calling it a magic wand."

"And I, Healer," said the cardinal, "remember you nearly stopping my heart by using it as a leg splint! But no matter. It is a hollow ceramic tube inlaid on both the inner and outer surfaces with circuitry in various precious metals whose purpose is first to transfer and reduce all of the ship's structure and contents beyond that outer surface and reassemble them inside the aft-facing end of the tube, and then to move it the required distance toward the other end before reversing the process. We should not be aware of anything happening, and the time required is too short for our senses to react to it. If we disregard the mathematical and philosophical aspects, think of the ship as entering the tube at one end, here in our present position in orbit, and when the process is reversed it will be emerging in our home system. To assist the guidance and astrogation, the tube is in exact alignment with the longitudinal axis of the ship so that we will move in the direction we are pointed. All else is simply a matter of calibration. Is that explanation simple enough for you?''

''Yes, sir,'' said Nolan, still looking at the ceramic tube. ''When will we know if it works?''

The captain sighed, and for the first time since they had rejoined him, his voice was that of an old and very worried man. He said, ''If Maeve had been less impatient for glory and forgiveness of past sins, and less influenced by the missionary zeal of Monsignor O'Riordan, and had she allowed the research to continue for another decade on Earth, we might not have needed cold sleep caskets and the other complications of a voyage lasting five centuries. We could have ferried the colonists to the New World, and kept them supplied during the early years, in ships a fraction of the size of *Aisling Gheal*. And if Hseng Hwa had succeeded in completing our work after I left, there should have been a well-established colony waiting here to greet us laggards. There was not, and one wonders if the reason was an accident to Hseng Hwa, a political change that brought our work into disfavor, or a flaw in the thinking on which the work itself was based.''

He shook his head in self-irritation at his momentary display of weakness, then in a firmer voice he said, ''By its very nature there can be no partial success or failure. If it works, we will be home again. The distance and direction, making allowance for planetary orbital motion and the stellar rotation about the galactic center, have been precisely calculated. But we will be going through, or around, or across, time as well as space. We left Earth orbit in the closing years of the fourteenth century, and now, as they reckon time, we are entering the twenty-first. It is *when* rather than *where* we will arrive that is my greatest uncertainty.

''And if my magic wand is a complete failure,'' he went on, ''and we do not move an inch from our present orbit, then the heat of my embarrassment will be felt in the colony below. But, Healer, if your question was when will it be ready for trial, it is ready now.''

For a long moment he looked at them, his features so lined and collapsed with age that only his eyes showed expression. He said, "Naturally, I am more impatient to try it than you two. But it would be no great hardship for me to wait for a few more days, or weeks, before leaving. Or are you already growing bored with too much of each other's company and are craving a new sensation?"

Their protests made him laugh aloud. "Very well, then," he said. "We will leave two days from now, and two hours after sunset at the colony so that they will have a clear view of whatever happens, or doesn't."

It was a long farewell. The monsignor had no reason to conserve his farspeaker's power cells, because soon there would be nobody in orbit to whom he could speak, and he, and seemingly everyone else in the colony, had much to say. There were personal good-byes and prayers for a safe voyage to their cardinal-captain from the senior ecclesiastics; and from the Healers and many ex-patients she had trained and treated in the House of Sorrows to Healer Dervla; and to Healer Brendan from everyone who had been on the lander as well as from Wanachtee, Ciaran, and, repeatedly and at length, from Allumlel. But it was Monsignor O'Riordan who had the most to say.

He wanted to give them the latest news, developments, and future plans of the colony for inclusion in the report they were taking home. When Allumlel was ready to leave them, which would not be for some time, Ciaran and a party of ecclesiastics, with Brenner and Ulechitzl as guides, would escort it back to its home lake and invite any Ull they met on the way to come to the Human school that was being set up in the colony. O'Riordan approved of Allumlel, and said that at times its grasp of philosophy, theology, and the principles of civilized debate were disconcerting. He did not know if Allumlel was the greatest Devil's Advocate ever born or if it was destined to become the Faith's first non-Human saint.

When he heard that, the captain said, "Dervla, my child, I would say that your Brendan has succeeded in making the monsignor a very happy man."

"I do not believe, Your Eminence," she replied, laughing, "that that was his intention."

And then suddenly there was nothing more to say because their departure was only moments away. The colony below them was already in darkness, apart from the dull red specks of the farewell fires that had been lit in their honor. As they lay strapped into their couches, the cardinal-captain's gaze moved constantly between the two Healers, smiling rather than speaking his reassurance, but they were unaware of it because their eyes were on each other.

And in the colony everyone watched the sky and the tiny, sunset-red star that was *Aisling Gheal* until there came suddenly a tiny explosion of light that grew slowly and radiated in great, circular ripples as though each one was a newly minted rainbow until the night sky was filled with them. And, briefly, from their center could be seen a spear of intense white light whose point tapered sharply to disappear into the region of space that contained the sun of Earth.

Epilogue

IT was the highest-level meeting of space scientists that it had been possible to assemble within the few hours since the tremendous ship had made its spectacular arrival and begun its first attempts to communicate. But in spite of their comparatively low rank within NASA and the Church, it was a communications engineer called Donovan and a fellow Irish expatriate and friend, Father O'Neill of a parish adjoining the launch complex, who were the center of attention and the focus of all questions.

"They are not alien and neither is their ship," said Donovan, not for the first time. "When we matched their signal frequencies and were able to receive their farseer and farspeaker messages—that is what they call their radio and television systems—it was obvious that they were human. And they insist that their vessel, the product of more than two decades of international cooperation, was assembled in Earth orbit more than five centuries ago. They say that no matter what has happened during the intervening centuries, surely we have not forgotten *Aisling Gheal*?

"I know it is impossible," he went on. "And, no, they do not speak English. But there were phrases they used which sounded like Gaelic and Latin. The Gaelic I learned as a boy in the old country is almost gone, as are the Latin responses taught to the altar boys serving Mass at the time. But Father O'Neill is proficient in both languages and was able to talk to and understand them. As to who they are and what they want, he can tell you that better than I. Father?"

The priest was young and painfully thin but with a voice that was deep and rich and could carry to the back of the church without need of a microphone. He said, "You can see from the VTR that there are three of them, a young couple and a very frail old man, who are, they say, the only people remaining on the entire ship because the rest of the officers stayed to work and teach on the world they colonized. The younger two identify themselves as Healers of the First Name Dervla and Brendan, a title they did not explain but which seems to be important, and it is they who do most of the talking because of their concern over the poor clinical condition of the third. He is His Eminence Padair, that is Gaelic for Peter, Cardinal Keon, onetime Head of the Confraternity for Space Exploration of the Hibernian Imperial Civil Service, and captain of the starship. I am, of course, taking their word for this, but I think I know a cardinal when I see one. What they want is another matter.

"The two Healers ask for food to be sent up," Father O'Neill went on, "because their landing vehicles are all grounded at the colony so that they are marooned on their ship. They also want the latest medication and literature covering the treatment of degenerative bone and cardiac conditions due to prolonged weightlessness, and they say that in the five hundred years since they completed their medical training there must surely have been significant advances in that area which will enable them to save the life of His Eminence. What the cardinal himself wants is . . . is impossible, crazy. At first I thought that extreme age had affected his mind, but the other two supported and expanded on everything he said."

The priest's voice grew quieter, but the pride and wonder in it stilled the tongues of his listeners more than could have any call for silence. He said, "That ship came from Earth, but not from the world whose history we know. On their Earth, sketches of the aeolipile of Hero of Alexandria found their way to Ireland, to the court of the High-King, and brought about a many-centuries-premature industrial revolution that made the country militarily unassailable and the most technologically advanced of its time. In their seventh century it was Brendan the Navigator who landed at what was to become the Redman metropolis of Brendan's Island, which we call New York, and who as the result of his personal example, honor, and enlightened statesmanship caused him to be adopted by the Algonquin and later elected their Paramount Chief. It was Brendan and his High-King, Dairmuid, who later brought into being the first of the many hundreds of treaties of friendship, trade, nonagression, and mutual defense that were, in the centuries that followed, to bind together Hibernia and the proud Redman nations of the two western continents, and ultimately the tribes of much of Africa. By the time our Columbus was about to embark on his expedition to the New World, the Hibernian Empire of the West had already sent out the first colonizing starship to what was, in fact, a new world."

"During that voyage," Father O'Neill went on, "Cardinal-

Captain Keon successfully completed his work on a new method of propulsion, a system which warps both time and space and enables his ship to make the journey of five centuries in as many seconds, and which will open up the farthest stars to human exploration. But what His Eminence wants, and repeatedly asks for himself is, well, impossible, and I don't know what to say to him.''

The priest stopped speaking and looked helplessly at the faces of the others in the room and on the television screens, then he said, ''His Eminence wishes to report directly to the person who now sits in the Chair of the High-King at Tara that the expedition sent out by the Seventh Maeve, Ard-Rioghan and Empress, has succeeded. That a human colony has been planted and is flourishing on the planet of another star, that friendly contact has been established with the intelligent nonhuman race indigenous to the planet, that a method of rapid interstellar travel has been developed that will open up the stars to human exploration, and that the starship *Aisling Gheal*, that is, the Bright Vision, has come home. He asks to speak directly and without delay to the Imperial Spaceport at Tara.

''But he has not come home,'' said Father O'Neill, in the voice of one who relates deeds both sad and glorious, and when he went on, the emphasis he placed on the first word told of his pride in the race that was his own and a history that was not. ''We have traveled to the stars, and made contact and are living in peace with an intelligent extra-Solar race. But we, we here, have not.''

''No, Father,'' said Donovan in a tone that exactly matched the priest's. ''Not yet.''

About the Author

JAMES WHITE was born in Belfast, Northern Ireland, and resided there until 1984 when he moved to Portstewart on the north coast. His first story was printed in 1953. He has since published well-received short stories, novellas, and novels, but he is best known for his Sector General series, which deals with the difficulties involved in running a hospital that caters to many radically different life-forms.